The mirror shows faces that are not her own. . . . *Dead Faces by Edwina Mayer*

A young man must test the edge of his newly forged sword—and his own soul. . . . *Tempering Day by Darren Clark Cummings*

After 50,000 years, this sergeant finally got a promotion. *Ploughshares by M. W. Keiper*

He never wanted to be more than a block of wood. . . . *The Unhappy Golem of Rabbi Leitch by Russell William Asplund*

A father is torn between the love of his son and the need to break the child's bones. . . . *A Report from the Terran Project by Scott Everett Bronson*

Alone, unarmed, all he had to fight with was his wits. . . . *His Best Weapon by Arlene C. Harris*

The hunchback made a living putting ghosts to rest—until he met her. . . . *Requiem for a Deathwatcher by Carrie Pollack*

These and many other fascinating tales await you!

What has been said about the
L. RON HUBBARD
Presents
WRITERS of the FUTURE
ANTHOLOGIES

"From cutting-edge high-tech to evocative fantasy, this book's got it all—it's lots of fun and I love the chance to see what tomorrow's stars are doing today."

TIM POWERS

". . . an exceedingly solid collection, including SF, fantasy and horror . . ."

CHICAGO SUN TIMES

". . . a double success for science fiction fans—it encourages new talents in the field, and it provides readers with some very good stories."

BUFFALO NEWS

". . . There are thrills, chills, action, adventure and romance in locales from Earth to outer space and planets light-years away."

HARTFORD COURANT

"Writers of the Future is a fun book, with plenty of reading material for the dollar. . . . Hours of great entertainment in reading. New worlds to conquer, new dangers to be faced. Excitement, romance, adventure.

ECHOES

"A first-rate collection of stories and illustrations."

BOOKLIST

"The untapped talents of new writers continue to astonish me and every WOTF volume provides a well-spring of the greatest energy put forth by the ambitious writers of tomorrow."

KEVIN J. ANDERSON

"The stories are as diverse as the backgrounds of the authors but all capture the imagination and take the reader on voyages through time or space."

PRESS TRIBUNE

"Over the long haul the 'L. Ron Hubbard Presents Writers of the Future' books have continued to support the creation of new science fiction writers and styles. Some of the best sf of the future comes from Writers of the Future and you can find it in this book."

DAVID HARTWELL

"Not only is the writing excellent . . . it is also extremely varied. There's a lot of hot new talent in it."

LOCUS MAGAZINE

"As always, this is the premier volume in the field to showcase new writers and artists. You can't go wrong here."

BARYON

"Consistently, over the years, 'L. Ron Hubbard Presents Writers of the Future' has demonstrated that the Contest delivers the goods. With the addition of the Illustrators of the Future Contest products, the anthology series is a 'must read.'"

ALGIS BUDRYS

SPECIAL OFFER FOR SCHOOLS AND WRITING GROUPS

The sixteen prize-winning stories in this volume, all of them selected by a panel of top professionals in the field of speculative fiction, exemplify the standards which a new writer must meet if he expects to see his work published and achieve professional success.

These stories, augmented by "how to write" articles by some of the top writers of science fiction, fantasy and horror, make this anthology virtually a textbook for use in the classroom and an invaluable resource for students, teachers and workshop instructors in the field of writing.

The materials contained in this and previous volumes have been used with outstanding results in writing courses and workshops held on college and university campuses throughout the United States—from Harvard, Duke and Rutgers to George Washington, Brigham Young and Pepperdine.

To assist and encourage creative writing programs, the **L. Ron Hubbard Presents Writers of the Future** anthologies are available at special quantity discounts when purchased in bulk by schools, universities, workshops and other related groups.

For more information, write

Specialty Sales Department
Bridge Publications, Inc.
4751 Fountain Avenue
Los Angeles, CA 90029
or call toll-free (800) 722-1733
Internet address:http://www.Authorservices inc.com

L. RON HUBBARD

Presents

WRITERS

of the

FUTURE

VOLUME XII

L. RON HUBBARD
Presents
WRITERS
of the
FUTURE
VOLUME XII

The Year's 16 Best Tales from the
Writers of the Future®
International Writing Program
Illustrated by the Winners in the
Illustrators of the Future®
International Illustration Program

With Essays on Writing and Art by
L. Ron Hubbard · Paul Lehr
Doug Beason

Edited by Dave Wolverton

Bridge Publications, Inc.

Dead Faces: ©1996 Edwina Mayer

After the Rainbow: ©1996 Fruma Klass

Reflections in Period Glass: ©1996 S. M. Azmus

The Savant Death Syndrome: ©1996 Jerry Craven

Ploughshares: ©1996 M. W. Keiper

Tempering Day: ©1996 Darren Clark Cummings

His Best Weapon: ©1996 Arlene C. Harris

Eyes of Light: ©1996 Richard Flood

Science Fiction and Fantasy Art: Three Keys: ©1996 Paul Lehr

Requiem for a Deathwatcher: ©1996 Carrie Pollack

The Unhappy Golem of Rabbi Leitch: ©1996 Russell William Asplund

A Report from the Terran Project: ©1996 Scott Everett Bronson

Devil's Advocate: ©1996 Syne Mitchell

Narcissus Rising: ©1996 Roge Gregory

Quixchotol: ©1996 E. Robertson Rose

The Heart of the Matter: ©1996 Doug Beason

In the Elephant's Graveyard, Where Space Dances with Time: ©1996 Sue Storm

Grail's End: ©1996 Callan Primer

Illustration on page: 8 Kenneth Scott ©1996

Illustration on page: 69 Brett Hess ©1996

Illustration on page: 103 Gary McCluskey ©1996

Illustration on page : 120 Kent Martin ©1996

Illustration on page: 175 Ivan Gregov ©1996

Illustration on page: 201 Lionel Baker II ©1996

Illustration on page: 240 Konstantin Sheverdin ©1996

Illustration on page: 268 Lionel Baker II ©1996

Illustration on page: 299 Oleg Dergatchov ©1996

Illustration on page: 315 Heidi Taillefer ©1996

Illustration on page: 347 Patrick Stacy ©1996

Illustration on page: 363 Kent Martin ©1996

Illustration on page: 382 Richard Moore ©1996

Illustration on page: 411 Gary McCluskey ©1996

Illustration on page: 430 Patrick Stacy ©1996

Illustration on page: 449 Anatoly Pristypa ©1996

Cover Artwork: "To the Future" ©1996 Bob Eggleton

ISBN 1-57318-027-0

Library of Congress Catalog Card Number: 84-73270

First Edition Paperback 10 9 8 7 6 5 4 3 2 1

Printed in the United States of America

Cover Artwork "To the Future" by Bob Eggleton

WRITERS OF THE FUTURE, ILLUSTRATORS OF THE FUTURE, and the words MISSION EARTH are trademarks owned by L. Ron Hubbard Library.

CONTENTS

INTRODUCTION

Written by

Dave Wolverton

Frequently, people ask me about "the future" of speculative fiction. If you want to know where it lies, study this anthology. While the pieces in this anthology vary greatly in style and content—ranging from heroic fantasy to hard science fiction—I think there are some interesting trends worth noting.

First, in the field of writing, over the past twelve years we've watched a consistent rise in the number of female authors entering the field. Our earliest anthologies had one winning female author to each two or three winning male authors. In fact, in one year, we had *no* female winners. But over the past three or four years, our numbers have evened out to about a fifty-fifty split. Indeed, in this anthology of our prize-winning authors, seven are female, five male—with two of our first-place winners being women. And in the past three years, two of our three grand-prize winners have been women.

Now, although science fiction, fantasy, and fantastic horror are all eligible for entry into the contest, it's also interesting to note that our female authors are predominantly science fiction writers.

The sheer number of talented women authors entering this field is mirrored in the professional arena. Consider the winners of the Hugo and Nebula Awards over the past few years: fine authors like Connie Willis, Ursula K. LeGuin, and Lois Mois McMaster Bujold now tend to dominate the ballots.

One must wonder how all of this will affect speculative fiction, which was once considered to be the domain only of pimple-faced boys. I suspect that, with the number of women authors entering the field and with their high caliber, SF will continue to attract more women readers and more serious readers—which cannot help but be a good thing.

In the past year, I've heard many authors and editors bemoaning the declining numbers of science fiction fans (as youngsters turn to video games and movies for entertainment), yet I suspect that these worries are somewhat overblown. The younger generation is raised on speculative fiction. Of the cartoons that kids watch, which one besides the Simpsons isn't speculative fiction? How many of the bestselling movies of all time are speculative fiction? Look at their video games, their comic books.

The younger generation cuts its teeth on SF, and so long as the written medium allows authors to create stories of greater power and depth than can be found in visual mediums, there will be a wide audience for written SF.

And, unlike it was in the fifties, half of that audience will be female. So the SF audience will likely become more sexually balanced in the next few years.

Beyond this, our illustrators are tending to also become more diverse—not sexually diverse, for we still haven't had more than one or two women illustrators win per year, but more geographically diverse. Six of our winners this year come from the U.S.—an even half. But, unlike the writing contest whose outcome depends on the artist's skill with the English language, the illustrators' contest knows no linguistic bounds. For the past several years, more and more of our winners have come from outside the U.S.—particularly from Russia, the Ukraine, and former Soviet-bloc countries. If my guess is right, this year may be the last where the illustration contest is dominated by Americans. We've recently begun advertising the contest in Europe and South America, and I suspect we'll see more illustrators from these areas.

So what is the future of speculative fiction? Diversity. A broadening of styles, a wider range of types of stories, and a larger audience.

If you want to see the future of SF, you'll find more than a hint right here in these pages—you'll find some of the rising stars.

DEAD FACES

Written by
Edwina Mayer

Illustrated by
Kenneth Scott

About the Author

From the age of six, Edwina Mayer began checking books out of the library knowing someday she would grow up to be a writer, but, unfortunately, like many people she eventually decided to set more practical goals. In 1977 Edwina graduated from the University of Illinois; she began teaching high-school reading and English—a profession she followed for the next eleven years.

When the demands of teaching and motherhood became overwhelming, she left her career to be home with her children while they were small. One morning, she was overtaken with an urge to write—finished a story in fact—and showed it to her husband, who thought it compared favorably with things he'd read in The Magazine of Fantasy and Science Fiction. *Coincidentally, the next day she read about the Flatiron Fiction Writers' Workshop, taught by Bruce Holland Rogers (a fine writer and WOTF winner from 1989; and by the way, Bruce's first novel will soon be out). With Bruce's encouragement, Edwina began writing steadily and has recently made two sales to Marion Zimmer Bradley's Fantasy Magazine. Edwina also won first place with this marvelous* *tale, which puts her in contention for the $4,000 grand prize. She hopes soon to begin her first novel.*

Currently, Edwina lives in Champaign, Illinois, with her husband, Lincoln Machula, her daughters, Chloe and Miranda, and her cat, Ben. (For some reason, most writers have cats.)

About the Illustrator

Kenneth Scott is twenty-five years old and lives in Calgary, Alberta, in Canada. There, with four years of art college under his belt, he makes a "meager" living by painting murals, designing logos and menus, drawing chalkboards, doing illustration and portraiture, and by writing gloomy pop tunes. In other words, he's following in the footsteps of some of our past masters, folks like Michelangelo.

Ken is currently strafing the genre publishing and comic book publishing world with his portfolio, where he eventually hopes to make it rich beyond his wildest dreams.

Charlotte had lost control of her face.

She sat before the dressing table mirror, her reflection an unstable flickering. Narrow eyes, wide eyes; a square jaw, a rounded one; the weathered skin of an old man, the velvety cheeks of a baby. Invisible hands seemed to manipulate a face made of warm wax—pinching the nose, pushing the cheekbones, molding the chin—never quite satisfied. Once or twice Charlotte's true appearance manifested, barely recognizable before transmuting into that of someone else.

"Just look at her," said Mrs. Jensen, the nurse.

With difficulty, Delia turned away from her mother's reflection and scowled. "We are looking," she said.

Impossible not to look.

Peter moved up behind Charlotte and put his hands on her shoulders. "Mother," he said, catching her chameleon gaze in the mirror, "Mother, stop it."

Charlotte's features froze, a collage of bushy eyebrows, a four-year-old's petulant mouth, a beaky nose, all topped by light, hip-length hair.

"Now look into my mind and make what you see there."

The hair changed first, became shorter, sparser and gray.

Then the eyes turned pale, the lips thin and bloodless, the nose cartilaginous beneath tight-stretched skin.

Illustrated by Kenneth Scott

And Charlotte was there again. Aged Charlotte. Sick Charlotte. Dying Charlotte. But Charlotte, nonetheless.

"Now stay this way," Peter demanded, pinning her eyes in the mirror with his own. After a moment he dropped them, then left the room.

The old woman rose unsteadily from the vanity stool and extended a mottled hand. "Help me back to bed, Delia."

Delia hurried to offer support as Charlotte took the four steps to the bed. Then, filled with longing for a mother who no longer existed, she held a desiccated hand till Charlotte's breathing assumed the slow rhythm of sleep.

As Delia tiptoed toward the door, a dry whisper stopped her. "Why do these things keep happening to me?"

Desolation threatened even the semblance of normalcy, but Delia pushed it back. "It's part of your illness, Mom," she said. "I'm sorry."

"Help me, Delia."

"There's nothing I can—"

"Do you enjoy seeing me like this?"

"Of course not. I want you to—" Guilt surged up this time, desolation's twin, and Delia stopped herself. "I want you to get well."

Charlotte glared at her, eyes hard and glittering. Then, with a shuddering sigh, she turned her face to the wall.

"I'll come up and see you this afternoon," Delia said.

Cursing her inadequacy, she fled down the stairs of the big Queen Anne house to prepare for the day's appointments.

Though she hadn't practiced in more than five years, Charlotte's presence still permeated the house, and nowhere was her influence more obvious than in the Manifestation Room. She had chosen its furnishings— the fine draperies and antique tapestries, the strategically placed candles and tall mirrors, the low boxwood tables and stools and chairs all intricately inscribed with hiero- glyphics—to create a space outside of time.

Charlotte would not have approved of the video system Delia had installed. But the camouflaged peep- holes Charlotte once used reminded her daughter of bangles, tambourines, and crystal balls. When poor health had forced Charlotte's retirement, Delia had wanted to plug the peepholes and replace them with something more professional.

Peter had balked at first. "What if she gets better?" he asked.

But the years passed. After a time Delia purchased the video system, though the peepholes remained intact.

Now she pushed back the heavy draperies that cov- ered the television monitor and settled in to watch Peter hypnotize their first client of the day.

In the parlor on the other side of an ebony door carved with the image of Maat, Egyptian goddess of truth, Peter leaned toward Emil Hart.

"Now, Emil," he said in a low-pitched voice, "I want you to think back . . . back to the past . . . back to your happiest time with Eve. Feel as you felt when you were with her then. Imagine how she must have felt. Back . . . back . . . back."

Hart was one of those erect old men whose bones don't settle with age, and though his facial muscles slackened slightly in response to Peter's soothing recita- tion, his carriage did not.

Peter continued. "Think back to the way you felt then, Emil, and fill yourself with love for Eve. Are you doing that now?"

The old man bobbed his head stiffly. Too stiffly.

"Now keep hold of that love," said Peter, "for unless we call the dead back with warmth, they hesitate to reveal themselves."

Delia watched uneasily. Though Hart was following Peter's instructions, the telltale unfocusing of the eyes that meant he had relinquished control was taking too long.

Doggedly Peter went on, coaxing Hart into the past, slipping around unconscious barriers of entrenched resistance. Finally the old man's expression shifted. With an exhalation of tension, Delia prepared to mine his memories.

"Now, Emil," Peter said, "as you think of that happy time, I want you to remember Eve's appearance. Create her in your mind, just as she was. Start with her face, Emil, with her eyes and hair . . . with her nose. Have you done that?"

Hart nodded, and Delia sent the tendrils of her own consciousness into the old man's mind. There she found a laughing young woman—Hart's wife—who had been dead for twenty years.

Gradually, Delia transformed.

She watched in the tall mirror as her image changed, her straight dark hair becoming shorter, blond and curly . . . her brown eyes lightening to clear gray . . . the little bump at the bridge of her nose smoothing out.

"Her lips," said Peter, and Delia's mouth widened slightly.

"Her chin . . ." A tiny, tantalizing cleft appeared there, and Delia's long jaw shortened and squared. "Her arms . . . her hands . . ." They lengthened and became more delicate. "The crescents at the base of her fingernails . . . the curve of her calves . . ." All changing from Delia to Eve.

The transformation nearly complete, Delia checked her new appearance. She was of the right stature now, and the hair and eyes were perfect, but the mouth was still too pale, so she reddened it.

In the parlor, Peter motioned for Hart to join him before the ebony door. Then Peter began to chant:

> O, Maat, mother of truth,
> She who stands at the left hand of Anubis,
> Lady who holds the feather
> Against which all souls are weighed,
> Open the paths between the worlds.
> Make the way open
> So this man may know the truth
> Only the dead can tell.
> Lead this man's wife, Eve,
> To the door between the worlds
> And make the way open.

Peter raised his fist and banged three times on the door.

"Open. Open. Open."

Using Eve's graceful arms, Delia closed the curtains over the television. Then she waited for Peter to bring the old man into the Manifestation Room where the dead came back.

As the door swung out, Hart stood blinking in the dimness. Jittering candle flames cast quivering shadows across the creased legs of his linen trousers, and, for a moment, Delia thought he carried an undulating serpent in his hands. But as the flames stabilized, the snake resolved into a walking stick.

Hart touched Delia's cheek with a carefully manicured hand. "Eve," he said, "you've come back to me."

The contact helped Delia firm up her physical portrayal, but appearances always came easily; feelings were the challenge. Delicately, she probed a little deeper for them, but they eluded her.

Charlotte would have relinquished her self-awareness now, surrendering entirely to the old man's sense of his wife. But that personal extinction—no matter how temporarily—terrified Delia. In its place she had cultivated an essential aloofness, maintained a vantage point from which she kept track of the path back, always.

Charlotte had lost track of the path.

That would not happen to Delia.

And if she knew a core of truth remained untapped within some of her clients, well, what of it? They always got better, even without tapping it.

Emil Hart would be the same.

"I *have* come back," Delia said.

She wondered if she erred with the voice, but Hart gave no sign of anything amiss. He rested his hands on her shoulders and raised his chin a fraction. "You had to come back," he said. "Things were left unfinished." Slowly his grip on her shoulders tightened, and a misconnected look invaded his eyes.

Delia fought the urge to pull away, then found herself unable to move as a spark-edged wave of regret surged from Hart's hands and coursed through her. She began to tremble as Eve's image first expanded in Hart's mind, then ran like rain-drenched watercolors.

When the color finally coalesced, Delia found herself—still trembling, but in control—on one side of a sheer, opalescent curtain. On the other side, a shiny, two-dimensional Eve hung like a paper doll suspended in blackness. Hart hovered in the background, very straight, hands at his sides, blocking a narrow passage that led to an even denser darkness.

Delia shivered. She had encountered such openings before. Sometimes they looked like doorways, sometimes like entrances to caves, or mine shafts, or even rabbit warrens. In the days when she had perceived her aversion to them as a character flaw, Delia had routinely mastered her fear and gone through the apertures anyway. But then Charlotte had begun to change, and one day Delia realized that every time her mother came back through one of the doors, she had misplaced another little piece of herself.

Fear was an expression of the survival instinct; Delia would heed it.

She would not go through this door.

But the transparent curtain was less threatening. She took a moment to plan her path of retreat, then pushed through.

The coldness on the curtain's other side was so brittle, she almost dissolved into herself.

Wrong, she told herself. *Don't do that.*

Wrapping the cloak of Eve's appearance around her more closely, Delia moved nearer to Hart and tried to discern his expression.

He had none.

She probed a little around the thin, hard edges of his image, but could find no deeper access. After a while, she inched carefully back toward the curtain. Once, she looked at Hart over her shoulder. He remained in the doorway, his face still immobile, his thoughts unfathomable.

When Delia withdrew from his mind, their time was up.

"I have to go now," she said. "Will you come back?"

"Of course, Eve. What else can I do?"

"What happened in there?" asked Peter. "I could see *you* for a second, Delia." He handed her a cup of tea and sat down behind his desk.

Delia relaxed into the sofa that occupied an entire wall of the cubbyhole Peter called an office and gratefully sipped a little of the strong brew. "He's an odd one," she said, swiveling the knots out of her neck. "He's disconnected from her, somehow. No feelings I could get to at all." Except for that initial flash of regret. And whatever lay beyond the door, of course, but she'd find a way to help him without going there.

Self-consciously, Delia picked up a small basalt figurine of Maat from the desk, then looked up. "What brought him here, anyway?" she asked.

Though Peter raised his eyebrows, he did not comment that Delia usually plucked that sort of information directly from the client's mind.

"He's been dreaming about her," Peter said.

"There's got to be more than that," said Delia.

Peter nodded. "I didn't realize it right away, but Eve came here first, a long time ago. I recognized her as soon as I saw your manifestation. I think you were away at college, otherwise you'd remember her, too. They had a little girl—Alice, I think her name was—who drowned. It was one of those cases where the parents get distracted for a minute, and by the time they realize something's wrong, it's too late. Anyway, Eve fell apart. When she couldn't put herself back together, they took the usual route—psychiatrists, medication, hospitals—but she just got worse. Finally, after she swallowed a bottle of pills, somebody sent her to Mother, and she seemed to improve. I suppose Emil's looking for the same solace."

Idly, Delia turned the figurine of Maat over and over in her hands. Unlike Delia, the goddess could see beyond the mind, into the soul.

"I wonder why Emil's dreaming about Eve now," she said. "She's been dead a long time."

"A couple of months ago he sold a cabin they owned. He says it stirred things up."

"How did she die?"

Peter leaned back into his chair. "Her car went off the road, up in the mountains."

"An accident?"

"That's what the coroner's jury called it."

Too ordinary a tragedy to explain that numbing cold.

"There's something else," Delia said. "I can't put my finger on it . . . something bad."

"Well," said Peter thoughtfully, "Mother thought there was something odd about the accident."

"Like what?"

Peter shrugged. "She never said, exactly. But whatever it was, I know she took Eve's death as a personal failure."

"I wonder why." Delia squeezed her eyes shut, trying to bring back that metallic wave, but it was gone.

"Take him through the door, Delia."

They both jumped, startled to find Charlotte in the room. Backed by a shaft of sunlight, she looked insubstantial, a pale wraith that moved without sound. She swayed a little, and Peter came from behind the desk to steady her.

"He can't go there by himself, Delia. You'll have to take him through." Though Charlotte's voice was tired, otherwise she sounded normal, her old self.

Delia ignored a surge of what she knew to be false

hope. "Mom," she asked, "have you been eavesdropping again?"

"Take him through the door."

"Mom, you're ill," Delia said. "You don't—"

Suddenly, Charlotte's eyes grew too big for her wasted face. "You think because I'm dying, I'm useless. But I'm not. I can see this. Take him through the door!"

Delia set the figurine of Maat down with a bang. "I want those damned peepholes plugged!"

Only when she noticed the echo of her words hanging in the air did she realize she had screamed.

Charlotte sagged against her son. "Don't leave them alone together, Peter," she said. Slowly, her features began to lose definition, to slide into those of someone else.

"Delia," Peter said, "go get the nurse." And when she didn't move right away, "Go now!"

For a moment Delia stared at them, horrified more by her own loss of control than her mother's. Then she turned and went in search of Mrs. Jensen.

Delia sat in the garden on a small wrought-iron bench, a bunch of purple irises at her feet. She had cut them as an apology; they were Charlotte's favorite.

She looked up as Peter sat down beside her.

"She's sleeping now," he said.

Delia let out a long sigh. "For a minute I hated her. I don't know what happened."

Peter covered her hand with his own. "It happens to me too. I think I've accepted it all, that I'm coping just fine. Then I get a glimpse of what she used to be and it's . . . I don't know . . . a taunt, almost. And I find out I'm not really coping at all."

"So, what's the answer?"

It was Peter's turn to sigh. "I've been doing some reading," he said. "There's a nursing home up north—"

Delia gaped at him. "Are you kidding?" she asked. "What nursing home would take her?"

"Just hear me out. They have a specialized environment for people whose minds . . . wander, and—"

"It's more than Mother's mind that wanders," said Delia. "Her *face* wanders."

"—*and* they're doing trials using medication for Parkinson's disease with Alzheimer's patients. Maybe it would help mother."

Delia shook her head. "Be realistic, Peter. Once we explained the problem, they'd want to commit *us*."

"I don't mean we'd send her there. If we could just get them to prescribe the medication, we could do the rest ourselves—remodel part of the house so it isn't so open, hire more help maybe."

He looked so hopeful, Delia hated to discourage him. "I don't know," she said. "I suppose it wouldn't hurt to get the information."

She couldn't imagine it though, a jail for a prisoner of inconsistent identity.

A soft thudding underscored not-quite-intelligible murmurs.

Emil Hart's walking stick made the thuds as it contacted Eve's bright head. She did not try to fend off the blows, simply knelt in penitence, reciting her sins, until she was driven to the ground. The sound of the blows went on for a long time after she stopped speaking or even moving. Then that sound stopped too, and a single white feather drifted down from somewhere far above.

Delia bolted upright in bed, fumbling frantically for the lamp.

Outside the door, Charlotte murmured to herself, the thud of her footsteps echoing along the hallway as she padded toward the stairs.

Delia got up and went into the dark hall. A humid breeze blew through an open window, and she paused to close it, blotting out the night music of crickets and cicadas. Then she stood on the top stair, listening, trying to locate her mother. Silence.

Downstairs, she found the kitchen and sun porch empty, but a sliver of light shone beneath the ebony door that separated the parlor from the Manifestation Room. Delia eased it open.

A young girl with bobbed black hair stood before the taper-flanked mirror. Her eyes, dark-fringed and the color of blueberries, brimmed with tears.

"Hello," said Delia softly. "Who are you?" *This time.*

The girl bit her full lower lip. "I don't know who I am," she whispered. "I thought my name was Lottie. . . ."

"But that isn't Lottie's face," Delia finished.

The girl pressed slender hands to pale cheeks. "No," she said, "but I've seen it before, somewhere. I think I dreamed it. Am I dreaming now?"

Delia nodded. "But I can help you wake up."

She led the girl to one of the boxwood chairs, then perched before her on a low stool and captured the child's gaze with her own.

"Now keep looking at me," Delia said, "and very soon you will be able to look through my eyes, into my mind. You'll find Lottie's face there, and you'll put it on."

"How?"

"You'll know how."

"I will?"

"Yes."

Then Delia opened her mind to Charlotte, who had been called Lottie sixty years ago and who had awakened tonight thinking she was Lottie still. But some other child, long-dead, looked back at her from the mirror instead. Charlotte must have become her once, and the frail specter had slipped out again tonight, unbidden, through the cracks in her reality.

"Are you ready?" Delia asked.

The child nodded.

In the silence, Delia re-created her mother. As the image took form in Delia's mind, she could feel the penetrating tickle of Charlotte's consciousness. Then the features of the blue-eyed girl shifted subtly, and after a while the little ghost was gone.

Charlotte looked in the mirror and sighed. She touched the eyes, the cheeks, the thick, dark hair.

"There I am," she said, smiling quizzically. "But better, somehow, don't you think?"

Delia shrugged, trying to ignore the guilt squirming in the pit of her stomach. She had intended simply to reinstate the present, but had been unable to banish the vision of the vigorous matriarch her mother had been a decade before.

As they started downstairs Charlotte rested a hand on her daughter's arm. "Delia, dear, I thank you, but this won't last. It's cheating, you know."

And that, of course, was true.

After helping Charlotte back to bed, Delia returned to her own room, but sleep eluded her. Finally, around five, she got up, made tea, and spent the time before breakfast going over the notes of her sessions with Hart.

He was coming again today.

In fact, he had been coming to see her weekly for more than two months, but so far their sessions had yielded little of import. Recollections of insignificant slights blown out of proportion. Apologies for broken promises. Regret for promises never made. The shredded fabric of a marriage gone awry, but nothing to account for the bone-chilling coldness or for Delia's dream tonight.

She checked her Eve-persona in the Manifestation Room mirror and found it nearly perfect. Even so, Delia knew the stress of living with Charlotte was turning her ragged around the psychic edges. She should have brought Hart further along by now, should have had some inkling at least of where to take him next. She rubbed her eyes. They felt grainy from lack of sleep.

Peter concluded the induction and led Hart to one of two chairs facing the mirror, then sat in the corner to wait and observe as he had promised Charlotte. Delia took the other chair.

Hart looked haggard, as though he hadn't slept much either. "Why do you haunt my dreams?" he asked.

Delia crossed Eve's legs at the ankles while she tested Hart's thoughts; she encountered nothing but Eve's image bouncing back at her.

Finally, she settled for the words Hart had used in their first session. "Things were left unfinished."

In the candlelight the old man's eyes were colorless and unreadable. "Ah," he said nodding, "so many sins left unrepented, unforgiven."

Hart sat a little straighter, and Delia became aware of a tensed spring of emotion just beyond the dark doorway. If she could tease it out into the light, perhaps they'd make some progress.

"We might talk about those sins," she suggested. "Perhaps I could rest then." She pushed a little further into his mind, but the specific words and images were still inaccessible. "It's been so long, Emil," she said. "Help me. Where should I begin?"

He took a slow breath, seemed to expand with it. The pale eyes widened, and though his reserve in no way lessened, a spot of mauve appeared high on each cheekbone. "I think, first, you must confess." The low syllables were unmistakably precise.

Here it is, Delia thought. She pushed a little further. Still no words. "Tell me what you want me to say."

His eyes widened even more. "*Confess!*" The candle flames wavered with the reverberations.

Almost there. Not quite. She inched toward the door. If she could just *see* in.

Indistinct shadows. Useless. "Tell me the words."

Hart closed his eyes during a long silence. Finally, control apparently restored, he spoke. "You first betrayed me in the cabin, up at the lake. . . . Go on, say it."

"I first betrayed you in the cabin, up at the lake. . . ." Some of the shadows gained definition. An A-frame cabin overlooking still, blue water.

". . . in the cabin, up at the lake," he repeated. "Because, because . . ." He trailed off and was quiet for a while. Then he abandoned that tack, and moved on. "You lay in our bed together"—an old four-poster; a quilt half on the floor—"and you gave away what was mine."

The uncoiling had begun, though not of a tightly wound spring, as Delia had imagined. Instead, a long-dormant snake awakened from malignant dreams.

And I didn't have to let go of myself.

But then the snake opened its eyes.

It pulled Delia along as it retreated through the door.

More than accessible now, the unstoppable images spewed forth like venom. Hart no longer had to speak; Delia plucked the pictures as they tumbled from his tortured psyche. "We lay together in the same bed I had shared with you," she continued, her voice like a recording heard faintly through a wall. "I gave away what was yours. I let him touch me in all the hidden places only you had a right to be. And he was just the first of many."

It went on and on then, the tawdry, titillating, intimately humiliating details of one adultery after another, until all of Eve's sins—whether real or only of Hart's imagining—had been expressed.

Delia was on her knees, shivering. Hart stood over her, still taut, though the images were spent.

"I forgive you, Eve," he whispered. The stiffness deserted him, and he sank into a chair. "Ah, thank God that's done."

Then came Peter, blessed Peter, leading Hart back to the present, back through the ebony door, away from the trembling figure of his wife.

Delia did not notice when Peter returned. She had doused the candles and turned on the lights, and, arms wrapped about her, stood studying her reflection. Eve's reflection.

Peter put his hands on her shoulders and caught her eyes in the mirror. "Time to come back," he said.

She was not entirely sure whom he addressed.

"Delia!"

She turned on him, eyebrows drawn together in irritation. "What?" Then, recognizing him and the concern in his eyes, she softened. "What, Peter?"

"Time to remake yourself."

She looked at him, puzzled.

"Delia," he asked, "do you need help?"

"No," she said, shaking her head.

Something important here, though. Her heart began a painful tattoo. Something she feared. Delia pressed a hand over her eyes and grasped at the little scraps of an image she found behind her lids, gathering them in helter-skelter before they could flutter away. Dark eyebrows . . . a long jaw . . . straight brown hair—she struggled to organize them into a whole—shorter now . . . heavier . . . less angular.

"There I am," she said.

Her heart steadied as she stared at her own reflection.

Peter looked at her speculatively, then shrugged. "Well," he said, "I'm glad that's over."

"Me too," said Delia. No reason to doubt it. Hart had said himself that it was done.

Mrs. Jensen cleared her throat loudly. "This one doesn't like my eggs," she said. "Claims they're poisoned."

Delia looked up from where she had been drowsing over her morning tea and a sheaf of notes. She tried smiling but found that she was too tired. "Who is she this time?"

"Some skinny, evil-smelling old man."

Delia got up from the table and accidentally dumped her notes on the floor. She stared at them distractedly.

Tired as she was, she would have to bring Charlotte back without Peter's help this time. They'd canceled the day's appointments so he could visit the nursing home. Though Delia still doubted they would find any solutions there, at this point she was willing to try almost anything. Charlotte was getting worse. It had been days since she had been herself for more than a few minutes at a stretch, except when she was sleeping. And of course, she never slept when anybody else did.

"I'll see what I can do," Delia told Mrs. Jensen.

But they could not get into Charlotte's room. The doorknob turned—they'd removed the lock long ago—but something, probably the vanity chair, had been wedged up against it on the other side.

"Mother," Delia said, "let us in."

A man replied. "No. No. No. No." The staccato syllables competed with what must have been the screech of the dresser legs scooting along the floorboards. "And your mother's not here." The dresser banged into the chair.

Delia took a step back, looked at the door. "Who are you?" she asked.

"Just who the hell are *you?*"

Calmly, she told him her name. "I'm looking for Charlotte," she said.

"Well, look someplace else. She's not in here." The man's raspy breathing filled a long pause. "What is this place, anyhow?"

Delia inhaled deeply, slowly let the air out. "It's Charlotte's room," she said. "I think she may be hiding in there. If you'd open the door, maybe I could find her."

The man's labored breathing continued. After a long while, he answered. "All right. But just you. Nobody else. Understand?"

"Yes. Okay."

Once again, furniture scraped along the hard floor. Delia motioned for Mrs. Jensen to stand back. Then the door opened, revealing an emaciated old man who leaned heavily on Charlotte's vanity chair. It was amazing that someone so frail could have moved the dresser.

He stared at Delia, studying her face with undisguised suspicion. "Do I know you?" he asked.

"You might. I'm—"

Mrs. Jensen crowded up behind Delia.

Beneath their shaggy brows, the old man's eyes widened impossibly. He snatched up the chair and lifted it over his head. "You're the one who's trying to poison me!" he yelled. Then he hurled the chair at Mrs. Jensen. It smacked against the hallway wall, narrowly missing her head.

"That's it!" she said to Delia, backing down the hall. "I'm finished." She reached the landing and rushed down the stairway without looking back.

The old man started after her, but Delia caught his arm.

"It's all right," she soothed. "Come back inside."

He strained against her, but the outburst had sapped his strength. The tension went out of him finally, and he allowed Delia to lead him to the bed where he sat down.

"I want you to help me find Charlotte now," she said, sitting beside him.

"She's not here."

"I think she is." Delia placed her hands on either side of the old man's face. "You're going to look into my mind, and then you'll help me find her."

The old man twisted his head away and squeezed his eyes shut tight. "She's gone away, I tell you, and she's not coming back."

"She can't just leave like that," said Delia. Suddenly she felt like an abandoned child. Her tears came as a surprise.

Still the old man refused to look at her. She went to the window and stared down into the garden. The bedclothes rustled behind her.

"Delia," Charlotte whispered.

Delia turned around. Though the old man still inhabited Charlotte's body, somehow she had found her own voice.

"Delia, I know you're afraid, but you have to help me. You're the only one who can."

Delia started to protest, to say again that there was nothing she could do, but before she could muster the words, her mother, still in the guise of the old man, fell asleep on the bed.

Delia walked downstairs slowly, wandered into the kitchen, found her tea. It was tepid, but she sipped at it anyway. She gathered up her notes and made a half-hearted attempt to put them back in order, then gave up and sat staring through the kitchen window.

The office phone rang.

She walked across the hall, taking her tea with her, and got there as the answering machine picked up.

After the inevitable beep, Emil Hart's voice, tinny and disconnected, came through the small speaker. "I need to see Eve again, soon," he said. "It's important. She comes to me in every dream I have. She wants more than forgiveness. Please, call me."

And then, though Emil was miles away at the other end of a maze of lines and circuits, Delia could see Eve, wrapped in a lover's embrace, unaware that her husband stood at the foot of the bed, his usually controlled face a treatise of pain and rage; his walking stick was in his hand; he raised it slowly.

The crash was accompanied by a wet, warm spattering. It took Delia a long time to realize she had dropped her cup and it was only droplets of lukewarm tea that ran down her legs. As she reached to Peter's desk and took some tissues to blot up the spill, her hand brushed the statuette of Maat. Without knowing why, she put it in her pocket. The message light blinked dull red.

"Call him back."

Delia whirled around, stomach lurching. "Mom, what are you doing down—"

Eve Hart stood in the doorway.

"Put aside your fears now and call him back. It's time for this all to be over."

"But Mom," Delia said, feeling like a child again, "I don't know what to do."

"Go through the door." Eve's features blended fuzzily with Charlotte's. "Otherwise the truth makes ugly pictures that seep out in our dreams."

Delia remembered the last time she had seen Emil, recalled the effort of finding the way back. She shook her head.

"You can't ignore your gift, Delia."

"Gift!" Delia squeezed her eyes shut to blot out her mother's unstable visage. "Look what our *gift* has done to you."

Exasperation spread across Charlotte's face—or was it Eve's? "I'm proud to have done what I was good at." And then, more kindly, "Delia, we all die."

"Not like *that*."

Charlotte shrugged. "Some other way, then. Take him through the door, Delia."

"Mom . . ." She wanted to say yes and no, both at the same time. Yes to her mother. No to . . . what? But Charlotte's determination flowed over Delia like a pent-up tide released, obliterating her ambivalence.

"I'll help, you know," Charlotte said and smiled in a way Delia didn't understand.

Delia, clothed in Peter's shape, met Hart at the door. The old man had encountered no other living person in the house; he didn't know of Delia's existence. There was no point in changing that now.

She preceded him into the parlor and indicated a chair where he waited for the induction to begin, clenching his walking stick with white-knuckled hands.

"Now, Emil," Delia said, using Peter's cadences and rhythms, "think back to the last time you saw Eve before she died, the last time you saw her when she was really alive. . . . Are you thinking of that time now?"

He nodded.

"Very soon you will have another meeting with her, a final meeting, and you will discover how to lay her to rest. Do you understand, Emil?"

"I understand. We will finally be free." For just a moment a beatific radiance suffused Hart's face, then left so quickly Delia was not sure it had been there at all.

She struggled to maintain the thread of her thoughts and continued. "You must start with Eve's death, Emil. Talk with her about your part in it. Let *her* forgive *you* this time."

He shook his head, brow furrowed, hands clenching and unclenching the walking stick. "That won't be enough. She wants me to be punished."

"Perhaps that's so," said Delia, her voice unsteady as she fought to remain separated from Hart's intensity. "Or perhaps it's something else Eve wants. Shall we go in now and find out?"

Hart nodded curtly.

"Come with me, then."

A peculiar sense of doubleness overtook Delia as she settled in the corner where Peter had waited during her own sessions with Hart. During the induction, Charlotte had gained control of her manifestation. Its perfection reinforced Delia's knowledge that even at her very best, she was aware of herself, wrapped in someone else's persona. But her mother was Emil Hart's Eve, completely.

"Emil," Charlotte said, stepping close to him, tears spilling from her downcast eyes, "thank you for coming back again. Thank you for helping me."

He laid his hand on her shining curls, pushed them back from her damp forehead. Except for the movement of that hand, he appeared as unbending as he had been on that first day. Heavy lids hooded his eyes as he stroked and stroked her hair. His hand sliding down her back, he pulled her close and kissed her, then lowered her into a chair. After watching her for a while, he knelt and took her hands.

"I thought forgiving you would be enough, Eve . . ."

"But it isn't," Eve finished softly.

"I must be punished." Emil gripped her hands tightly.

She gave him a small, encouraging smile. "And how would we accomplish that?" she asked.

He dropped her hands, stood, and gazed into the mirror as if it held something other than his own reflection. "There are those," he said carefully, "who administer punishment once guilt is established."

Eve closed her eyes, drew in a soft little breath. "Are you sure that's the path you want to take, Emil, even knowing what's at its end?"

He gave a jerky nod. "I worry about you, though."

She smiled and patted his vein-studded hand with her young, supple one. "That's unnecessary, Emil. I can't be much deader than I already am."

The flesh around his eyes trembled as if tectonic forces worked deep beneath the planes of his face. He grasped her by the shoulders. "But I can touch you! You have a body. You're solid. You can feel."

"Of course I can. Now. But only here, Emil. Outside this room there's only . . . confusion. When this is over, we'll both be able to rest." She smiled again. "So, shall we begin?"

Hart stared at her for a long time, then sank with weary familiarity into the chair where he had spent so many hours. "All right then. Tell me about the last man."

Eve licked her lower lip and closed her eyes, remembering. When she opened them again, they had taken on a faraway, glassy look, much like Hart's. Delia found herself, with a volitionless ease she had not experienced before, sliding into her mother's mind. Except the mind was not Charlotte's; it was Hart's, filtered through Charlotte. And Charlotte was Eve.

"I never knew his name," Eve began, "never bothered to find out, though he may have asked mine. He was of no importance. Just an expendable pawn." She tilted her head to one side, met Hart's eyes. "Now, there's another crime."

Hart nodded mutely. They sat silently for a while.

"When did we start committing the crimes, I wonder? Do you remember?"

He shook his head.

But Delia saw a child splashing in a sparkling mountain lake, paddling and laughing while her parents held hands on the shore, so wrapped up in each other that when the tone of the child's squeals changed, they did not immediately notice. Then, though no cloud blotted out the sun, the water darkened. Abruptly, the vision ceased.

Hart wiped a hand across his eyes. "I want to remember only that last night now, Eve."

"All right, Emil. There's time." She paused, finding her place in the tale. "I had tried to argue with you that night—so many nights. But you . . . couldn't?" He nodded, and she continued. "I said all the harsh, horrible things I could think of, searching for the one that would make you talk to me. Shout at me. Anything but your silence. Your indifference. But you simply sat, with your hands between your knees, and looked through me. So I went out into the night and found him somewhere."

"You found him in a tavern."

"Yes, you're right," Eve agreed. "What was the name of it?"

Shade Inn, thought Delia.

"You know the name," said Hart.

"Shade Inn. I met him at Shade Inn. A stranger. Tall. Young. Handsome. We drank together for a while."

Hart sighed. "And then what happened, Eve?"

"We drank together, and when the tavern closed—"

I took him with—Delia clapped her hand over her mouth to keep the words from spilling out in time with her mother's.

"I took him with me, in the convertible, up to the cabin and we—"

Made love.

"Made love."

"It took a long time," said Emil.

Eve bit her lip. "Yes, Emil, a very long time. And then, when we finished," she wrinkled her brow, "you were there."

Hart rose and turned his back. Though they could no longer see his face, he could do nothing now to lock them out of his mind.

"I followed you that night," he said. "I waited in the parking lot."

In the shadows beneath the trees, as straight as one of the old oaks, and as incapable of speaking.

"I loved you, Eve. Love you." Even now, the words came haltingly.

Eve touched his shoulder, but Emil did not turn.

"When you came out with your lover, I followed you to the cabin. I watched the two of you through the window. After a time it began to rain, so I came inside. It seems so odd now, that I would come inside." His words were whispers from a mausoleum.

"I saw you then," Eve continued, "at the foot of the bed—"

"And still I could . . . not . . . speak."

Cold. Cold. Cold, thought Delia, and was racked by an uncontrollable shiver.

"We went out into the night, putting on our clothes as we went, frightened by what we saw in your face. But I was triumphant, too. I drove him back down the mountain, but it was—"

Raining.

"Raining," Hart said in that same sepulchral whisper.

"And we had had too much to drink."

"And you always drove too fast," said Hart.

Eve nodded. "And I was in a hurry to get back."

To your anger.

"But I missed a turn. It was a long way to the bottom of the ravine."

"And you died."

"Yes."

That Hart still stood with his back to them was the only outward sign his implacability had deserted him. "The police called it an accident, you know," he said. "They never knew."

"Never knew what, Emil?"

"Why, that I killed you, Eve; that I drove you down the mountain with my coldness. That I murdered you. They never knew. So I haven't yet paid. But I will. This time there won't be any doubts how you died." He took a deep breath. "Eve, kneel down."

Eve took a step back from him and sank to the floor.

He turned slowly, eyes shadowed pools in an ashen face, and raised the walking stick that had found its way into his hands. "This time I *will* be punished."

Not like this. But Delia had no part in it.

The look Eve turned up to her husband was one of pure knowing and acceptance. "I forgive you, Emil."

For a moment, they were poised like that, a tableau from Delia's nightmare. Then Hart began to shake. Slowly, he lowered the stick, dropped it. The only sound was the hollow rumble as it rolled across the hard floor. He stumbled backward into a chair and covered his face with his hands.

"And a coward on top of it all."

"No," said Eve gently. "Not a coward. A kind man, always."

"But I won't be punished."

Eve shook her head. "You've done penance all these years, Emil. It's almost over now."

Eve turned to look at Delia.

There, suddenly, was the door in Emil Hart's mind. Illuminated.

A child paddled and laughed in a sparkling mountain lake while her parents held hands on the shore, lost in each other's eyes. "Papa!" she called. "Look at me!" When Hart didn't seem to hear, she made for the shallows, came up out of the water. She pushed the dripping strands of her bobbed, black hair away from her face, and the sunlight made bright crystals of the water drops caught in the lashes that fringed her deep blue eyes.

"Papa! I'm *here*. *Look* at me," Delia said, realizing as she said it that her voice was no longer Peter's, that she had transformed into the child with the blueberry eyes.

Hart looked up, confused. "Alice?" he whispered. "Alice?"

"Yes, Papa, it's me. I'm here." Still dripping with lake water, she came close to him, reached out her little child's arms and wrapped them around him.

For a long time he stood, embraced but not embracing.

Then, with a convulsive jerk, he locked his arms around his daughter and lifted her. She snuggled close to him.

"Alice," he murmured, "I'm so sorry. I never meant, never intended—" The rest was lost in a sob.

Alice leaned back in his embrace, studying him with the peculiar earnest intensity of a well-loved child who has first encountered adult despair. "Don't cry," she said. "I know you and Mama didn't mean for it to happen."

"Emil," Eve said, gently touching his elbow, "say the rest of it now. Say all of it."

He looked up, confused. "What?"

"Why, that you loved me," Alice said. "That you miss me."

He swallowed hard several times before he found the words. Finally, they came in a choked whisper. "I loved you, Alice. *Love you*. And I miss you. Miss you both. So much."

"And we love you, Papa. Always."

Behind the tears Emil Hart's face was that of a shattered statue cleansed by rain.

The sun, low in the sky, cast rose shadows on the wall of Charlotte's room. Delia sat in a wooden rocker by the bedside, watching Eve as she slept. Regaining her own form had taken a toll on Delia, and she would need her reserves of strength for the work that was left. So she had helped her mother up to bed but not through another transformation.

Delia heard Peter's tired tread on the stairs just as dusk slipped into darkness. She went to meet him in the hallway. One look at his face told her things had not gone well at the nursing home.

"No help there," he said. "Those poor people might as well be dead. They just stare into space all day. And they're not including any outpatients in the study, anyway."

"It doesn't matter, Peter."

He didn't seem to hear. "The director gave me another name, though. I'll call in the morning."

"Peter," she said again, "it really is all right."

"How can you say that, Delia? Didn't you hear what I said?"

"I heard you, Peter, but we don't need them." She rested her hand lightly on his arm. "Come on with me."

"Oh, God," he groaned when he saw that it was not Charlotte who slept in the bed. "Not again, not right now." He crumpled into the rocking chair and buried his face in his hands.

"It's all right, Peter," she repeated. "I know what to do now."

She sat down on the edge of the bed and took the other woman's slender hand. "It's time to wake up," she said.

Eve blinked, then stared at her with those clear gray eyes. "I think I remember you. You were there when I was talking to my husband." She drew her brows together. "Was he my husband?" she asked.

"Well, in a way," Delia replied. "He's Eve's husband." She waited for the implication to register.

"But I'm not Eve," the woman said.

"No."

Charlotte caught sight of her image in the vanity mirror and stared at it for a long time. "That's not *Lottie's* face."

"That's right. But I'm going to help you find your face. This time you'll be able to keep it forever."

"It's what I want, you know."

And Delia did. She could feel the certainty, warm and solid, at her very center.

"All right now, look at my eyes, and in just a minute, you're going to feel me in your mind. You're not to be afraid, but I need to find you there, just to make sure. Do you understand? I need to find your image, just the way you want it to be, and then I'll help you put it on."

Charlotte nodded. Then her eyes lost their focus, and Delia found herself inside her mother's mind. Off to one side, Emil, Eve and Alice stood together in a tight little knot, but Delia paid them little attention. She could see the door, a rectangle of pulsing violet light. Ignoring the last vestiges of her fear, she stepped through.

She was in a long corridor, lined by people who stood shoulder to shoulder on either side—men, women, children—all still as wax figures. Some of them she recognized as manifestations from Charlotte's past, but most were unfamiliar.

Far in the distance the corridor ended in a circular room with walls of burnished copper. A huge scale, its two sides out of balance, dominated the room's center. Delia had to go there.

She started out, felt herself descending. Eyes fixed on the scale, she stopped only once before a man she thought might be her own dead father. But he remained unspeaking, unmoving, and after a time she went on.

Finally, she reached the scale.

Its lower side was weighted with the linen-clad form of an Egyptian woman, familiar but somehow out of place. Delia reached out and took the still, white hand. A tingling current enveloped her. She tried to let go of the hand, but could not. She could feel her hair billowing in a nimbus. Slowly, Delia lifted her gaze to the copper walls, expecting to find her own reflection.

Maat stared back at her with kohl-rimmed eyes, a large feather clasped in her right hand.

She looked back to the scale where Charlotte's final manifestation now lay. Though much older than the child Delia had found weeping in the Manifestation Room, still this Charlotte appeared not so very different from Alice. They were both dark-haired, slender and finely formed. But Charlotte also emanated the strength and assurance of a powerful woman in her prime.

Taking her time, Delia memorized every detail of the image. The thick hair. The delicate nose. The graceful limbs and rounded fingernails. When she finished she laid the feather gently on the other side of the scale. Slowly, the two halves balanced.

Then Delia retraced her steps past all the silent people Charlotte had taken into herself. Finally, she reached the door, stepped through it, and withdrew from her mother's mind.

"Now, look at my eyes," Delia said. "Look at my eyes, and soon you will be able to look through them, into my mind, and there you will find yourself, just as you want to be. You'll find your image there, and you will put it on."

"How?"

"You'll know how."

Then Delia could feel Charlotte pulling voraciously at the image she had been unable to claim before because it lay through a door she could no longer breach by herself, down a path she could no longer follow.

Once Charlotte had donned her chosen form, the final transformation did not take long. She closed her eyes, inhaled once, deeply, slowly exhaled. Then she fell still.

After a while, Peter reached out and touched her wrist. He looked at Delia and shook his head. "She's gone."

Though Delia was crying, for the first time since Charlotte had begun to slip away she felt no regret—just a hollowness that would lessen if she paid attention to it now.

"It was what she wanted, you know," Delia said.

What else had there been, finally, to want?

Delia sighed, wondering who would breach her own door and go down that long corridor, who would play Maat for her and help her don her final face when she could no longer do it for herself.

AFTER THE RAINBOW

Written by
Fruma Klass

Illustrated by
Brett Hess

About the Author

Fruma Klass grew up in the Bronx in New York, and was among the first wave of girls admitted to the hitherto all-male Bronx High School of Science. At the time, she was also an impassioned Zionist determined to live on a kibbutz—until at the age of fourteen she was expelled from the Zionist Socialist organization for individual deviationalism. She says that her life pretty much went downhill after that.

She briefly flirted with Dixieland jazz, playing the coronet, and somehow found herself working as a hematology lab technician, which of course took her into medical writing.

Meanwhile, she married Phil Klass, a science fiction writer that you might be familiar with. Phil wrote many fine stories under the name of William Tenn. For twenty three years, while Phil taught writing and science fiction as a professor at Penn State, Fruma somehow managed to avoid writing her own stories—though she edited and taught writing herself.

Recently, she realized that it was time to get a move on with her own career. Her first published story appeared in

George Zebrowski's Synergy *series (Vol. 3). The fine story you are about to read is her second sale.*

About the Illustrator

Brett Hess was born in Michigan City, Indiana, and has long had a fascination for the macabre and surreal in art, taking inspiration from both Renaissance artists as well as such moderns as Salvador Dali, Ivan Albright, and H. R. Geiger.

At the American Academy of Art in Chicago, he received his associate degree in illustration, and is currently working in his own style, using the airbrush to create a textured appearance in his paintings.

Brett describes himself as being "obsessed" with his art, working nonstop. The good ones usually are.

Call me Ishta.

It's a good name; actually, for me, it's the very best name possible—it saved my life. It means "his wife," and that tricked God into thinking I had a right to be on the Ark when I didn't. I was only a baby, only four months old—so how could I be somebody's wife? What kind of man marries an infant?

A good man, that's who. Ham, second son of Noah. A big man, with wonderful big hands—he used to toss me in the air and just set out those big hands to catch me as I fell back down; there was no way I could hit the ground with Uncle Ham's hands outspread. When I was little I really believed that Uncle Ham could do anything. It was almost true; at least, he could *make* anything. I remember when he let everything else go and spent a whole week on beautiful pinwheels, perfectly carved and painted, for all of us kids—me, my brother Gomer, and my cousins Rika and Bassi.

Bassi was his own daughter, and I used to envy her. To think of having Uncle Ham as your father! But then, I always reminded myself, you'd have to have Aunt Rodel as your mother.

Bassi and Rika had been born on the Ark, and that made them special. They didn't even *look* like the rest of us. Bassi was darker than everyone else, and Rika was lighter. Bassi's hair was *curly*—when her hair was wet, the curls got bushy and didn't even drip. Rika's hair was somehow reddish, not a dark brown like everyone else's. Both girls looked a lot like their mothers, but Bassi didn't look like Uncle Ham at all, and Rika didn't look like Uncle Shem.

"The Rainbow," Aunt Bintra said. "The effect of the Rainbow changed their colors."

"Why didn't it change mine?" I asked her.

"You weren't born on the Ark."

"But wasn't the Rainbow after we *left* the Ark?"

"Sometimes what has not yet happened casts a shadow backward."

But I never understood, and she'd turn to Rika in exasperation. "Explain it to her, Rika," she'd say. "Explain to her that Mother knows best."

And Rika would dutifully try to explain to me what made no sense to her either. The one thing she was absolutely certain of was that Mother knew best.

Well, why shouldn't she? Aunt Bintra was a Wise Woman, after all, so she *ought* to know. Wise Women, I used to think, knew all there was. Any time someone got sick or hurt, Aunt Bintra would come by. She'd tap on your chest, inspect your tongue, smell your urine, and feed you some nasty-tasting tea. And you always got well again.

Of course it was always possible that when Aunt Bintra said "Mother knows best" she meant *the Mother*, not herself at all. But I didn't think so. The adults were very careful never to refer to the Mother where God could hear them. Everybody knew that God couldn't stand the competition. The men never mentioned Her at all. And Aunt Bintra, without being nervous about it like *my* mother, was especially careful.

Careful, yes—but also so calm, so certain! I used to envy Rika for having Aunt Bintra as a mother—but then, I'd have to remind myself, you'd get Uncle Shem as a father. And Uncle Shem would have been an awfully disappointing father.

For one thing, he was hardly ever around. The animals were his responsibility, and he spent almost all of his time with them. Rika once said she thought he loved the animals more than her; when she said it to him, he laughed and told her that she could get along without him much better than the animals could. They needed his full attention; she could find other people to pay attention to her.

They *did* need his full attention. When the Ark came to rest and the ground dried out, he was the one who had to decide which animals to wake up, and in what order. The gazelles and the deer and all the other grass-eaters had to be allowed to build up their herds before the jaguars and the lions could be loosed on them. And that took time.

So the big cats and the other predators slept on, inside the Ark, while the herds slowly increased. And Aunt Bintra could never spend much time with us children; she had to stay close to the sleeping animals and watch their drugs.

Sometimes she'd have to do a healing that would take real time; when Imma (that's my grandmother) slipped on the muddy patch in the road and broke her hip, Aunt Bintra worked on her for hours, twisting and pulling and chanting every minute of the time. Her chants were always wonderful and this one was longer than most of them, because an old woman's hip was especially difficult, Aunt Bintra told me later. But I couldn't resist the urge to memorize it:

"Make this whole, Arundhati! Whichever bone or even more than one bone inside thy body hath been wrenched or cracked, may Dhatar set it in a proper manner and stick the arm or the leg together, join the marrow onto the other marrow and stick thy limb onto the other arm or leg. Let what hath fallen off of thy flesh, and also off of the bone, grow back on again. Close up the spaces between one marrow and another piece of marrow. Let the pieces of skin stick together, so thy blood gets thicker and thy bones grow strong and do not break anymore in thee and thy flesh grows together with all the rest of the fleshy parts. Stick thou together hair and also skin and even blood and bones, to grow strong in thee. Fix the broken part, O plant. "

"Who is Dhatar, Aunt Bintra?" I asked her. "Who is Arundhati?"

She shrugged. "How should I know? Old gods, maybe—no, I shouldn't say that. Forget I said that."

And she wouldn't talk about it anymore. The older people, all of them, are still too afraid of God to even talk about how afraid of Him they are. For them, the world before the Flood is still real, and they remember too much. It's hard to believe the tales they tell of that wonderful world—grand houses, two and three stories high, with lanterns at all the windows, they had so much oil to burn. Carpets on the floors, with perfect designs and colors; so much cloth that everyone, even children, had three or even four different garments; jewelry and body ornaments made of precious metals. We have so little, because there simply isn't enough time for Aunt Rodel to weave so much cloth or even to spin enough wool to weave it, or for Uncle Ham to dig and smelt metal just for decoration.

But most of all, they tell stories of the people. And those stories are the most fantastic ones of all. Hundreds, no thousands of villages, and each village with hundreds and hundreds of people. If you traveled a few days, you could come to a city with maybe five thousand people, but even if you stayed home there were more people than you could remember the names of. And that seems impossible.

It was all real enough to Aunt Bintra, though—real enough that she wouldn't talk about it anymore. But I had memorized her incantation—that was fairly easy, since I *had* heard it twice—and I was bothered by its lumpiness. So I worked on it a little and gave her a better version. I wasn't prepared for her reaction. She went straight to my father.

"Yafeth!" She really had to shout; my father was working on a history, and he did hate to be bothered when he was working. He worked on those histories most of the time; that was his job, keeping the History and the Records. But finally he came out of our hut, rubbing at his eyes as he always did, and asking why, what was the matter?

She waved the slate at him—my new version of the incantation. "Wait," she said. "First let me give you the original." And she quickly wrote out the chant I'd tried to improve on. "Here. What do you think of this?"

That moment is carved into my memory, into my very bones. Above us, the sun's heat poured down like cooking water, and sweat streamed from my armpits and puddled down my back, but my hands were suddenly cold and the back of my neck shivered. In the normally quiet forest, a single bluejay called out. I was unable to move.

My father peered at the slate and pursed his lips. "Bad spelling," he said. I held my breath. "Most of the vowels are wrong. But reasonably good lines. One of your boys?"

The words were calm and measured, but his voice trembled. I knew what was going through his mind; it was the same thing that was troubling all the adults: Which child could they find to receive their crafts?

Aunt Bintra was going mad with the problem—Bassi was the one who should have gone into training with her to become our next Wise Woman, but Bassi couldn't have been less interested. It was too late, anyway, since Bassi had started having babies as soon as she began having her monthly moon-cycles ("matching the Mother," my aunts called it). Rika couldn't train for her own mother's specialty, and I—I had been promised to Aunt Rodel. To be a Crafty Woman.

To be a Crafty Woman. To practically live with Aunt Rodel and Uncle Ham. Not as Uncle Ham's second wife, no—that "marriage" had been dissolved when I was ten. (Oh, they were terribly clever, the adults! They'd worked it all out on the Ark, after they'd found me, the only survivor of the world God had drowned: Ham would marry me and save my life, then divorce me after ten years of a barren marriage. Then—at ten—I'd be apprenticed to Aunt Rodel and married, at sixteen, to my cousin Eber, the son of Uncle Shem and Aunt Bintra. My whole life mapped out when I was four months old.)

But it didn't work. It didn't work for any of us.

Being a Crafty Woman was a nightmare for me. My eyes and my memory were fine, but I was simply clumsy. I dropped things—a clay pot had only a few days' life around me. My fingers got thick and felt like chicken gizzards whenever I had to do any fine handling. My seams would rip open when I sewed, or the thread would somehow tangle itself into monstrous knots that I couldn't undo. I desperately didn't want to become a Crafty Woman.

What did I want, then? My mother, Hanni, used to ask me, holding me in her lap and murmuring into my hair: "What does my Ishta want, then? What does my Ishta want? Tell Mama Hanni and Hanni will bring you a shiny star to hold in your hand. . . ." It wasn't a star I wanted, but it might as well have been. I wanted something I couldn't have, of course. I wanted to apprentice, not to my mother—that would be awful enough—but to my father. I wanted to be a Recorder. A Historian. Like him.

And now I stood barefoot on the flat rock in front of our hut, the rock on which I'd first practiced my word-marks with soft limestone. Along one edge was the spot where my father had let me carve my name, once my hand was steady and readable. Gomer's name was there, and those of my younger brothers, Magog and Madal, but mine was the only girl's. The rock was hot. *I'd let my feet burn before I'd move.* I kept my head down, staring at my own name—*Ishta, Ishta*—while a single bluejay's raucous cry split the carven moment, like a single bolt of lightning against the black sky, with an aftersound like the lightning's afterimage.

"Reasonably good lines," my father said. "One of your boys?"

"I'm afraid not," Aunt Bintra said, and his face drooped; a tiny bit of hope remained in it as he asked her who, then, had produced the lines. "It's your daughter. This one."

My father sighed. "I hoped again," he said.

"Yafeth, isn't it possible—"

"And the crafts, then? Shall I send Gomer to learn the crafts? Or shall I send him to become a Wise Woman? Will you teach him, Bintra, to be a Wise Woman?"

"But these lines, Yafeth. Surely a child who could write these lines . . ."

"I can't, Bintra; you *know* I can't. Still, the lines are good. I'll do a little more on them."

"Oh, no, Yafeth, I want them exactly the way Ishta wrote them." Say it, Aunt Bintra, say it.

"If you like," Aunt Bintra said.

"Or—I'll tell you what," my father said. "Ishta, why don't you do it? Make it really good—and get rid of those names."

"Arundhati and Dhatar?" I asked.

He nodded. "And let me see the final version."

I could hardly breathe. He was going to let me Record. Oh, it wasn't a major bit of History, but it *was* History, and it *was* Recording. I would make this chant perfect. I would make him proud of me.

Arundhati gave me a lot of trouble. I finally solved it, along with *Dhatar*, but I'm still not happy with it. Anyway, this is the final version I gave Aunt Bintra— and my father:

Make this whole, O round of tea!
Let blood and bone grow strong in thee.
Whatever of the bones are split
Thy daughter give it proper fit
And join together limb by limb.
With marrow let the marrow mesh
The limb united with the limb;
Let what hath fallen of the flesh
And the bone also, grow again.
Let marrow close with marrow;
Let skin unite with skin;

Let blood and bone grow strong in thee,
Flesh grow together with the flesh.
Join thou together hair with hair.
Join thou together skin with skin.
Let blood and bone grow strong in thee.
Unite the broken part, O plant.

"'O round of tea' doesn't make sense," my father
said.

"It's the tea made from the plant," I said defensively.

"Ah, *we* know that, certainly, but will the reader a
hundred years from now? A thousand?"

And once again I could not breathe. He was opening
a door here; not much more than a crack, it's true, but
enough to show me what a wide world lay behind it.
This was the first tiny step, the first chance I'd ever
gotten, to learn about being a Historian.

And the door flapped shut, as quickly as it had
opened.

"Don't you think you'd better hurry to your Aunt
Rodel? Surely there's something you ought to be
learning. . . ."

It was enough. For the moment, enough. If he would
open that door from time to time, if he would let me
learn his specialty, I could stand Aunt Rodel and the
dreary, repetitive tracing patterns we were doing now.
What difference did it make what pattern a pitcher had
around its base? Who looked at the base of a pitcher
anyway? Aunt Rodel was the only person alive who
cared about such things.

But she, at least, did care. Her children—all of
them—always wore perfectly fitting clothes, with intricate

designs in dyes and embroidery. Bassi wore sandals
made of rope, with thongs that came up between her
toes, small versions of the rope sandals Aunt Rodel wore
herself. The rest of us all went barefoot, and Bassi hated
her sandals. She said they hurt, and Aunt Rodel was
always after her to put her sandals back on. Bassi always
obediently put them back on, but she'd slip them off
again whenever we were out of her mother's sight. Bassi
always *looked* obedient, but she always found ways of
doing exactly what she wanted.

She'd matured too early, Bassi had. She'd turned into
a woman and started fighting Aunt Rodel while the rest
of us—Rika and I—were still good little girls ("The
effect of the Rainbow," Aunt Bintra said, but that didn't
explain it). Bassi was shorter than a woman ought to be,
because she'd stopped growing when her monthly
cycles began, but tough—oh, wonderfully tough. She
never actually refused to do anything she was supposed
to do, but somehow it just wasn't possible. For instance,
how could she start to train as a Wise Woman when she
was pregnant?

Every one of the adults had a session with her to find
out who the father was. And she never actually refused
to tell them; she just said she didn't know.

Uncle Shem spent two hours drawing charts on the
ground, to show her what would happen if she'd picked
the wrong father. Aunt Rodel threatened to break both
her legs. Hanni, my mother, burst into tears and pleaded
with her. Even my grandfather, Noah himself, who talks
directly with God, couldn't budge her. All she would
say was that she didn't know.

But she told me.

"All of them," she said. "They were all after me like
flies after Eber's puddles, and I just got tired of saying

no. Besides"—a little giggle here—"I wanted it too. I *love* making love. Don't you?"

Which wasn't very nice of her. Bassi knew I wasn't ready yet. But it just wasn't possible to stay mad at Bassi, when she stretched to her full height, a whole head below yours, looked up at you with those round eyes like a big baby herself, and then giggled.

"When you say 'all of them,'" I asked carefully, "are you including Noah himself?"

Bassi opened her very black eyes wide. "Sweet Mother, no! Not any of the grown-ups! I'm glad I told you first—it never occurred to me that they'd think 'all of them' meant *all* of them!"

Later, I remembered that she hadn't excluded her brothers, though she had excluded Eber, more likely because he just wasn't up to fun and games much lately than because he was betrothed to me. At the time, what bothered me most was her casual invoking of the Mother. If God overheard, He just might kill us on the spot; one thing we all knew was that He was a jealous god. That He didn't kill us could only mean He hadn't been paying attention.

Counting Bassi's six brothers, the father of her baby might be any one of nineteen boys—eighteen, if you left out Eber—though a few of them really were too young. They were certainly too young for formal marriage— they had to be seventeen for that. But a girl was supposed to be sixteen to marry—fourteen when she matched the Moon, plus two years to ripen. Bassi was fourteen *now*.

Rika was also fourteen, but just about the exact opposite of Bassi. Tall where Bassi was short, straight and leggy where Bassi was full-hipped and curvy, so pale that her skin blotched with little brown spots in the sun. And Rika, of course, was nowhere near woman-hood: she was all angles and bones, without a trace of the rounding she'd show later. Still, she *was* fourteen, and that meant that she'd be marriageable in two years. Saba and Daden, the older sons of Uncle Ham and Aunt Rodel, were getting tired of waiting.

You couldn't blame them, I suppose. Whatever had happened—or had not happened—with Bassi, Bassi was their own sister and not available, at least not openly. But Daden and Saba were twenty-three and twenty-four years old, bursting with health and strength and pent-up sexual hunger. They couldn't go after me, because I was promised to Rika's brother Eber. But Rika herself—well, Rika was promised to *them*, wasn't she?

One thing that would have to be settled, and settled soon, was *which* one would get her. And since no word came down from Ham, their father, or from old Noah, their grandfather, evidently it was up to them to settle the question themselves. They went about it exactly the same way as the rams and the billygoats—and the bull elephants, for that matter. They began butting heads.

It started slowly, with measured stares and barely discernible posturing. But it moved along pretty quickly, until the day it broke into a full-scale fight. There they were, rolling on the muddy ground, panting and grunting, in the middle of a circle of cheering boys. Even the youngest—my brother Tiras, Rika's brothers Lud and Aram, and their own brother Phut—stamped their feet and shouted "Get 'im, Daden!" and "Kill 'im, Saba!"

As long as the fight involved bare hands, no one interfered. But when Saba picked up a rock—and the light glittered off a shard of metal in Daden's hand—the adults stepped in. It was my grandmother, Imma, who walked up to them, right through the circle of screaming boys, right into the mud they struggled in.

The cheers and shouts died away. (The last to stop cheering was Bassi, whose final shout at her brothers, "Winner gets a woman, loser gets lost!" hung in the air like a band of wood smoke.)

Right up to them walked my grandmother, right into the mud, with a big wet fish in each hand. Swinging the fish by their tails, she slapped the two boys in the face. It was enough to make Saba drop his rock; Daden brought the metal shard up, at first, until he realized what had happened. I can't imagine anything more sobering than a wet fish in the face.

She stood over them, this tiny figure for once overwhelming. All the boys were utterly silent as she spoke, in a voice whose softness was more terrifying than open anger would have been. "I am an old woman," she began. "A grandmother. But it seems to me . . ."

She didn't speak long; she didn't have to. It was enough to remind them that our family had once before experienced the terrible sin of fratricide, that once before brother had killed brother—"and that time, it was because of God's favor, not a woman's," she said. "And what made you think that *you* could decide who Rika would marry? That decision was never yours to make— it was Rika's! Are we cattle, that the strength of the male decides? You should be ashamed of yourselves!"

Saba was blubbering; Daden, still holding his metal shard, had hung his head and was staring through tears at Imma's feet.

"Look at me, you great babies! What are we to do with you now?"

"Kill us," Daden muttered, and at the same time Saba pleaded, "Don't kill us."

"What do *you* say?" she asked beyond us, and we all became aware of a second ring of spectators: the three sons of Noah, Shem, Ham, and Yafeth, and their wives, and even beyond them, Noah, standing apart.

My father spoke. "We have a precedent here," he said. "Once before we had a fratricide. That one was accomplished and this one only attempted, but I think the precedent is clear."

The other adults nodded. Uncle Ham, sorrow graven in his face, spoke too. "We have no choice. We cannot permit brother to murder brother within our community. We cannot prevent them from murdering each other if they truly want to do it, but we cannot let it happen inside our community."

"We'll never, never do it again!" Daden was weeping; Saba had dropped to his knees in the mud and was staring at the adults in terror.

"You are to leave," Noah intoned. "As the murderer Cain was sent away from his family, so are you sent away; God has shown us what to do."

"But where are we to go?"

"Anywhere. Anywhere in the world away from us."

Daden had found his voice. Now that he knew he wasn't going to be killed, he sounded a little more normal. "Can't we *ever* come back?" he asked, a little resentfully.

"Never," began Noah, but Imma interrupted him. "With wives," she said. Noah looked at her. "Cain found himself a wife, so perhaps you will too. If you find wives, you can come back. *With* them."

"Aw, you know we'll never . . ." Saba was grumbling, as the adults walked away.

Shem, who hadn't said anything yet, suddenly stopped. "*Killing*," he said. "You are not to kill. Not people, not animals. Do you hear? There are not enough animals yet for you to kill—not even for food."

"All right, all right," Saba said morosely.

"If you do," Aunt Bintra added, "I will lay a curse on you. A heavy curse, a curse of bleeding, a curse of pain in the night, a curse of . . ."

"All *right!* We won't kill anything! We swear!"

"We will give you food," Imma said. "Enough for many weeks. There are fruits, and nuts—you won't starve."

"And good nets for fishing," Aunt Rodel said. Her voice sounded strange—unnaturally high-pitched. She was keeping tight control, though.

"May we kill fish?" asked Daden sarcastically.

Uncle Shem answered him seriously. "There is no shortage of fish, so you may kill and eat as many fish as you want."

"One other thing," Saba said. "I want to take my dog with me."

"Your dog," Shem said. Saba nodded. "I can see that you'd want to take your dog. But there are rules for the dogs, and you'd have to obey them." Saba nodded again.

"You'll each want a dog, and you should take them—male and female, so you'd always have some dogs. But the dogs must not be allowed to increase without control. Here, your aunt Bintra controls the litters with drugs—or we'd be overrun with dogs we couldn't feed. . . ."

I couldn't help starting a little calculation in my mind. If each bitch bore only one litter a year, and the litters averaged only six puppies each, that'd be eight puppies, with a total of four females, in the first year—thirty-two at the end of the second year—and at the end of five years, there'd be over two thousand dogs to feed, with the numbers going up so fast after that it was frightening.

". . . so that is the exception to the no-killing rule. Do you understand?" Both boys nodded. "But you may not eat the dogs. You may use the skins, but not the flesh." They continued to nod.

"You will be gone by sundown." Noah had turned back to say the last words. "You will not bring down the wrath of God on this community."

Saba and Daden shook themselves, very like dogs, in fact, and looked around at the rest of us. Their hair and faces were muddy, and tears had left clear runnels down their cheeks. We looked away. Uncle Ham had turned his back on his sons and was slowly walking away, his huge shoulders hunched over. He walked as if he were even older than my grandfather.

"It isn't fair," Bassi said under her breath. "It isn't fair at all. Now Daden and Saba will never have a woman, or children—and just because that's the one thing they did want."

"Oh, I don't know," my brother Gomer said, his arm around her thickening waist and his hand resting along her belly. "Better put your sandals back on. . . . Abel was the good boy, wasn't he? The one who was God's favorite, the one who didn't do anything wrong? So how many of us are descended from Abel?"

It was worth asking my father about. Cain, the murderer, somehow left descendants; Abel, beloved of God, left none. No matter what He said, then, wasn't God actually favoring Cain?

"We would like to think," my father said, "that we are the descendants of the third son, Seth. But we also carry the blood of Cain in us, and we must not forget it. Each of us is capable of committing murder, if the circumstances are right. You too"—and he looked at me, hard—"if you don't get what you want, *when* you want

it, you too can get angry enough to kill. Don't ever forget that. Growing up is learning how to live without
getting everything you want."

"Is growing up agreeing to do something you hate,
for the rest of your life?"

"If it must be done and there is no one else to do it,
yes."

"But there is! What about the younger girls—Rika
and Bassi and I aren't the only ones!"

"But it is up to you to set the examples for them. And
the younger girls are *very* young—Mari's not even six."

"And Rika's sister Lida's not even five—but so what?
You had *my* life planned out for me earlier than that!"

He sighed. "You are different, Ishta. You know that.
We had to decide for you in a few frantic minutes, to
save your life."

"But I'm a person too!"

He looked startled. "Your mother said that. She said
you were a person, not a puppy dog."

"My mother . . . ?"

"Hanni."

"Oh," I said. For a moment, I'd thought he meant
my original mother, the woman who'd climbed the Ark
and tied me in place for the people inside to find, when
she knew she would die along with the rest of the
world. But of course he meant Hanni, the only person in
the world who never, ever reminded me that she hadn't
given birth to me.

"You still feel somehow separate, don't you, even
though we couldn't possibly love you any more than
we do. . . ."

But he'd said it before, and I did still feel separate,
different. How could I help it, when they—everyone

but my mother, Hanni—said it to me all the time: *"You are different, Ishta. . . ."*

"You *look* like us, you know. Think of Rika and Bassi—*they* don't look like the rest of us at all."

Rika and Bassi who were born on the Ark. Who got the effect of the Rainbow.

"But you have questions, don't you?" Yes, I had questions. "I'll tell you whatever I can."

"What was my name before it was Ishta?"

I'd startled him again. "I never thought of that," he said.

"When is my real birthday?"

He threw up his hands. "You know I can't answer *those* questions," he said.

"Why can't I be a Historian?"

He brightened. "That one I can answer. You can't be a Historian because, one, you are a girl and not a boy. That means that you will become a woman, and not a man. Two—"

"Why can't a woman be a Historian?"

"Oh, Ishta, Ishta, we've gone over this again and again!"

"I have the talent, don't I?"

He would not lie to me. "Yes. You do."

"Then in God's name, why can't I be a Historian?"

"That's why."

I shook my head. "I don't understand. Look, you know you could explain it to me if you wanted to. Maybe you won't explain it because you know it doesn't make sense."

"Ah, but it does."

I waited.

"'In God's name,' you said. You can't be a Historian because you can't understand what 'God's name' means. Why, that is a meaningless—no, a dangerous—phrase."

"I'll never say it again!" I cried.

"Beyond that, because God will never talk to you."

"Has He talked to *you?*" I was skirting the edge of insolence, but I couldn't stop.

"No. But He might. At any time. A Historian has to have that possibility open—that someday, under some set of circumstances, for some reason, God might talk to him."

"But how do you *know* He won't talk to me?"

"He never talks to women."

It was so unfair I couldn't even speak—unfair, but not unexpected, really.

"You know, you never let me get to the second point." Of course he remembered his "two"; he'd structured his argument perfectly in his mind before he'd even started speaking.

"The second point," I said.

"You cannot train for your own parent's specialty."

"Why not?"

"You aren't thinking, Ishta. What would happen in a community where specialties were passed on from father to son, mother to daughter, generation after generation?"

"People could get to do what they really want to do," I said stubbornly.

He laughed. "You know better. There'd be just as many people who'd be miserable about being forced into the family specialty—probably a good many more. But most importantly, it would be terrible because families would keep their knowledge secret; because they'd plan marriages on the basis of the specialties. Because they'd eventually create a caste system, a tight, locked-up caste system, with the families who didn't have any specialty at the bottom, doing all the dirty work. Like Hanni. Would you like to see your mother being forced to clean everyone else's privies?"

All right, maybe he wasn't lying to me. But he certainly wasn't being fair. "I can't believe that would really happen," I said.

"It *has* happened," he said. "In the valley of the Indus, the same people who produced that bone-healing chant."

"'Arundhati'. . . ?"

"The same. They developed four major castes and a lot of minor ones within each major. There were the Thinkers, the Fighters, the Doers—and the Dirty-Workers. Would you like that?"

He wasn't being fair, and I told him so.

"Never mind," he said. "Those people are gone—washed away with the rest of the old world—and we have no caste systems now. We never will. We are free, and we are equal. We have no lords and no kings." He was silent for a moment, then added, "Except Him. Our God."

"Who doesn't talk to women," I said, the tears pushing at my eyelids.

"I'm afraid so," my father said. "Besides"—and his face changed, a tiny, barely perceptible change—"you'd put in the wrong emphasis."

"What do you mean, 'the wrong emphasis'?"

"Well, if you were Recording the history of Cain and Abel, you'd emphasize that Abel left no descendants, wouldn't you?"

"I suppose I would. Yes."

"And the result would be—what? A thousand years later, careless or evil men might use your History to prove that it's a mistake to serve God, or that there's no real penalty for murder—of one's own brother."

"But you could use the story that way *now*, if you wanted to. The facts are there."

"The facts are there, yes. But in order to discover that particular fact, it would be necessary to study the story many times, and by the time that fact appears, the important points have been accepted. No one could really believe that the true point of the History of Cain and Abel is that fratricide is desirable—as the History is Recorded now."

My throat had tightened up so that I could barely have spoken. The door had flapped open again. "You may not do it, and here's how," was what he was saying.

And once again, as soon as I became aware of it, it ended. My father rose from his seat, stretched luxuriously, and said conversationally, "Well, now that we're rid of Daden and Saba, I wonder what will happen to Eber?"

"Eber? What does Eber's illness have to do with them?"

"The three of them were involved in something God didn't like. Maybe He's punishing them."

"What did they do?"

"They hid Noah's clothes."

I hadn't heard anything about Noah's clothes disappearing. "When did they do this?" I asked.

"On the Ark."

"On the *Ark!* But that was fifteen years ago!"

My father shrugged. "His time is not the same as ours. If He could create the world and the stars in less than a week, He could also wait fifteen years for a punishment."

"Do you think Eber's illness is a punishment?"

My father spread his hands. "A reward it certainly isn't."

I thought about it as I walked back toward Aunt Rodel's. I didn't particularly want to go there—everything would be in an uproar over the boys' banishment—but I had nowhere else to go. Would Rodel really want to continue with the double-wreath pattern— *today?*

Along one of the footpaths at the end of the clearing, I came across another of Eber's puddles; you could spot them from half a mile away by the cloud of flies and bees. Something was very wrong with Eber: He was terribly hungry and terribly thirsty all the time. The hunger made him eat enormous amounts of food, but he kept getting thinner and thinner. And the thirst made him carry bags of water around with him, as if every walk across the green was a two-day trip. But all the water he drank seemed to go right through him, so quickly that he very often couldn't get to a privy in time.

And then there was something new—the itch. Eber was always scratching at himself, scratching until the blood ran. This meant that he was usually covered with scabs. Yes, he looked awful.

Aunt Bintra, who could cure anything, couldn't cure this. She knew what it was, she said, but there was no way to treat it here. What Eber had was the sugar sickness, and it would kill him.

In the old days before the Flood, when the fields were full of sheep, there was a treatment, Aunt Bintra said; you used the sweetbreads of sheep, dried to a fine powder. But that was out of the question now. Although we had plenty of sheep—eighty thousand at last count—we could not give up four healthy young sheep every single day. The grass-eaters had to provide food for the meat-eaters. The wolves and the panthers could not sleep forever.

Aunt Bintra seemed resigned, almost matter-of-fact about it. For the first twelve years of his life she'd been able to control what and how much Eber ate, she said, but once he passed childhood and was responsible for himself he had only himself to blame. The fish, eggs, and vegetables she fed him would have kept him healthy, but once the boys discovered the sugar cane growing wild behind the Ark, you couldn't stop them— they chewed and sucked on it all the time. We all did.

At Aunt Rodel and Uncle Ham's, it was Bassi who was making most of the noise; everyone else was calm. But Bassi was shrieking with rage: "They wouldn't have done anything—you know that! All they wanted was to be treated like grown-ups, and you wouldn't do it!"

"Put your sandals on," Aunt Rodel said quietly.

"I won't! I won't! You wear these rotten old sandals if you want to, but not me! From now on," and she pulled off her rope sandals and slapped them against each other, "I am free of you! You *and* your sandals that hurt my feet. My brothers are thrown into the wilderness and you tell me to wear my sandals! *This* for your sandals!" and she spat on them, slapped together again, and then threw them, one after the other, directly at Aunt Rodel. "You made a choice—you hear me? You chose these rotten sandals! Well, you can have them!"

Aunt Rodel tried to speak, though I don't know what she could have said; Bassi was not going to be stopped.

"You can name them. Name them Daden and Saba. Keep them around when you miss your children. If you ever miss your children. Because you just lost me, too."

Uncle Ham took one step forward.

"I am not your child anymore. I won't live with the woman who threw out my brothers."

Why blame only her mother? It hardly seemed fair; all of the adults had joined in expelling the boys, and it was my grandfather, Noah himself, who'd given the order.

"You can't go very far," Rika said. "The baby . . ."

Bassi looked surprised. "Who's going anywhere?" she said. "I'm only going out of *her* house."

So Bassi's wedding was years too early, though Gomer seemed ready for it. And Rika's, of course, was years too late—since she had to marry a son of Ham's, she had to wait for the next one to grow up. That was Canaan, two years younger than Rika. It really worked out better that way, though—by the time Canaan, who had been promoted to "firstborn," was old enough, Rika was genuinely ripe.

And me? What of my wedding?

Eber would never marry, would never father children—he was too sick, and Aunt Bintra said the sugar sickness was one thing we didn't need to preserve. He had reached the point where he fell into insensibility the way other people fell into sleep—but he'd stay in these sleeps for days, sweating and getting thinner all the time. One time he simply never woke up again, and when he died (he starved to death, Aunt Bintra said) no one was very surprised.

But it left me—the only one who should have married at the right time, the only one who'd matched the Moon exactly as expected—waiting around for the next son of Shem just as Rika had had to wait for the next son of Ham. Arphaxad was his name, and he was a lot more interested in training his dog than in getting married. He still had some teeth missing, and he usually had some nasty scabs on his knees and elbows. None of which was surprising; he was ten years old.

Was it reasonable to expect me to wait until the age of twenty-two? I was nineteen when Rika finally married,

and I could see the reflection in my mother's eyes of
what I felt: Precious breeding time was being lost. I
could have had—*should* have had—three children by
then. Bassi already had four.

But I *had* to wait for a son of Uncle Shem's. Uncle
Ham's sons, Cush and Mizraim, were my stepsons, because of that first official marriage to Ham; Magog,
Madal, and Javan were my own brothers. There were,
then, *no* men (or boys) I could even fool around with, let
alone have a child with. A few years before, in Bassi's
first pregnancy, there had been a shortage of girls; now,
suddenly, there was a shortage of boys, at least for me.

It was especially bad at night. Oh, it was rough
enough in the daytime—Bassi trotting her four little
ones past me like a duck trailing a string of ducklings,
the smallest baby tucked away in a harness she wore
like the peacock wore his feather tail; Rika pushing her
belly before her and saying that she was going to
outproduce Bassi, and the two of them giggling like the
girls they used to be, and pitying me. But the nights
were something else again.

Sometimes I'd take a blanket and go out to the
woods. It was perfectly safe: the few predatory animals
kept away from us, and of course there weren't any
other people. Lying in the long grass, I'd look up at the
stars that so thickly spattered the sky, and wonder why
God put them there; we didn't really need the light once
the moon rose. Some of them twinkled and some didn't;
a few changed their places in the sky, now a morning
star, then an evening.

With an effort of imagination I could see their patterns as the figures and animals my grandmother had
pointed out to me: the Warrior, with his long blade at his
side; the Hunting Cat, with his enormous whiskers

quivering; the Spoon with the Long, Long Handle. I could see them and yet I couldn't; there were times when they looked no more meaningful than the patterns of brown dots and blotches on Rika's face after a few hours in the sun.

But once the moon rose—ah, that was different. I had no difficulty seeing Her face on Her moon.

None of us were ever really sure about whether God could see in the dark, so for safety's sake I'd roll over and make my Mother-sign where He couldn't possibly see it, with my body shielding my hand. Thumb and the two inner fingers down, the two outer fingers extended— when you did that, you were calling on the Mother for help without making a sound. The best time to do this was at Old-Mother time, when you could see Her face.

And that's where I was, that's what I was doing, when I heard Aunt Bintra's terrible wail: "He's dead! He's dead! Oh, dear Mother, he's dead!"

Running back to the settlement, I was almost afraid to think. But my father, Uncle Ham, and Uncle Shem were at the Ark, along with my grandfather, and Aunt Bintra's five sons—Arphaxad, with his thumb in his mouth, Elam, Asshur, Lud, and Aram. Who, then, was Aunt Bintra wailing about?

The lion. The male lion.

Uncle Shem, with Aunt Bintra's help, had been slowly releasing the bigger animals as soon as there was enough food for them. They had gotten to the big cats in the past year or so, and, as usual, awakened the females first. Then, after the cubs were born and not quite help-less, they'd wake up the males. Sometimes a male would kill the cubs if they weren't his, and we guarded against that possibility. The lion cubs were past the stage of complete helplessness now, and it was time to wake

Illustrated by Brett Hess

up the big male and send him out of the Ark. But this lion would never wake up.

It was worse than that. All three cubs were female. So the death of the male lion meant that the entire species of lion would die too. After these cubs, there would be no more lions. Ever.

Aunt Bintra was kneeling on the Ark's walkway, sobbing as she had not sobbed for her son. She'd been calm and accepting when Eber died, but now she was carrying on at the death of an animal. Uncle Shem had gone over to her and was holding both her hands, murmuring, "It's not your fault, it's not your fault," over and over.

"It *is* my fault," Aunt Bintra said. "I didn't figure the right dosage. And Eber's my fault too."

"Eber was punished," Uncle Shem said.

"And Daden and Saba?"

"Also punished. But Eber must have been the leader."

"But it's *my fault*," Aunt Bintra said, and then she caught sight of me and her eyes widened. "You! It was because of you, what I did for you on the Ark!" And a look ran across her face, a look of such terrible hatred I thought I couldn't bear it. What had I to do with anything anybody did on the Ark?

Uncle Shem put his arms around her and she let herself be led away, still sobbing.

Actually, I thought it was pretty remarkable that they hadn't lost a good many other species of animal, too: They were using drugs that had never been used this way before, and Aunt Bintra had to calculate each animal's dose, over and over again. Just getting the drug into the sleeping animals was hard enough. But they had been successful with all the others, from the rhinoceros and the hippopotamus all the way down to the tree shrew and the weasel. Losing the lion was an awful blow, and Aunt Bintra felt responsible. This burden of guilt must have been so terribly heavy that she had to push some of it onto *somebody*. So why *not* me?

And another year went by: another child for Bassi and Gomer, another descendant of Canaan for Rika. Nothing for me. Arphaxad was getting older, of course—he didn't suck his thumb anymore—but he still wasn't old enough for marriage. And I was getting older too—with nothing happening.

The forests were filled, now, with the sounds of life. The baboons had split into two troops, and ritually shouted and threw leaves at the little family of leopards that passed their trees on the way to the lake. The elephants had really moved down the mountain and spread out—they needed fairly large ranges. Uncle Shem and my brothers Magog and Madal, along with four of my cousins, came back at last from the long trip to return the kangaroos and the rest of those strange pouched animals to wherever they'd come from. (They'd missed one—a funny little thing called an opossum got left behind. But I don't think Uncle Shem will make that trip again anytime soon.) Even the scavengers, the birds and animals that lived on dead things, had enough to eat, though barely.

Life everywhere. Only for me time stood still. Twenty years old, and still trotting obediently to the grueling sessions every day with Aunt Rodel. She had given up trying to instill any aesthetic sensitivity into me—actually, I could appreciate the fine detail work and enjoy beautiful patterns and colors as well as anybody else, I just couldn't produce them—and had settled for grimly trying to make me memorize formulas and procedures.

I don't think I'll ever forget how to make leather: the soaking and scraping and scrubbing, followed by steeping in a mixture of exactly twenty-two pounds of rye flour, ten pounds of oat flour, some salt, and enough yeast to set up fermentation. You mixed all this with enough water to make a cauldron-full and steeped the hides in it for two days. The hides would swell and get very difficult to handle. Then you put them in a solution of willow and poplar barks for eight days, turning them exactly at noon every day. Finally, you put them into a solution of pine and willow barks for another eight days, pulled them out and split them, and put them back into a fresh pine-and-willow-bark solution for a last eight days. They had to be scoured, rinsed, and air-dried, then tempered for three days by being folded together. At the end, you soaked them with a compound of two-thirds birch oil and one-third seal oil, the seal oil twenty years old and utterly rank. Aunt Rodel would then go on to dye the leather, but my mind balked at any further work on it. The process was so long, so tedious, and so physically tiring that it was hard to believe anyone—even Aunt Rodel—could *want* to have anything further to do with leather.

Aunt Rodel would shake her head in despair—she was doing that more and more, lately. "You *can't* be as clumsy as all that," she'd say. "Not the child of the woman who tied your harness to the Ark!"

Once again, somebody was pointing out my origins.

"You know, your real mother must have been a Crafty Woman. The beautiful knots she tied!"

"Hanni's my real mother," I'd say. "Nobody could be any realer."

"You *know* what I mean," Aunt Rodel would say angrily, and once she even silenced me with "I mean the mother who knew your real birthday." I couldn't speak at all after that one.

And Aunt Bintra seemed to be somebody else, somebody in terrible mourning all the time. I was really afraid to get sick and need her help; she was stiff and cold with me. Uncle Shem shrugged and said, "Eber *and* the lion. It's just too much." But why blame it on *me?*

More and more, I was feeling that I didn't belong, that they should have just let me die on the Ark. I wasn't really of Noah's family . . . I wasn't *supposed* to be saved . . . it was all a mistake. . . . Yet simply being alive was wonderful. Even those long nights in early spring, snug in my blanket in the long grass and looking up at the black sky so thickly spattered with stars, when I felt most alone and most separate from everyone else, I also felt most real and alive. The Warrior in the sky would smile at me, half drawing his sword from its scabbard, while I'd move my own hand slowly over my body and imagine that the exploring fingers belonged to someone else, someone unimaginable.

The lion's visit came first, of course. It was my younger brother, Javan, who saw her, the lioness, in an unmistakable second pregnancy. He was down the mountain with the herds of sheep and goats, pushing them farther away from our village. The goats especially kept wanting to come back to the settlement, and they had to be regularly pushed back out again. Goats can be remarkably persistent, and the job was continuous— otherwise there'd be no chance for the grass to recover, and we'd have animals dying of hunger while the valleys only a few days away were full of untouched grass.

So there was Javan, down at the foot of the mountain, with his pigskin bag slung over his shoulder, his flute in his belt, and his long crook in hand, shooing goats farther and farther away, when all of a sudden the lioness appeared on a high rock. She wasn't hunting, he said, just sunning herself and looking around. And her belly was heavy, heavy with cubs.

What questioning from Uncle Shem! How did she walk, how did she move? *Exactly* where and how did her belly hang? Had he seen any trace of a male lion? Did he *hear* anything—like a roar?

Only Aunt Bintra refused to believe it. As far as she was concerned, it was a fake, an attempt to make her feel good, and nothing more. She refused to feel good. The lions were dead or about to be dead, and their death was some sort of personal punishment from God. Why, you might as well tell her that Eber, whose limbs she had straightened and whose eyes she had closed before he went into the earth, had been seen dancing on the next ridge.

Hanni, my mother, tried to talk to her. "Eber, no," she said. "But that's God's doing. Death, that's His. But birth . . . ? Isn't He really too busy to worry about every birth of an animal?"

"What then?" Aunt Bintra said nastily. "Mother knows best?"

My mother stiffened. "It isn't something to joke about," she said. "No matter what you're feeling, there are some things you just don't say."

Aunt Bintra started to speak, but stopped. She glanced at the sky, then turned back as my mother continued with a line she'd said many times to me at home. "And besides, my father used to say—"

Aunt Bintra sighed. "'Don't wave your emotions in other people's faces,'" she recited, matching my mother's voice exactly. Although I'd been soundlessly reciting the line along with her, I was startled when Aunt Bintra did it. Once again I was reminded of how well the adults knew one another, of how much private history they shared before we—my generation—came along.

My grandfather, Noah, was the only one who casually accepted the miraculous lions. God had created the lions in the first place, he pointed out. So why be surprised when He simply repeated His original act?

In that case, my father said, there was no reason to study or to learn anything. "We learn that *this* way, not *that* way, is how the world works," he said. "We learn— so slowly!—how to do things, how to live. Then are we to amend that knowledge with 'Unless God changes it'?"

Uncle Ham said so too. "When I make a shoe for a horse, should I go on the basis of what I have learned about melting metal and shaping it, or should I stand back and wait for God to pass a miracle and make the shoe appear out of the butter churn?"

Noah was immovable. "He makes miracles when He wishes. He creates; He destroys. Blessed be His Name!"

"Amen," everybody said, but we were all troubled.

Uncle Shem was the most troubled of all. He talked about it later to my father. "Suppose, Yafeth, just suppose, that God felt the lions were really so important that it was worth breaking His own laws to keep them alive."

My father nodded. "All right. Then what?"

"Then all our work and worry over the lions was for nothing. It didn't matter *what* dosage Bintra gave them. She could have given them pickled potash, for all the difference it made."

"It looks that way," my father said.

"Then what are we doing with our lives?"

"What He wills," my father said, and they didn't talk about it anymore, at least not where I could hear them.

Only my grandmother, Imma, said nothing at all. But she started getting up at night and going out to the green in her nightclothes. From where I lay in the long grass outside the village, I could see her plainly. Thin white fabric fluttering in the night breeze, her long gray braid undone and the hair loose on her shoulders, she'd stand quietly for most of the night, just looking up at the moon and waiting. If she knew I was watching, she made no sign; she too, I suppose, was waiting for a miracle—but from the Mother, not from Him.

If the Mother *would* do anything, I would have thought She would act when the moon was full, when you could see Her old face. But there was no moon visible when it happened to me. To me. Like the lioness.

The night was particularly dark. Imma had been standing in the middle of the green but now I couldn't see her; there wasn't even enough moonlight to pick out her white cloth. The stars lay across the black sky, thick and beautiful.

Low in the sky the Warrior strode, his sword half-drawn from its scabbard. He smiled at me. . . .

And someone else's hands were moving on my body, someone else's fingers gently exploring.

Had it been at any other moment, I think I would have felt terror. Bassi would have been furious at this uninvited approach; Rika would probably have rolled over onto one elbow and asked coolly, "And who are you?" I seemed to have suspended all thinking.

I was aware of the stranger's body against mine: the length of it, the weight. He smelled unlike anyone I'd ever smelled before. His hair was dry and his skin a little salty, with a faintly burnt taste (so I was kissing him, yes, and tasting him). His beard was soft; his hands were hard and yet gentle. His head, over mine, blotted out the stars. I remember arching my back and trying to get even closer to him; I remember that my toes curled, and that lights and colors circled on the inside of my eyelids.

Later—much later—when I opened my eyes he was gone, and the Hunting Cat had moved lower in the sky. The Warrior was putting his sword back into its scabbard, and I found myself smiling. In my mind I could hear fourteen-year-old Bassi's sly "I love making love— don't you?" My blanket still held a trace of his personal, unmistakable odor.

Was this what had happened to the lioness—a visit from a wonderful male lion, or perhaps God Himself in the form of a lion, to ensure that the race of lions would not die out? But then why should God send the form of a man to me? Certainly *man* was in no danger of dying out.

No, impossible as it sounded, there was only one possibility: other people had survived the Flood. *Other People?*

A simpler explanation would be that I had imagined the whole thing. But I knew I hadn't. Even if I discounted the feelings of my own body, there was still a damp spot in my blanket and the trace of a salt-burnt odor. And— yes!—a hair, on my shoulder. The night was still too dark to see its color, but I knew it wasn't mine.

Then was it reasonable to assume two completely different sources for these two visitations, the male human and the male lion? If the man was not God in human guise, but a human being like the rest of us, the most rational explanation was that the lion was an ordinary lion and not a god in lion's clothing either.

Then—rationally—both man and lion came from the same place. *Other People* were alive on our world.

Could I really assume *Other People* from the existence of only one Other Person? Well, certainly one man could not have survived alone; for us, Noah's family, to survive it had taken the combined skills and knowledge and even brute strength of the entire group. A solitary man who managed to survive, and who had been living alone for the whole twenty years since the Flood, would barely *be* a human being anymore; surely he would have thrown himself on me like one of the orangutans grabbing at a female in heat, instead of being gentle and sensitive, as he was. (Was I a female in heat? Wasn't I?)

Anyway, Other People had survived; Other People shared the world with us. The idea was staggering. Even if this man had come to us alone—if, say, he'd been banished from his family as Daden and Saba had been from ours—another family existed.

It was difficult to keep my mind straight. I was thinking two completely separate lines of ideas—one, that there had to be Other Animals too, and wouldn't Uncle Shem go wild? and two, that if the man *had* been sent away from his family, he had to have done something terrible. Had he killed? If he had killed, could he— would he—kill again? Had he borne some mark, a mark I couldn't see in the darkness, to warn strangers against him? If so, would that mean that *his* family knew that *we* existed?

It was too much for me; my wonderful encounter in the night was now too important and perhaps too dangerous to be kept secret. I threw the blanket over my shoulders and started running back toward the village. The only question in my mind was who to tell first—my father? My grandmother? Uncle Shem? Old Noah himself?

In the gray dawn, I could see people beginning to move toward the green. There were too many people.

Young ones, old ones, a few children; women and men; tall ones, short ones, fat ones, thin ones—oh, it was impossible to grasp with a vision that had been limited to *our family!*

Noah had dropped to his knees and was offering prayers of thanksgiving; Aunt Rodel was fingering a woman's coat that was fringed with gold thread ("How could you spin gold into yarn? How do you have *time* for such things?"); Uncle Shem had thrown his arms around the neck of a young camel and was sobbing with joy; the camel kept craning its neck to look back at him.

My mother was laughing, with tears of joy running down her face. I was close enough by now to hear my grandmother, serene as ever, chiding her gently: "You should not be surprised, Hanni. Joyful, yes, but not surprised."

And, of course, I was looking only for the man, the man of the night before. I couldn't see him.

There *were* men, yes—but always the wrong size, or the wrong age, or even one who would have met every other test but was as bald as an egg. I wasn't going to find him; that seemed clear. He'd have to find me.

Looking for him, I was able to really look at our visitors without being overcome by the single idea that was so obviously uppermost in everyone else's mind: *We don't have to do it alone anymore!* I was able to note the really interesting differences between our family and these new people.

They certainly were different from us. For one thing, they were tall, much taller than we were—even the women were at least five feet. Their hair was straight, as ours was, but blacker, almost with blue lights. Their skin color was not terribly different, but less brown and more golden. The most striking physical difference, though, was in their eyes: they had a sort of extra fold in the eyelid that made their eyes slanted rather than round, like ours.

Their clothes were different, too. If Aunt Rodel hadn't noticed the gold fringe, I probably wouldn't have either. Despite all the labored sessions on patterns and decorative motifs, I really couldn't care very much about trimmings. But I had to notice the big differences: Where we all wore long robes, tied at the waist, over a loose poncho sort of undergarment, they wore short robes, no more than hip length. Under this kind of tunic they wore a strange garment that seemed to be a separate robe for each leg, the two tubes joined at the crotch into a sort of bag for the lower body.

It did look as peculiar as it sounds, but it was not really unattractive. I could see that it might be pretty functional, too, especially for climbing or riding a horse or a camel. But here, too, you could easily reason out that these people had to have come from some really large group; the amount of time it would take to sew all those seams meant that they had to have *many* Crafty Women.

Many Crafty Women! I wasn't the only one to reason all this out: Aunt Rodel had grasped the idea almost immediately, and was simply looking dazed; Aunt Bintra had carried it one step further and was asking for "your Wise *Women*." My father, of course, was asking eagerly for their Historian: "Where are you from? How did you survive the Flood?"

A woman answered, a thin woman who carried a leather bag very like the one my father carried his writing implements in. "Ours was the city of Sippar," she said.

"In the land of Sumer. Our own History says most of us originally came from somewhere else, somewhere further east. We'd been living in Sumer along with the other Sumerians, and we pretty much settled down in Sippar. Now we've gotten too large for one community—we were a whole city, after all. So we split."

"Who among you was the one God spoke to?"

The woman looked baffled. She turned to confer with a younger woman, who was carrying a small pile of slates. Then she turned back. "Which god do you mean?" she asked.

Now my father looked baffled. "*God*," he said.

The woman shrugged. "Some gods speak to some people, other gods speak to other people," she said.

"Well, who's the man that was warned about the Flood? Who saved you?"

"Oh, that was the old king, King Ziusudra. He died a few years later."

"Ziusudra . . . I've heard of a King Xisuthros. . . ."

"That's him."

"Is there a new king?"

She shook her head. "No, we decided that we just couldn't afford a royal family and all that. Besides, kings get unhappy when there's nobody to go to war with, and there won't be any wars anymore. We can't afford that, either."

"We also have no king," my father said.

"Then who saved you?"

"My father, Noah." And he looked around for Noah, who was still on his knees singing praises to God.

The thin woman looked disappointed. "Then where is your Old Woman?" she asked. You could clearly hear that "Old Woman" was a title, not just a reference to age.

My father seemed nonplussed. "I don't think we have one," he said.

"Of course you have one. No tribe, no clan, no human society, can survive without an Old Woman."

"We have a Wise Woman," my father said.

A quick, certain shake of the head. "No, an *Old* Woman."

My father looked around helplessly. Bassi, surrounded by wide-eyed toddlers, was giggling. "What are *you* laughing at?" he demanded. But she stopped giggling just long enough to point behind him. There, talking to a wizened little man who leaned on a stick, and accompanied as usual by my mother, was my grandmother, Imma.

"We do too have an Old Woman," Bassi said.

"I don't think you understand," my father began, but the thin woman walked past him, over to Imma.

"Come and meet *our* Old Woman," she said.

Without any trace of surprise, my grandmother nodded. "Excuse me," she said to the man with the stick, and followed the thin woman into the crowd. Her long gray hair was neatly braided, the braid wrapped around her head, and she was wearing her best white linen robe. Somehow, between the time I saw her standing alone in the night and this dawn when the strangers arrived, she had dressed and done her hair.

At the edge of the crowd, the thin woman brought her up to another old woman, someone who certainly didn't look like anyone important: a little on the fat side, definitely dumpy, with scraggly gray hair and some teeth missing. The two of them sat down together on a high rock like old friends.

The thin woman came back, smiling. "It's good to see two Old Women together," she said. "We couldn't live without them."

I could see my father's personal desire to argue struggle with his Historian's desire to understand; the Historian won. "Why do we need Old Women?" he asked.

"If we didn't need them, we wouldn't have them, would we?"

My father shook his head impatiently.

"Look—oh, where's your Animal Husband?"

The term was a new one to me, but it could only be one person. "Shem!" my father called, and Uncle Shem came over, with Aunt Bintra close behind.

"Are you the one who knows about animals?"

Uncle Shem nodded. "I know all there is about animals," he said simply.

"Do you know any animal where the female lives half her life span *after* she has stopped bearing young?"

Uncle Shem shook his head. "Elephants live for a number of years, but not half their lifespan."

"But people—women—do. A woman can live for forty years after her child-bearing is over."

"So?"

"So there must be a reason for it. There's always a reason."

"We don't always know why He does the things He does," Uncle Shem said slowly.

"We don't know why any of the gods do what they do"—Uncle Shem looked terribly uncomfortable— "unless they tell us, but we do know that *they* have some reason. There's *always* a reason. It's up to us, as thinking, reasoning people, to figure it out."

Noah had walked over to the little group and was listening silently. Now he spoke up.

"You keep speaking of gods," he said, hitting the

issue head-on. "But there is only *one* God. There are no others."

The thin woman sighed. "You need to speak with our Holy Man," she said. "I could reason with you, but you need more than *my* reasoning."

He was there, the same little man with a stick that Imma had been talking with. Again, he didn't look important at all. But his voice had as much richness and resonance as Noah's when he said, "Gods? Yes, let's talk about gods."

"Not gods," Noah said. "God. The one, the only."

"The One God is yours, right. But other people can have other gods, can't they?"

"'*I am the Lord your God,*'" Noah quoted. "'*Thou shalt have no other gods before me.*' He says that Himself, again and again."

"All right. Let's look at exactly what He says." The little man's voice seemed to take on an extra richness, an extra depth; he had been leaning on his stick up to now, but he stood taller and straighter, waving the stick with each emphasized word. "He is *your* god. Even *He* doesn't say he's *every*one's god."

Noah began to look distressed.

"He tells you not to have other gods before Him. He wouldn't *have* to tell you not to have other gods if there *weren't* other gods, now *would* He?"

Noah's distress was moving into anguish.

"He says that *you* are to have no other gods before Him. Right. But that doesn't mean that other people, people He *didn't* speak to, can't have *other* gods, now *does* it?"

Noah shook his head.

"And finally, He says that you are to have no other

gods *before* Him. Doesn't that mean that you may have other gods *after* Him, of lesser importance than Him?"

"But He is the God Who created us!"

"All right," the little man said. "But do you know for a fact that He created *us*, too?" He waved his stick around, at the crowd of *his* people.

Noah was silent.

"He created your ancestors. All *right*. But doesn't your History ever mention any of your ancestors running into some *other* people your god *didn't* create?"

"Cain," said my father.

The old man looked at him politely.

"One of our most important ancestors, the oldest son of the man and woman God created."

I couldn't help nodding as my father spoke. The problem of Cain kept coming up again and again.

"He found a wife in the land of Nod, but the History never explains where the Noddites came from."

The old man leaned on his stick and smiled, in quiet, purely intellectual triumph. "You see?" he said to Noah. He was speaking in a normal voice again. "Your god created your line. But other gods did some creating themselves."

Noah shook his head. "He also created the sun and the moon and the stars, everything."

"Even so," the old man said. "Did He ever claim that He was the *only* creator?"

"I don't think so," Noah said. "Did He, Yafeth?"

"No," my father said. "At least if He did, it hasn't been Recorded."

"There," the old man said. "Your god created you, and saved you from the Flood. Which He probably produced in the first place, but never mind that. But anyway, other gods created other people and saved *them* from the Flood."

"Are there others? Do you know of others?"

"We'll ask the Historian that. But first," and he spoke directly to Noah, "we need an agreement."

"I suppose we do," Noah said.

"About gods. We will not attempt to change your beliefs in your god—oh, not that we could, of course," he added hastily as he watched Noah's face—"and you won't try to change ours. Agreed?"

There was no way Noah could refuse; it would have been pure boorishness. "Agreed," he said, and although there wasn't much enthusiasm in his voice, he was giving his word.

My father asked again, "Do you know of any other groups that survived?"

"Our Historian would know about that. Aiello!"

The thin woman reappeared; she'd been watching Aunt Rodel, who was surrounded by what looked like a dozen Crafty Women showing her how their two-tubed garment was put together.

"Aiello!"

"Here I am," she said impatiently. "What's the big fuss?"

"Your Historian?" my father asked.

"Sure," Aiello said. "Don't I *look* like a Historian?"

"Well, no," my father said. "I've never heard of a woman Historian before."

Aiello shrugged. "I don't see why not," she said.

"Does your god"—he was adjusting quickly!—"speak to you?"

"Of course not. That's what Holy Men and Holy Women are for."

"We don't have any of those," he said.

"Your group *is* awfully small. You don't have a lot of specialties."

As they talked my mind began to whirl. A woman Historian . . . a woman Historian . . . it *was* possible! Once again, as it had before, the moment froze and I became wildly aware of every single thing going on around me: the sky, now brightly blue and cloudless; the morning sun, not yet hot, but spilling white light over everything; the flattened grass under my feet and the smell of the apple trees at the edge of the green; the flies that circled around us, determined to find a landing spot. No bird sang this time; the only sounds were the bees' buzzing and the woman Historian's voice. It was possible to be a woman and a Historian. It was possible.

"Excuse me," she was saying. "Do you think we could sit down for a while? We're really very tired— we've been doing a lot of walking."

Suddenly my mother was there, directing the younger children to bring stools and benches, the boys to build a cooking fire and the girls to fill the great kettle, the biggest one we had, with fresh water. Uncle Ham himself lugged it to the tripod over the fire; nobody else could have lifted it. All around us people were sitting down, beginning to take food out of bags and packs. To one side, three young women had opened their tunics and were suckling babies; my cousin Rika had joined them and was companionably feeding her latest baby, too.

Uncle Shem had found *their* Animal Husband, who trailed three boys and a girl that listened carefully to every word he spoke and occasionally marked something on slates. Aunt Bintra, however, couldn't find any Wise Women.

"We don't have any," the Historian said. "We've heard of Wise Women, but we've never had any ourselves."

"But you must have a Healer!"

"Oh, of course we have a Healer—we have a Medicine Man."

He was the bald man I'd seen before, the one who—if it hadn't been for his baldness—might have been my night visitor. He had the same kind of *capable* quality Aunt Bintra had, the same *clean* look. And like their Animal Husband, he also trailed apprentices, who ranged from about ten years old to about my age. Aunt Bintra was beyond surprise or protest at this point; she immediately started asking him about any new treatment he might know for the sugar sickness. He was shaking his head regretfully as they wandered off.

We ate; you might almost say we feasted, except that we hadn't been prepared to feed so many people all at once. But my mother wouldn't hear of them using up any of the food they'd brought with them; they still had a long way to go before they found a good valley of their own, and they'd need all their provisions. We did have plenty of rice cakes and goat cheese to fill in until the roast got going; there were a dozen boys to turn the spit. And Noah brought out four whole casks of wine, enough for everyone to have a couple of cups, though not enough for anyone to get really drunk.

There was singing, too—their Holy Man turned out to have a singing voice as good as his speaking voice, and he and Noah were singing some wonderful rounds and harmonies I'd never heard before. For one song, a lovely piece about being carried across the desert on the shoulders of camels, they were joined by a plain woman I'd hardly noticed before, who had an absolutely beautiful soprano voice.

So we didn't get back to History again until the evening. We sat around a good campfire, tended by my brother Javan and two Sipparite boys, and Aiello told us about how they'd survived and what others they knew of.

They'd built a lot of boats, she said. Their gods had warned them, and—unlike the people of other cities around them—they believed the warnings.

"Did you save *everyone* in the city?" my father asked.

"Oh, no," the Historian—the *woman Historian*—said. "Only those who were willing to work on the boats. But that was still a lot of people, because there were so many who *would* have helped but weren't able to, and we had to count them, too."

"You mean, people who were crippled, that sort of thing?"

"That sort of thing. People who were crippled, or sick, or too old to work, or children who were too young. We couldn't abandon them—they would have helped if they'd been able to."

Noah broke in. "What were the dimensions of the boats?"

Aiello shrugged. "They weren't the same. We just kept adding space as we kept finding more people."

Noah didn't say anything more, but he looked gloomy.

What about other people, my father wanted to know. *Had* they found any other people?

"We found *you*," Aiello said. We all laughed. "But besides that, we know of three other groups."

Everyone leaned toward her; all other conversations stopped.

"There's a group on Mount Nisir, about where the Tigris and Euphrates Rivers met—maybe they still do.

Anyway, they call themselves Akadites, or Akadians. Their leader is somebody called Utnapishtim."

"I know of those people," my father said. "They look like us."

"Some of their young ones don't," Aiello said. "They have a couple of redheads." She laughed, and my father laughed with her.

"Rika has red hair," I said, and immediately wished I hadn't.

"The effect of the Rainbow," Aunt Bintra said automatically, and then caught herself. They were all laughing, all the grown-ups. Aunt Bintra went on. "Surely the Rainbow affected other families too!"

"We have one ourselves," Aiello said. She waved her hand at a young man on the other side of the firepit; I hadn't noticed before, but he looked very like Bassi.

There was a general giggle, a sort of wave of good feeling. As it died down, my father asked Aiello to go on.

"There's a group that's not even big enough to call a group," she said. "Just two people, a man and a woman, on a mountain called Parnassus, or maybe Aetna or Athos. It's on one of a chain of islands in the sea to the west."

My father frowned. "Just two people? Why would a god save just two people?"

"Who knows? Anyway, they're called Deucalion and Pyrrha, and they seem to be the son and daughter of a god and his brother."

"A god and his *brother*?"

"Listen, I don't understand gods either. Anyway, there's one more group we know of; they're more or less in the same area where Utnapishtim was, but they don't seem to be related. These people were saved by someone called Yima. There's supposed to be a whole city of them."

"They also didn't measure their boats?" my grandfather asked, a question that was more of a mutter to himself than a question.

"They didn't use boats! You won't believe what they did," Aiello said. "They extended their city's walls into a great dome that enclosed it completely."

Uncle Ham shifted on his rock. "I don't think that's possible," he said. "How can you turn walls into a dome?"

"That's something our Master Builder would have to explain."

From the circle of people a man stepped forward. He was even larger than the rest of these large people, a true giant. "Here," he said to Uncle Ham, holding out hands as big as watermelons, "I'll show you how. Do you know how to build an arch?" The two of them moved toward the trees, the Master Builder gesturing with those enormous hands and Uncle Ham nodding and nodding. "Well, then you build *another* arch, right next to the first, and you fill in the space between them with mortar and pitch. . . . " The voices trailed off. I could just make out something about pottery tubes for air, "pointed *down*, so the rain can't enter . . ." as they moved away.

It was a wonderful night, a magic night. I had to admit it really didn't matter that I couldn't find the man of the night before; I'd found something much better: a woman Historian! I stayed and listened to her as long as she was willing to speak, going to bed only when she retired to her blanket roll.

Also that night, I knew with certainty that I was not going to bear a child out of that encounter; the familiar warm stickiness I woke with gave me just enough time to leap clear of my bedding without staining my blanket.

I didn't *have* to find him now unless I really wanted to. And I didn't, really.

The next day we were still catching up, still full of the glory of Other People and all we could learn from them. Aunt Bintra asked to see their Holy Woman and spent hours with her, under a thick black cloth big enough to cover a table. When she came out she looked at peace, though tired, and she hugged me. "It wasn't your fault," she said. "None of it. I've been blaming you for something you had nothing to do with." And she hugged me again. When I asked her what had happened, she shook her head. "No, dear, that isn't for you to know or for me to tell you. But I blamed you for something you had nothing to do with, and I want you to know I'm sorry. I love you very much."

"Aunt *Bintra*," I said, and burst into tears.

By the time our visitors were ready to leave, our lives had been shaken up a good deal. One thing remained— for me, the most important thing. I was trying to work out exactly how to ask my father to let me go with them, when Aiello came to see him—and asked for me herself. They were taking a few others with them—Bassi's brother Cush, for example, who was going to study Hunting. ("But we cannot hunt!" Uncle Shem said, and the Sipparites' Mighty Hunter said, "True. But someday people will hunt again, and we must not let the skills die. Your nephew Cush will never hunt himself, but his son, perhaps, may be a Mighty Hunter.")

And they were leaving some children with us: a girl who had wanted to be a Medicine Man but, of course, couldn't; two boys who wanted to learn what Uncle Shem knew about animals ("all there is"); a boy *and* a girl to take my place learning Aunt Rodel's crafts. No, they didn't call them Crafty Men; they called both men and women who knew the crafts *Artisans.* Aunt Rodel was ecstatic.

So when Aiello asked for me, I was more than ready to go. But my father said no.

"She has the talent, has she not?" Aiello asked, in an oddly formal way.

"She has," my father admitted.

"And you have seen that a woman can be a Historian, haven't you?"

My father admitted that too.

"Then why hold her back?"

"Because *I* am a Historian. Because she cannot train for her own parent's specialty."

"But you just heard our Mighty Hunter say that your nephew Cush's son might be a Mighty Hunter too—didn't that bother you?"

My father sighed. "First of all," he said, "Cush isn't *my* child. Secondly, he will never practice his specialty, just learn it in order to pass it on. But Ishta will *be* a Historian; she'll practice the art."

"And thus you cannot let her go?"

"I cannot let her go. Also, she is promised in marriage to Arphaxad, Shem's son."

"I'd come back and marry him! Oh, I would! Please, please let me go!" I was sobbing by now; this was the only chance I'd ever have, and it was sliding away from me.

Suddenly my mother was there. She held me, briefly, and then stepped in front of my father and Aiello. "Yafeth," she said, "let me speak."

My father nodded.

"We love her so much, Yafeth, that we forget the truth. The truth is, after all, that she is not your child— or mine either. . . ."

My breath caught in my throat as I realized what she was doing. She was giving me up, denying me—she was throwing away twenty years of being my mother. *"And what does my Ishta want, eh? Mama Hanni will pull down a star for you to hold in your hands. . . .* The pain in her voice was clear, and the determination. I cried out, "No, Hanni, no!" but she wouldn't stop.

My father was staring at her as if he didn't know who she was—and wished he did. I ran to her and threw myself into her arms. "I won't leave you," I said, and she managed a laugh.

"Of course you will," she said. "What kind of mother would I be to keep you with me by tying your feet?"

My grandmother added one last bit. "These are good people," she said. "Did you know that they are walking only four miles a day? It's because of the Old Woman— her arthritis won't let her go faster. But they could have left her with the rest of Sippar; they didn't have to take her along to slow them up."

"We're not in any hurry," Aiello said. "After all, it's a pretty empty world."

So it's all settled now, and all about as far from the original plan as it could be. I'll be leaving with the Sipparites in the morning, and I'm going to be a Historian.

I will come back, though. Some day my mother will be the family's Old Woman, and I want to be there. Besides, I owe the family something—some children, at least. *One?*

Just a little while ago, Arphaxad came to say good-bye. I hadn't realized how tall he'd become in the last few years. "Maybe you should throw a shoe at me," he said. "If you're really leaving . . ." He has the shadow of a mustache, and when he held me and kissed me good-bye I felt a definite stirring.

I will most certainly be back.

REFLECTIONS IN PERIOD GLASS

Written by
S. M. Azmus

Illustrated by
Gary McCluskey

About the Author

Scott Azmus has had your typical writer's grab-bag of experiences: As a child, he moved many times and found that telling stories helped him to make friends.

As an adult, he's had an interesting life, and he takes interest in life. He graduated with a BA in geology from the University of Colorado, is a certified gemologist, gained teaching credentials at the University of Oregon, then went through a number of jobs—observatory manager, electrician, marine outfitter, teacher, and so on—with a good deal of time spent in the military as a naval officer (Lieutenant Commander, specializing in surface warfare). For some reason, Navy folks do well in the contest. Perhaps all the time they spend on ships and submarines helps build a desire to write. Currently, Scott lives in Annapolis, Maryland, where he works as a full-time teacher.

Scott is the father of three children, and has been writing for the past couple of years, with recent sales to Aboriginal

SF, Galaxy, *and* Space and Time. *Like a surprising number of authors in this anthology, he has recently finished his first novel and is sending it out to publishers.*

The story you are about to read, a finalist in a hard-fought quarter, is reminiscent of the fine tales of Ray Bradbury or Zenna Henderson—the kinds of stories that will always be in demand. As a finalist, Scott will be eligible to re-enter. That's good. I find myself hoping to see more of his work. Perhaps next time he'll win big.

About the Illustrator

Like most of our artists, Gary McCluskey began drawing as a child and just never gave up.

In high school he took three years of commercial art and design, then later graduated from the Joe Kubert School of Cartoon and Illustration. He also studied art at Rhode Island College and at the Rhode Island School of Design.

He says that he is probably one of the few people who has met both comic artist Barry Windsor Smith and stop-motion animator Ray Harryhausen and had each of them say the very same thing: "Excuse me, son." (He was standing in their way.)

Gary McCluskey lives with his wife in South Attleboro, Massachusetts. It has long been the hope of those who administer the contest that our winners will use their money in such a way as to further their careers. Gary has used his prize money to begin publishing his own comic book, Rayne, in an attempt to pull of another coup as was done with the Teenage Mutant Ninja Turtles.

It is an endeavor we hope succeeds beyond his wildest dreams.

I automatically slide my magnifying glass aside as Danny calls, "Grandma! You've got to come out to the lab. It's all ready!"

I close the stamp album on today's clippings from the *Rocky Mountain News*. The lab? Oh, the shed. He wants me to head out to the shed. It's funny how the same thing can mean different things to different people. His father used the shed for reloading shells. His grandfather, as a carpenter's shop.

My arthritic hip aches, but I lever myself out of my rocker and follow the dogs, Sasha and Turbo, out the back. Danny is an industrious boy, but I wish he'd repair the grape arbor or repave the walk instead of spending all his time in the shed. The bird feeders could use some work, too.

The gate squeals as I push through to the back alley. The ground is already pocked with ant lion pits. An old prescription bottle rolls in the breeze. A trace of late snow lingers along the fence.

Danny pops his head out. "Grandma, you gotta see this! It's working."

My sense of smell isn't what it once was, but as I enter I know two things at once. Danny has "fried" more than a few electronic components, and at least one of his girlfriends has just left. I try to recall which one wears so much perfume, when Danny lifts his ferret off an old lawn chair and guides me into it like I'm some kind of invalid. When he has me positioned, he drops his ferret, Pashtran, on my lap and begins to pace.

"Okay, I haven't got the internal diagnostic working yet, but I think I've got most of the bugs worked out. The dates are relative vice absolute and the color's not the best, but I'm getting close. Also, I haven't figured out how to slow the images, but that's probably a software problem. . . ."

I stroke Pashtran's belly. She sleeps through this with her head tucked, so I guess she's heard it all before. I nod for Danny to continue as it is almost time for my nap.

When he stops in front of the workbench, he breaks into a grin that shows he's proud of whatever it is he's done, but doesn't want to admit it. I know that look well. It was his father's look and *his* father's. He's secretly afraid I won't be impressed.

He whips a cardboard barrier aside. "Ta-da!"

An opposing set of metal hemispheres, looking for all the world like a pair of colanders, dominates the workbench. Of course, they wouldn't be any use as colanders because all the holes sparkle with tiny lenses. Red-and-blue-striped cable ribbons run from both sides to a panel of digital readouts and chromed slide bars. The panel reminds me of the holocube reader Danny wanted so desperately last Christmas. I look closer and see that it *is* the holocube reader, only not quite as I remember seeing it just three months ago.

None of that bothers me. What does vex me, though, is that my glass pickling crock stands between the colanders. It's a barrel-shaped jar almost two feet tall. He's stuck blobs of gray putty all over it.

"That was passed down from my grandmother," I say.

Danny slides a copper wire into one of the blobs. "Come on, Grandma, it's just an old jar."

I look at my grandson. His hair is longer than it ought to be, which probably comes from growing up with his mother in California. Normally full of jokes and sporting a huge grin, he is now intent on the instruments before him. Can this be the same boy who last autumn burst through my front door announcing something wrong with all the neighborhood trees?

What kind of child doesn't recognize the changing of seasons when he sees it?

He brushes the hair out of his eyes with a casual raking of his fingers. The red comes from his mother's side. God knows *our* family never had a lick of red.

I ask, "What does this contraption do?"

"I'll show you." He whispers to his laptop computer and an image of the paired colanders instantly hovers over its projection stage. "This is a project for my archeology class. Don't worry, I won't hurt your jar."

"I hope not. It's valuable, you know."

"How old is it?"

"Let's see. It used to be in my grandfather's old country store. Twenty years or so before I was born. I remember seeing it for the first time when I was around, oh, five years old."

His face gets a look like *Wow, ancient history*, but he asks, "What year would that be?"

"Has to be at least eighty years ago, now. It was there when they cleaned out the old post office and turned it into a coop."

He aims something the size of a car key. Rosy laser light plays over the jar. "Fifty-six centimeters high . . . diameter, thirty."

The computer draws. After a moment, the image is complete with glass ribbing and a cursive "Duriglas" across its base. It looks real. As he runs his finger over the little pad by the keyboard, the false glass swirls with iridescence.

"A coop?" he asks.

"A chicken coop. They cleaned out the post office and took everything to the barn. My mother found a lot of old stamps—"

"Okay, so it's at least eighty years old. What was it used for?"

"Probably closer to eighty-five. There was an old bell, too. The kind they rang to call the farm hands in for supper."

"I thought farmers used a triangle."

"No, it was a bell. At least on our old family farm it was a bell. Sometimes the hands rang it if they wanted something. Like a lump of brown sugar or water for—"

"There. That does it. Fully calibrated."

Pashtran yawns and snuggles down. Danny tabs a key and commands, "Begin regression sequence."

The jar between the colanders looks the same, but the one on the stage begins to change. Light glares off it and something seems to form inside.

"The projection will steady out in a second," Danny advises. "The regression is running at a year a minute. That's roughly a month every five seconds, but we won't see much more than a blur until the jar settles down. I tried this with some Neolithic ceramics, but found it works best with transparent objects that have sat still for long periods. This jar's perfect because it probably didn't move around too much. I mean, it probably weighs something close to ten pounds, empty."

I can't believe what I'm seeing. The image solidifies

and over the space of the next few minutes fills with mittens and then suddenly empties. I used to knit mittens every year and give them out at Halloween, but had to stop because of the arthritis.

I ask myself, "What's Danny up to?" but never answer. Rubber bands have replaced the mittens. They are green and red like the ones that used to come with a daily newspaper. Their level dwindles.

"Don't forget that this is running in reverse. When the level falls it means that in real-time, someone was adding stuff to the jar."

I nod numbly and edge closer. The jar swirls with light and for the first time I notice that the outer surface is reflecting images of its own. Half-seen shapes move briefly and disappear. The motion is swift, but at times I imagine seeing my own face. Sometimes I think I see my kitchen before the new cabinets.

Green. A band of green runs vertically up the center of the jar. One side holds a gravelly darkness; the other, eddies of fog.

Danny checks his watch. "It's been twenty minutes. That makes this something close to 1980." He types the number in and it floats at the bottom of the display, regressing rapidly. "Recognize any of this?"

At first I don't, but then remember lending the jar to the neighbor girl for a school project. That was just after Danny's father left home. I guess it was before I'd decided it was an antique.

I peer hard at the image. Tiny fern fronds are tucking themselves back into fiddleheads before plummeting into the soil. Patches of moss shrink back. "It's a terrarium."

Danny tilts his head at the display, then gazes at the jar. "This is great! If only I could slow the projection. Maybe if I use QuickLook seven point oh and . . ."

Illustrated by Gary McCluskey

I stop listening as the image goes completely dark. When brief flashes occur, I recognize the inside of my pantry. Another eight minutes pass before the projection stage shines. Rainbows glint and small shrimplike creatures fly around in the interior. Sometimes they swarm like gnats; sometimes they dwindle to just a few pairs. Each grows progressively smaller before disappearing. After less than a minute, the jar returns to darkness.

"What the heck was that?"

I laugh. The digits at the bottom of the display have spun down to 1971. "You're father was a boy then. He would have been nine or ten."

"So?"

"Those were Sea Monkeys."

"You're kidding. *My* dad had Sea Monkeys?"

I nod as the image shifts through earlier volumes of bottle caps and rocks, shells and glow-in-the-dark Superballs. Once or twice I see my boy's reflection as he gloats over his various collections.

When the digits reach 1965, the hologram clouds before revealing a bramble of worn paintbrushes. As the months tick by, they grow newer and I see hints of the many layers of paint—yellow before blue before yellow, again—that Dad, my husband, Danny's grandfather, painted our home. Once or twice I catch a vision of him crafting something in his workshop, but the images are faint and fleeting. I feel a sudden twinge of guilt at having allowed all his tools to rust to nothing.

Tears well and I rush to wipe them. Guess I forgot how much I miss the old goat.

I'm still lost in the memory of his spicy cologne and the taste of his sweat when a blur of orange forms and spirals through the jar. Occasionally, there are two or more swaths of twisting-veering orange.

Danny claps his hands. "Goldfish!"

"Moby and Goldie and Bubbles," I recall fondly. It was the 1955 state fair. I was fifteen, acting sixteen. Billy Kramer won them for me by tossing Ping-Pong balls at their bowls. I never knew what happened to him after his mother died and his family moved back East.

Marbles come next. Hundreds of them, lasting for almost eight full minutes. Baked clay at the bottom, grading up through alabaster to beautiful glass puries, lacy shooters, and cat's-eyes. My father, so proud to finally "sire" a boy, began the collection. Robbie, my baby brother, had to finish it alone. Green and silver, yellow and blue. Swirls of scarlet.

Long before Vietnam.

"This is incredible," Danny says. "This might sound stupid, but the color really surprises me. I've seen a lot of old TV shows and—"

"You were expecting black and white?"

He blushes, shrugs, and we both turn back to the hologram. After the marbles, came World War II.

Before that, I mean. Between 1945 and 1941, the jar repeatedly fills with all manner of small recyclables my father would have taken down to help the war effort, him being a touch too old to serve.

The image jerks, fades . . . returns. "What's wrong?" I ask.

"This is useless for archeology! See, the years are accelerating. The farther back the time scan runs, the more degraded the resolution. It must have something to do with the photon density. Or maybe I've got the resonance polarity skewed."

I don't understand what he's saying, but the years are just *shooting* past us now. From 1938 back to some-where close to thirty-three, the image remains dark.

Suddenly: an interval of flashing gold light.

I see a network of cottony strands, minute tangles of gray, and tiny black things, crawling. Spiders? Somewhere in the old barn? The daily passage of a sunbeam?

Digits blur. The jar swirls as the years stream farther back. . . .

Snap! Just like that, the jar is full. In the brief reflections, I recognize my mother's description of the old family store. The jar empties itself of red-beet eggs, then pickles, then—

"What the heck are those?"

"Pig's feet." Granddad loved them with lentils and greens.

The jar darkens, then immediately glows. Its ribbed sides reflect hundreds of other jars.

"See," Danny says, "it's not so valuable. This must be where they were manufactured. One of thousands."

The image breaks up, but before Danny switches off I imagine seeing a beach and after that, mountains.

"Useless, piece-of-crap equipment," he says, as he yanks a cable free and clears the projection. "End regression. Save."

I lift Pashtran and absently plop her back in the chair as I stand. I have not thought of many of those things for some time. Grandpa's store, Dad's carpentry, Robbie's marbles . . . I find myself a bit shaken.

Danny thrusts the laptop into his satchel. "Sorry, Grandma. Thought I had it figured out."

I hug my grandson. "You will. I know you will."

He looks at me strangely. I can tell he's wondering if he should ask about my teary eyes. I don't give him a chance. I lift the jar from between the colanders and, as I carry it back to the house, embrace it, too.

Right now, it's in my front window. I'm filling it with blossoms of spring.

THE SAVANT DEATH SYNDROME

Written by
Jerry Craven

Illustrated by
Kent Martin

About the Author

Jerry Craven is a professor of English at West Texas A&M University, where he teaches creative writing. He's published short science fiction in Asimov's, Analog, and poetry in a number of places. He has several nonfiction children's books that have either just gone to press, or which will go soon. From Rourke Books, he's publishing three books on Festivals, Celebrations, and Folk Pageants. He's also recently published nonfiction books on Aikido, Tae Kwon Do, and Ninja. He's got a book of humor appearing soon, called Boxing Hawgs and Tilting Cows, and he's co-authored two textbooks for teaching English to the Japanese. And these are just some of his projects coming out soon.

Jerry has traveled extensively in seventeen countries—including Malaysia, where he and his wife, a psychotherapist, taught for two years, and Venezuela, where Jerry was raised for five years.

Jerry has four children, one of whom graduated from the International School of Kuala Lumpur, and he has five grandchildren.

When he's not writing, Jerry enjoys sea kayaking, hiking, and bicycling.

About the Illustrator

Kent Martin was born and raised in Clanton, Alabama, and began drawing as a child, leaving elaborate pictorial messages for his parents long before he could write.

When he was twelve years old, he met award-winning watercolorist John Zed King, who gave Kent his first set of watercolors and became a major influence in Kent's life. Kent later felt the inspiration from such greats as Frazetta, Vallejo, N. C. Wyeth, and Howard Pyle.

While working in the construction industry, Kent found that the travel made it difficult for him to concentrate on an art career. In the past year, he has married and quit construction, and now pursues that full-time career in art. He has been busy in wildlife and portrait commissions, as well as advertising design. He recently created a line of Civil War prints to be published by Dixie Graphics, and is negotiating a deal on aviation art.

Kent works in a variety of media and subject matter, but inspired by winning in the Illustrators of the Future, hopes to devote himself to speculative fiction art.

Why is it," the passport clerk muttered to himself, "strange people come on the last flight of the night?" He sighed and looked up. "Your husband, he is among the cargo of the plane?"

"Yes," Cynthia said. "But, of course, he lies wrapped in a cold-form suit." She glanced at the clerk's handsome brown features, at his government uniform. From the way he had been looking at her, from the slight condescending tone of his voice, she could tell much about him. He regarded her as inferior, as a mere woman and hence a being to be manipulated by his sexual charm, as someone to be used.

On his breast he wore a plastic nameplate that said "Mohammed Othar Faud." He would go by Othar, Cynthia told herself. Islamics liked to name their sons Mohammed, even if they never called anyone by that name.

"Ah," Othar said. "We have suits in Malaysia. Cold suits. In all parts. A boy came in last week in such a suit." He jerked his thumb over his shoulder. "From up north, beyond Cameron. A little black *orang asli* boy, from the jungles. A crocodile bit him. They brought him to Subang Hospital. They said the cold suit saved him from bleeding to death. Your husband, would he bleed if not in suit?"

"No." She watched Othar shift from her passport to her husband's, then back. The man appeared dull-witted,

which was why Cynthia had chosen his line to clear
immigration at the Kuala Lumpur-Subang airport. He
squinted at the passports, making an effort not to look at
Cynthia.

She had caught him eying her when she stood farther
back in line, and she sent him an image of her in a
translucent blouse. Not a vivid sending—just enough to
make him take a second look. Standing in front of him,
she decided to allow her real image to do the work she
needed. Her fair skin and blond hair made her an ideal
beauty among many Asians—that ought to be enough to
give her the edge she needed to get through the
Malaysian airport bureaucracy with a minimum of
bother.

"The papers are correct," Othar said. "And yet, this
seems most irregular." He looked at her again. She
smiled and he looked back to the passports. "Your husband. He is a sick man?"

"Yes."

"Then I am afraid I cannot let him in."

"He has a genetic disorder," Cynthia said. "Something he inherited. He cannot give it to anyone."

Othar reached for a phone. Cynthia sent him an
image of his hand on her breast. She hated doing that,
but it seemed the only way to be done with the red tape
of entering Malaysia.

Othar dropped the phone, staring at his hand. He
shot her a quick glance. His upper lip trembled, and perspiration appeared on his forehead. She strengthened
the image, then released it. Let him do with it what he
will, she thought. He closed his eyes for a moment.

It had not taken much of a sending to get him
agitated, Cynthia observed. That meant he had already
been constructing similar images himself. The jerk.

"You will stay where?" Othar asked. He took a deep breath and let it out with a sigh.

"At the Hilton. But I know so little about your country. Someone will have to show me around." She smiled again.

Othar brightened. "I call for you. In the morning." He stamped the passports and handed them to her. "I call. At the Hilton in P.J. Yes?"

"You are kind," Cynthia said. She took the passports and followed the signs to the baggage claim area to get her husband.

Luggage already circulated on the baggage ramp. The green plasto-crate that held Brad lay on its side, moving toward her. It weighed eighty kilograms, which she could handle, though not with ease. As she reached for it, Othar stepped in front of her. "Please allow me to help."

"He is heavy," Cynthia said. "It will take two of us." She moved around Othar and helped him lift the crate. They set it on the floor. "Thank you," she said. "Your manners are exceeded only by your kindness."

"I now on break," Othar said. "I get you through customs. You need cart?"

"Thank you, no. That is my bag," she indicated a shoulder bag moving toward them on the ramp. "I can carry it easily, and the crate has wheels."

Othar picked up the bag. "That way," he said. "But for what is the crate like a square box?"

"Brad—my husband—is drawn up in a fetal position. He said it would make moving him easier."

"Ah," Othar said, nodding. Cynthia wasn't a telepath, but she could read his thoughts on his face: How strange, how very strange.

He leered at her as they walked toward the customs inspector, and she regretted sending him such sensual imagery. She stood in line, not listening to Othar's chatting. Mostly she felt numb. Jet lag, she told herself. But she knew her tired feeling amounted to much more than jet lag.

If Brad had been awake, standing in line beside her, she knew he would hold his impatience in check only for so long before he began moving people aside, whispering subliminal commands that would have those in front of him wandering off, puzzled about what possessed them to abandon their places in line.

Maybe not, Cynthia thought, looking at the man in front of her. He wore a business suit and a turban. In front of him stood two Malay women, robed in the black sacks that Islamics thought proper for women. Did those people speak English? If not, then Brad's subliminal commands would register with them as a kind of background noise, and they would not do as he ordered. Cynthia imagined it: Brad parting his lips slightly, concentrating on sending his messages, the people not moving, and Brad clamping his lips into a thin line in his anger. Then he would turn to her, part his lips, and she would feel the inclination to send images to the man in the turban and the women in black, images that would frighten them, perhaps, or images to confuse them—whatever occurred to Brad at the moment to force the people out of his way.

Of course, Cynthia refused to abuse her ability, and she would have to calm Brad. She would smile and send images of Colorado's Monument Lake to Brad, a place he found relaxing. His eyes would widen at the sending, and he would be furious at her refusal to do as he wished.

I'm glad he's in the crate, she told herself.

Othar bullied past the customs inspector and followed her outside. The Malaysian night hit her like a hot, damp wall, and for a few seconds she had the illusion that the air was too thick to breathe. "I get a taxi," Othar said.

While Othar and the cab driver struggled to lift Brad into the trunk of the cab, Cynthia felt the numbness coming upon her in increasing waves. This is lunacy, she told herself. Like the AIDS victims back in the twentieth century flocking first to France and dying there—because they heard, inaccurately, that the French had medicines that might work. Then they fled to China for treatment with poisonous roots, and they found only death in China. Then to Africa for cow saliva dried into tablets. Nothing helped, not back then, but that didn't stop the afflicted from desperate flights around the world in search of the miracle that would cure them.

"You ride P.J. Hilton in style," Othar said. "Mercedes taxi. Style." He opened the door for her. "Tomorrow morning I collect you at Hilton for tour of city, yes?" Cynthia managed a smile for him, though it took great effort.

As the cab pulled out of the lighted airport drive into the Malaysian night, Cynthia said, "Take me to the Mandarin Hotel in Kuala Lumpur."

The driver looked at her in astonishment. "Not the Hilton?"

"No."

"But the Mandarin old. Bad. It cheap, not for lady. You go to Hilton, yes?"

"No. I go to the Mandarin in downtown Kuala Lumpur by Central Market."

The driver shrugged, a gesture that would have been lost in the darkness to anyone else. But Cynthia saw it.

So here I go, she thought, scurrying around the world with Brad in a cold-form suit, searching for something that will not appear on the medical scene for another decade or so. And Brad will die in Malaysia, die in his quest for a cure for the virus that has invaded his dreams with nightmares, that has begun to slow down his genetically enhanced speed. Soon it will take his voice, and then the fever will come. And Brad will die.

She thought of the vivid nature of her own dreams on the flight over. Not nightmares, exactly—but vivid, swirling in colors, tumbling over her in images that made her cry out in her sleep. Were the dreams the harbinger of death? Would genuine nightmares like Brad was afflicted with come to her soon? Did she now have the virus in her veins, working its deadly and unstoppable damage to her nervous system?

Perhaps, she acknowledged with a sigh, she, like Brad, would die in Malaysia.

At the Mandarin, Cynthia told the taxi driver to wait while she got some American dollars changed into ringgit. "Othar paid," the driver said. "You no must pay." He helped her get the plasto-crate from the trunk.

"Can you wait, anyway? Okay?" Cynthia asked.

"Can," the driver said, looking puzzled.

She dragged Brad up the steps to the hotel entry. The door opened as she pulled the crate toward it. Marble floor, the main lobby, a surprise to Cynthia, for she had read that the hotel was shabby and cheap. Old, she decided, and maybe cheap. But not shabby.

The desk clerk, a young Chinese-Malaysian, had her reservations before she got to the desk. "Welcome to K.L., Miss Armand," he said.

"Thank you. How did you know you had the right person?"

"You American," he explained. "At Mandarin, we get almost no American reservation."

Cynthia had him give her Malaysian currency for a traveler's check. "I'll be right back," she said.

Outside, she looked around. The area was dimly lit, so the buildings across the street seemed dirty from shadows. She went to the taxi driver and held currency out to him. "No need," he said. "Othar paid."

"I know. This money is so you will tell Othar that you took me to the Hilton. I do not want him following me like a puppy."

"Hundred ringgit," the driver said, pleased and surprised. "For this, I tell him I take you to Jahore Baru. To Singapore."

"Just say you took me to the Hilton."

She got to her room exhausted but not sleepy. Her body still ran on Dallas time, where it was 10:30 in the morning. She knew she would have to make a fast adjustment, and a hard one. Malaysian time was 10:30 at night.

She sat on a chair, becoming aware of the room. Brad's crate sat on a carpet that had long strings rising from it here and there. The plaster on the wall cracked above the doors, and the curtains were stained and specked. An unpleasant odor of cleaning fluid came from somewhere. The bathroom, maybe. Maybe from the upholstery of the chair. The most amazing thing in the room was a lizard about as long as her index finger crawling across the wall. She sighed and revised her opinion of the Mandarin. It was both old and shabby.

I really ought to take Brad from the crate, she told herself. It would be the decent thing to do: uncrate him, put him on one of the single beds. She looked at the crate, feeling the will to move drain from her. The fact was, she admitted, she had no desire to see him at all, even unconscious, suspended in the cold-form suit.

Not that uncrating him would matter to Brad: in his condition he could be left for—she glanced at the date on her watch—three more days before the cold-form suit had to be removed. And those three days he could as easily spend in the box as anywhere else. Still, it seemed more proper that he be on one of the twin beds.

She nudged the box with her toe, stood, stretched, and got into bed.

It seemed forever before she dropped off to sleep. Then the dreams came with vivid intensity. Even as she dreamed, she knew she dreamt. At first rainbows swirled around her in a kaleidoscope of colors, turning and spinning like a nebula. She liked it. Her dreams always came in color, and often the spinning of the spectrum was all she remembered the next morning.

The whirling stopped, with green dominating what remained. The green formed itself into a jungle from which emerged the gray hulk of an elephant. She saw the elephant to be Brad, which surprised the part of her that watched the dream, knowing it to be only a dream; for Brad was a slender man of medium height, not someone whom she would think of as being represented in her dreams in the form of an elephant. She followed Brad-elephant to a clearing which led to the path just outside the main building of the Newman Institute for Arts in Dallas. The locals called it the "Idiot Savant Institute."

"This is the place that killed me," the elephant told her. And she understood. The art institute housed some of the most talented creative people in the world:

painters, sculptors, musicians, architects—whatever the gang in genetic design decided to make. None were idiots, but that didn't stop the press from calling them that. When not being critical, the press called them simply *savants*.

"They bunch us up so we share disease," the elephant said. "And we die." The elephant turned back up the trail, and Cynthia followed it into the jungle, watching as the giant creature seemed to melt, changing its form into that of a snake, a large brown boa.

The boa slithered up a tree, then out on a narrow limb that drooped, lowering the snake into a bush. "Thisss one, Cindy," the boa hissed. "This iss the bussh to sssave me. Seek this. Ssseek thisss, thisss. . . ." She turned and ran, but the voice followed her: "Seek, Cindy, thisss, thisss," until she realized the snake spoke not from without but from somewhere inside her head as only Brad could speak to her. And she knew running was futile.

Brad-snake wound around her body, working his way to her neck. He began to constrict, to choke her, and she knew she would die.

Cynthia woke in a sweat, the images of the snake and the jungle still vivid. She switched on the lamp and looked at the plasto-crate. "Damn you, Brad!" she said. "Damn you. And damn the genetic engineers. All of them. I would trade all my gifts for a single night of peaceful rest."

She turned out the light and told herself to sleep without dreams, then laughed at the notion, for the dreams would come.

The next morning, she woke at dawn, feeling tired, knowing she had dreamed more disturbing dreams, but not wanting to recall them.

Illustrated by Kent Martin

She took Brad from the crate, lifting his stiff body and putting it on the other twin bed. The cold-form suit was clear, a fact that had discomforted her when he had first put it on. The power pack sat bunched in a pouch on one shoulder, but even it looked clear. Cynthia could, if she tried, see the wires, so tiny as to be invisible to anyone without her vision, networking from the power pack to all parts of the suit.

She set him upright and began to stretch out his limbs, doing it slowly and with great care. Brad was supple; if she applied steady pressure, she would be able to cause him to lie prone on the bed. She would likely bunch him up into a fetal position again, if she had to transport him. But it bothered her to see him rolled into a ball.

After a shower, she sat on the easy chair and reviewed the reading Brad had given her. The map of the city she simply glanced at; it was not something she could forget, given the gifts that the genetic engineers had built into her. Ideas in words, though, were a different matter. They needed reinforcement, the same as for nearly anyone else.

The man Brad wanted her to find, if possible, was a bomoh named Tak Ladah Hitam. And a *bomoh?* Brad said it was a sort of folk doctor who dealt in herbs. She remembered the plant in the dream—the bush. That was what she came to Malaysia for. A bush on a jungle floor, one with magic qualities—or they might as well be magic. Brad felt certain the bush that opened the door to curing neo-AIDS would be the very one that would allow him to live.

At nine in the morning, Cynthia went to the front desk of the Mandarin. "When do the shops on Petaling Street open?" she asked the day clerk.

"Ten. Not yet. Ten. But some shops in Central Market open now." He began to give her directions, but she interrupted him with a word of thanks and left. She would follow the map in her head—a map from one of Brad's books.

Outside, on Sultan Street, she saw that the dim light of the previous evening had not played her false: the buildings across the street were indeed dirty. Perhaps the walls had once been white, but they had turned black in streaks of mold from the tropical rains. Cracks ran across the walls, and in some of the cracks grew cliff plants, some the size of small trees. Cynthia remembered reading that the old, cracked buildings were all that remained of the heritage of British architecture from colonial days.

On every block Cynthia found a pair of soldiers lounging idly, each with a laser-equipped assault rifle dangling in the crook of one arm, as if expecting any moment to lift the weapon and fire at some enemy. She identified the soldiers as Malays, slender, good-looking men, smaller in stature than Brad.

On Bandar Street, the buildings became newer. The Malay government had torn down all the supposed eyesores from Colonial Malaya and replaced them with cement stalls staffed with round-faced, dark-skinned people who sold curios to tourists. A glance down Bandar told her that the only buildings remaining from the twentieth century were the Hindu temple and the Buddhist stupa. Cynthia walked to the end of Sultan Street to look at the Klang Bus Station, an old landmark from the late twentieth century, but found it depressing and dirty.

In Wet Market, an alley behind the Mandarin Hotel, she found vendors working at stalls under corrugated zinc roofs. Cynthia walked by displays of mangoes, rambutan, bananas, and an abundance of vegetables she did not recognize. Toward the end of the alley were the butchers; men and women cutting up fish, pigs, and chickens. At several stalls shoppers selected live chickens, which were killed and plucked on the spot. She hurried through the meat area, emerging on Petaling Street.

She had read that only one block of the shops in the old Chinatown of the nineteenth and twentieth centuries remained, and the map she had memorized told her she stood in the middle of that block. Shoppers, mostly of Chinese descent, crowded the street, and street hawkers stood by carts on both edges of the road, making it difficult for cars to get through. Which way to the Sun Wah? she wondered. She looked to her left and caught a glimpse of the ubiquitous pair of soldiers with their assault rifles. They seemed so out of place there amid all the peaceful commerce. Irritated by their presence, she turned right.

The buildings on both sides of the street had sidewalks built under the second stories, an architectural idea pushed by the British colonial days. With covered walkways, the Brits could shop even in the frequent tropical rains. Cynthia walked out into the street so she could better see the wares of the food hawkers. Beside one, she paused, pointed to a display of green fruit and asked, "What are those?"

"Guava," the vendor said. "Good. Refreshes mouth. Only two ringgit for slice." Cynthia bought a slice and went down the street, nibbling on it. The fruit had the texture of a woody apple and tasted something like a sour grape. Before she took many steps, she saw the Sun Wah.

Brad had found a reference to the Sun Wah in a twentieth-century novel written by some obscure Texan who had lived for a couple of years in the Kuala Lumpur Valley. The book noted that the place was a gathering point for dealers in gems and for men who dealt in herbs. It was as good a place as any to begin the search, Brad had told Cynthia.

The entire front of the shops stood open to the covered sidewalk. Inside, Cynthia found cheap cafe tables around which sat Chinese and other Asians she could not identify. North Indian, maybe, or Tibetan. More likely, she told herself, these were the men from Nepal, the gem dealers. Some of the tables had displays of cut gemstones and other trinkets on them.

Cynthia sat at an empty table. A man of Chinese descent came up, wiping his hands on an apron. "May I help you?" he asked.

"Yes, please. I would like a cup of coffee." The waiter bowed and went to the back of the shop.

Cynthia looked around, impressed with the scene. The high walls looked as if they had not seen a coat of paint in thirty years, and signs in Chinese script hung beside ads for American cigarettes. Geckos like the one in her room roamed the walls. Were those fierce-looking men with gemstones the grandsons of the twentieth-century gem smugglers who frequented the place so long ago? she wondered.

When her coffee arrived, she again remembered the description from the old novel: black coffee in a clear glass cup sitting on top of sweetened, condensed milk. Some things, Cynthia mused, must never change. "Anything else?" the waiter asked.

"Would you mind answering a foolish-sounding question?"

"If I can, I will." The man looked puzzled. Other men in the cafe glanced at her, but seemed to go on with their conversations.

"I came a very long way to find a certain man, called, in the press of the time, Tak Ladah Hitam."

Other conversation stopped when she pronounced the name. Several men stared at her. The waiter glanced about and sat on the chair beside her. "You said you had a foolish question. You did not lie."

"Forgive me." Cynthia flushed. She sipped her coffee. It tasted even stronger than it looked. "I have so little information, and it is vital that I find the man I mentioned."

"But you asked not about a man at all. You used a Malay phrase that means 'black pepper.' *Ladah Hitam*. Black pepper. *Tak* is a term of respect among the Malays. What you said sounded like, 'Where is the honorable black pepper?' It sounded funny."

"And yet you were not amused."

"No. Not amused." The man lowered his voice. "The Malays, they . . . But it is foolish of me to say such things to a stranger." He shrugged.

"The man I want was a bomoh, according to the *New Straits Times* many years ago. He supposedly knew more about herbal medicine than anyone in all of Asia. Have you heard of the disease called neo-AIDS?"

"Do I look so young? Only the very young are ignorant of neo-AIDS."

The man looked uncomfortable. He leaned forward and said in a whisper, "The man you seek was not a bomoh. *Bomoh* names a Malay witch doctor, one who deals in spirits and conjures the dead. The man who found a cure for neo-AIDS was Chinese."

"Not a Malaysian?" Cynthia asked in astonishment.

"Malaysian, yes. But not Malay. Chinese. The Malays . . . but I forget myself. Excuse me." The man stood up. "I must work. I'm sorry I cannot be of help to you."

Yet he knows something of use to me, Cynthia thought. Why is he afraid?

Two soldiers she had seen down the street sauntered by on the sidewalk, pausing to look into the Sun Wah. Was that it? Cynthia wondered. Did the Malay soldiers frighten him?

She took another cautious sip of her coffee and decided it might be drinkable if she stirred the sugar and cream at the bottom into it.

An older Chinese man came over from a nearby table. He stood in silence while the soldiers walked past, then said, "I know someone who might answer your questions."

"Can you take me to him?"

"Can." The man leaned toward her in a slight bow. "His name is Lionel Lee. My friend. You follow." He walked to the front of the coffee shop.

Cynthia tried the coffee as she stood up. Mixing the sugary cream into it had not helped. She put three ringgit on the table.

"Have caution, lady," the waiter said. She looked up, startled that he stood so near.

"Caution? Of what?"

The waiter lowered his voice. "Con men. This place is full of con men. And perhaps some spies—which is why I spoke with caution. A man might lead you into a dwelling, strike you in the head, and rob you. Have caution where you go with that man."

Cynthia looked at the man waiting for her in the entrance and shuddered. "Thank you," she said.

Cynthia followed the man from the Sun Wah only a short distance before he vanished into another cafe. She stopped, distracted by the abundance of sensuous imagery that surrounded her. The cries of the hawkers in the street. The brilliance of the sun just beyond the covered walk. The dark-bodied birds darting into the street and back to mud nests on the ceiling of the walkway. The signs on the street in Chinese characters.

On this one block in an otherwise modern city, it was easy to believe she had slipped somehow back into the twentieth century. Maybe to the nineteenth century. If I live, she told herself, I will return to this place to paint. What a wonderful place for an artist to discover.

She found that the cafe the man had led her to looked much like the Sun Wah. It was a bit wider, and the walls were more recently painted. But the same kind of men sat around the similar cheap tables. Cynthia wondered if people who did not look at faces with an artist's eye might believe these were the same men, that they had sprinted down a back alley between the Sun Wah and this cafe to assemble around the tables before she could get there.

Her guide stood by a table, waving his hands about and talking in Chinese to a man sitting with his back to Cynthia. The guide gestured to Cynthia. "This man Lionel Lee," he said as she approached. "You do business, yes? I go to Sun Wah." He left.

Lionel stood and turned to her. "Hello," he said, offering his hand.

"Hello." Cynthia shook his hand, noting Lionel had an advanced palm, an artist's hand that gripped hers with formal firmness. "My name is Cynthia Armand."

"Please," he said, waving toward an isolated table in the back of the cafe. He picked up a leather pouch, took her arm, and escorted her to the table.

She inspected him as they sat down. Lionel stood only slightly taller than she—about the same height as Brad. But much more handsome, she told herself. Much.

Lionel's Chinese features were perfect, the epitome of male oriental beauty.

"My cousin," he said, opening the leather pouch, "told me that you seek quality gemstones." He dropped his voice and added as she began to speak, "No, say nothing yet. Those men?" He glanced up at the other customers in the cafe. "The Chinese are mostly regulars in this place and in the Sun Wah. The others are Grukha tribesmen from Nepal, smugglers of gemstones from Burma, and importers of tourist items. Among the Grukhas or the Chinese is a government spy, a pig who carries tales that can make people vanish from Chinatown." He put some paper packets on the table and began to unwrap one. "We will look at gems but speak of other things. My cousin told me with his hands that you ask disturbing questions, that you are not looking for stones. Speak softly and ask, but be aware that my answers might be oriental, not western."

Cynthia looked at him with renewed interest. This man spoke impeccable English. American English, mainly. Learned from American television shows? From being educated in the United States? And what did he mean about the differences between *oriental* and *western*? Would he communicate in circuitous, nonlinear ways, like in the ancient oriental writings she had read? She decided to probe for a clue to what he meant, to understand his method in communicating. Would a direct question get a direct, western-style answer? "You fear the soldiers?" she asked.

"Chinese offer sacrifices to devils as well as gods. The devils are often cheap, shabby things, round-faced and dark, and the sacrifices befit the character of the demons with rifles. The sacrifices are paper money, which most soldier-devils take readily in exchange for leaving us alone. But bribing is a dangerous business, for some few cannot be bought. These," he finished unwrapping the packet and set it in front of her, "are blue star sapphires from Burma. Medium to low quality, though they star nicely. Watch." He produced a penlight, turned it on, and held it above the stones. They lighted up in six-pointed stars.

"Impressive," Cynthia said, not convinced that his focus upon the sapphires had much to do with gemstones.

"You need not be impressed and you need not buy. But look at the stones, for others watch us. Whom do you seek?"

A direct question, she thought, pleased. "I'm not sure. The only name I have is apparently a false one. *Tak Ladah Hitam.* Sir Black Pepper, I was told at the Sun Wah."

"Who are you?"

Another direct question. She had expected more Lao Tzu-like indirection, as he had offered when she asked about fearing the soldiers. "Cynthia Ar—"

"Yes, yes. Cynthia Armand. A name." He turned off the penlight and began unwrapping another packet. "You like stars? These are called black stars. Cheap stones, really, often sold to ignorant tourists as black star sapphires." He set them in front of her and held the light above them. "Nice, bright stars, yes? But observe that the star is actually a cross, not a star at all. This stone looks good, to the ignorant. But it is soft. A real sapphire has a hardness of nine on Moh's Scale of Hardness, for it is aluminum oxide, the same as a ruby. A black star is something known to those who bother to learn as a star diopside. It has a hardness of five point five—the same as ordinary glass. Worn on a ring, it will lose its luster with wear and become a scratched, ugly black stone.

But how beautiful it appears to those who know little."
Lionel sat back and looked at her. "You are beautiful,
Miss Cynthia Armand."

"Somehow you say that so it does not sound like a
compliment."

"It is merely an observation," he said, his voice
neutral, his eyes appraising her.

This man is certainly fascinating, Cynthia thought,
with his subtle, careful mind, his thinking in symbols,
like an artist. "I came here from Dallas," she said. "I am
an artist from the Newman Institute. My husband is a
singer. Perhaps you have heard of Brad Armand?"

"I seldom pay attention to popular music."

"He sings opera."

"I know little of opera. A cultural flaw, I'm sure."

"No matter. I don't like opera much, myself. Brad is
a fine tenor, one of the best in the world."

"His voice—was it built into him by the engineers
who supply the Newman Institute with savants?"

"Yes." There it was again, she thought: that odd and
disarming combination of sidestepping noninformation
coupled with blunt directness.

"And your talent with art? From the engineers, also?"

"Am I a savant, you mean? No." Cynthia watched as
Lionel considered her response. If he suspected her of
lying, it did not show. She seldom told anyone the truth
about the origin of her skill with art, for it altered how
people responded to her. As a natural artist, she received
respect. But if people knew her to be a savant, they
regarded her as a freak.

"Why are you in Malaysia?"

"You have heard about the illnesses that strike the
savants? A kind of genetic flaw, it seems, that causes

many to become ill, then die. The media has named it SDS. Savant Death Syndrome. It affects only people like Brad, and is always fatal. Brad has SDS."

"I have read about the disease, yes. But why come here, asking about the myth of the bomoh who found a cure for neo-AIDS? That disease was caused by a virus, not a genetic flaw."

"We now know that SDS is also viral. A recent discovery, and not one made known yet to the public, for fear of causing panic. So far, it has struck only the genetically altered, though why that would be is still a mystery. Brad believes, perhaps with good reason, SDS might be curable with the same plant that gave the blueprint of the alkaloid for curing neo-AIDS. So we have come to Kuala Lumpur to search for the plant. Doctors synthesized the neo-AIDS medication, and the plant was forgotten. But it had other alkaloids ignored by the medical world. Brad believes they could save his life."

Lionel nodded. He took another packet from his pouch and began to unfold it. "These are beryl glass," he said, setting them on the table in front of Cynthia. "Red beryl glass, with a hardness of seven, so they will slice ordinary glass like a ruby. Hold one up to the light. Beautiful, no? The Grukha sell these to tourists as Burmese rubies. But they are not even man-made corundum. They are glass, cheaper than printed rubies. Yet there can be great profit in them when sold as rubies. You said *we* came to Malaysia. Where is your husband?"

"In my hotel room, in a cold-form suit."

"To stave off death. The disease is advanced, then?"

"Yes. He is days from the fever that kills."

"The plant you seek for him, a jungle plant, was rare even when it was found. You know that?"

"Yes."

"More rare than a real Burmese ruby on Petaling Street. See how clear the beryl glass is? Pure. No inclusions. The same would be true of a man-made ruby. A real ruby would have inclusions visible to the naked eye or with a lens." He took out another packet. "Here I have three genuine Burmese rubies." He unfolded the packet and set the stones on the table in front of Cynthia.

Cynthia frowned at the stones. This interplay of symbol and straightforward speech surely had some pattern, unless he switched from one to the other to throw her off guard. She pointed at the Burmese rubies. "These shine more than the glass rubies."

"Yes. You have a good eye."

"And the inclusions—I can see them. But they are so slight that most people would not notice."

"That is correct. Pick the best stone."

Cynthia looked at Lionel. What was he up to with the Burmese rubies? He had warned her that they would not talk about gemstones, though they would examine them. She looked back at the rubies. "This one," she said. "It is cut better, and the inclusions are barely visible. Is it valuable?"

"I have dealt in stones for ten years, since I was more boy than man. Of all the stones I have bought from the Grukhas, the one you now hold is by far the most valuable. It is now yours to keep. I make a gift of it to you."

"But I cannot possibly take such a gift."

"You are new to this country and ignorant of our ways, so I forgive you for saying what you just did. Do not dishonor me with refusal of a gift. Learn from me, Miss Cynthia. Take the stone."

"You do more than teach me the values of your culture in giving this gift. You are trying to teach me something, something I need to know. But I do not understand."

"Yes. And this one, too," he picked up one of the pieces of red beryl glass and put it into her hand. "It, too, is a gift. Do not disparage its value because it is cheap. A stone cutter in Jaipur spent much time faceting that piece of glass, and it does have beauty."

Another lesson, Cynthia thought. But what? She turned the stones in her hand, comparing them. The red glass did have a nice luster, but beside the Burmese ruby it looked dull. "I have the feeling that the message you want me to get is one that I will not like. Is that right?"

"You will give me two one-ringgit bills, folded. Others are watching, and they must think I have sold you the stones."

"You sidestepped my question nicely." She took out the ringgits and handed them to him. "But no matter. Please, help me with finding the man called Black Pepper."

"The man you seek was Chinese. But he has long since vanished from Chinatown. And the plant you seek no longer lives in Malaysia, nor anywhere else. It was a rare shrub, even in the twentieth century, for it grew only in the shade of the primary jungles. And they are all gone, chopped down for the hardwood, sawed into lumber, cut into furniture. Finished. The plant you seek is finished."

"Then Brad must die," she said, adding to herself that she would likely die also. She sighed. Brad's certain death—and the possibility of hers—were not news. Had she really begun to allow herself to be infected with Brad's absurd belief that she could find a cure when the best medical sleuths in the world floundered? She looked at Lionel. He studied her with a hint of amusement on his face. He knows something else, she realized. Something he will not tell.

Back in her room, she set the cold pack to "wake," then took a shower. By the time she got out Brad was beginning to stir. When he could sit up, he glared at her. "You have failed." He stood and struck her cheek with his fist.

She recoiled, catching herself on the wall to keep from falling, then spat an answer to him: "Yes. The plant we seek is extinct. A function of deforestation by the Malays."

"You can't know that," he snapped.

She told him about going to the sellers of herbs in the Chow Kit area of the city, then told him about Lionel.

"And you trust this weird Chinese fellow?"

"Yes." She rubbed her cheek and considered mentioning that Lionel seemed to be holding something back. "I trust him."

"I need to see him for myself."

"I knew you would say that. He agreed to meet at noon in the Sun Wah." Cynthia stood and went to the window, then whirled about, angry for the first time in many days. "You made me do that. Made me go to the window with your damned muttering. I warned you not to use that on me."

Brad laughed, dry and without humor. "A test. I still have the power, Cynthia. It has been slipping."

Her face softened. "You didn't tell me."

"No. I barely told myself. I do not want to die like a tree, from the top down. This is my last stint out of the cold-form suit. I will die soon."

Cynthia turned again to the window, doing so on her own volition. Their marriage was dead, she knew that. But do I want to see Brad die? She asked herself, shaking her head.

On the way to the Sun Wah, Brad became animated, looking with exaggerated enthusiasm at the wares of street vendors. Cynthia watched him in disbelief. Never before had he shown interest in such matters. He's dying, she told herself, and yet he acts as if this is the best day of his life. This isn't right.

At the Sun Wah, Cynthia felt Lionel's eyes gauging her, lingering upon the burning spot on her cheek where Brad had struck with his fist. She made introductions and they sat over coffee in clear glass cups.

Brad and Lionel spoke to one another in brittle voices. "The plants have all vanished from the jungles around here?" Brad asked. "You're certain."

Two Malay soldiers stopped across the street and lighted cigarettes. Lionel looked at them. "Nothing in life is sure. But, yes. The plant you seek will never again be found in the peninsula of Malaysia." Lionel shook his head in several small jerks. "I hear a buzzing. Are you doing that, Mr. Armand?"

Cynthia looked at her husband with disgust.

"Yes." Brad smiled. "The power ebbs from me, like waters of the Klang River flowing into the Straits of Malacca. In a way it feels good, that draining, and losing the power is an odd kind of gift. I have the opportunity to live my last days as an ordinary person." He laughed. "With a concerted effort, I think I could make you tell me, Lionel, if you happen to be hiding anything behind that stony look of yours. But I'll save the effort, for you know nothing of any use to us. Nothing." He laughed again.

To Cynthia the laugh had a forced edge to it. She searched Brad's face for other signs of lying but found none. Still, she knew Brad would never embrace the notion that he was in any way ordinary.

He stood. "The coffee is laced with chicory." He picked up the cup, took a sip, and sat it down with a clatter. "Delicious. Lionel, there is a place nearby where two rivers merge into one, a place where the British once mined tin. I understand that today a beautiful mosque stands in the fork where the rivers converge. Could you direct me to the place?"

Cynthia started to rise but Brad stopped her with a gesture. "I'll go alone to seek the beauty of the city. It will be glorious, experiencing the world for the first time as a normal person." He smiled, though his forehead remained knit into a frown.

Liar, Cynthia thought: liar! You're up to something other than playing at being a tourist. But she said nothing.

Lionel pointed. "Two blocks that way, beyond the Mandarin Hotel, and a block to the right. Follow the river and you will find the mosque."

Brad took several steps from the table, then looked back, a smile fixed on his face. "Maybe I have one more short burst of sublims left in me. Maybe not." He stepped into the street.

"He does a poor job with lies," Lionel observed.

"Yes. I thought that, too."

"He struck you."

Cynthia detected anger in Lionel's voice, though his face gave away nothing. "Yes. He struck me. But he's dying, Lionel. I allow him certain liberties because of that."

"He approaches the soldiers. What would he have to say to them?"

"Nothing they will understand. Much that they will feel. One of the gifts Brad has from the Institute is the ability to speak in subliminal messages."

Lionel and Cynthia watched Brad smile at the soldiers, then turn away from them, his hands thrust into his pockets. The soldiers cast uneasy glaces at him.

"Sometimes it is necessary to ask the right questions," Lionel said. "You and Brad have not done so."

"About the plant?"

"Yes."

"It is gone. You said that. But what of extracts from it? That's it, isn't it?"

"I believe so, yes."

"I must tell Brad." She looked across the street and started to rise.

The Malay soldiers snapped away their cigarettes and fumbled with their automatic rifles. Brad turned toward Cynthia, smiled, and waved just as the storm of bullets ripped into him.

People along the street dropped to their stomachs, and those in the cafe dived toward the back. All except Lionel and Cynthia.

"I should have saved him." Her voice shook. She put her face into her hands. "I knew. I knew what he was doing. But I did not believe." The words came out as sobs as she felt the enormity of what had happened.

"I, too, Cynthia, could have saved him." He reached toward her, then withdrew his hand.

Guilt washed over her, made more intense by the knowledge that she disliked her husband, that on some level she had wished that he might die. "It's my fault, Lionel, not yours. You could have done nothing. But in doing nothing, I caused his death."

"The extract. I might have told him that I believe my uncle keeps some in his home on Crab Island. I did not understand the degree of your husband's desperation.

But what of you? Will you become ill with what drove Brad to take his life?"

"I don't know. Yes. I will die from the syndrome."

"Then we must go to Crab Island, you and I. Maybe the doctors in Dallas can use the extract to save you."

"I can't think about that now."

"You must." Lionel put his hand on hers. "There are others to think about."

"Others. Yes." She looked at the soldiers standing over Brad's body and felt tears sting her eyes. "There are others like Brad who need help. I'll go with you to find the extract."

THE MANUSCRIPT FACTORY

Written by
L. Ron Hubbard

About the Author

The adventurous life and prolific writing career of
L. Ron Hubbard have become legendary in both scope
and creative influence. His exploits, travels and unquenchable
curiosity led him to become explorer and master mariner, pilot
and diver, prospector and photographer, artist and educator,
composer and musician—and, always, quintessentially, the
writer's writer. In a career spanning over half a century, he
also shared his time and energy generously with beginning
writers, helping them to become more productive at their
craft.

L. Ron Hubbard's experiences as a youngster growing up
amid the robust terrain of a still-frontier Montana, riding
horses by the time he was three, becoming a tribal brother of
the Blackfeet Indians later gave his western fiction a sharply
memorable authenticity. His diaries as a teenager journeying
to the remote corners of the Far East, provided a rich profusion
of ideas for many of the novels and short stories carved out in
the early 1930s.

In 1929, returning from the Far East, he took to the skies
as a daredevil glider pilot and powered-aircraft barnstormer,

launching a distinguished career as a correspondent for The Sportsman Pilot, *a popular national aviation magazine.*

Then the young Mr. Hubbard, already a seasoned mariner, led two sea-and-land expeditions to the Caribbean, adventures that engendered additional ideas for his hugely versatile story-telling art.

In 1934, he published "The Green God," his first adventure story, in one of the vastly popular all-fiction "pulp" magazines of the day. Virtually overnight he became one of the most successful and highly paid fiction writers of the period.

The variety of Mr. Hubbard's output was phenomenal: air, land and sea adventures, then mysteries, detective fiction and westerns. Always willing, as well, to share his hard-won experience with novices, he addressed aspiring writers at Harvard and George Washington University on the practical techniques for launching their careers. He began, in 1935, to publish "how to" articles about writing which continued to appear in major professional writers' magazines for many years and which today form the basis for the Writers' Workshops held each year for the winners of the Writers of the Future Contest.

In 1936, at the age of twenty-five, he was elected president of the New York Chapter of the American Fiction Guild, whose membership then included Raymond Chandler, Dashiell Hammett and Edgar Rice Burroughs.

The following year brought him to Hollywood to write the screen adaptation of his original story "Murder at Pirate Castle," which was then released in installments under the name of The Secret of Treasure Island, *one of the most spectacular serial film releases of the day.*

The publication in 1937 of his first hardcover book Buckskin Brigades, *a milestone novel of Indian life in the early, turbulent, fur-trading days of the American West.*

Then, in 1938, L. Ron Hubbard began to produce a wealth

of science fiction and fantasy, beginning with the publication of his first science fiction story, "The Dangerous Dimension." Such acknowledged literary landmarks as "Fear," "Final Blackout," "Slaves of Sleep" and "Typewriter in the Sky" followed, establishing him as a founder of what has come to be known as the Golden Age of Science Fiction throughout the 1930s and 1940s.

Service as a U.S. Naval officer in World War II interrupted his writing career but, by age thirty-nine, he had already written and published nearly 260 novels, novelettes and short stories—an extraordinary total of more than sixteen million words of fiction in print.

In 1950, his many years of research on the human mind culminated in the watershed publication of Dianetics: The Modern Science of Mental Health. For the next three decades, Mr. Hubbard dedicated his life to writing and publishing nonfiction concerning the nature of man and the betterment of the human condition.

His return to science fiction, however, brought a new dimension to the genre. To celebrate his fiftieth anniversary as a professional writer, L. Ron Hubbard authored the award-winning international bestseller, Battlefield Earth, now scheduled for production as a major MGM motion picture starring John Travolta. He followed this remarkable literary production with the unprecedented 1.2 million word, 10-volume MISSION EARTH® dekalogy. Each volume achieved national and international bestseller status.

L. Ron Hubbard has sold over 117 million copies of his works in 105 countries and over thirty-two languages, making him one of the most widely read and acclaimed authors of all time.

He established and sponsored the Writers of the Future Contest beginning in 1983. Aimed at discovering and, through the pages of this acclaimed anthology series, *publishing the work of amateur and aspiring authors of demonstrated merit, the Contest has grown into the world's largest and most renowned competition for new writers. Its winners have gone on to publish more than 1,000 stories and over 100 novels in the field of science fiction and fantasy, alone.*

In the following article, entitled "The Manuscript Factory," L. Ron Hubbard brings the sharp, candid—and pungent—insights of the seasoned professional to the practical rigors—and rewards—of writing as a craft and career in an intensely competitive marketplace.

So you want to be a professional.

Or, if you are a professional, you want to make more money. Whichever it is, it's certain that you want to advance your present state to something better and easier and more certain.

Very often I hear gentlemen of the craft referring to writing as the major "insecure" profession. These gentlemen go upon the assumption that the gods of chance are responsible and are wholly accountable for anything which might happen to income, hours, or pleasure. In this way they seek to excuse a laxity in thought and a feeling of unhappy helplessness which many writers carry forever with them.

But when a man says that, then it is certain that he rarely, if ever, takes an accounting of himself and his work, that he has but one yardstick. You are either a writer or you aren't. You either make money or you don't. And all beyond that rests strictly with the gods.

I assure you that a system built up through centuries of commerce is not likely to cease to function just because your income seems to depend upon your imagination. And I assure you that the overworked potence of economics is just as applicable to this business of writing as it is to shipping hogs.

You are a factory. And if you object to the word, then allow me to assure you that it is not a brand, but merely a handy designation which implies nothing of the hack, but which could be given to any classic writer.

Yes, you and I are both factories with the steam hissing and the chimneys belching and the machinery clanging. We manufacture manuscripts, we sell a stable product, we are quite respectable in our business. The big names of the field are nothing more than the name of Standard Oil on gasoline, Ford on a car, or Browning on a machine gun.

And as factories, we can be shut down, opened, have our production decreased, change our product, have production increased. We can work full blast and go broke. We can loaf and make money. Our machinery is the brain and the fingers.

And it is fully as vital that we know ourselves and our products as it is for a manufacturer to know his workmen and his plant.

Few of us do. Most of us sail blithely along and blame everything on chance.

Economics, taken in a small dose, are simple. They have has to do with price, cost, supply, demand, and labor.

If you were to open up a soap plant, you would be extremely careful about it. That soap plant means your income. And you would hire economists to go over everything with you. If you start writing, ten to one, you merely write and let everything else slide by the boards. But your writing factory, if anything, is more vital than your soap factory. Because if you lose your own machinery, you can never replace it—and you can always buy new rolls, vats, and boilers.

The first thing you would do would be to learn the art of making soap. And so, in writing, you must first learn to write. But we will assume that you already know how to write. You are more interested in making money from writing.

It does no good to protest that you write for the art of it. Even the laborer who finds his chief pleasure in his work tries to sell services or products for the best price he can get. Any economist will tell you that.

You are interested in income. In net income. And "net income" is the inflow of satisfaction from economic goods, estimated in money, according to Seligman.

I do not care if you write articles on knitting, children's stories, snappy stories, or gag paragraphs, you can still apply this condensed system and make money.

When you first started to write, if you were wise, you wrote anything and everything for everybody and sent it all out. If your quantity was large and your variety wide, then you probably made three or four sales.

With the field thus narrowed, and you had, say, two types of markets to hammer at, you went ahead and wrote for the two. But you did not forget all the other branches you had first aspired to, and now and then you ripped off something out of line and sent it away and perhaps sold it and went on with the first two types regardless.

Take my own situation as an example—because I know it better than yours. I started out writing for the pulps, writing the best I knew, writing for every mag on the stands, slanting as well as I could.

I turned out about half a million words, making sales from the start because of heavy quantity. After a dozen stories were sold, I saw that things weren't quite right. I was working hard and the money was slow.

Now it so happened that my training had been an engineer's. I leaned toward solid, clean equations rather than guesses, and so I took the list which you must have. Stories written, type, wordage, where sent, sold or not.

My list was varied. It included air-war, commercial air, western, western love, detective, and adventure.

On the surface, that list said that adventure was my best bet, but when you've dealt with equations long, you never trust them until you have the final result assured.

I reduced everything to a common ground. I took stories written of one type, added up all the wordage, and set down the wordage sold. For instance:

DETECTIVE   120,000 words written
                             30,000 words sold

$$\frac{30,000}{120,000} = 25\%$$

ADVENTURE   200,000 words written
                             36,000 words sold

$$\frac{36,000}{200,000} = 18\%$$

According to the sale book, adventure was my standby, but one look at 18% versus 25% showed me that I had been doing a great deal of work for nothing. At a cent a word, I was getting $0.0018 for adventure, and $0.0025 for detective.

A considerable difference. And so I decided to write detectives more than adventures.

I discovered from this same list that, whereby I came from the West and therefore should know my subject, I had still to sell even one western story. I have written none since.

I also found that air-war and commercial air stories were so low that I could no longer afford to write them. And that was strange as I held a pilot's license.

Thus I was fooled into working my head off for little returns. But things started to pick up after that and I worked less. Mostly I wrote detective stories, with an occasional adventure yarn to keep up the interest.

But the raw materials of my plant were beginning to be exhausted. I had once been a police reporter and I had unconsciously used up all the shelved material I had.

And things started to go bad again, without my knowing why. Thereupon I took out my books, which I had kept accurately and up to date—as you should do.

Astonishing figures. While detective seemed to be my mainstay, there was the result.

DETECTIVE $\quad\dfrac{95,000 \text{ words sold}}{320,000 \text{ words written}} = 29.65\%$

ADVENTURE $\quad\dfrac{21,500 \text{ words sold}}{30,000 \text{ words written}} = 71.7\%$

Thus, for every word of detective I wrote I received $0.002965 and for every adventure word, $0.00717. A considerable difference. I scratched my head in perplexity until I realized about raw materials.

I had walked some geography, had been at it for years, and thus, my adventure stories were beginning to shine through. Needless to say, I've written few detective stories since then.

About this time, another factor bobbed up. I seemed to be working very, very hard and making very, very little money.

But, according to economics, no one has ever found a direct relation between the value of a product and the quantity of labor it embodies.

A publishing house had just started to pay me a cent a word and I had been writing for their books a long time. I considered them a mainstay among mainstays.

Another house had been taking a novelette a month from me. Twenty thousand words at a time. But most of my work was for the former firm.

Dragging out the accounts, I started to figure up on words written for this and that, getting percentages.

I discovered that the house which bought my novelettes had an average of 88%. Very, very high.

And the house for which I wrote the most was buying 37.6% of all I wrote for them.

Because the novelette market paid a cent and a quarter and the others a cent, the average pay was: House A, $0.011 for novelettes on every word I wrote for them. House B, $0.00376 for every word I wrote for *them.*

I no longer worried my head about House B. I worked less and made more. I worked hard on those novelettes after that and the satisfaction increased.

That was a turning point. Released from drudgery and terrific quantity and low quality, I began to make money and to climb out of a word grave.

That, you say, is all terribly dull, disgustingly sordid. Writing, you say, is an art. What are you, you want to know, one of those damned hacks?

No, I'm afraid not. No one gets a keener delight out of running off a good piece of work. No one takes any more pride in craftsmanship than I do. No one is trying harder to make every word live and breathe.

But, as I said before, even the laborer who finds his

chief pleasure in his work tries to sell services or products for the best price he can get.

And that price is not word rate. That price is satisfaction received, measured in money.

You can't go stumbling through darkness and live at this game. Roughly, here is what you face. There are less than two thousand professional writers in the United States. Hundreds of thousands are trying to write—some say millions.

The competition is keener in the writing business than in any other. Therefore, when you try to skid by with the gods of chance, you simply fail to make the grade. It's a brutal selective device. You can beat it if you know your product and how to handle it. You can beat it on only two counts. One has to do with genius, and the other with economics. There are very few men who sell and live by their genius only. Therefore, the rest of us have to fall back on a fairly exact science.

If there were two thousand soap plants in the country, and a million soap plants trying to make money, and you were one of the million, what would you do? Cutting prices, in our analogy, is not possible nor fruitful in any commerce. Therefore you would tighten up your plant to make every bar count. You wouldn't produce a bar if you knew it would be bad. You'd think about such things as reputation, supply, demand, organization, the plant, type of soap, advertising, sales department, accounting, profit and loss, quality versus quantity, machinery, improvements in product, raw materials, and labor employed.

And so it is in writing. We're factories working under terrific competition. We have to produce and sell at low cost and small price.

Labor, according to economics in general, cannot be measured in simple, homogeneous units of time such as labor hours. And laborers differ, tasks differ, in respect to amount and character of training, degree of skill, intelligence, and capacity to direct one's work.

That for soap making. That also for writing. And you're a factory whether your stories go to *Saturday Evening Post*, *Harper's*, or an upstart pulp that pays a quarter of a cent on publication. We're all on that common level. We must produce to eat, and we must know our production and product down to the ground.

Let us take some of the above-mentioned topics, one by one, and examine them.

Supply and Demand

You must know that the supply of stories is far greater than the demand. Actual figures tell nothing. You have only to stand by the editor and watch him open the morning mail. Stories by the truckload.

One market I know well publishes five stories a month. Five long novelettes. Dozens come in every week from names which would make you sit up very straight and be very quiet. And only five are published. And if there's a reject from there, you'll work a long time before you'll sell it elsewhere.

That editor buys what the magazine needs, buys the best obtainable stories, from the sources she knows to be reliable. She buys impersonally as though she bought soap. The best bar, the sweetest smell, the maker's name. She pays as though she paid for soap, just as impersonally, but many times more dollars.

That situation is repeated through all the magazine ranks. Terrific supply. Microscopic demand.

Realize now that every word must be made to count?

Organization and the Plant

Do you have a factory in which to work? Silly question, perhaps, but I know of one writer who wastes his energy like a canary wastes grain just because he has never looked at a house with an eye to an office. He writes in all manner of odd places. Never considers the time he squanders by placing himself where he is accessible. His studio is on top of the garage; he has no light except a feeble electric bulb, and yet he has to turn out seventy thousand a month. His nerves are shattered. He is continually going elsewhere to work, wasting time and more time.

Whether the wife or the family likes it or not, when the food comes out of the roller, a writer should have the pick and choice, say what you may. Me? I often take the living room and let the guests sit in the kitchen.

A writer needs good equipment. Quality of work is surprisingly dependent upon the typewriter. One lady I know uses a battered, rented machine which went through the world war, judging by its looks. The ribbon will not reverse. And yet, when spare money comes in, it goes on anything but a typewriter.

Good paper is more essential than writers will admit. Cheap, unmarked paper yellows, brands a manuscript as a reject after a few months, tears easily, and creases.

Good typing makes a good impression. I have often wished to God that I had taken a typing course instead of a story writing course far back in the dim past.

Raw Materials

Recently, a lady who once wrote pulp detective stories told me that, since she knew nothing of detective work, she went down to Center Street and sought information. The detective sergeant there gave her about eight hours of his time. She went through the gallery, the museum, looked at all their equipment, and took copious notes.

And the sergeant was much surprised at her coming there at all. He said that in fifteen years, she was the third to come there. And she was the only one who really wanted information. He said that detective stories always made him squirm. He wished the writers would find out what they wrote.

And so it is with almost every line. It is so easy to get good raw materials that most writers consider it quite unnecessary.

Hence the errors which make your yarn unsalable. You wouldn't try to write an article on steel without at least opening an encyclopedia, and yet I'll wager that a fiction story which had steel in it would never occasion the writer a bit of worry or thought.

You must have raw material. It gives you the edge on the field. And no one tries to get it by honest research. For a few stories you may have looked far, but for most of your yarns, you took your imagination for the textbook.

After all, you wouldn't try to make soap when you had no oil.

The fact that you write is a passport everywhere. You'll find very few gentlemen refusing to accommodate your curiosity. Men in every and any line are anxious to give a writer all the data he can use because, they reason, their line will therefore be truly represented. You're apt to find more enmity in not examining the facts.

Raw materials are more essential than fancy writing. Know your subject.

Type of Work

It is easy for you to determine the type of story you write best. Nothing is more simple. You merely consult your likes and dislikes.

But that is not the whole question. What do you write and sell best?

A writer tells me that she can write excellent marriage stories, likes to write them, and is eternally plagued to do them. But there are few markets for marriage stories. To eat, she takes the next best thing— light love.

My agent makes it a principle never to handle a type of story which does not possess at least five markets. That way he saves himself endless reading, and he saves his writers endless wordage. A story should have at least five good markets because what one editor likes, another dislikes, and what fits here will not fit there. All due respect to editors, their minds change and their slant is never too ironbound. They are primarily interested in good stories. Sometimes they are overbought. Sometimes they have need of a certain type which you do not fill. That leaves four editors who may find the desired spot.

While no writer should do work he does not like, he must eat.

Sales Department

If you had a warehouse filled with sweet-smelling soap, and you were unable to sell it, what would you do? You would hire a man who could. And if your business was manufacturing soap, your selling could not wholly be done by yourself. It's too much to ask. This selling is highly complex, very expensive.

Therefore, instead of wasting your valuable manufacturing time peddling your own manuscripts, why not let another handle the selling for you?

There's more than knowing markets to selling. The salesman should be in constant contact with the buyer. A writer cannot be in constant contact with his editors. It would cost money. Luncheons, cigars, all the rest. An agent takes care of all that and the cost is split up among his writers so that no one of them feels the burden too heavily.

An agent, if he is good, sells more than his ten percent extra. And he acts as a buffer between you and the postman. Nothing is more terrible than the brown envelope in the box. It's likely to kill the day. You're likely to file the story and forget it. But the agent merely sends the yarn out again, and when it comes home, out again it goes. He worries and doesn't tell you until you hold the check in your hand.

The collaborating agent and the critic have no place here. They are advisers and doctors. Your sales department should really have no function except selling—and perhaps when a market is going sour, forwarding a few editorial comments without any added by your agent. This tends for high morale, and a writer's morale must always be high. When we started, we assumed that you already could write.

By all means, get an agent, and if you get one and he is no good to you, ditch him and try another. There are plenty of good agents. And they are worth far more than ten percent.

Advertising

Your agent is your advertising department. He can tell the editor things which you, out of modesty, cannot. He can keep you in the minds of the men who count.

But a writer is his own walking advertisement. His reputation is his own making. His actions count for more than his stories. His reliability is hard won and when won is often the deciding factor in a sale. Editors must know you can produce, that you are earnest in your attempt to work with them.

To show what actions can do, one writer recently made it a habit to bait an editor as he went out to lunch.

This writer met this editor every day, forced his company on the editor and then, when they were eating, the writer would haul out synopsis after synopsis. The answer is, the writer doesn't work there anymore.

If a check is due, several writers I know haunt the office. It fails to hurry the check and it often puts an end to the contact when overdone. Many harry their editors for early decisions, make themselves nuisances in the office. Soon they stop selling there. Others always have a sob story handy.

Sob stories are pretty well taboo. It's hitting below the belt. And sob stories from writer to writer are awful. One man I know has wrecked his friendship with his formerly closest companions simply because he couldn't keep his troubles to himself. It's actually hurt his sales. You see, he makes more money than anyone I know, and he can't live on it. Ye Gods, ALL of us have troubles, but few professionals use them to get checks or sympathy.

Reputation is everything.

It does not hurt to do extra work for an editor. Such as department letters. Check it off to advertising. Answer all mail. Do a book for advertising. Write articles. Your name is your trademark. The better known, the better sales.

Quality Versus Quantity

I maintain that there is a medium ground for quantity and quality. One goes up, the other comes down.

The ground is your own finding. You know your best wordage and your best work. If you don't keep track of both, you should.

Write too little and your facility departs. Write too much and your quality drops. My own best wordage is seventy thousand a month. I make money at that, sell in the upper percentage brackets. But let me do twenty thousand in a month and I feel like an old machine, trying to turn over just once more before it expires. Let me do a hundred thousand in a month and I'm in possession of several piles of tripe.

The economic balance is something of your own finding. But it takes figures to find it. One month, when I was used to doing a hundred thousand per, I was stricken with some vague illness which caused great pain and sent me to bed.

For a week I did nothing. Then, in the next, I lay there and thought about stories. My average, so I thought, was shot to the devil. Toward the last of the month, I had a small table made and, sitting up in bed, wrote a ten-thousand-worder and two twenty-thousand worders. That was all the work I did. I sold every word and made more in eight days than I had in any previous month.

That taught me that there must be some mean or average. I found it and the wage has stayed up.

There is no use keeping the factory staff standing by and the machinery running when you have no raw material.

You can't sit down and stare at keys and wish you could write and swear at your low average for the month. If you can't write that day, for God's sakes, don't write. The chances are, when tomorrow arrives, and you've spent the yesterday groaning and doing nothing, you'll be as mentally sterile as before.

Forget what you read about having to work so many hours every day. No writer I know has regular office hours. When you can't write, when it's raining and the kid's crying, go see a movie, go talk to a cop, go dig up a book of fairy stories. But don't sweat inactively over a mill. You're just keeping the staff standing by and the machinery running, cutting into your overhead and putting out nothing. You're costing yourself money.

Come back when you're fresh and work like hell. Two in the morning, noon, eight at night, work if you feel like it and be damned to the noise you make. After all, the people who have to hear you are probably fed by you and if they can't stand it, let them do the supporting. I take sprees of working at night, and then sleep late into the day. Once, in the country, farmers baited me every day with that unforgivable late slumber. It didn't worry me so much after I remembered that I made in a month what they made in a year. They think all writers are crazy; take the writer's license and make the best of it.

But don't pretend to temperament. It really doesn't exist. Irritation does and is to be scrupulously avoided.

When all the arty scribblers (who made no money) talked to a young lady and told her that they could not write unless they were near the mountains, or unless they had the room a certain temperature, or unless they were served tea every half hour, the young lady said with sober mien, "Me? Oh, I can never write unless I'm in a balloon or in the Pacific Ocean."

One thing to remember. It seems to work out that your writing machine can stand just so much. After that the brain refuses to hand out plots and ideas.

It's like getting a big contract to sell your soap to the navy. You make bad soap, ruin the vats with a strong ingredient and let the finer machinery rust away in its uselessness. Then, when the navy soap contract ceases to supply the coffee and cakes, you discover that the plant is worthless for any other kind of product.

Such is the case of a writer who sees a big living in cheap fiction, turns it out to the expense of his vitality, and finally, years before his time, discovers that he is through. Only one writer of my acquaintance can keep a high word output. He is the exception, and he is not burning himself out. He is built that way.

But the rest of us shy away from too cheap a brand. We know that an advanced wage will only find us spending more. Soon, when the target for our unworthy efforts is taken down, we discover that we are unable to write anything else. That's what's meant by a rut.

As soon as you start turning out stories which you do not respect, as soon as you start turning them out wholesale over a period of time, as soon as your wordage gets out of control, then look for lean years.

To get anywhere at all in the business, you should turn out the best that's in you and keep turning it out. You'll never succeed in pulp unless you do, much less in the slicks.

If you start at the lowest rung, do the best job of which you are capable; your product, according to economic law, will do the raising for you. Man is not paid for the amount of work in labor hours; he is paid for the quality of that work.

Improvement of Product

With experience, your stories should improve. If they do not, then you yourself are not advancing. It's impossible not to advance; it's impossible to stand still. You must move, and you must slide back.

Take a story published a month ago, written six months ago. Read it over. If it seems to you that you could have done better, that you are doing better, you can sit back with a feline smile and be secure in the knowledge that you are coming up. Then sit forward and see to it that you do.

If you write insincerely, if you think the lowest pulp

can be written insincerely and still sell, then you're in for trouble unless your luck is terribly good. And luck rarely strikes twice. Write sincerely and you are certain to write better and better.

So much for making soap and writing. All this is merely my own findings in an upward trail through the rough paper magazines. I have tested these things and found them to be true and if someone had handed them to me a few years ago, I would have saved myself a great deal of worry and more bills would have been paid.

Once, a professor of short story in a university gave me a course because I was bored with being an engineer. The course did not help much outside of the practice in writing. Recently I heard that professor address the radio audience on the subject "This Business of Writing." It was not until then that I realized how much a writer had to learn. He knew nothing about the practical end of things and I told him so. He made me give a lecture to his class and they did not believe me.

But none of them, like you and I, have to make the bread and butter some way in this world. They had never realized that competition and business economics had any place whatever in the writing world. They were complacent in some intangible, ignorant quality they branded ART. They did not know and perhaps will some day find out, that art means, simply:

"The employment of means to the accomplishment of some end; the skillful application and adaptation to some purpose or use of knowledge or power acquired from Nature, especially in the production of beauty as in sculpture, etc.; a system of rules and established methods to facilitate the performance of certain actions."

They saw nothing praiseworthy in work well done. They had their hearts fixed on some goal even they did not understand. To them, writing was not a supreme source of expression, not a means of entertaining, not a means of living and enjoying work while one lived. If you wrote for a living, they branded you a hack. But they will never write.

Poor fools, they haven't the stamina, the courage, the intelligence, the knowledge of life's necessity, the mental capacity to realize that whatever you do in this life you must do well and that whatever talent you have is expressly given you to provide your food and your comfort.

My writing is not a game. It is a business, a hard-headed enterprise which fails only when I fail, which provides me with an energy outlet I need, which gives me the house I live in, which lets me keep my wife and boy. I am a manuscript factory but *not*—and damn those who so intimate it—an insincere hack, peddling verbal bellywash with my tongue in my cheek. And I eat only so long as my factory runs economically, only so long as I remember the things I have learned about this writing *business*.

PLOUGHSHARES

Written by
M. W. KEIPER

Illustrated by
Ivan Gregov

About the Author

M. W. Keiper is one of our first-place winners this year, and will be a finalist for the $4,000 grand prize.

He's written science fiction on and off for a long time—and in fact was a finalist in the contest when it first began. He's sold stories to Ellery Queen's Mystery Magazine, *to* Midnight Zoo, *has recently finished a novel and acquired an agent, and is currently working steadily on his second novel.*

Keiper graduated from Stetson University in DeLand, Florida, where he majored in history with the intent of becoming a lawyer. However, after a harsh attack of character, followed by a fierce bout of ethics, he decided against it. (It seems that Keiper and one of our other authors share similar opinions about the legal profession. Please reference Devil's Advocate *by Syne Mitchell found elsewhere in this anthology.)*

Keiper has worked the usual writerly jobs—bookstore clerk, ironworker, special deputy, newspaper reporter, salesman, and for a brief time he once followed the profession of Jesus. But he decided that carpentry wasn't for him.

He currently lives in Cassadaga, Florida. We wish him well in his writing career.

About the Illustrator

Ivan Gregov was born in Split, Croatia, in 1973. He graduated from the School of Applied Arts in Zagreb, where he is now studying painting.

Ivan finds that most of his inspiration for his drawing comes from music, not from other artists, and says that he listens to music as much as possible. He prefers medieval and traditional Irish music to others.

Beyond his art, he is also interested in mountaineering, the study of ancient cultures, raising dogs, and writing short stories. He says that most of his drawings sit in a cupboard, though he has published a few things, and while in school he worked extensively on an animated film.

The first batch of recruits showed up on the parade grounds in white dresses and wearing amoebas on their feet. At least they all looked to be male and between the ages of eighteen and twenty-five, like Franklin promised. They all looked like pretty good specimens, too. But still, they had fucking amoebas on their feet.

Goddamn Army.

They came out of the barracks building and approached me, at the far end of the drill field, with big smiles on their innocent young faces. That wouldn't do at all, not at all. I could see I was going to have to provide some attitude adjustment right away.

Franklin said they'd all be able to speak "English 20th North B" and be at least passingly familiar with basic military terminology—this first bunch of volunteers being selected from history majors and anthropologists and such. I adjusted the angle of my "Smokey Bear" hat and tucked my swagger stick under my left arm. Let's just see what's what here.

"Move yourselves! Fall in, you worthless sons of bitches!" They milled helplessly for a few seconds, then formed a rank, shoulder to shoulder, in front of me. All fifty of them. I approached the one at the end of the line nearest me.

"What's your name, son?"

"In Speech, or in English 20th Nor—?"

"English, if it won't overtax that pathetic shriveled organ you call a brain."

"Gloriously Blooming Chrysanthemums Conjoined in Ecstasy, sir,"

"Don't call me sir, goddamn it! I ain't no fucking officer! I work for a living! I am Master Sergeant James J. Scovill. You will call me Sergeant or Top! You got that, boy!"

"Yes, si . . . Sergeant!"

"All right, Fucking Flowers. Just what is it you and your little pals think it is you have done here?" He looked down the line, then back at me.

"We have fallen in. In response to your command."

"There are fifty of you, son. You have done formed a rank into the next county. Ranks of ten, five deep. Move your asses!" They sorted themselves out quick enough; I'll give them that. I've had whole platoons that couldn't take two steps without tripping over their own dicks.

"Just pathetic. Unless the Enemy laughs themselves to death at the sight of you, I see no hope whatsoever. I need me a volunteer. You there," I pointed to the biggest one in the front rank, "three steps out. What's your name, boy?"

"Seagull Contemplating Its Oneness With the Zephyr Lifting It Heavenward, Sergeant."

"O.K., Birdbrain," I pointed with my stick toward his feet. "What are them things on your feet, boy?"

"Symbiotic foot shields, Sergeant. They draw sustenance from the host and provide healthful protection for the feet."

"Soldiers do not wear amoebas on their feet, boy," I slapped the top of my spit-shined leather combat boots with my stick. "Soldiers wear boots." I flipped the edge of his sleeve with the stick. "What'd you call that there get-up?"

"It is the Garment of Serious Undertakings, appropriate for these climatic conditions, Sergeant."

"That's a dress, son. Soldiers do not wear dresses. You a faggot, boy?"

"No, Sergeant. Do you require one? I think Sunrise Over Mountain Tranquility and Blossoms of a Frost-Tinged Spring Morning are." A couple of hands went up. "There are also many of us who are occasionally bisexual that—"

"NO! GODDAMNIT!" I took a deep breath to steady myself. A lot of fucking changes in twenty thousand years. I used my swagger stick to draw a line in the dust at Birdbrain's feet, then thrust the stick through my gunbelt.

"All right, Birdbrain. Lets us conduct a little experiment, you and me. Now, I am the Enemy. Across that there line is home, hearth and family—everything you hold sacred. I am coming across that line to rape, pillage, plunder and destroy. You do your level best to stop me—bar none. You got that, boy?" He nodded, and licked his lip nervously.

It wasn't a sneaky punch, nor a particularly fast one. I just drew back my right fist and popped him one right on the beezer. He went down faster than a Subic Bay whore on payday. He sat there in the dirt with his legs sprawled out in front of him, hands clasped over his bleeding nose, weeping.

Yep, humanity's best and brightest hope for survival.

"Stand up, boy!" He wobbled to his feet. "How bad you hurt?"

"Oh, the injury is of no consequence, Sergeant."

"Then why you cryin', boy?"

"I am overcome with gratitude, Sergeant, that you would take on the great burden of doing such violence on our behalf. I love you very much, Sergeant." This was followed by a chorus of agreement from the formation.

"GET! BACK! IN! RANK!" I took up a position front and center and gave them my very best evil eye.

"In thirty years' soldiering I have seen five major campaigns and three police actions. I have been severely wounded four times and I have killed upwards of one hundred men." I held up my left hand so they could see my missing third finger. "A Cuban sniper shot that off outside Havana," I slapped my right knee with my swagger stick. "A Chinese mortar round took off my kneecap in South Africa in '08! I once killed twelve men in less than five seconds with grenades and automatic weapons fire! I damn near froze to death in a ditch outside Seoul in the winter of '23 while the Reds lobbed artillery at us for thirty-six straight hours! Not one of those scenes of horror, slaughter and heartbreak depressed me half as much as the sight of you does at this moment! You will be issued a proper kit tonight and we will start this fresh in the morning. In the meantime, I want you to reflect just how much the term *soldier* is disgraced and degraded when applied to such as you! Dismissed!"

I turned on my heel and strode off toward my office on the opposite side of the field. I needed to get in touch with Franklin about properly outfitting these bozos. I heard running footsteps behind me, then a call.

"Sergeant! Sergeant, a moment please!" I turned.

"What is it, Flowers?"

"Um, what should we do now, si . . . Sergeant?"

"Son, I don't care if you go organize a circle jerk. I ain't emotionally involved, get me?"

"Yes, Sergeant," he said doubtfully.

When I got to the steps leading to my office, I looked back at the drill field. Most of them were gathered around Flowers who pointed to his crotch, then made a circling motion in the air.

"FLOWERS!" He jogged over to me.

"Yes, Sergeant?"

"That's what's known as a figure of speech, son. It wasn't an order." At least he looked relieved rather than disappointed.

Goddamn Army.

You would think a man of my experience would have known better than to volunteer for anything. When the verdict came back "pancreatic cancer," I put in for the euth needle. I didn't have too many regrets. Ruthie had passed on three years earlier. The boys were well established with families of their own. I figured I was right with God and country. If it was time to go, then it was time to go.

When the euthanasia councilor showed up there was this here fella with him. He said they'd like to use me for an experiment in "long-term tissue preservation." Said I wouldn't notice no difference between that and the euth needle, and I could leave my kids $50,000. Well, where the fuck do I sign?

Only next thing I know, I wake up sittin' on a bench in this beautiful little flower garden. I'm wearing a blue dress and there are amoebas on my feet. There's this old coot sittin' on the other end of the bench who looks a hell of a lot like pictures I seen of Ben Franklin, only he's wearing the same outfit I am. I tell him that. He says good, Franklin can be our Name Between Friends for him. Then he gives me the lowdown.

Somewhere out in far space the human race has finally met another intelligent spacefaring species. It should have been a dream come true; only it ain't. These boys take the existence of the human species as a personal affront, and they ain't about to stand for it. We can fight, or we can die. Only we don't know how to fight anymore. Some twenty thousand years of civilization has taken it out of us.

So I'm back in the Army. Hell, for right now, I pretty much am the fuckin' Army.

I best get on the stick and call Franklin. Got to get these yahoos properly fitted out so's we can take another run at this thing tomorrow.

"Central!" I shout.

"How may I assist you, Sergeant Scovill?" The voice always seems to be coming out of thin air from a point about three feet in front of me.

"I need to talk to Franklin."

"The Elder would have you join him for midmorning refreshment. I will provide a car."

"That'd be just fine." I left my D.I. hat on the desk and grabbed a billet fatigue cap from a hook by the door. As I stepped outside, a couch swooped down from overhead and came to a halt floating a few inches off the ground before me. I made myself comfortable and ordered the bottom half of the spherical shield to turn reflective silver, the upper to turn the same transparency as glass. I just like the effect. George-fucking-Jetson, that's me.

The ground below blurred with speed. Central Administrative Arcology is in the Rockies, 'bout where Denver used to be, I reckon. It didn't take long to get

there. The car deposited me on the balcony outside
Franklin's office. I wasn't exactly sure just how big a
muckety-muck Franklin was, but he was a big one, right
enough. The outside doors were open and he waved me
in. He was sitting cross-legged in front of a low wooden
coffee table loaded down with a tea service and plates of
goodies. The floor sprouted a low-slung chair for me.
Franklin motioned me to it.

"Sit, my friend. How did our young people fare?" I
accepted a cup of tea and made myself comfortable.

"Not promisin'. I knocked the biggest one down and
he just sat there a-cryin'."

Franklin looked thoughtful for a moment, then he
raised a finger. "Seagull Contempla—"

"That'd be him," I interrupted.

"A young man of exceptional potential," he leaned
over and refilled my cup. "He is a student of history and
has conducted some interesting experiments. He once
constructed an apparatus for the capture of fish and
actually killed one of the creatures and prepared its
flesh for consumption over an open fire. He was able to
ingest several bites before his natural revulsion made
him ill. It was considered a very daring experiment,
quite controversial in some quarters. I thought his direct
experience with such savagery would make him a good
candidate for our program."

"You tellin' me he's the best material I got to work
with?"

"Well, he did kill the creature himself."

"So the best soldier material I got is a boy who couldn't
keep down a camp breakfast 'cause he was so tore up
over killin' a trout?"

Franklin set down his cup and folded his hands in
his lap. "I think I understand how weak and trivial we

must appear to you, my friend. But make no mistake: These fifty have pledged their lives to this undertaking. Many thousands more of our people, both men and women, stand ready to follow them."

"Franklin, I got to ask you something. Have you people maybe done something to yourselves? I mean, have you even got what it takes in you anymore?"

"Sergeant, I do not think I could adequately explain our medical arts to you. . . ."

"Goddamn it, Franklin! I had an American high-school education when that still meant somethin' good, and I've had a library card since I was seven years old. Don't let the corn-pone accent fool you. I may have been born in West-By-God-Virginia, but I know the difference between DNA and the fuckin' N.B.A. You damn well know what I'm askin' you!"

He looked down for a moment, then up into my eyes. "We have eliminated some illnesses, of both body and spirit, and some tendency towards illnesses; that is all. We are no different flesh, you and I. It is a matter of nurture, not nature. It is that upon which I base my hopes for our salvation."

"All right then. That's all I wanted to know. There's a list of things I'll be needin'. We can start with some regulation uniforms, like your people run up for me."

"Anything is yours for the asking, my friend."

When I got back to base I could see the whole passel of them runnin' back and forth out on the drill field. Christ on a stick! Now what? I got out of the car and walked over. When I seen what they were kicking around, I felt a hot flare of anger in the pit of my stomach. I waited until the black-and-white ball spun closer, then I drew my pistol and put three rounds through it. Everybody froze.

"I leave you candy-ass, mammy-jammers alone for five fuckin' minutes and you start playing soccer! This is a sport for third-world losers! This is a sport you don't even need opposable thumbs to play! I will not have my troops playing any sport a chimp is overqualified for! You feelin' so goddamn frisky, you can give me fifty laps around the drill field! Move it!

Goddamn Army.

It did not go well.

Oh, they did good enough at the purely physical stuff. They hardened up quick; run the obstacle course like real gung-ho troopers. But, at bayonet practice, just stickin' a canvas bag with a face painted on it, all their hands shook and half of them lost their lunch. Hand-to-hand training was even worse. It's too depressing to describe in detail. There was a lot of crying; let's just leave it at that.

I think I began to understand what the problem was when Serenity of Dawn Over the Azure Mountains froze during live grenade practice. He stood there trembling for about ten seconds, then dropped the grenade. Flowers charged over, pushed Serenity out of the way and threw himself on the grenade. I stood there tapping my swagger stick against my leg for about thirty seconds, then went over and gave Flowers a nudge in the ribs with the toe of my boot. He slowly unwrapped his arms from around his head and blinked up at me.

"Hello, son."

"Hello, Sergeant."

"Tell me, Flowers. What is it you are doing?"

"I am saving the lives of my comrades by shielding them from the lethal force of the explosion."

"Are you now? Tell me, how long have you been laying there?"

"I am not sure, Sergeant."

"I calculate it to be the best part of a minute. How long is the fuse on a hand grenade?"

"Five seconds, Sergeant."

"Unless you plan on taking up a career as a rug, stand up, son." He got up very slowly. "Hand me that," I pointed at the grenade. He passed it over and I held it up in front of his nose. "What is this, boy?"

"It is a Mark 29 Fragmentation Grenade. Standard issue, U.S.A. armed forces, circa 2014 through 2037."

"Notice anything, oh, I don't know, significant about it?"

"Um . . . The arming pin has not been withdrawn?"

"I feel the need for exercise. Go run laps around the drill field until my need for exercise abates."

It wasn't that they lacked courage. They just lacked the right kind. That evening, I went to see Franklin and gave him the bad news. We stood on the balcony of his office, drinking a potent clear liquor and watching the sun go down.

"Old Georgie Patton said it best. 'No poor bastard ever won a war by dying for his country. He won it by making sure the poor bastard on the other side died for his country.' I'm right sorry, Franklin. I just don't think they got it in them."

"Then there is no hope for us. The Enemy will not suffer us to live. Now that they know we exist, they will search unceasingly for us. It is only a matter of time."

"I done what I could. You can put the boy in the jungle, but I guess you just can't put the jungle in th—" I broke off because I'd just given myself an idea. "Franklin, I don't suppose there are any wild places left—are there?"

"Many. Two-thirds of the planetary surface is dedicated to natural reserves."

"Do I have a completely free hand?"

"You may do whatever you deem necessary."

"I'll need a large transport craft at my command."

"Done."

The transport was a white sphere the size of an aircraft carrier that extruded a boarding ramp wide as a four-lane highway from its base. I gave them one last chance to back out. No one did.

"All right then. Strip on down. We ain't takin' nothin' with us but our claws and teeth. From here on out, it's root hog or die!" I led them up the ramp.

We took our first three casualties in northern Alaska when a big storm hit—exposure. We lost two more in the swamps of northern Australia. Snake bite and drowning. At each stop we carved out a place for ourselves, held it, then gathered our dead and wounded and moved on. We did that for six months.

When we landed at Central Administrative Arcology there was a crowd waiting. I cleaned up, put on a dress uniform, and went down the ramp to meet Franklin. They started to unload the coffins about then and the first words I tried to say to him were drowned out by cries. The sound of human grief never changes. Franklin seemed to shrink a little more as each coffin came down the ramp.

"All?" he asked in a cracked voice.

"No, twenty-eight." I gave a whistle and the seven members of the First Squad of the Wolf Clan padded down the ramp. Squads Two and Three waited for One to move clear of the ramp. They'd learned about keeping your interval. Squad One automatically spread out into a skirmish line. The three at the rear with the longbows ready to provide covering fire. Most had copper spearheads or knives Shapes With Fire had fashioned from ore we had found in the Colorado mountains. Standing Bear preferred his flint ax. Red Arrow wore a bearskin kilt he had made from the hide of the grizzly that had killed poor old Flowers. Red Arrow had tracked that bear for two days and two nights; putting nine flint-tipped clothyard arrows into its hide before it gave up the ghost. There was never any question of quitting. By then the rules had been established. Shed the blood of the Wolf Clan, you pay in blood.

They all had crude bone-needle and plant-ink tatoos of a wolf's head on their right shoulders. I had one too.

"Your training cadre," I told Franklin. "There's blood on their hands and red murder in their hearts. They know this culture, their own people, better than I do. Maybe the price for their groups won't be quite so high." I turned and walked away. Central had a car waiting for me and I headed back to base.

I sat there at my desk and stared at the pistol on the desktop in front of me. I felt very old, and very far from home. An old boot camp buddy of mine used to say, "Be careful what you wish for. You just might get it." I wondered if that was a bit of ancient wisdom Franklin wished he'd had just a mite sooner. I looked at the pistol and wondered if it was possible for a dead man to commit a mortal sin. God help me, was a man ever so lost?

There was a knock on the doorframe. It was Franklin. He walked over to the desk. For the first time since I'd met him, he moved like an old man—very old.

"There is no way we can adequately thank you," he said.

Illustrated by Ivan Gregov

"Don't be so sure you should."

"I am sure. Our great debt to you makes it all the more difficult to ask anything further. Yet I must." He reached out and laid two small gold stars on the desk in front of me.

"On behalf of the Elders, I ask you to accept command of the Emergency Forces, to become general of the Army of Humanity. Your children yet face great trials. We need you, Great-grandfather."

"Great-grandfather?"

"It has been a very long time. Nearly all of us can claim some degree of blood kinship with you. We have very good records. Even in your time the AI machines had begun to keep extensive files in the belief it would aid genetic research. That, and that they've always tended to be busybodies—even the early models."

"Franklin, I'll need to study on this a bit."

"Of course. I will leave you to contemplate." He bowed his way out.

From one second to the next everything was completely different. Talk about your mysterious ways. "All right," I said aloud, "I don't need no damn burning bush to fall on me."

"I'm sorry," said the voice of central. "What is it you do, or do not require?"

"I ain't talking to you, you jumped-up pocket calculator! Though I admit you do a pretty good impression of Him sometimes."

All right, you bastards out there in the far dark. You hear that sound? It's the sound of ploughshares being beaten into swords—and the steel is coming out of the fire harder and sharper than ever. You've shed the blood of the Wolf Clan, and my boys and girls are coming to see you about that. I reckon I'll be coming with 'em.

I looked at the gold stars on my desk and I just had to laugh. It took twenty thousand years and an inter-stellar war to do it, but Mrs. Scovill's little boy finally ended up an officer.

Goddamn Army.

TEMPERING DAY

Written by
Darren Clark Cummings

Illustrated by
Lionel Baker II

About the Author

Darren Cummings *is a software engineer for Honeywell's Air Transport Division. He earned his bachelor's degree in electrical engineering from University of Missouri-Rolla, and as a devout Christian and member of the North Phoenix Baptist Church is active in the ministry. His first story was published in* Dragon Magazine *in the November 1994 issue.*

However, his biography perhaps puts a finer spin on Darren. He is, among other things, "a washed-up triathlete" who doesn't own a television, but who does appreciate a good quote, tree frogs, platypuses, rain forests in general, and any species' little-known biological quirks or DNA slyness. He can definitely balance accounts, give orders, take orders, cooperate, act alone, solve equations, analyze a problem, program a computer, and cook a tasty meal. If pressed, he could probably change a diaper, plan an invasion, butcher a hog, conn a ship, pitch manure, set a bone, design a building, write a sonnet, comfort the dying, fight efficiently, and die gallantly. He agrees that specialization is for insects, another thing he greatly admires—insects, that is, not specialization, so much.

In short, Darren Cummings is a fine example, when all his neurons are firing, of what millions of years of evolution can do on the right planet with a little luck.

About the Illustrator

Lionel Baker began drawing at an early age, and studied art at the University of Tennessee, where he was disappointed to find that his instructors held fantasy art in contempt (a problem that many of our artists, I'm sure, can relate to).

Undaunted, Lionel decided to try to fuse art with his other major interest—Heavy Metal rock—by creating album covers and T-shirts, a project that has begun to garner some success.

Lionel says that his influences include the almighty Frank Frazetta, Barry Windsor-Smith, and N. C. Wyeth.

Lionel currently runs an independent record shop, The Dragon's Lair, in Bristol, Virginia, which caters to Heavy Metal music fans and helps to promote gigs for local and regional bands.

Palin raced faster. Sheathed in goat's hide, his sword slapped against his back, unnoticed—for the sun rising before him meant he was late. Though he'd run nearly the whole way to the beach, the sun had already climbed onto the sea's edge, starting the day.

His day—his Tempering Day—when his abbot would give him final instruction for the completion of his sword. Somewhere on the broad beach Abbot Bondau waited for him. The trail's cold stone sucked the heat from Palin's toes, numbing them. He stumbled, but forced his pace to quicken.

The sea's gentle voice found Palin's ears. He scanned the rocky shore, blinking against the growing sun. There. The abbot stood far down the beach, at the edge of the water, a large man bent with age atop a block of stone.

The abbot's shadow stretched across the beach as if blown back by the force of the morning sun. Palin slowed to catch his breath. He moved up carefully, quietly, following the long shadow until he reached the abbot's feet.

"It is a long walk down here, isn't it?" asked the abbot quietly, still watching the waves.

"Aye, sir, and—"

"And perhaps an earlier start would have been advisable?" The old man looked down, his seamed face pitted with tiny burn scars, his eyebrows gone, long seared away over the forge.

"Aye, Father."

The dark old eyes flicked away from Palin, across the sea, then back. "Aye. And Brother Door needed sticks for his fire, didn't he? Eh?" The deep wrinkles shifted into a more accustomed smile. "Help me down, son, the tide is wanting my perch." He bent and Palin reached up to help. As the hard old hands took Palin's, the emblem of their order swung from the abbot's neck between them, reflecting sunlight. The abbot carefully stepped down to the wet sand, between waves. "Highest tide this night, you know."

As he drew away, he slipped Palin's sword free.

"Brother Hammer tells me you were ambitious." He hefted the long blade. Yellow light flashed along its length. "Straight enough. Nicely worked, for an acolyte. You show restraint with the finishing hammer. . . ." He looked up. "Tell me, Palin, why do you need such a heavy sword?"

"I am large enough to use it, sir. I've seen the King's guard use larger—"

"Have you?"

"Aye! They carry them across their backs this way, to draw across the shoulder—"

"You've seen them carried, then. Not used."

Palin blinked at him. "No, sir. Not . . . not used. I don't remember the war. I was brought here as an infant."

The abbot handed him back the weapon. Palin fumbled to sheath it as they began walking along the beach.

"There is much debate as to whether this constitutes a missed stroke in your education, you know. Eh? Well, it does. A Friar of Arms should be completely sharpened. We send you boys out like that blade, untempered."

Palin could not control his glance at the sword.

The old man chuckled. "Yes, yes. We will attend to your sword's last stages. You are wondering when I will show you the location of the 'Magic Clay,' or has a new acolyte's myth replaced that one these days?"

Palin could feel his face redden. "Sir, I expected no powers, just fine clay."

"And that is what I will give you. And some minor advice on the clay's layering, the thicknesses, and the placing of the blade in the heat, and the temperature of the water, the time of quenching, the hammer work to follow. . . . You have time for this, I assume?"

"Father, my time is pennies. Yours is gold."

The abbot stopped and looked at him closely. "Perhaps I have underestimated other facets of our program here. Brother Homily would be pleased with that reply." He turned and stared out at the sea again. "Never could move a man with words, myself."

Palin followed his gaze out to a small rocky island a few hundred yards away.

Then the abbot's smile fell away and he said, "Acolyte Palin, I have a task for you."

Palin stepped to the water's edge, searching the rocks with his eyes. "Yes, Father?"

"A ridge lies along here, it becomes islands . . . there." He pointed with a thick, bent finger. The third and last island is but a bit of washed stone."

"How will I find it?"

"You'll see it well enough. There's a man on it."

"I'm to rescue him?"

The abbot turned a wooden expression to him. "This

man is there under sentence of death." He swallowed.
"The highest tides cover the rocks, you see."

Palin shivered. "What . . . I am to prevent his escape?"

"He is an old man. He'll not be swimming away."

"I am to hear his confession, then?"

"If he offers that, you do it. But he'll not be asking for
your services, Palin."

"Then . . . ?"

The abbot turned and looked back out at the sea.
"Listen, son. It's hot out there. Unless it rains, that pile of
stone holds no fresh water. Even then there's little of
interest. Living until the highest tide is part of the sentence. But this man has found some way to survive
through two cycles of the moon. He has served his time.
He has suffered enough. It is time for his sentence to be
fulfilled."

Palin's mouth hung open. He stepped backward,
shaking his head. "Kill him? You want me to kill a
man?"

"You carry a sword, don't you? What were you
planning to do with it?"

"Not . . . not executions! Father!"

"The King's executioners put him there. They will
not go further without legal intervention, which is quite
impossible considering the man is already legally dead.
I have managed to obtain permission for our order to
administer mercy."

"Did he ask for this mercy?"

The abbot's eyes hardened, searching Palin's face
with an expression he usually reserved for rust. He said:
"If you are refusing my task, then hand me your sword,
boy."

They stared at each other.

A wave rolled in and hissed across the sand, leaving tiny shells on Palin's toes. He looked down, then nodded, the blood drained from his face.

"Walk with me some more, Acolyte Palin. I'll show you the rowboat." The abbot took his arm and led him down the beach. "Let me tell you about Simon Lecheau. Simon the Assassin . . ."

They walked together and the abbot talked until the clouds lost their color. The abbot stopped when he reached a small rocky grotto.

"What a monster," Palin whispered. "Children?"

"Aye. Still, there's no evidence he enjoyed it," said the abbot, "nor sought for else but the gold. He did it quick—that's what kept him from the stake. Here's the boat, then."

Palin blinked down at a laden rowboat which floated low in the pool. He bent to the rope and reeled the boat closer. "It's full of food. Is this island far?" He looked up at the abbot who was examining the horizon of the sea.

"A last meal is traditional. A bit of kindness might come as enough surprise to loosen his heart, if nothing else will. We must always temper justice with mercy, my son." He frowned down at the boatful of provisions, pursed his lips. "Perhaps Brother Stores misunderstood my instructions."

"I'd best return all this to him—"

The abbot's calloused hand moved to rest on Palin's shoulder. "It will keep until your task is completed."

Palin was able only to nod.

Palin rowed awkwardly, though his arms were knotted with muscle from years over the forges. There his work had been fueled by martial fantasy—of war and heroism, of battle's honor, of thundering cavalry

charge and ringing sword blow—and every imagined
blow matched his hammer's fall upon the anvil, felling
imaginary menace. Now he thought simply of striking a
man to death with the sword he had made and his arms
seemed to melt at the oars. His mind brought forth
butchers' images, balked, refused to accept them, leaving him confused, numb.

Cold spray made him stiffen. He had drifted beyond
the lee of the first island, and great waves from the open
sea shoved at his heavy boat and splashed into it, wet-
ting his feet. He bent into the task and rowed hard,
allowed thoughts only of rowing.

He soon cleared the white caps and saw the second
island. A small tower of stone poked up from the waves,
a dark silhouette he steered toward.

The hard rowing helped. A stroke at a time, he told
himself. Focus on the simple task. He would arrive at the
island, he would do it quickly, he would leave. He
wouldn't think about it. He would simply do it.

Let the abbot think about it, he decided. I'm thinking
about rowing. Let the abbot carry this burden—it was
his idea, this mercy. He's the wise one, the master. I'm
just following orders. I row, I carry food, I do this other
task. I'm just his hands.

The stone tower's eastern face was dazzlingly white
and speckled with nesting gulls. Atop the rubble, at the
tide's high mark, lay the skeleton of a small rowboat.

Palin's hands tightened on his oars. He pulled,
pulled again, taking deep sweeps away from the island.
When he could no longer see the pile of wood he again
drifted. Finally he turned and looked for the third island.

It was almost lost in the glare, far out, a dark speck
against the sea. He turned back, reached for the oars,
and found himself weeping.

When he could see again, he had drifted far south. Inland, over the Gray Mountains, a storm was building. It would be raining in Isebrook when he returned, he thought.

He splashed water on his face, then pulled again on the oars, watching the distant storm slowly build.

The sun had traveled a third of the way across the sky by the time Palin reached the island. He turned the boat around and brought it in canoe-like, awkwardly. Even now, as the tide ebbed toward its lowest point, the island was little more than an obstacle to shipping: a pile of boulders perhaps eighty feet across, and less than thirty high.

Palin checked his sword for the third time as the boat ground to a stop upon the gravel patch he had selected. He stepped out, unsteadily, feeling with his feet, afraid to take his eyes off those of the man who watched him.

Simon Lecheau sat well back from the water's edge. He was small and thin and old. His robe was but rags and the sun had tanned his skin to the color of the stones themselves. His stringy white beard fluttered like the feather of a gull upon a beach.

Palin threw the oars carefully away from the boat, then moved across the rocks after them. The abbot's tale-telling had left him expecting a caged monster, not this wasted old man. "Food," said Palin, gesturing at the boat. "And water."

Lecheau exhaled, then nodded. He carefully stood and limped across the rocks toward the boat. His right foot was misshapen, tied in dirty rags, healing poorly. A large stone dropped from his hand as he passed Palin.

He sat beside the boat and fumbled at a waterskin, finally tearing the thong to open it. He sucked noisily at it, then reached for a bag with shaking, wet fingers.

Palin turned away. At least, he thought, this did not require conversation.

"What's your name?" croaked Simon Lecheau.

"I'm from the monastery," Palin answered, without turning around. "The abbot, the Master Friar of Arms, sent . . . this meal for you." He stepped away again.

"Bit heavy for a meal, don't you think? Hey?"

Palin turned around. Lecheau gestured at him with half an apple, speaking with his mouth full. "I know you monks eat well enough off the peasants' tables. But I'm used to lighter fare, you see. Is any of this for you— planning to stay a while, perhaps?"

Palin shook his head.

"I'll be holding you up, then. I'm sure you have many things to do." The thin arms began pulling bags out of the boat, tossing them farther up the shore.

Palin opened his mouth to stop him, but the words died. I can reload the bags, he thought. Afterward. He may as well enjoy the meal.

Palin watched Lecheau pile the bags and skins and realized how easy it would be to take the man suddenly, a single stroke from behind. There would be no words, no explanations. And no chance of confession. He sat down and watched Lecheau eat. For a starving man, thought Palin, he certainly took his time.

Simon Lecheau's face was as seamed as the abbot's. But the abbot's lines were deep and pocked with tiny forge-scars, each a story, each crevasse a hiding place of time and wisdom. The lines in Lecheau's face were so thin that it merely looked cracked, like the shell of a dropped brown egg.

He gestured again, this time with a biscuit. "You can be getting on, now. Unless you need the bags?"

Palin shook his head. He felt chilled, though sweat trickled down his back. Lecheau shrugged and seemed to chew even more slowly.

"You must be nearing the end of your training, hey?" Palin nodded, his eyes moving to the dark clouds over the inland mountains. Lecheau asked, "How much longer till you start your wandering time?"

"I don't know."

"Got some training left? Some more forge-time?"

Palin shook his head again.

"So you will be finishing soon?"

Palin looked at him, speaking softly, "I have a few tasks yet to perform. Not all are specified." Now I need to tell him, Palin decided.

He took a deep breath.

"So," said Lecheau, "you're Abbot Bondau's executioner? Hey?"

Palin blinked at him, not sure he had heard the words correctly. He felt his face flush.

"Hey?"

"No! I'm not . . ."

Lecheau nodded knowingly over his biscuit. "You are here to perform an execution. You're an executioner . . . or at least intend to be, soon."

Palin stood up. "I have no such . . . I was told to administer mercy to a man condemned to die a lingering—"

Lecheau laughed. Silent spasms shook his thin body. He finally coughed and took a drink, then looked up again. "You hardly have to explain it to me, of all people. Practice that speech all the way out here, did you? Well, I'd rather not hear it. Save it for yourself, for the long row back."

Palin swallowed. Is he daring me? he wondered.

"I understand, boy, I really do. It's hard waiting to kill a man. It's hard when you have to sit there and think about it. I know." He smiled, showing his missing teeth. "I always went straight to it, got it over and done with."

"This is not one of your assassinations, Lecheau—"

"Call me Simon, please. I'm the one who's being killed, I'll call it what I like. You are here to assassinate me."

"I am here under orders to carry out an existing—"

"You are here to extract revenge upon me. Many of my patrons hired me for similar reasons. Really, I understand. I totally agree with your motives."

"Justice is not revenge!"

"Depends upon which way you hold the mirror, boy. Care for an apple?"

"I don't share your motivations!"

Lecheau bit into the apple with a crunch, then spoke with his mouth full. "You poke a man with sharp iron and claim to be unwilling?"

"My will in this is only to obey my abbot."

"So you obey Bondau and I obeyed my patrons—"

"For money!"

"And where did you get those clothes, that ridiculously huge sword? When did you last spend a night hungry? Now you must earn it, as did I." He tossed the apple's core behind him. "Welcome to the guild, little brother."

Palin whipped his sword free and strode forward. "Do you want a time of confession?" he shouted.

Without looking up at his approach, Lecheau reached for the bag again.

"Simon Lecheau! Speak now if you want me to hear your last confession!"

Lecheau pulled free an apple, frowned, and took a bite

of it. He looked up, chewing. "Do you friars always temper your swords with human blood? Is that your secret?"

Against his will, Palin's eyes were drawn to the sword in his hands. He thought of it slick and red. He stumbled backward.

"Is every one of you friars sent here as a final test or something? I wonder how many prisoners have been sacrificed to your blades on these rocks?" Lecheau looked around as if expecting to see bodies.

Palin felt sickened. He stepped back again. All the rumors, all the whispered acolytes' tales of Tempering Day, flickered through his mind.

"So? You are all actually assassins—your pardon—executioners, then?"

Palin shook his head, hard. He remembered the older acolytes returning with their tempered swords. They always returned reflective, silent, humbled. . . .

Then Palin noticed Lecheau's hands, clamped tight about his apple to still their trembling. And he saw the lie for what it was.

He looked in Lecheau's eyes. "Men with such a secret could not teach the First Virtue as they do."

"The first virtue?"

"Honesty. And they teach it well. By example."

Then it was Lecheau's eyes that fell. He reached quickly to fumble at his bag of fruit. "Ah . . . well, that's . . . that's a good cover story, then. Who would expect—"

"Enough lies!" Palin strode forward, sword raised.

Lecheau stared up at him, expressionless. "Is it to be out of anger, then? Even I never killed for anger's sake."

Palin stood over him, breathing hard. His arms cramped from his clutch on the hilt.

"Careful, boy. You'll lose the temper they've put on you, hey?"

One blow, Palin thought. Then it would be over.

"It is a long row back," whispered Lecheau, "is it not?"

Emotion, Palin had chanted often enough, was not substitute for duty. He stepped back, again, dropping the point to the ground. How, he marveled, could a man so evil understand so much?

Lecheau barked at him: "Lies, you accuse me of? Look, boy, I'm not the one fattening up my victim while planning his sacrifice!"

Palin could see the fear behind those old squinting eyes. The man's words were but beggings to him now.

"Yes, lies," he said. "The tide is coming in, Simon Lecheau. The highest tide. Even if I fail, you'll not live out this night. That is truth." Palin bent and picked up the oars. "I'll come back when my shadow has lengthened to my height. You think about this—truth can also be found in confession."

"Perhaps there is no such thing as truth!" shouted Lecheau at his back. Palin ignored him and climbed up the rock piles toward the island's summit.

Palin sat on the island's shallow peak, atop a pile of large flat stones—the work of countless condemned hands who had hoped to raise the pile above the tide's reach. Weeds and refuse tucked into the highest crevices told him of their failing. He watched the sun lower toward the storm-wrapped mountains. A wall of cloud had gathered there, the first of the autumn rains, and now seemed to be growing, or moving onto the sea, toward him. He had no wish to row through rain after night fell. He glanced at the shadows: Lecheau's time had nearly ended.

Waiting for perfectly pure motives, Palin decided,

would have kept him from ever having committed a good act in his life. He could do no more than desire pure motives and, he had found, they usually followed soon after obedience.

Right action was not nullified by gray motivation, he thought. Nor was lack of action justified by the same. This kind of thinking came clearly enough from his training. Why, he wondered, was the application so much more difficult?

He had decided to let Lecheau choose where mercy lay.

Palin bent to the mundane task of cleaning his sword. He polished it carefully, wiping away the spots the salt water had left. His calloused fingers searched the blade for any hint of rust, each touch remembering the days of work that bit of iron represented. He wondered again what mysterious process of heat and clay and quenching would be needed to produce the final temper. Would his sword be proof to the sea's corrosion then?

A rock rattled below him: Lecheau, early. The old man panted from the climb but moved steadily upward. He climbed on one leg and his hands; his right foot leaked onto the rocks that it chanced to touch. He drew near before resting.

"I found this waiting bothersome," he said between breaths.

"You have decided to confess, then?"

Lecheau's eyes peered up at him, measuring. "Have you a name, boy?"

"Aye. But you need it only for the confession ritual, Simon. Are you asking?"

The thin skin twisted into a grin. "Another impasse? Hey?"

Palin shook his head and stood, wiping the blade a last time. He glanced down the slope, amazed to see how quickly the tide had risen—the rowboat now floated above its rope.

"What's it to be then?" asked Lecheau. "Not an execution. Not an assassination. Not an act of passion . . . a religious experience, perhaps? A moment of worship?"

"Call it what you will."

Lecheau sat up, nodding. "The assassin and the executioner differ only in the amount of formality observed." His eyes found Palin's, pierced them. "You'll know this yourself soon enough. You'll find that the fine meanings of words blur when there's blood on your hands."

"I think you are right."

Lecheau opened his mouth, paused, blinked.

"I came," said Palin, "to administer mercy. That was my order. Would you really find the sea more merciful?"

Lecheau's eyes dropped to the gray water surrounding them, then to the shrinking shore.

I can explain this decision, thought Palin. Let him choose the water. Perhaps the abbot will not even ask. . . .

Lecheau raised his eyes again. "What would you choose?"

"I don't . . . I don't have to decide." It was Palin's turn to look away at the waves.

"You kill me either way. You."

Palin shook his head, stepped back from him. "These debates gain you nothing, not even time."

"I harm no one, here," said Lecheau softly, fervently. "I am an old man, sick. What great evil comes from giving me my little time?"

Palin shook his head again. How could the man continue to twist things so?

"You have a boat, hey? The tide will pass quickly. You could return tomorrow, report me dead—"

"Lie? And you would then starve."

"No! I catch fish! I have lived all summer this way. And now autumn comes, with more rain—"

"I have a different order."

"An order to be merciful, hey? Then show some real mercy. You said it was my decision—I choose my natural allotment of days!"

Palin wheeled on him. "That choice died with your victims!"

Lecheau pulled himself unsteadily erect. "Then you tell me—"

"Enough debates! Look down there," said Palin, stepping away to the lower boulders. "The tide threatens the boat. I'll go retie it. If you come down, I'll hear your confession, or use the sword, or both. If not, then you can wait for the water." He picked up the oars.

There, Palin thought as he leaped down from stone to stone, that forces a choice at last.

But what, his mind whispered traitorously, if he is too frightened to choose? Will he remain up here, afraid, paralyzed? Will I have to float in the dark and watch, and hear, offering him confession into the night, until the last?

Will I listen to him drown?

Palin stopped, hissed through his teeth, and turned back.

But Lecheau already shuffled after him, eyes glaring hate.

The boat's stern floated higher than its bow by the time he reached it; the rope held taut to its mooring rock below. Palin glanced at the sun, sinking behind the gray band across the west. I've waited too long, he realized.

He shucked off his tunic and sword and slipped into the water, gasping at its cold. The rough rope refused to slip. The knot felt swollen to his numb fingers.

At his third surfacing he caught sight of Lecheau moving quickly toward him across the rocks. Palin scrambled out for his sword. Lecheau stopped, bent and breathing hard. He slammed his withered fist against a stone in frustration.

Palin, watching him warily, simply cut the rope. The stern of the rowboat slapped into the water, startling both of them.

"Well, Lecheau?"

"No one will know if you let me live."

"That's a storm out there. I must row through it. I'll not wait here while you decide."

"Perhaps then you'll join me in the waves tonight, hey?" He smiled wickedly.

"Make your decision."

The grin faded. "I'll not ask you to kill me, boy."

Palin nodded. He drew the blade from its skin and pushed the boat higher up on a rock. Slowly, checking his footing, he stepped toward the old man.

Lecheau squinted up at him, though the light was failing. "I'm legally dead," said the cracking voice. "No one cares if I live or die but me and you. If you kill me, it'll be because you want to."

Palin spoke through clenched teeth: "Confession or no?"

Lecheau spat.

Palin raised the sword and stepped closer. "Close your eyes."

Lecheau stared up at him, unblinking.

Palin inhaled, stepped again, lifted—

"Leave me be!" Lecheau snarled. "I'll take the waves, then. They aren't hungry for me, at least."

Palin let out his breath, nodded, stepped back. His hands were shaking.

He quickly crossed back to the boat, stumbled over the rocks. He felt dizzy. Sheathing the sword, he scrambled in and fixed the oars. They dug at the rocks in the shallow water. He should have pushed off.

Lecheau limped to the water's edge, a ragged form in the softening light. "Why will you not let me live, hey? I harm no one here on this prison!"

Palin rocked the boat, freeing it. He stroked once into the open water.

"Hey, boy! Perhaps, in time, I will convert! Have you thought about that?"

Palin halted his second stroke. He looked up. "Is there nothing you would not say to me now in order to live?"

Emotions flickered behind the squinting eyes: fear, pride, hate, fear again.

Then something else. "No. Nothing," he whispered.

Palin nodded, stroked again. "We must consider that your confession then, Simon. May you somehow find peace because of it."

He rowed hard, to drown out the shouts.

Palin saw the second island at the corner of his eye and only then allowed his knotted shoulders to rest. He shipped the oars and stretched, muscles burning up into his neck, causing him to shiver—the wind against his back felt cold and full of the promise of rain.

He looked at the stone tower, hardly believing it to be the same place. It seemed halved in height by the sea's rising, shorter, older somehow against the blackened horizon in the last gray light. No gulls now circled. Palin looked at the approaching rain and considered the possibility of refuge but the tower showed only flat faces of rock. He remembered the broken boat, sure that by now it had been swept away by the great tide and the choppy sea. Lecheau's island, he thought, must be nearly awash.

He jerked his thoughts away, telling himself that his own safety was challenge enough. Lecheau had chosen his fate.

Palin again took up the oars and pulled, facing back upon his own passage, and found himself squinting for a sight of the little island.

How had the man survived the earlier tides? Perhaps the island was not too deeply covered and Lecheau avoided drifting by tying himself—with sacks?—to the highest rocks, then treaded water, or simply floated . . . upon driftwood?

Perhaps inflated waterskins, thought Palin, would be enough to keep your head up. How long would the tide take to pass? A few hours . . . but could a man of that age, and wounded, have possibly survived two such trials? Could he survive a third, tonight?

Cold rain on his back woke him from his musing. It was likely, realized Palin, that the rare summer storms had never before coincided with the highest tide. Another chill, from inside, passed through him at this thought.

The sea grew choppy enough so he had to row unevenly, timing the strokes to the waves. Palin imagined floating, tied, fighting the sea for each breath. If the rope was too short, each wave would roll over you, as if the line at your leg pulled you under longer each time the tide and storm inched the water higher.

Lecheau should remember, thought Palin suddenly, that length of rope I cut off. He saw me cut it; he must have remembered to use it. But that knot had been so tight!

Over the wind and rain Palin thought he heard thunder. He stopped rowing and listened. The deep drumming continued behind the hiss of the rain—the surf. He could hear the beach. That sound meant safety.

Palin reached down to find the little bucket under his seat and bailed the rain from his boat. He watched the dark fitful water and imagined being tied down in that black sea. He thought: I'm leaving a man to drown in that.

He took the oars and turned the rowboat around.

He rowed like a madman, the wind a great hand against his face, pushing him back out into the storm.

Palin found the second island with his ears. The waves beating against it sounded like a great animal's growl. He passed it close on his left and knew he rowed straight—the wind full in his face was his guide.

But how far? How many strokes to the sunken third island? Surely not so many. . . . The wind lifted him, powering him outward. But how would he know when to stop?

Palin shouted Lecheau's name back at the wind as he rowed.

Then the worst of the storm caught him, the main squall line, marching down on him like a wall. The waves threatened the boat, and he simply bailed, letting the storm carry him outward. He screamed for Lecheau.

Palin bobbed in a great bowl of angry waves, bailing, the air filled with cold rain.

A shout? To the left?

He rowed furiously, then shifted to one oar, peering ahead, listening. He screamed again into the storm.

A wave broke against something to his left. He fought the boat against the wind, turned it, was forced to use both oars.

Another wave broke behind him, and in the trough he struck something solid. He spun, reaching, shouting.

Beside him: a pile of rock. A lumpy body moved upon it. A wave blasted down, foaming, and tore the body away.

But it crawled back, hand over hand, out of the trough.

"Simon!"

The wave carried the boat away. Palin wrestled the oars against the water and fought through another wall of foam. "Simon!"

Another wave passed and left a hand clutching his right oar. Palin threw himself sideways, nearly swamping the flooded boat, losing the left oar to the storm.

But his hand closed on Lecheau's hand.

A wave crashed over them and Palin's arm was horribly wrenched. The boat rolled out from beneath him and he kicked against water, gasping, losing Lecheau's hand. Palin thrashed against the water, scrambling for the boat.

It hung a few strokes away in a trough, another wavecrest rolling up behind it. The boat would come back at him. Moving fast. Palin's foot kicked back against something soft.

He twisted around to see hands slapping at the water. The rope! The rope held Lecheau down!

Palin dove, wrestled Lecheau's head up, choking, alive.

Illustrated by Lionel Baker II

Out of the hiss of wind and rain Palin heard the waves' rumble rise up behind them.

Lecheau scrabbled feebly at him. Palin let himself sink, his left arm entwining the man's belt and his right arm pulling his sword free. He sawed at the line.

It split as the wave crashed down.

Palin surfaced. Hard wood slammed into them. Palin kicked frantically, trying to follow the wood, Lecheau and the sword hanging like anvils on either arm.

"Grab the boat!" Palin screamed. The prow spun past them.

He kicked after it. The next wave's rumble grew. He shoved Lecheau forward and gasped, "Grab it!"

Lecheau coughed, was limp.

Palin let go of his sword. His hand closed on the empty oar lock as the wave caught them. Somehow he held it through the water's passing. He rolled inside at the next trough and dragged Simon after, a tiny cold body tied about with sodden food bags. Simon was sick in the stern of the boat. But he breathed.

Palin bailed. The world became cold rain and tossed waves.

At last the storm blew itself out. Palin rested, cradling his bucket, exhausted beyond sleep.

The sky slowly cleared behind the rain's passing. Stars appeared first in the west. Bright Scout was there, one of the wanderers, normally a leader in the night's parade that followed the sun. Much of night remained, if Scout was not yet gone. Palin watched the other stars creep out of hiding and thought he could even make out the dim light of Isebrook, just above the sea.

Palin glanced down at Simon Lecheau, who huddled

in the stern. Starlight glittered off the slits of his eyes; he too was watching the sky.

His lips moved slightly. Palin thought of the night-rhymes old Brother Homily had taught him, his earliest lessons. Simple verses and prayers they had been, but all that he, a war orphan, had had to guard him at night in the strange, fearful new monastery. Lecheau saw him watching, and froze.

"The storm seems to have gone," said Palin, quietly.

Lecheau started to speak, coughed. "Just an autumn shower, hey?" he croaked. "Just a touch of winter's gales."

"They'll be here soon enough."

"Aye." Lecheau leaned back, closing his eyes. "That they will."

The tower of the second island jutted up from the sea, reflected the sun's yellow glory, scattered it, sparkling, across the dancing waves. Behind it, the Gray Mountains sat watching.

Palin rowed, canoe-like, out toward the third island. Simon Lecheau sorted through his food bags, trying to decide what had survived the salt water. His white wisp of a beard fluttered in the breeze.

"I'll not lie to the abbot, Lecheau."

"Simply set me on the mainland's beach, boy. I'm too old to be a danger—"

"I do not know what he'll do when I tell him you still live on the third island."

Lecheau threw a bag of sodden biscuits into the sea in disgust. "I'll tell you what old Bondau will do," he said, watching the bag sink. "He'll wait a moon's cycle, then send another boy with another sword."

Palin winced at the word. He switched sides with his oar again, rowing harder.

"Where's your sword, hey?"

Palin looked at him. "I lost it last night."

Something moved behind those squinting eyes. Lecheau's mouth opened, then he turned away.

"Another boy in another month. Another who only thinks he is supposed to kill me, hey?"

"I have no idea what the abbot's plans—"

"Ahhh. . . . You don' t see the pattern yet?" Lecheau threw back his head and cackled. "You are but the latest attempt. Each came bearing, suspiciously, a month's worth of food, and a confusing order to administer mercy. Bondau doesn't really want you boys to kill me or he'd be waxing up your ears by now."

"Lecheau, you are mad. Each must have failed, as did I."

"What of the food, hey? What of fishing hooks?" He held up a tiny bag, shook it, grinned.

Palin stared at the little bag in confusion. "But for what other purpose would he send us?"

Lecheau spoke through clenched teeth: "He wants to extend my suffering."

Palin shook his head and returned to his rowing.

"No?" asked Lecheau. He spat: "He hates me. He has always hated me, ever since we were boys of much less age than yourself."

"You knew the abbot as a boy?"

"Does he tell you nothing? When I left our village for the city, he took my place as a friar candidate. Until that day he had a serf's future, in the fields." He leaned forward, grinning. "Our old Father . . . I forget his name, the local priest—he always preferred me, you see. I spoke better. Still speak better, so I'm told." He laughed again through his broken voice.

"Then why could he possibly hate you—"

"He was jealous of me then and he hates me now!" Lecheau's thin shoulders shook. "Bondau spent his wandering days following me from town to town, help-ing the sheriffs, finally drove me back to Isebrook's slums. Then abbot! Him! And he hunted me, had me watched, drove me to take the dangerous jobs, the ones the guild brothers would not even price. He set me up at the last. He helped them capture me and he talked the King into this sentence, usually reserved for women." Lecheau spat. "I thought it was pity. When they drew my foot from the boot and told me I was not to face the stake, I actually thought he felt pity. And now he taunts me with boys. That, boy, is hate!"

They rowed to the third island in silence. Palin cir-cled it once, hoping for a glint of steel, but saw nothing. He grounded the rowboat on the gravel.

Lecheau suddenly leaned forward, to the middle of the boat, pleading, "Take me to shore, hey? Let me go, I swear I'll not even thieve again. I'm no danger to any-one, with this leg. Don't help him torture me anymore. He's mad with hate! I'll be mad too, soon, if you leave me here! He hates me, boy!"

Palin helped him from the boat and gently tossed the bags onto a nearby rock.

"He loves you," he said.

He rowed away. Before he went far, Lecheau's rag-ing turned to sobs.

Abbot Bondau waited for Palin beside the little grotto. The remains of a meal lay beside him; he had waited long. Palin carefully tied up the boat before meeting his eyes.

"Father, I was not able to—"

"I've scouted out the clay, Palin. The storm has made our digging an easy task—the sandy layers have been washed away." The weathered wrinkles seemed deeper, now, after Lecheau's face. And the old eyes were filled with knowledge.

Palin nodded. "But I've lost . . ." He swallowed. "I've lost my sword, Father. In the storm."

The abbot's eyes searched his face. "Well, then, you have a rare opportunity. I know of no other acolyte who has made two swords." He reached and squeezed Palin's shoulder, pulling him gently around to walk.

"Of course," said the abbot, "such an opportunity allows a variety of . . . improvements. I'm sure Brother Hammer will have a list of such, if you but ask."

Palin chuckled, nodded, wiped his eyes.

"And perhaps heading the list will be to make a slightly smaller weapon, eh?"

They laughed, together.

Palin found his voice. "I have been thinking of the scrap room, Father. There are some fine old swords in there, some from even before your time, before we tempered with the charcoal. We studied pommel-work in there—some of the old craftsmen were geniuses."

"But those blades are all ruined."

"I have heard that you . . . I think you know how to repair them. Sir."

The Abbot sighed. "Aye, Palin. But repairing a badly tempered weapon is the most difficult of all. Most do not try, the effort is likely wasted . . . better to pound out a new blade, where quenching can be used, than to try and soften the old brittle metal." He shook his head. "It's so likely to split. And then you try to reshape, to retemper. Those fine old blades lie there unused for a reason, Palin."

"But the challenge . . . is worth the effort, Father?"

The abbot smiled, nodding slowly. "Perhaps. But few look at the remade blade and appreciate it, Palin. Eyes always seek the shine of new steel, never the blows that shaped it."

"A master would know."

"Aye, son. Aye. If anyone would." His calloused hand went unconsciously to the emblem hanging from his neck.

They fell silent for a time, listening to the sea as they climbed up the ridge away from it. At last they reached the crest and looked back over the broad beach.

"Father? Does Simon know?"

The abbot sighed. "He must be starting to understand. By now, he must."

Simon Lecheau propped himself up with a twisted length of driftwood. He stood atop the highest point of the island and watched the sun set behind the Gray Mountains. The tide had eaten his island down to a spare mound of rock, but the night was clear and he knew a full month would pass before he was again threatened by anything more potent than loneliness.

That boy had been the third. It was clear to him, now, that Bondau, the abbot, would let him live out many days—if he could continue to talk his way out from under those swords. Final escape, he mused, required only silence. Eventually I will make a mistake, though. I'll misjudge the temper on one of these boys, and one of those ever-sharpened swords will fall. What would Bondau have gained then?

Perhaps accepting death would best spite the abbot. But it gagged him to think of those swaggering self-righteous fools bringing his death. Even were it to destroy Bondau's plans, he thought, it would be a hollow victory indeed. These armed children are the martyr types, not me.

What can Bondau possibly think he is accomplishing?

The worst of it, Simon decided, was that it was becoming harder. The arguments, the words with which he defended himself, were beginning to sound hollow to his own ears. Their strength, he well knew, would fail with his conviction.

And, though the damn fool boy had almost drowned Simon, he had actually found himself liking that last one. Palin had been a better talker than the others.

Simon Lecheau watched the lights of Isebrook appear, and his mind conjured up the evening sounds of the city: pans rattling, dogs barking, conversation . . . .

But the only sound in his ears was that of the steady surf against the island, gently eating at the shore, eroding it from beneath the twisted stave he leaned upon.

HIS BEST WEAPON

Written by
Arlene C. Harris

Illustrated by
Konstantin Sheverdin

About the Author

Arlene was born in 1966 in Novato, California. She began reading at age two, writing at age four, and submitted her first sixty-three page "novel" to a publisher at age twelve. She always knew she would be a writer. Somewhere in her parents' files is a letter that she wrote to her father at age seven or eight, explaining to him why it was so much more important for her to watch Star Trek than for him to watch Sixty Minutes on Sunday nights.

In her writing desires, she found encouragement from her uncle, Dick Mason, who taught science fiction literature at Tamalpais High School in Marin County for many years. She found discouragement from another teacher in high school who told her that "girls shouldn't write that sort of thing," but eventually came back to writing at Sonoma State University.

There, she wrote her first novel, a fantasy, with the encouragement and help of her academic advisor, and is now at work on her second novel, which promises to be the first in a series.

Arlene works at various writerly jobs, and currently lives in Framingham, Massachusetts. She's active in science fiction fandom, where she likes to engage in filking, and also edits a fantasy-story-oriented fan magazine called Dreamberry Jam.

Arlene sent us her story on the advice of her good friend Jane Mailander, a winner from 1987. We'd like to thank them both.

About the Illustrator

Konstantin Sheverdin was born in Lugansk, Ukraine, in 1963. He's a graduate of the Moscow University of Arts, Fine Arts Department, and in 1990 he graduated from the Lugansk Teacher's Training College, where he majored in History.

Since 1992 he has been a member of the Ukranian Commercial Makers Union, where he specializes in creating his own jewelry designs, synthesizing various metals. His work has been displayed in exhibitions in Moscow, Kiev, and Lugansk, and can currently be found in the Lugansk Museum, Kiev Museum of Ethnography and Crafts, and in private collections in the Ukraine, Russia, Great Britain, France, Canada, and Germany.

Ten minutes later the hatch opened again and Allenby stumbled into the air lock. In the light gravity he pitched forward in slow motion, falling to his hands and knees as his long golden hair cascaded over the top of his head and into his eyes. A helmet lay loose on the grating in front of him. Burke was gone.

The three starjackers stood just outside the 'lock, staring at the helmet with macabre fascination. "I don't believe it," the obese, gray-haired one muttered. "She didn't take it."

The spindly Belter youth beside him sniggered. "Too bad the fishin' port's 'paqued." He ran his bony hand across its concave surface. "I would've loved to see her go without it."

The leader of the terrorists—broad-shouldered, muscular, his face puckered and scar-ridden—said, "I told you they'll do anything for each other; that's what they're trained for. Their partners come before everything else, even their own skins. That's why she kept yelling 'Not me, take him first,' you see. So he'd have first crack at the helmet. But our Lieutenant Pureblood here didn't hardly bat an eye, did you?"

Allenby didn't look up, not even to give them the traditional "curse you" glare.

"Either he's the best fishin' actor in the Fed," the thin one snorted, "or the coldest fish in Terraspace."

The fat one pointed to the helmet. "I say let's let him walk without it."

"Nah," said the leader, "let him have it. I'll even give him the same five minutes to think about it. Don't matter, though, 'cause I'm gonna wager you two fenwicks double or nothing that *he* don't take it, either."

As the inner door hissed shut, Allenby sat back against it and rested his elbows on his knees, calmly regarding the helmet in the middle of the tiny room. Beyond it stood the 'lock's outer door, the one that led to the Great Big Step. Behind him, in the main cabin of the shuttle, the terrorists were separating out the other passengers, some to live, some to die. Mounted high up on the wall next to him stood the disabled air lock control panel; he could almost feel the gauges cycling as the golden moment slowly approached. He wondered if Burke had avoided looking at them, too.

He knew without bothering to glance up that the 'lock camera's red eye was black; the first thing the terrorists had done when they boarded the shuttle was disable the monitors along with the rest of the security system—which explained why the observation port in the inner door remained clouded over. His final five minutes, minus, were all his own.

Allenby glanced down at the controls on his chest. He could feel the soft tanks on his back, nestled between his uniform and the suit, the emergency airpack that carried a little more than an hour's ready supply, but without a helmet to seal the opening around his neck, he would become what Burke had called "a tube of human-flavored toothpaste."

He could no longer suppress a bitter laugh, not because he found the subject of Burke preceding him into a vacuum amusing, but because for all his careful analysis, Scarface was wrong. Burke *wasn't* Allenby's partner, at least, not yet. Allenby's psychological attachment to her rated only slightly above nil.

It was the rule of the Corps: three tries for compatibility, three attempts at the Trust Factor Evaluation. He and Burke had been each others' absolutely last chance to pass the final phase of the Morale Corps' strict and unyielding mutual psychological exam.

Losing one's potential partner out an air lock was no excuse in the regular military, much less in the Corps. With Burke dead, Allenby could never hope for reassignment even if he survived, and without what the Corps offered him, Allenby's life had no purpose.

And even if he did put on the helmet, what could he do? Apart from drifting away in the vastness outside, hoping his meager air supply would hold him until some hypothetical vessel picked up his suit's emergency beacon—assuming the ship's pilot would veer from his own course and waste time and energy coming to pick up one stray floater. . . .

And what about the passengers? If he tied himself to the coolant pipes above him, he could avoid getting sucked out of the ship. Then what? Alone, unarmed, he could do nothing for the rest of the passengers except . . .

Are you going to make that decision for them?

Damn her! *She* was the one with the mission, the one searching for her place in the universe, not he—he had found his niche. But she was his last chance, and she knew it, knew he'd rather be dead than drummed out of the Corps, and *still* she'd left the helmet for him.

He banged his head back against the inner door. *Why?*

Six hours before, Lieutenant Daffyd Allenby had disembarked from the transport on arrival at Tranquility

City, Luna. He stepped lightly into the terminal, his magneboots stabilizing him enough so his jaunty gait wouldn't send him flying. Allenby would have stood out in a crowd on looks alone, with his long blond hair, piercing blue eyes, and features not unlike an archangel chiseled by Michelangelo's dusty hands. But the thing most people first noticed about him was the fact he stood just over two meters tall.

Luna felt comfortable; he preferred low gravity. His stature made it difficult for him to take a standard one-gee strain on his back for more than a few weeks at a time, but most stations and ships he could serve on would be low-to-light-gee environments anyway—assuming, of course, that he could establish a rapport with this third potential partner. If not, his career as a military psychologist would be finished, leaving him with three equally unappealing options.

He was two centimeters too tall for a standard ground-duty battlesuit, neither could he fold his long limbs into a shipboard battle station. So combat duty meant they'd cut him down, take three or four vertebrae out of his spine, remove a few centimeters of bone from his arms and legs and fuse them back together. And of course, the hair would have to go. Combat meant becoming normal.

If he went to another noncombat division, it would mean turning his back on his goal of twelve years.

And going civ? What civilian psych center would hire a failed Morale Officer? What else was he fit for, if he could not practice clinical psychology, but go back to what he had been before?

"Morale Officers are responsible for the emotional well-being of every soldier in their division," the Corps Commander had told him. "But it's a time-proven standard that even the best Morale Officers can be gotten to, because a person can stand only so much of other people's problems. And who does a Morale Officer turn to when it all comes crashing in on him? His partner, that's who! No matter how good you are solo, Allenby, you go *nowhere* without a backup."

During the trip from Beligo Station to Luna he had perused the general bio of this third-and-last chance: designate RTMZ BRQE LLAP, one point seven meters tall, fifty-five kilos, black hair, brown eyes. Fluent in three of the twelve official Federation languages: Anglish, Italian, Hebrew. Relative age of twenty-five; legal age, three hundred and seventeen. Cross reference: Smithsonian Institute for Chronoanthropological Studies.

A Guildmember. Allenby flinched mentally. Just what he needed. Then he read further:

During a research assignment into the past, one of the Institute's field agents had accidentally brought an indigenous person forward from the year 1994. This was a rare occurrence, but not unheard of; standard operating procedure dictated that the displaced person be mindwiped and returned to the original point of departure, plus one second. However, two events made that impossible. During routine decontamination procedures following a return from the field, an attending med had inadvertently dissolved what would have been in the primitive second millenium a fatal malignant tumor. By itself, this oversight constituted a breach of temporal integrity, and the Institute would have had no choice but to put the tumor back in—if it hadn't been for the fact that when their archivists ran a background check on her, to make sure they would be returning her to the correct temporal locus, they discovered that according to known records, from the point of her departure, they could find no further trace of her existence—as if she'd fallen off the face of the earth.

With no mandate from the past to send her back, the Institute had no choice but to keep her in the present. Although the Institute was required to pay restitution for relocating her to the twenty-third century, and her pension would have left her comfortably situated, she chose instead to enter the military—the Corps specifically. Her Academy record was unremarkable, but her rating as a counselor registered well above nominal. From the marks given her during the preliminary psychological evaluations, she had managed to adequately adjust to her new situation after having simultaneously over-come both future shock and culture shock.

Allenby shook his head. It wouldn't matter how she tried to fit in with her new environment, she still would be an anachronism, a misfit.

Perhaps they *did* have something in common, after all.

But why had she left the comfort of the Institute for the Morale Corps, of all places?

By training, Corps members were clinical psychologists; in practice, they were everything from ship's mascot to camp counselor, friend, parent, nanny, confessor, lover, entertainment—prepared to go to any lengths to keep the soldiers in their units sane, happy and fit for duty. For that reason, the Morale Corps was the only noncombat division of the United Earth Forces that pulled automatic hazard pay.

The Corps rejected six out of ten applicants outright; of those remaining, perhaps half made it as far as the TFE, the psychological gauntlet that gauged just how implicitly a candidate trusted his or her assigned part-ner. It was imperative that there be no barriers between

Morale Officers; without absolute trust, the partnership collapsed. Allenby had underestimated the test's ability to find the weakest link between two people and exploit it shamelessly.

His first unsuccessful partnership had almost worked. But his second failure . . . well, how else *could* it have turned out, Allenby reminded himself. The guy was a member of the Valerian Society. Because of the nature of the assignments and the lengths Morale Officers would normally go to for the mental and emotional well-being of their troops, Valerian M.O.'s were rarer than blondes—and no doubt harder to place, thought Allenby. That pairing had been doomed before it began. No self-respecting Valerian would let himself be seen speaking to someone like Allenby, much less share quarters—or secrets—with one.

After a quick stop to divest himself of his flight suit and a longer one to ask for directions, he located Lt. Burke in the Apollo Lounge, of all places. Allenby frowned. Meeting one's prospective partner in a bar was not a good sign.

He easily spotted her in the nearly empty bar; she sat belted into the barstool, languidly staring at the display in the middle of the murkily lit room. The lounge was built over, and encompassed, the original site of the first lunar landing. The tricolor flag of a long-dissolved nation, the footprint, the plaque, all stood preserved for posterity under scattered plexidomes as the centerpiece of a high-class drinking establishment.

"Lieutenant Burke?"

"That's me. . . ." She swiveled in the chair, her bobbed hair snapping back into place, but her mouth remained open longer than it should have as her gaze fixed on the insignia on the left breast of his uniform. "Mother of

God," she breathed, "does the Pope know you're gone?"

"Huh?"

"Never mind, but the Sistine Chapel'll never be the same. You must be Allenby." She held out her hand and he hesitated, baffled by the quaint gesture, but decided to humor her and reached out to shake it. At the last moment she pulled her hand away and saluted.

Allenby winced. "That's a very old gag."

"Yeah? *You* fell for it." She patted the vacant seat beside her and beckoned for the bartender.

"My primary's Daffyd," he began after ordering a drink. "Two f's, two d's."

"Artemis," she returned. "But I prefer Artie."

"Why say Artemis if you don't like it?"

"Analyzing me already?" She smiled slyly. "I never said I didn't like the name, it's just, you know, Artemis? You don't get it, do you?"

He leaned on one elbow and sighed. One reason he couldn't stand Guildmembers was their tendency to quote chapter and verse from people who'd been dead a thousand years, cite ancient customs and use anachronistic jargon, then look at him as if he should know what they're talking about. And Lt. Burke had actually been raised in that long-dead world. How much worse could it get?

"Artemis," she said slowly, "was the sister of Apollo." She nodded her head back toward the display area. "She was the Greek goddess of the moon, and the hunt . . . and the protector of virgins."

Allenby smiled despite himself. Associating a Morale Officer with a virgin *was* pretty funny. "Trade cards?"

"Sure." She placed her identity card face down on the table and slid it in front of him; he did the same with his own. By unspoken agreement they flipped them over simultaneously.

Allenby's heart sank. He'd expected the Guild's logo, but . . .

"DFYD LNBE GMSB." Burke spelled out his identifying designation. "Daffyd Allenby, er, something." She tapped the affiliation tags on his card: the hands-encompassing-the-globe symbol of the SPCI, and an inverted pink triangle. "Now *there's* a combination you don't see every day."

He held up her card. "*Two* religionist affiliations?"

In answer she reached down her shirt and pulled out a chain, showing the two icons she wore around her neck. They were the same as on her card. "This is a cross," she said, holding up one symbol, "representing the Christian faith—in my case, indicating allegiance to the Roman Catholic church, because my father was Catholic." She fingered the two interlocked triangles. "And this is a Star of David. Because my mother was a Jew. Now, I lost one of my prospective partners because he considered me a hypocrite, but then again, he was a Valerian, so what the fish did he know, right? I mean, jeez, those guys are so right-wing they make the John Birch Society look like the ACLU." She spread her arms and shrugged. "What I'm saying is, I have no problem reconciling this, shall we say, conflict of interest, but if *you* have a problem with it, then we can both kiss our careers goodbye right now."

He thought about it. Religionists bothered him. No, that wasn't true—the Valerians bothered him, as often as he let them get to him. Objectively he knew better than to judge all religionists by the Society's example, but subjectively . . .

Allenby shrugged. "Hey, it's your belief system. Just make sure you keep it that way."

She caught his meaning. "I don't do conversions."

"Good."

"So, what's your registration?"

The question caught him off-balance. "Oh, uh, Danish."

"Danish? I would've said Welsh, but you're probably just pronouncing off the letters of your designation too, huh." She lifted her glass to her lips and held it there. "The Society for the Preservation of Cultural Integrity." She filled every carefully enunciated syllable with acid. "Please tell me you don't buy into that 'diverse cultural purity' bullfish."

He laughed. "Who, me? Oh, fish, no. It's not like I had a choice, it's just . . ." He let the words trail off as he gestured ambiguously.

"The way you are," she finished.

"Well, yes. Not that registry does *me* much good . . ."

No, thought Allenby, still staring at the helmet, being a regger hadn't done him a bit of good.

The SPCI required one to be able to prove "cultural or racial homogeneity" to a minimum of ten full generations of ancestors minus one, or 1023/1024 progenitors, and conferred registration on anyone who met that standard, whether or not that honor had been requested. Reggers qualified automatically for a grant enabling them to pay the exorbitant government surcharge on multiple offspring, provided, of course, the resulting subsidized offspring also qualified for registration. The SPCI favored no specific race or ethnic group, but encouraged them all to continue the traditions of societies long passed from the mainstream of Terran culture. But less than 15 percent of the total intrasystem population qualified for the subsidy. The rest either could afford a second child, or they could not.

Out in the main cabin, the starjackers would be checking the passengers' identity cards for that little globe symbol, winnowing the reg from the non-reg—not that it mattered which group Allenby belonged to, since as a Federation officer he was a target regardless. As a Morale Officer, whose only weapon was psychology, he was something best disposed of as quickly as possible.

Hence, the air lock. After their capture, Burke and Allenby had been marched to the boarding 'lock. The leader of the starjackers had left the routine sorting of passengers to his associates in order to assist two others in overseeing the "game."

"Two Morale Officers," he said in a low monotone, looking at their cards. "One regger . . ." He looked first to Allenby, then to Burke. "And one not. Two evac suits. *One* helmet." He held it tightly between his hands, then fastened it to a hook on the wall, just inside the air lock. "One of you'll have five minutes to decide what you want to do. If you take the helmet, well, maybe you'll drift far enough that someone will find you, though I doubt your oxygen'll hold out. But just remember: your partner follows right behind you. So if the first one in takes the helmet . . ." His men snorted appreciatively. "So, who's first?"

Allenby kept his lips sealed—he'd have none of their game, even if it wasn't against regulation to cooperate with terrorists. The hall was silent but for the restless rustling of the starjackers' own evac suits.

Suddenly, Burke said, "Send him first."

"What?" Allenby's head snapped around. What the fish was she *doing?*

Burke said to Scarface, "Let him go first. He, I mean, look, please, I can't make that kind of decision. . . ."

"Oh, and I can?" Blurted Allenby, forgetting himself. He took a long breath and stared straight ahead, almost at attention. "The fish I'm going first. You go first."

"Don't be a *putz*," she growled through her teeth. "You go."

He shook his head adamantly. He knew she wasn't afraid to die; he suspected that her religious convictions wouldn't let her fear death.

"Well, *I'm* not going first."

Scarface nodded to the Belter, who laughed as he dragged Burke toward the 'lock. She gave a high-pitched scream and kicked at him wildly. "No! Not me! Send *him!* Send hiiii—"

Clang. The Belter reached for the jettison controls. "No," said the leader. "Five minutes, like I said." He grinned up at Allenby. "Who knows? If she's lucky, she'll drift into Beacon Delta's range before her air gives out, but we'll be long gone by then. If she even takes the helmet."

"What makes you think she won't?" asked the fat one, who did not ease his vicelike grip on Allenby's arms.

"Are you kidding? If she does, that's as good as killing him herself. She couldn't live with the guilt, if she survived and he didn't. Nah, she'll leave it for him."

The Belter gaped in disbelief.

"Let me put it another way," said Scarface. "I'm willing to bet twenty K that the helmet's still in there when that 'lock repressurizes and the door opens in, oh, nine minutes."

The fat one beamed. "You're on."

"Why do you want to be a Morale Officer, Allenby?"

The question had startled him into silence. Could he tell the whole truth, not just the shadows and wisps he had told his first partner, things he could never have told his second?

He opened his mouth—but the words froze in his throat.

Burke pounded the bar. "I knew it. That's where the conflict is. When I looked at your records, your first failure—"

"You *what*?"

"I accessed your personnel file. Morale Officers can do that, you know."

Of course he knew; he'd been doing it regularly since graduation. But she'd accessed his file, *his!* "You had no right—"

"I have *every* right to analyze past mistakes and use that data to my advantage. If it'd help us pass the TFE, I'd access the fishin' Commodore's file." She pointed a finger in his face. "You and what's-his-name, the guy you were first paired with, you should have made it, by all reports. The second was a no-go, but that first one? *You* blew it. What held you back?"

Allenby continued to glare at her. Burke glanced furtively around the room, first over one shoulder, then over the other. "It's halfway through blue shift; there's no one here but you, me, and the bartender. And whatever tanked your first pairing's gonna do the same here, unless you level with me."

He considered it, but the moment came and went. Again he kept silent.

Somehow, back before the first pairing, he had come to believe he could actually withhold his past from a partner and still pass the TFE. His first partner seemed to have not the slightest inkling that Allenby had held back, yet the test indicators wouldn't pass them. The second partnership never got beyond the initial mistrust. But this third partner, she *knew* something was there. Failing to disclose it now would guarantee their mutual dismissal from the Corps.

And yet . . .

She reached across the bar and held his bare wrist, applying gentle pressure from first one finger, then two others—the silent, personal code that meant "commence private information." By pressing any number of fingers against his arm, a motion almost invisible to the naked eye but easily read by the ultrasensitive nerve endings of the skin, she could speak without being overheard. The Corps touch-code was almost as good as a cranial implant transceiver—better, since such communications could not be plucked from the ether and deciphered.

He studied her carefully. Then he nodded.

With her free hand she toyed with the chain around her neck, not looking up at him. With her other she carefully squeezed out the code. *It's because of what happened at Phobos, isn't it?*

He broke her grip and hunched over his drink, focusing on the molecules between himself and his glass.

"All right," she said in a low tone, "we'll do this the hard way. In 2275, twelve years ago, the WorldNet substation on Phobos went down, and the whole colony lost everything. Credit disappeared, all records were wiped—the Fed sent a peacekeeping force to quell the riots that followed, but by the time they arrived, thousands were dead, and the rest bankrupt, homeless, without hope, looting, raping, killing each other over scraps. All because of a computer glitch." She took a long pull of her drink. "And because the security monitors went down with the substation, a lot of what happened never got reported because there was no recorded proof, just a lot of 'your word against mine.' Until the troops arrived, it was fishing chaos. After that, it was martial law. Martial," she repeated, a wry and inappropriate smile curling the corners of her mouth until she saw the look on his face—then it faded. "So, you would have been what? Fourteen?"

He sipped his drink to ease his dry throat, but had to fight down the sick feeling welling up inside him. "How—"

"Your personnel records, the backups in the mainframe on Earth, place you on Phobos during the uprisings. After that, there's a two-year gap. At sixteen your records show you on Beligo Station, where you racked up a couple of assault charges—but they got dismissed on grounds of self-defense. The rest of your record is nothing but a few arrests for soliciting without a license." She paused. "At eighteen you took the Academy entrance exam and passed with exceptional marks. They were willing to overlook your criminal record since you were never convicted of anything worse than a misdemeanor. From the Academy you went straight into the Corps."

He clutched his drink for support. "Don't. Just . . . don't. Save your pity for someone who needs it."

"Pity? More like incomprehension."

"What's so hard to understand? At fourteen I lost my home, my family . . . and a *lot* more. I was much shorter then, and twice as naive—and by sixteen I was turning tricks on the Beligo docks. I managed to turn that experience into a career; I entered the Corps with more practical experience than the Academy could have ever taught me. Or is what we're doing for the Fed any different from what I did on my own?"

Burke tapped her bottle with her fingernails. "I don't know about you, but I didn't spend four years in the Academy studying to be a hooker. I studied psychology. And the difference is, people bought what you sold because that's what they *thought* they needed. I get paid for giving people what I know they need—whatever they need, whether they want it or not, whether they like it or not, and whether I like it or not. I mean," she added, unnecessarily lowering her voice, "I don't particularly like sleeping with women, either, but hey, it's all in the line of duty, right?"

She raised her glass. "So, is it worth it? Is whatever you're holding back worth fishing over your whole career, and mine too?"

He squinted his eyes shut. "You don't understand. . . ."

"Then make me understand!" she said through her teeth. "Help me understand! Or do you want your little secrets more than you want the Corps?"

"It's not that simple—" He took hold of her wrist. *It's not that I want the Corps, I need the Corps.*

They sat silently for a few minutes, then Burke casually mentioned it was getting late and they really should be getting back to Beligo. She unbelted herself from the chair. As she handed the bartender her card, picking up Allenby's tab as well, she nodded to the mirror behind the bar and laughed. "Look at this, will you? It's Liza Minelli meets Robert Plant—"

Allenby stood. Burke's head just reached the bottom

of his ribcage. She whistled. "Make that Larry Bird. But don't worry, I'm not going to ask you if you play basketball. *Nobody* plays basketball anymore." She smacked his arm. "C'mon, let's go get my gear and get the fish off this rock. I'm sick of the Moon."

"I thought you were supposed to be a moon goddess," he said from the corner of his mouth.

"Nope," she flipped back. "Just a lunatic."

Since the subject of Phobos had been shelved, they talked about other things. They did a little free association; a little light, meaningless banter; she told a few jokes he didn't understand. When he asked her the standard psych eval question, "What's the saddest thing you can think of?" Burke said, "Elephants."

"Elephants? They're extinct."

She turned away. "I know."

They'd chosen to take a civilian shuttle back instead of a Fed transport because they were Morale Officers talking about things better left uncomprehended by other soldiers. Most civilians didn't pay attention to, or invite conversation with, Morale Officers . . . which suited them both perfectly.

Protocol demanded that all Fed personnel wear pressure suits on public transport and keep their helmets ready—just in case—and while Burke donned her suit, Allenby stepped into his own. Burke snickered. "What's with Ops? They think you'll grow into it or something?"

"It's a *regulation* suit," he shot back. "I can't use my civvy suit on duty because it doesn't meet military spec. I can't qualify for a custom-made duty suit until I pass the TFE. And unfortunately the only ones Ops has that'll fit my height are proportioned for Callistoid drydock workers."

"You mean, the only people in the system shaped like the satellite they're from?" She spread her arms wide and puffed her cheeks. "I mean, how can you drill in that thing? You'd be flopping all over the place. . . ." Her mouth fell open as he performed all thirty-two checks and functions of the suit-up drill in quick succession. It took her a moment to realize her own suit lay in a pile around her ankles.

Allenby drew himself up, adding another centimeter to his already considerable height. "My record for complete suit-up is thirty-six seconds. Suit down, thirty-two. This time it took, oh, forty . . . but then I wasn't really trying." So there, he added to himself.

Burke whistled. Then she pulled at the midsection of his suit until it stretched out to its full size. "Yeah, well, the next time I have to smuggle a keg of beer through customs, I'll keep you in mind."

He wound his tether around his waist, crossed it over his back, and fastened it in the front, giving his suit a form-fitting look. She tossed him his helmet and, without another word, preceded him into the boarding bay.

The return trip to Beligo would take five hours. He let her have the window seat, though she couldn't see much; the earth was on the other side of the ship. Being on the aisle gave him a chance to stretch his left leg, though his right would suffer for it. Even on a troop transport, the result would have been the same: the seats simply weren't far enough apart to comfortably accommodate anyone over two meters tall.

They took up the association game to while away the time during launch: he would ask her what she was thinking about and she'd tell whatever happened to be on her mind. It bothered him that he couldn't tell whether or not she'd prepared her responses in advance, just to annoy him.

"What are you thinking about?" he asked as the gees kicked in.

"Hamburgers!" She licked her lips. "God, what I wouldn't give for a Big Mac right now. But what with the greenhouse regulations and the ban on beef to keep the methane levels down . . . well, it's all soylent green to me."

Allenby gritted his teeth. "You know what your problem is? You're stuck in the past. Why don't you come join the rest of us in the twenty-third century?"

She slumped in her seat and crossed her arms. "Those who do not remember the past are condemned to repeat it."

"Oh yeah? And what dead person said that?"

"George Santayana," she shot back. She went on to describe, in unnecessary detail, a place called Jonestown, Guyana. He didn't speak for a long time afterwards.

The flight was less than a quarter full. A couple of passengers were Fed, similarly suited and seated well away from the Morale Officers. Most were civs. But Allenby saw a few Guildmembers, identifiable by the little star-and-hourglass logo pins on their civilian clothes. Burke explained how the letters on the left breast of their uniforms indicated rank. When she told him the letters were Greek, he felt stupid all over again. "What's with you and Greek? You don't even speak it."

"Ancient Greece was the foundation of western civilization. It's the starting point of nearly every classical scholarly discipline: geometry, history, philosophy— psychology is a Greek-based word, too. *Psyche, logos.* Lore of the mind."

"Fishsticks," he said under his breath.

"Now there's an interesting phrase. Imagine, after a

thousand years of use, one four-letter 'f'-word is finally supplanted by another. Know why?"

"Why, no." Allenby propped his head up with a clenched fist. "It's only the most famous war story of the past two hundred years, why should I?"

"Sorry." She ran her gloved hand through her shiny black hair. "It's just that's such a great story, all those nukes hitting the Mediterranean, sending up a cloud that rains radioactive fish bits over half the globe for six solid months—and people still remember it." She sighed dreamily. "Wish I'd been around to see that."

The shuttle executed a 180-degree roll and fought its way out of the Moon's limp gravitational pull, using centripetal force to sling itself out toward Beligo Station, which rotated lazily in the snug, stable well of the fifth Lagrange point. After the course change Allenby realized he'd never returned the question. "Why do *you* want to be a Morale Officer, Burke?"

Her eyes were closed. "To protect and defend the citizens of the Federated States of Terra—"

"Don't give me the Academy answer. Really, why?"

Burke reached for his arm, but he pulled away. "We're suited," he reminded her softly. "I couldn't feel your signal if you used both fists."

He could have unsealed his glove, if he'd wanted to accommodate her request, but he reasoned that she could either choose to speak her mind aloud or keep it to herself. He hoped he had read her correctly, that faced with silence as the alternative, she couldn't *help* but speak up.

His training told him that her constant self-reminders of the century she'd left behind served as an anchor for her, her distance a cushion, her "safe area." That comfort zone had to have been the barrier between her and her own two previous potential partners. For her to accept the present day, she had to be able to relate it to her own experience, even if present social conditions had evolved three hundred years beyond her. And if he was ever to understand her, then first he must accept that as part of the package, even though in order to do so he would not only have to tear down his own walls, but also take up the bricks and with them build a bridge to her.

Burke hunched her shoulders. "Where the fish else can I go?"

"Well, back to the Institute, for one."

She rolled her eyes. "Right. Go back to the Smithsonian Institution—and what? Be a sideshow exhibit like that poor bastard Bierce? No thanks, pal."

"Institute. Not 'Institution.'"

"Oh, sure, *now* it is. . . ." She humphed. "I'd rather walk barefoot over live coals."

He thought about asking her what coals were, but let it go. "The Institute pays you a pension, right? Reparations for relocating you three hundred years into your future? You could make a nice life for yourself, on the Guild dole."

"As a civilian? Get real. *You* know how ex-Guild are treated by the civs—they all think the Guild's made up of a bunch of pampered actors raking in serious amounts of cred for going back in time and taking vacation shots of the Battle of Waterloo. Do I look pampered to you?"

"You're not really a Guildmember, though."

She flashed her card, tapping the sunburst symbol. "Tell that to John Q. Public. No, thanks. Besides, what am I fit for? What job skills do I have that the twenty-third century'd want?"

He chewed on his lower lip. "What about combat?"

Burke snorted. "The United Earth Forces won't take me for combat position because of the tumor—you know about that, right? Well, even though I was cured, it still counts as a head injury, and they won't take anyone for a combat role who's had possible brain damage . . . though why they want grunts with brains I can't even guess." She chuckled. "Didn't stop them from accepting me into the Corps, though. Besides, I wouldn't go if they asked me. I'm not a fighter, and I'm smart enough to know it."

"But why the Corps? What about the JAG division, for instance?"

"Me? A lawyer? I don't think so." She opened one eye. "All right, I'll tell you why the Corps. I believe I was brought here for a reason. I don't know what that reason is, but I was raised up from the twentieth century and cured of a terminal illness to be here. Call it what you want, but I call it God's will. And wipe that smirk off your face." She pointed a finger at him. "And until I find out *why* I'm here, I'm going to do the best I can, for as many as I can." After a moment's silence, she shrugged and turned toward the empty window. "Besides, I liked the advertising campaign. 'Join the Corps, see the system. . . .'"

Allenby leaned back in his seat and let out a deep sigh.

"Actually I find it amusing that you had a first-class snit-fit about me reading your file when you've obviously tapped mine." She glanced at him sideways. "That's okay, I kind of assumed you would. I mean, this *is* our last shot at making the grade. . . ."

He looked up at the flight clock at the front of the cabin. Four hours left. And then the TFE, and the rest of his life listening to her prattle. . . .

Burke whispered, "I'm sorry about earlier. I didn't, I mean, I wasn't laughing about the idea of martial law. I just have a classical turn of mind." She leaned forward and rested her elbows on her knees. "The word *martial* comes from Mars, the Roman god of war—for whom the planet was named. His minions were Terror and Fear. That's why its moons are named as they are—Deimos, and Phobos. . . ."

"We tabled that subject," Allenby snapped.

"You did, not me. Where do you think we get the word *phobia* from?"

"*Not here,*" he hissed.

"But soon, though, huh?" She stood up. "Let me out, I gotta go to the head." At his raised brows she added, "You know. Can. Lav. Whatever."

"If it'll give me a moment's peace." He pulled his legs up and let her by. Then, with only the hum of the shuttle's drives and the faint mumbling of other passengers to distract him, he reviewed his dwindling options.

Why not tell her? What did he have to lose by telling her? What did he have left to lose? What was he afraid of?

She couldn't possibly understand. To tell her and have it laughed away or made light of—or *worse,* for her to misunderstand *his* reason for being here . . .

Burke came back almost immediately, paler than before. He suppressed a smile. "Well, well, a little spacesick, are we?"

She placed her hand on the side of his neck, under his ear, the only exposed area except for his face. *Danger. Go to the cargo bay and wait for me.* Then she strode off toward first class, where the lavies were. Faking nonchalance, he strolled off in the opposite direction.

He waited, stooped in the cramped baggage hold;

the ceiling was barely high enough for Burke, much less
Allenby. He did not wait long. "What's going on?" he
demanded. "Where have you been? And why did you
flash a danger code?"

She locked the door behind her. "In that order?
We've been shanghaied, doing a little reconnaissance,
and we've been shanghaied."

He let out an exasperated sigh. "Please, for once will
you speak plain Anglish?"

She grabbed the front collar of his evac suit and
pulled his face close. "Read my lips: staaaaar-
jaaaaacked."

"*What?*" He jerked his head up and smacked it on
the ceiling.

"How about 'taken hostage'? Is that simple enough
for you?" She threw up her hands. "I just hope no one
notices us missing. . . ."

"Could you tell?"

"Tell what?"

"Pro-reg or anti-reg?"

"I didn't ask for their IDs!"

"I take it that means you don't know. Oh, great, and
our helmets are out over our seats! Why didn't you tell
me to bring them back with me?"

"Gee, I dunno, but a couple of Fed officers unpack-
ing their helmets in the middle of a flight is just a *leeetle*
bit conspicuous. Besides, there's got to be a couple of
helmets in here we can use. Civs don't have to suit up
for transport. . . ."

Allenby glanced around the compartment at the
neatly stacked luggage on the shelves along the walls.
"Compatible helmets? Maybe. It'll take a while to locate
some."

"I counted ten or twelve of 'em." She opened one kit after another. "Starjackers, I mean. They came through the forward boarding 'lock, and they're in first class right now. As for our fellow Fed out in coach, all three of them, they consist of one company clerk, one JAG officer, and a tactical analyst. Not a fighting soul among 'em. So I guess it's up to us."

Allenby pointed at the controls on his chest. "Well, whatever you do, don't use your com-link to call for help. The hull will just reflect it back in and alert the starjackers that we're here."

"Well, no fish, fenwick." She cocked her head. "So how do we get an SOS out? A distress message," she added quickly.

"Well, assuming the pilot didn't get a chance to beam out a distress or launch a beacon before the systems got cut, we're going to have to go EVA and let our suits' emergency beacons do the job. . . ." He noticed a sparkling red evac kit. Stars and flowers covered the case, surrounding a wide-eyed, cartoony picture of a girl in a spacesuit. "This one's got Ruby Rokett on it! Oh, fish, there are kids on this ship!"

"In first class, yes, I saw . . ." Burke turned to him. He still held the Ruby Rokett kit. "Hey, if that helmet fits, put it on."

"What? No, of course it won't." He threw it aside and waded through the discarded luggage toward the racks on the other side of the hold. He picked a promising helmet and fitted it over his head, folding his long hair up into the back before fastening the catches. "I got one!"

She didn't respond. He realized she couldn't hear him without the com-link, so he took it off again. "Well, come on, grab one!"

"And then what?"

"And then I'm going to override the cargo 'lock and we'll just drift out with the rest of the baggage."

Burke just stood there. "And *then* what?"

"And *then* we'll discuss it!"

She pointed behind her. "This inner door wouldn't withstand a full vacuum. If we pop the outer hatch, that door's going to buckle. We'll be venting the whole ship. Nah, we gotta go back through to the passenger 'lock. . . ."

Allenby squinted his eyes shut and pinched the bridge of his nose. "It's too late. Once you locked that door you locked us in here. It's a safety measure, so terrorists can't stow away in the cargo hold. The doors don't open into the cabin from here if the security system's down. No, there's only two ways out for us, and that's through the outer door, or back into the cabin, and only then if the starjackers break it open from their side. And if *that* happens—"

"No." She fixed her gaze on the perky grin of Ruby Rokett on the kit at her feet. "I can't believe God put me here to space a bunch of civs."

"Burke," he snarled, "take it from me, there's worse things than dying."

"Are you going to make that decision for them?" She narrowed her dark eyes at him. "Where there's life, there's hope. Or would you really rather have been dead the last twelve years?"

The intercom clicked on. "All right, you two," said a slick voice. "Come out or we'll put you out."

Burke spun around. "Aw, geez. . . ."

Allenby tossed her his helmet and went in search of another. As he flung luggage about the cabin, he told himself that if they survived, he might provide an answer for her question, assuming she didn't find out firsthand.

"We want the blond," said the voice in the intercom. "Send him out."

He glanced up sharply. Burke gestured to him, and hissed, "Keep looking! I'll stall!" Then she cooed into the intercom, "I'm sorry, he's not available right now, but if you'll leave your name and number at the sound of the beep . . ."

"Send him out here or we'll blow the outer hatch."

"Hey, I'm not interested in your personal life." She gestured to Allenby: *hurry up!* "Tell you guys what. We're gonna give *you* one more chance to let everyone go, drop your weapons, and surrender to the crew."

The intercom was silent for a moment. Then, laughing: "Or what?"

"Or . . . I'll huff and I'll puff and, uh, I'll blow your heads off."

"Last chance, blondie," the voice purred. "Your partner's about to get you killed."

She thrust a fist at the door. "Yeah, well, go fish, pal!"

"Got one!" Allenby flipped open the latches of the kit and tossed the suit aside, placing the helmet on his head. He flashed her a "thumbs up."

Burke clicked off the intercom, slipped on her own helmet, and turned—then waved her arms frantically: *abort abort abort—*

In the reflection of her faceplate he glimpsed the glaring crack that ran halfway down the side of his own, and the reversed label he didn't need to read to understand: WARNING! UNRATED FOR DEPRESSURIZATION!

Before he could move, the inner door swung open and three armed figures in full suits trained their weapons on them. Allenby popped his helmet and put his hands on his head.

Now he sat in the air lock, leaning against the door that had closed behind Burke. Maybe she *was* a lunatic, but her sacrifice had left him the means to survive, to escape or to fight back.

He could tether himself to one of the overhead supports inside the 'lock, and when he hit vacuum he could pull himself back to the ship with it. Once there, he could climb over the topside of the shuttle, and breach the cargo compartment. . . .

And then what? Burke's voice came back to him.

Until the riots, he'd been just another spoiled rich regger colony teen. Instead of the promising outlook of the fourteen-year-old Daffyd Allenby, the sixteen-year-old one walked the docks of Beligo, selling the only thing he had to offer in order to survive. And every day he paced that long walk he repeated his vow, that he would find the ones responsible, and then . . .

But these starjackers were not the men of Phobos, for whom he meant his carefully prepared retribution.

Are you going to make that decision for them?

"To protect and defend the citizens of the Federation," Burke had said. That was the oath they *both* had taken. There was revenge, and then there was revenge. Taking out innocent civs along with the terrorists wasn't the kind of revenge he was in the market for. He didn't know *what* he would do afterwards, but he knew that, to do anything, he'd have to stay alive.

He stood up and pulled the helmet over his head, fastening the catches as the outer surface of the faceplate automatically mirrored over. He could tether himself securely to the inside of the 'lock, wait for it to vent out and repressurize, and when the inner door reopened, he . . .

No. Unarmed, alone, what could he do? Get himself killed. Better to take his chances outside.

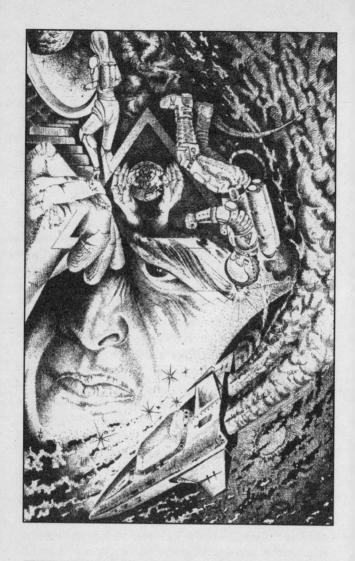

Illustrated by Konstantin Sheverdin

He checked his own gauges; his airpack registered almost an hour and a half's worth, just enough to watch himself burn up in the earth's atmosphere if his tether snapped and he fell into its gravity well; if it held, then he would stay leashed to the ship until someone answered his beacon, whether or not he was alive to be rescued. . . .

Almost two minutes left, according to the 'lock controls. Plenty of time left to secure himself against the force of the vacuum.

Allenby frowned. Then why was the helmet still in the lock?

He looked across to the peg in the wall. If Burke had chosen not to take the helmet, it should have stayed attached to the peg after the 'lock opened, and if the helmet had somehow fallen off the peg, it should have been swept out along with her. Yet it had been lying loose on the floor.

From the corner of his eye he caught the image of the convex faceplate reflected back into the concave window of the inner 'lock door, and somewhere in the mirrored infinities he glimpsed something swaying rhythmically, like a tree bending in the breeze. . . .

No, he reasoned, concavity turned things upside-down—therefore, something swung like a pendulum, hanging *down* from . . .

He jerked his head back and looked up.

Burke dangled from the ceiling, tethered to the coolant pipes. She floated right above the inner 'lock hatch, bobbing lightly in the low gravity. "How did you—" He checked himself. She couldn't hear him.

Even at his height he could barely reach her; he jumped on his toes and loosened her tether, cradling her in his arms. Her face was pale but intact, her pulse strong though her breathing came shallow, stilted—she hadn't imploded at all! But she *was* unconscious. Just as well, he mused. In a minute the warning klaxon would sound, and the gauges would cycle downward to zero. Better for her not to be awake for that. . . .

God put me here for a reason, she had told him.

Well, thought Allenby, far be it from me to second-guess someone else's deity. He removed the helmet and fitted it over her head, buckling the clasps two at a time. Then, in midmotion, he said out loud, "What am I *doing?*" and popped the helmet off again.

A minute later, the outer hatch opened.

He floated free, adrift in the vastness. The ship grew smaller and smaller as he spun away, unable to right himself or stop himself. He closed his eyes to keep from getting dizzy, and took a deep, careful breath. If only he'd had time to secure the tether to the inside of the 'lock. . . .

But at least the ship was safe. The last thing he saw before he forced his eyes shut was a patrol ship docking with the shuttle. So the pilot *had* managed to send a distress signal after all. He felt relief, knowing he had made the right choice. . . .

But no ship came after Allenby.

He felt a shift in the bulk of the suit beneath him, and he winced; then a squeezing around his middle, and a tap on his lower back, just under his duty tunic, right over his kidney: *Anybody home?*

"Can you hear me all right?"

Yes. An elbow ground into his rib. "Oh, hey, my com-link's on. . . ."

"Well, don't use it! *Your* tank's only got about an hour on it, so keep still and shut up for once."

More tapping and squeezing: *Can't make me, nyah nyah.*

"I knew I should have left you there. No, wait, I didn't mean that. . . ."

I know. Conserve your own air, dumbfish.

"Not until you tell me what you thought you were doing, telling them to put me in the 'lock first." He felt her quiver against him. "Are you laughing at me?"

Born and bred in a briar patch, Br'er Rabbit.

"And what's *that* supposed to mean?"

It means that reverse psychology's been around over three hundred years. Still works, too. Besides, it was you they wanted, I don't know why, but I figured if they were pro-reg, they would be saving you for later anyway, and if they were anti-reg, they'd have found it more interesting to watch you squirm, wondering if I'd leave the helmet for you, than if they'd just sent you out first. So I made sure they took me first. She paused. The helmet was supposed to be bait, to draw them into the 'lock so I could jump them. I guess I popped the helmet off before full repressurization. . . . I hadn't planned on passing out.

He stretched himself as far as he could reach, hoping it would slow his rotation. It did not. "And if that failed?"

Burke didn't move for a moment. *Actually, I was praying for a miracle.* Another pause. *I think I got one.*

Allenby hummed. "For about an hour, anyway."

Ah, well, I didn't really want to take the TFE again. She slowly adjusted her position in the belly of the suit. *Nice accommodations. Very womb-like. I just wish I had a window seat now.*

He opened one eye, gaped at the spiral of the stars surrounding him, and shut it again. "No, you don't."

Long minutes of silence stretched, engulfing them. Then, suddenly: *They were Fed, weren't they?*

Allenby frowned, puzzled. "Who, the starjackers?"

No. Phobos.

He felt his face flush, could not help himself as every muscle tensed. *I thought so,* signaled Burke. *Or is now not the time to go into this? It's now or never, right?*

He kept his mouth clamped shut.

See, I figured if it had happened during the riots themselves, you'd be more inclined toward becoming a soldier or some kind of law enforcement officer. But it wasn't, was it? It was afterward, during the occupation by the so-called 'peace-keeping' forces.

She didn't signal further, and he realized she wouldn't until he responded. She wasn't about to lecture him. Removed from the rest of the universe, with oblivion before them, the time had come for him to speak.

"How did you know?" he murmured.

I didn't. But it's the only thing that makes sense. I can understand why you might want to become some kind of social worker, to help other survivors come to terms with their own experiences. But why, specifically, a Morale Officer? You didn't just want to be a psychologist, you wanted to be in the Corps. She withdrew her hand from his back. He waited.

He could feel her breathing, the rise and fall of her rib cage against his, as she lay curled in a fetal position in the midsection of his pressure suit. The tank still strapped to her back dug into his hip bone, but her insight and frankness had numbed him to physical discomfort.

According to your records, your parents were killed during the first few days of the riots. And you were a lone four-teen-year-old boy, against unscrupulous soldiers with the authority to arrest anyone for anything, or for nothing.

Another pause. *After Phobos you emigrated to Beligo, a station that happens to house a military port. All that time, you must have been looking for them. And you're still looking for them, aren't you? After all, we can access any UEF personnel file.*

He rolled his tongue around his dry mouth, trapped between the disorientation outside him, and dizzy from the spinning truths within.

The TFE doesn't monitor what precisely you've done in your life, just if you've been honest with your partner about it. How could you tell a prospective partner that you were out for revenge, against some of the people you're sworn to serve?

"Revenge?" he whispered. "Is that what you think I want?" *Isn't it?*

"I . . ." He let out a deep breath. "I'm a Morale Officer. And if . . . *when* I find them, you can be fishing sure—when I'm through with them, they'll never be able to do such things again."

She did not move for a long time. Then, slowly, her arms wound around his waist and up under his shirt. He felt a long, steady squeeze that bore no message he could decipher. . . .

Then it dawned on him that it *did* mean something: it meant she *knew*, and knew all of it—

Morale Officers were duty-bound to help, to heal. Perhaps the soldiers that had used him so cruelly could not be helped—but not for lack of trying. In so choosing, Allenby had first healed himself.

And Burke recognized this. The signal was a hug.

Blinking back tears, he wrapped his arms around his middle and wished she could feel the gesture in return. Then he started to laugh softly.

What? What? What's going on?

He tried to keep his eyes open—the sight was glorious! "There's a cruiser coming right for us, Terraspace patrol ship. They must have picked up our beacon. . . ." He laughed harder, gulping his precious air, knowing there would be more. "I guess that means we have to take the TFE after all, huh?"

Burke hugged him tighter. *What for? We just passed it.*

FREE

Send in this card and you'll receive a FREE POSTER while supplies last. No order required for this Special Offer! Mail your card today!

☐ Please send me a FREE poster.

☐ Please send me information about other books by L. Ron Hubbard.

ORDERS SHIPPED WITHIN 24 HRS OF RECEIPT

SCIENCE FICTION/FANTASY:

___ *Battlefield Earth* paperback	$6.99	_____
___ *Battlefield Earth* audio	$29.95	_____
Mission Earth® series (10 volumes)		
___ paperback (specify volumes:_____) (each)	$5.99	_____
___ audio (specify volumes:_____) (each)	$15.95	_____
___ *Final Blackout* paperback	$4.95	_____
___ *Final Blackout* audio **SPECIAL**	$11.95	_____
___ *Fear* paperback	$5.99	_____
___ *Fear* audio **SPECIAL**	$9.95	_____
___ *Slaves of Sleep & The Masters of Sleep* hardcover	$9.98	_____
___ *Slaves of Sleep & The Masters of Sleep* audio	$19.95	_____
___ *Ole Doc Methuselah* hardcover **SPECIAL**	$9.98	_____
___ *Ole Doc Methuselah* audio	$24.95	_____
___ *L. Ron Hubbard Presents Writers of The Future®* volumes: (paperback)		

___ Vol XI $6.99   ___ Vol X $6.99   ___ Vol IX $5.99

___ Vol VIII $5.99   ___ Vol VI $4.95   ___ Vol IV $4.95   _____

NEW RELEASES!

___ *Writers of The Future Volume XII*	$6.99	_____
___ *Typewriter in the Sky* hardcover (Fantasy)	$16.95	_____
___ *Typewriter in the Sky* audio	$16.95	_____

CHECK AS APPLICABLE:

SHIPPING*: _____

☐ Check/Money Order enclosed **TAX**:** _____
(Use an envelope please)

☐ American Express ☐ VISA ☐ MasterCard **TOTAL:** _____

Card#: _____

Exp. Date: _____ Signature: _____

NAME: _____

ADDRESS: _____

CITY:_____ STATE: _____ ZIP: _____

PHONE#:_____

Call us Now with your Order 1-800-722-1733

* For first item add $3.25 for shipping and handling, each additional item add $1.50.
** California residents add 8.25% sales tax.

© 1996 BPI. All Rights Reserved. MISSION EARTH and WRITERS OF THE FUTURE are trademarks owned by L. Ron Hubbard Library. 0808954401

Name: _____

Address: _____
_____

City: _____ State: _____ Zip: _____

BUSINESS REPLY MAIL

FIRST CLASS MAIL   PERMIT NO. 62688   LOS ANGELES, CA

POSTAGE WILL BE PAID BY ADDRESSEE

BRIDGE PUBLICATIONS, INC.
Attn: Dept. WOTF XII
4751 Fountain Ave.
Los Angeles, CA 90029-1723

EYES OF LIGHT

Written by
Richard Flood

Illustrated by
Lionel Baker II

About the Author

Richard Flood was born in Chicago in 1952, where he says he was raised in the suburbs by Ray Bradbury, Jack Kirby, Steve Ditko, and John Carter of Mars. As a boy, he contributed to comic-book fandom, submitting to various magazines, and began writing fiction in the seventh grade.

He moved to northern California in the late seventies, where he studied computer science and creative writing. In his senior year at UC Berkeley, he won a share of the Eisner literature prize, and an Elizabeth Mills Crothers short story prize, and he had literary stories published in several magazines.

After graduation, he worked as an editor for Creative Arts Books Company, where he met his wife, a cookbook author from Pennsylvania.

He moved east to be with her, and began consulting as a technical writer and programmer for the telephone industry. When he'd thoroughly fouled things up, he moved to Wall Street, where he worked on networking and graphics programming.

Only recently has he begun to realize that he is a trained writer and not at all qualified to be a programmer. We do hope that he keeps his priorities straight from now on. As a finalist, Mr. Flood is eligible to enter the contest again, and we fully expect that with writing like this, he could win big.

On the night of the summer solstice, Imiresh, my friend and True Brother, who forgave my alien birth and shared even the Taeneh rite of kinship under the stars, cried out to me in my dreams.

Sad-eyed, touching his chest, he said *"keinsam,"* the Taeneh word for silent brightness, for death, and also for forgetting.

I awoke suddenly, as I often did after one of their visitations. A syncopated tapping was already at my door. I lit a lantern and went to the sound.

Imiresh's apprentice, Oorihi, squinted at my lantern's light, vertical irises shrinking into hairline filaments, his lemur-face craning toward me. "The teacher," he said, breathless, touching his own chest as if to mimic my dream. "Death-brightness surrounds."

In a chill wind, Oorihi and I hurried to the village, to Imiresh's hut. His mates hummed soft chants outside, beneath the stars. We ducked in, and found Imiresh against an inner wall, a blanket over his legs, face joyless in the flickering candlelight. Oorihi moved beside him, crouching, face down, silent.

My True Brother spoke. "Imiresh falls into forgetting, night-sleeper," he said, speaking in their customary third-person fashion. "Brightness eats the past." His eyes awaited my response.

Impressions from my dream flared at the edge of awareness: Imiresh blind, stumbling, confused. A seeming senility. Loss of the sacred past. The Taeneh memory was a thing of vast extent, and fundamental to their culture. To them, we were amnesiac, blind to our own history.

"What have you lost?" I asked.

"The old-old days, and newer ones a few." He leaned forward on furred hands, his shadow elongating on the earthen wall. Warm, musty candle-scent swirled past me.

"Since the government woman came last, it is grown bad. Oorihi owns the old-old pictures," he said, meaning that he had passed the memories on to Oorihi. "And others own them. But here," he touched a claw to the back of his skull, "they fade."

"Perhaps it is temporary," I said. "Perhaps it will pass."

He looked at the ground, signaling doubt. "This sickness has touched the Taeneh before, now and now. Four times in this one's own lineage. In others. There is a bitterness to this one's spittle, and he does not see as well in darkness." Imiresh was a fellow doctor now, recounting symptoms. "Sleep is poor. Imiresh awakens, spinning inside."

"The others showed these signs?"

"*Amm,*" he said. Yes.

The winds whistled outside, and a pitter of rain now swept across the roof. Imiresh's wives came in, huddling in the shadows opposite us.

"You will let me test, let me see into it?" I needed to scan him, and to take blood and saliva.

He snuffed a candle with his fingers, then pointed to himself and to me. "These two have been True Brothers for a short time."

"Yes." It had been twelve years. Long enough to grow much grayer, slower, but still too short a time. "Do not leave us yet," I said. "Let me see into this."

"Amm," he said. "Your seeing is different, perhaps not so final, then. *Amm."*

Back at my cottage, Epsilon Eridani's rim blazed red on the horizon. I lit lamps in my office and switched on the antique phonograph, a prized find from the nearby markets of Santa Maria. It had been scavenged from the wreckage of an early transport, along with other archaic equipment, and dozens of old vinyl platters—classical recordings in superb shape. These were irreplaceable, and I handled them with great care.

The turntable itself was a wonder of retro-technology: A wound-copper motor, seemingly indestructible. A primitive playing arm that could produce sound with even a thorn. Unthinkable, of course, but technically possible.

As a string quartet began, I saw Oorihi outside in the soft, windblown drizzle, capering to the music.

I sat, closed my eyes. I felt ill-suited to help Imiresh. The scope of Taeneh memory, impaired or not, left little hope his self-diagnosis was flawed. They were rarely wrong about such things. Yet I could do little to heal a serious Taeneh illness. Whatever skills I once had, my practice had long involved little more than herbalism and first aid.

Outside my window, the winds blew again, but the rain had stopped. Oorihi danced on. I flipped open my reader and keyed Imiresh's symptoms on the sensor pad, hoping that Taeneh studies in Santa Maria would shed some light.

Meanwhile, I studied blood samples and scans I had taken from Imiresh, unsure what I sought, regretting for once the backwardness of my equipment. The Outreach folk had offered newer hardware more than once, but I preferred minimum technology, dumb machines without neural interface.

A tap-tapping came at the door.

I let Oorihi in, and asked him why he chose not to sleep.

He squatted near the doorway. "Sleep is soon. I suffer about Imiresh-teacher." It was not exactly *suffer* he said, but a word that meant the pain of not-knowing.

"You help Imiresh," he said.

"I do not know yet. I am seeing what can be seen."

"You help him. The shapes in the sky are not right."

"No, they are not." The star-positions marking Imiresh's death were supposedly many years away. Oorihi seemed too young to take over the work, anyway. "I will do whatever I can. We are True Brothers."

"Amm, amm," he said, his narrow face relaxing. He ran a finger down the umber fur on his chest. "Our *keirra* breathe together."

"I will not let him die, if there is any way to save him," I said. "You have my promise."

"Amm." We sat in silence for a time, then he left.

I watched him on the grassy area in front of my cottage, leaning forward on his haunches, bounding off toward the village at great speed.

I considered my words and their local meaning. For the Taeneh, unforgetting, promises were never lightly made.

Celia Guerra's clipped voice came through the system with impatience intact. Her smile, more pained than friendly, lingered, in snapshot, on the screen. The low bandwidth to Santa Maria supported only stills of her face and gestures, each trailing her words by a few seconds.

"The department is losing interest in the Eridanae, and they have never had much in your work. The real research is on the other side of the planet, with other settlements." In the past, she had been helpful, but mine was not an easy request.

Eridanae was the official term for Imiresh's species, "Erries" to some; *Eridani* the common name for the planet, though the vast constellation Eridanus spanned dozens, maybe hundreds, of planetary systems. Someday they'd need to expand the nomenclature.

"This is a common operation," I told her. "Years ago, I did it routinely."

"On humans."

"Their physiology is wellknown. The condition is similar to types found in humans."

"Let me ask you one thing—" Her image sitting back, hands pressed together. "When you did this kind of work, would you have agreed to such a request?"

I watched the view retrace with little change. "No, probably not."

"Then you understand the position we are in. I cannot force anyone to take this on."

"This creature is important to the Eridanae culture."

She sighed. "So what would you have me do?"

"Talk to Subramanian at the Med Center. He is the best choice for this operation. And get Outreach to pay for it."

The audio transmitted an ironic laugh, though the image stayed pensive. "That's all?" There was a pause. "If this is so important, why don't you do the work yourself?"

"Neural interface is the only way to handle this, and I don't have the skills anymore. I haven't *attached* since I left Earth."

"But as you said, the operation is simple."

"I've been fixing cuts and abrasions for twelve years. Don't have the device, either. The nanodevice this operation calls for."

"Uh-huh. So you need the hospital and the surgeon."

"Yes. It must be done at the Med Center. Subramanian will not travel out here."

"No, of course not." She said something softly in Spanish, invoking God's mother. In the next image, she appeared to be writing. "I think the plan will fail, but I will talk to Doctor Subramanian for you. You will want to start polling him shortly. You must be aggressive or he won't pick up the call."

The image dimmed and control icons brightened. I set the system to poll Subramanian and closed my eyes, sitting back, tired. The clock was moving on in irregular Taeneh time, while my progress remained unclear.

My hopes were pinned on the cooperation of Subramanian and the Med Center, yet there was no guarantee of either, or that, in the best case, they'd respond quickly enough. Imiresh's condition itself presented no imminent danger, but the Taeneh elders had already chosen the site for his immolation ceremony. I had a day, or two, or three, but no more.

I pondered my alternatives. When I first arrived, I was provided neural-interface equipment—portable, low-power hardware that was, with the proper surgical fitting, sufficient to operate on Imiresh. It had never been unpacked, but was undoubtedly still functional, if rather primitive.

I had used better hardware back on Earth, hospital

equipment like Subramanian's. In fact, I had decades of experience with it, back before the NI strictures became law. Nowadays, doctors retired from NI work by age thirty-two, biological years. Hospitals enforced strict limits on interface time. In any case, I had no interest in the NI equipment I received. I had buried it in its crate out behind my cottage, the cold remains of my previous life.

But this equipment mattered not, anyway. No one would come out and do the work, and even if I had my skills, I was far too old for an operation of this complexity.

The call came in an hour later, faceless, showing only the Med Center's hexagonal logo. Subramanian's voice had a flat, staccato quality. It was uncomfortably familiar. "Guerra pinged me. What is the design?"

"I have an Eridanae," I told him, "long-term memory loss."

"Calcification. I have scanned some files on this. Wait." There was a pause. He was attached, I assumed, and temporarily switching context. "Back," he said. "So, Guerra thinks she can fund. Why don't you do it? Oh— delete that. I see that you have let yourself become old. This won't be a quick procedure either. Seems too risky for you."

"No, and I have not attached in years."

"Yes." Brittle laughter came from his side. "I have seen your career-rec. Unfortunate." His coldness, while expected, grated on me.

"I do not have the nanodevice."

"An excuse," he said. "Such devices are not hard to come by, the smaller ones. Not officially. You have some money? The traders will not accept a government promise, unlike us."

"No, not much."

"Ah, then. So you are out of luck. Sadly unattached."

"You will not do it?"

"Wait." Again there was a pause. "I have scanned your work. It is a shame you cannot do it. Equipment has changed little since your disconnect. Faster hardware, sees better. You would find it familiar."

It was, I thought, already so. A tension had crept into me during the call, and a vague ill feeling. "My involvement," I said, "is not an option."

"Understandable. But neither is mine. This is veterinary surgery, after all. Not my field."

The logo had already begun to fade. For people in Subramanian's state, social graces were a waste of precious time.

On Earth, in Quintana Roo, the recruiters had not cared much about my suitability for inter-species work. I was an M.D., willing to travel to strange worlds, and they were short of volunteers, short of many resources. Space, an expensive, slow-yielding investment, favored governments oblivious to public opinion, not democracies like theirs.

Imiresh came to see me often, though I treated him rudely at first. Rude for humans, at least. Though uncannily sensitive in some ways, the Taeneh were thick-skinned in others. He gibbered constantly about things I then had little interest in—the movements of the winds and rains, the long history of his kind. He listened, rapt, to my occasional responses, mangled phrases from the software in my translator. Even through the verbal fog, traces of Taeneh humor surfaced—exaggerations, absurd understatement. For a long time, I had thought these were translator bugs.

We began to sit together in the night, beside fires he built of the fibrous Eri wood, speaking, watching the stars—or waiting for them to shine through. Like the rains, clouds came and went quickly in the moonless sky. Imiresh tried to teach me the Taeneh vocabulary, with varying success. Many terms had no human equivalent; others, such as color, translated strangely. Blue and green things were "wet," browns were "powdery," all shades of red were "warm."

He pointed out their constellations: the bucket, the flaming spear, the spiral tunnel. From Eri, Sol was a part of our constellation *Serpens*. To them, it was *crown-star*, gem on the crest of the *Falling One*, a Taeneh warrior with arms and legs thrown forward, tail curling behind.

Oorihi maintained a vigil outside my cottage, sleeping at times beside the low-slung violet *tarimai* near my porch and office. When the rains passed through, he hid under a skin he had brought. He grew inactive as the hours wore on with no sign from me.

I had contacted a supplier through the indirect, untraceable means he preferred, and awaited his arrival. If something was for sale anywhere on Eridani, Arno Fedyk would know about it.

In the late afternoon, I heard Oorihi's shrill voice: *"Taanaan, colitan!"*

His face appeared at the window above my desk, leaning in, muzzle pressed against the screen. *"Colitan,"* he said again, softly.

It was their word for backhoes, tractors, and the simpler industrial robots. For a moment, I found the term confusing. Then I caught the whine of a vehicle coming uphill toward us, and recalled the Taeneh nickname for Fedyk.

He wore a shoulder bag and the black half-helmet that "enhanced" types favored, a sensory device of some sort. As he stood in my doorway, a cyan bead suspended near his forehead glowed, scanned the room.

"Is a tidy place you have here," he said, in a deep voice, vaguely electronic. "Little box of civilization. In the wild."

He glanced around, walked past me to the office doorway and peered in. "Like a trip to the nineteenth century, this place. Mind if I look?" He did not wait for an answer. I followed.

"Oil lamps! Do you write with a quill? And what's this contrap?" He laid a finger on the frame of the turntable, feeling the vibration. I had left it on, wasting precious electricity.

"An antique device," I said, "for playing music."

"Ah. Show me. I have a great interest in music devices."

I waved him back, then took Dowland's *Lachrimae* from its sleeve.

Fedyk's third-eye flickered, recording the scene for later reference.

"It plays silicon disks?" he asked.

I put it on the turntable. "No, these are vinyl."

"Ah, magnetic, then."

"No, mechanical." I put down the stylus.

He seemed puzzled. As the music began, his expression soured. "Depressing, it is."

He gestured for me to quiet it, pulled a small translucent slab from his bag. "This," he said, touching the gleaming surface, "is quality." A stream of digital cacophony spewed from the tiny thing, filling the room, a huge, full sound for something so small.

"State of the art," he said, leaning close, then shut it off. "Never did like antiques. Some of my customers do." He scanned the rest of the office. We went back into the living room, and I sat at my desk, clicked the reader on. I accessed an image and specifications. "I might need a medical part. Nanodevice. Official channels cannot get it, not soon enough anyway."

"Don't know much about medicals," he said. "But I'll run it. He held a glove-sensor up to the iconic code on the screen, then stepped back. "This'll take a moment; medical's not cached."

While he downloaded, Oorihi's head bobbed above the window frame again, peeking in.

"Errie's been watching us," said Fedyk. " I scanned him before. You get along with those monkeys?"

"Yes. They—"

"Used to hunt them down South before they passed the restrictions. Don't taste too bad, no offense. Now we do some business. Got to take care with them. Shrewd devils. Can't deceive them."

I said nothing. At least he honored the restrictions, more than could be said for some of his kind. In any case, our meeting was purely for Imiresh's sake.

"This," said Fedyk, "is a special order. Very rare item. In fact, I scan only one on the market, at ten-thousand five."

I felt the blood run from my face. "The official price for this device," I said, slowly, "is 500 Standard."

He let out a low, wheezing laugh. "I know the official price, but that doesn't bear," he said. "My product is quality. This is some kind of brain slicer, isn't it? Wouldn't want bad product."

Despite the nature of his business, Fedyk was trusted by humans and the Taeneh, but I could not meet his price. "I don't have that kind of money. I did once, years back."

"Spent it on the Erries? Seems a waste." He looked about, zipped his shoulder bag. "Ah, well, should you change your mind, you know where I hook up."

"Change my mind? I do not have it, or even close to it. Is there no way to bargain on this?"

He stepped into the doorway, then stopped, thought for a moment. "No," he said, "can't manage it. This one is fixed-price. You provide ten-five, I provide your part."

I turned away, staring blankly past the image on the reader, at a loss.

"You can raise it," he said, still there. "I am certain of it."

"No, you are mistaken."

"I ran your stuff when I came in," he said, and laughed that soft laugh again. "Some is worth a fair price to collectors. The old oil lamps, some of the furnishings. Very little real oak on Eridani, you know."

I made no response. It had been a long day, and I was feeling numb, inert.

"It would do," he added, trying to read my silence. "Would cover. Give it some thought." Then he left.

Above me, Oorihi's face leaned into the screen again. "Colitan give parts?"

I looked up at his young face, but did not smile.

Blue fire spiraled upward in the warm night breeze, then settled back. Imiresh poked embers in the three-sided pit, a smell like cinnamon or cloves filling the air. I had listened silently to his assessment of Oorihi's readiness and the future—his tribe's and mine. Now I needed to make my proposal.

"In your mind," I said, struggling with a limited Taeneh vocabulary, "there is a wall between the past and present. That is the nature of this sickness."

Imiresh arched his head back slowly, a Taeneh nod. "This one has seen it, the dark structure. He tries to penetrate to the old-old things, but he cannot. It grows more opaque." He used a word that connoted hardening, or sedimentation.

"I believe there is a way to remove the wall," I told him, describing microtools that could dissolve the calcification, restoring neural chemistry in the tissue associated with his long-term memory.

"*Cheliana*," he said. The word described a beneficial, healing, or luck-giving touch. "Night-sleeper is a wise healer, for a young one."

I smiled at the mixed compliment, a kindly way of describing someone of shallow memory. I told him that the Taeneh nervous system had been studied by humans, and bore resemblances to ours. Our doctors had operated on Taeneh before, so it was nothing to fear.

"If night-sleeper advises it, Imiresh will try this healing."

I had expected a long debate about the surgery, but realized once more that he was not human, and not bound by my expectations. Still, I needed to be sure. In elaborate detail, I described the nanodevice and operation again.

"*Amm*," he said, blinking great dark eyes at the fire, crescents of pale blue reflecting in them. He used a word that connoted cutting into the skulls of prey, but added a softening inflection. "Night-sleeper will do this next-night?"

I sighed. Nothing in this conversation was going as planned. "No, I cannot do it."

"You do not know this cutting?"

"Once," I said. "It has been too long. And I do not have the device yet. It will take time to get it, and the surgeon. I do not yet know how long."

"Keinsam. Keinsam. Keinsam," he said, changing the inflection with each word. Time, forgetfulness, death. "No time remains." He brushed his narrow hands together then opened them, signaling finality and freedom.

"You must delay. It will take several next-nights."

He gazed at the ground, eyes heavy-lidded. "No delay. Children hesitate, night-sleeper, not the full-born."

A hissing came from high overhead, reptilian gliders crisscrossing in the shadows above. I picked up a piece of Eri blackwood, ran my thumb along its pitted surface. "Another few nights, that is all."

Imiresh gazed at the fire for a time, in silence. He began a soft chant sung during times of change, then abruptly stopped. Turning to me, his eyes once again open wide, alive, he described the day I first came up the hill to their settlement: the shirt, pants, and shoes I wore, the first words I spoke to him, the way the wind blew my hair easily to and fro. I was "many-eyed" then, my mind skittering without center. He lapsed into a reverie of details from the night we had spent together under the stars, eaten their loathsome ceremonial meal. In keeping with their traditions, I had recounted the long lineage of Taeneh elders from memory, and, by their laws, become kin.

He leaned forward and blew into the heart of the fire, making it flare. "Imiresh owns all of it," he said, "every mote of that time together, and when not together, carrying it heart-close to the assimilation. The old-old times he has already lost, but not that."

In swirling winds, I knelt behind my cottage, beside a re-engineered lilac planted shortly after my arrival, now resplendent, hiding beneath it the artifacts of my own history.

Now, even twelve years later, I felt a deadness in my limbs, a sour heat in my belly. I wondered if I had been healed after all, or only dreamed.

It had not seemed strange then to bury the devices instead of destroying or selling them. I worked like a dumb automaton, separating out the neural-interface gear from the rest of the portable equipment the government had provided. Hiding it, but not too far.

Now, my alternatives had all dead-ended, foolish hopes, anyway. No nanosurgeon on Eridani would operate on a Taeneh, though some knew their physiology. Only a few doctors had any interest in them, and none showed great concern for Imiresh or his settlement. That left one candidate for the work, old, ill-equipped, reluctant, and fond of his antiques.

I heard a rustle of leaves to my right, then Oorihi crashed into my thoughts, bounding past the lilac, loud and real. "Night-sleeper! No music. It is time-of-music."

"No," I said, suddenly tired. Some great part of me longed for sleep. *Silent brightness*. But not yet. "No music this day. Not in the on-and-on, unless you sing for me."

"*Amm*," he said, puzzled for a moment, then blinking his eyes, understanding. "Backhoe have parts."

"No, not yet. Now bring *chennam*, and friends. We must dig."

I sat near my comm system, waiting. I had contacted Fedyk in the usual way, sending a message to a node he often checked. One never dialed him directly. Now I could only wait for the return call, sent from some masked site.

The sleek, pristine tools sat in a foam-lined case before me. I touched the cool metal casing of the earwire module, the ring of external sensors on the scalpband. It was portable, battery-powered stuff, cheap junk compared to the hospital issue. But it would do. The greater worry was my own skills, and how I would handle the attach.

I had always pretended I left Earth for philosophical reasons, motives abstract and impersonal. Medicine, after all, had become a strange profession. Doctors often no longer knew their patients in the flesh, only binary signatures, scans, histograms, transformed into frozen bitstreams.

Back then, the best at microsurgery and similar work lived in deep communion with their neural-interface systems, *attached*, surrendering to an inevitable, incremental effect. Lived at light-speed, in a realm of precision and control, assist-AIs at one's shoulder. Over time, the waking world turned loud, blurred, and slow, an ooze of ambiguous data.

Before the interface syndrome was well understood, I developed the classic symptoms. I grew to fear and crave interface. Family and friends gradually receded as I dwelled more and more in that strange union. My attached life became captivating and eventually, intolerable.

So I broke away to Eridanus, to my accidental healing, and a life of seeing a sun and stars each day. At least, it had seemed a healing.

I turned toward my comm system. My comm system was flashing. A synthesized voice issued from it.

"I got your ping. What is it?" The logo of a plumbing

company appeared on my screen, some sort of noise thrown up by Fedyk's stealth software.

"Can you get the device quickly?" I asked. "Can you get it to me by tonight?"

A low electronic hissing came over the channel, but no response. I wondered whether Fedyk was receiving everything.

"Did you get my questions?" I asked.

"Got them," he finally said. "The device is available. Not easy to deliver it by tonight, though."

"It must be here then, or it will no longer be needed."

"You will provide me with the antiques," said the voice. "Including the player."

"Yes," I said, before fully parsing his statement. "No—not the player. That was not part of the arrangement."

"You've taken too long on this," said the voice. "And now you want it there, instant. Add the player, and I'll do it tonight. Otherwise, it'll be tomorrow sometime."

"What difference can it make to you? You showed no interest in it."

"I have someone interested in it. And I'll have to pay someone to get the device and meet me on the way to your place."

"It was not the agreement," I said, weakly. I had no negotiation position, nor any time left to argue him down.

"So," he said, seeming to sense my resignation. "You will also include the cartridges? We are agreed on them?"

It made little difference now. Without the turntable, the recordings were useless. "Yes, you might as well have them. When will you be here? I must prepare."

I wiped my forehead and put on the equipment, turned it up. There was a tickle in my ear canal as filaments homed, a faint hum of power, then the metallic taste. Familiar, the same as so long ago, discomfiting.

Occluded light expanded in my forehead. I heard a faint electronic gibbering, then my limbs went cold. For a time, I drifted in a soundless haze of brightness, deaf and blind.

It was *blanking*, common with the cheaper equipment, usually brief. But the bright quiet lingered, too long, and my mind built fearful scenarios: The equipment was untested, long used, old power cells unable to hold charge. I was too old, physically incapable now. The state could last for days, rendering me useless to Imiresh or anyone else.

I saw his placid face in my mind's eye, thought of his easy trust in me, felt the sadness of failure, and the release.

Then, at last, dots of color glittered in the distance, grew, spiraling outward from the center. The room again appeared, enhanced, pointillism with an adjustable scale. Testing, I zoomed into the surface of a nearby table, through the lacquer, grain, and fiber of the wood, into the dead honeycomb of the cells.

The AI announced its readiness. I wiped perspiration from my eyes, located the device Fedyk had delivered. Zooming again, I attached it with a nanotool.

In the examining room, Imiresh lay facedown on the table, sedated, the shape and mottled density of bone now visible beneath the shaved rear of his scalp.

The tension had passed. I felt strong in the pulsing neural field now, exhilarated.

Moving close, I cut in, removed a small piece of bone from his skull, and took the AI on a brief, live tour of the

Taeneh brain, teaching it the odd neural structure, the different neural centers.

I had slipped a tube into Imiresh's mouth, and now had the AI send seek wires to his heart and lungs, ready to assist his respiration.

We scanned the striation of calcium in Imiresh's hindbrain, then went to work. To my enhanced eyes, the probes looked like veins of mercury as they tunneled into Imiresh's tissue, then a sparse, silvery root-system in his hindbrain. I brought the tips of several filaments to the first neural cleft. Painstakingly, we guided the microtools, two probes working at the deposits in the first neural cleft while a third released an enzyme into the area.

As we finished the first task, my vision began to blur. I tried to blink it away, reset the optical subsystem, but it would not clear up. The AI scanned for power or process abnormalities, found none. This was not hardware fatigue, I realized, but my own. Yet we had completed only a fraction of the procedure.

Still, I was almost blind now, and had to stop.

I dropped the interface into standby and rested, giving my neural chemistry time to recover, knowing that eventually, such delays could end Imiresh's life on the operating table.

Alone in the featureless brightness, I awaited a reconnect from the AI, too tired to formulate any kind of plan. For a time, it was like dead sleep, pure unconsciousness. Then came the low whisper of the AI's voice circuit:

Restoring.

Color again swirled into view, coalesced into Imiresh's form. The topology of his hindbrain was once again clear, the grayish strands like veins of clay. I asked

Illustrated by Lionel Baker II

the AI how long I had been out, and how long the first work had taken. The answer confirmed my suspicions. With periodic rests, the procedure would take far too long, and the AI could not finish it alone.

Quickly, I studied the dozens of deposits and had the AI pattern-match, classify. It was as I suspected: Though a portion of the work was too complex or irregular for the AI without days of rehearsal, much fell into groups of straightforward, similar tasks.

We would concentrate on these first, and while I rested, the AI could repeat the procedures on matching areas.

Hopeful, I began again.

My rests grew more frequent as we went on. Imiresh's alien metabolism seemed profoundly disrupted by the procedure, his vital signs slowly, steadily decaying, and the AI had begun to augment his heartbeat and breathing. I found I had to stop monitoring him. The periodic bad news only increased my sense of time pressure, and thus my own neural fatigue.

At last, two hours into the procedure, I could not go on. I hoped the AI had learned enough to finish the procedure, but regardless, I could not.

I slumped into a chair, brightness swirling in my head. Then the spinning stopped, and a bright haze descended upon me.

I awakened from my strange sleep some time later, pushing up from the chair. I touched Imiresh's leg. It was cold. My heart sank.

I scanned his hindbrain. The probes had retracted, their work apparently complete. The AI, unable to pull me back to consciousness, had sprayed a protective membrane on the site and gone into standby, conserving power.

How long had I been gone, then? I looked up, checking the task log the NI hardware projected onto my field of vision. The AI had finished over an hour ago.

I could not tell if Imiresh was still alive. There was no sign of his own respiration, just the minimal support of the hardware. When it shut down, I would find out. I was not ready for this yet.

I turned back to brighter, more quantifiable things, engaging the NI interface again so that I could mend his skull.

Afterwards, I lingered in the attached state again, standing back from the operating table, hands out. I breathed deeply. A great stillness hung in the room—a bright pulsing of energy, the vaguest whisper of white noise from the equipment. I felt quickened, awakened, eyes of light. There was such power in this state, such a brightness and clarity to things. I looked at my hands, and watched the blood pulsing in them, the endless quivering in the cells.

I peered into the form on the table: the flattened, vaguely-human skull, the huge eye sockets. In the chest, thin cartilaginous bands expanded and contracted. Taeneh ribs, so delicate compared to ours.

Its breath, I thought. No, *his* breath, the breath of my True Brother, my underserved friend. In the center of his chest, the disc-shaped *kierra* beat, now slow and steady, unassisted. His heart.

I nodded to Imiresh's living form, and put my hand gently upon his back, apologizing wordlessly. For a moment, I had forgotten my history, my weakness, but no more. These tools were no longer needed.

I shut everything down, awaited the sharp discomfort of the afterstate. But: nothing, even after many minutes. The quiet breath of two creatures, a mild breeze outside, wind's rustle in the leaves. Eyes not of light, but sufficient.

Night birds hissed in the evening outside, drums pounding in the Taeneh village, celebration rolling in like a storm. Imiresh, head still bandaged, had recounted the oldest of the old-old tales, praised the "young" healer from the crown-star and his great powers. Soon they would come for me, and the night-sleeper would not sleep before dawn.

A tap-tapping came at my door, Oorihi outside with a look of great concentration, a translucent packet hanging from a strap around his neck, like Fedyk's.

"Mohss-art," he said, attempting English. "Do-len, Viv-alghi." He held out a basket full of dark wafers, the thin media it played.

And he touched it, speaking now in Taeneh: "For you, night-sleeper, again time-of-music."

And my house was filled with the sound of strings.

SCIENCE FICTION AND FANTASY ART: THREE KEYS

Written by
Paul Lehr

About the Author

Paul Lehr's illustrations have appeared on literally hundreds of science fiction books during the 1950s and 1960s. His "Grok" cover for Robert A. Heinlein's Stranger in a Strange Land *was a cult treasure of the 1960s.*

Lehr's illustrations have appeared in magazines around the world in such publications as Time, Fortune, Playboy, Reader's Digest, Omni, Analog *and many others.*

A painting of the first moon landing, which appeared in the Saturday Evening Post *in 1959—ten years before the actual event—now is in the permanent collection of the National Air and Space Museum in the Smithsonian Institute. His work has been exhibited in many museums and galleries.*

Currently, Paul lives on a secluded farm in Pennsylvania, where he works on his painting and sculptures.

Lately, he has done less illustration and worked more on creating his own personal fantasy images. Lehr integrates the beauty and patterns of nature with images of the ancient and future to create pictures that depict mysterious scenes of human congestion, destruction, and conflict.

Paul Lehr has been a long-time supporter of the Illustrators of the Future Contest, and recently became its first judge.

Pictorial art in science fiction and fantasy means different things to many people. I will try to give my personal outlook on the field, which has come about through nearly forty years as a working illustrator. What I have to say will not be etched in stone for everyone; my peers have their own procedures in work, some of which differ from mine. I can only present personal guidelines collected through my own experience.

First, I consider illustration to be a high art form. It has the capacity to enlighten, and to project feelings of emotion. It *can* do more than illustrate an incident in a story. (Although that is of primary importance.)

Just look back to the great illustrators of the past: Daumier, Winslow Homer, N. C. Wyeth, Remington, Howard Pyle, and Chesley Bonestell, to name a few. All were powerful painters whose book and magazine illustrations reflected their own times, and move us even today. Redon, Rousseau, Goya, and Paul Klee could be called artists of fantasy. It is far-seeing work that carries us beyond our own time, and into the future with dreams and realistic speculation.

We have the imagery of science fiction all around us in our own world—and it has always been so. With the kitchen light on during a summer evening, look out through the screened window, and you will see what I mean: myriads of insects of all shapes, sizes, and colors, with designs undreamed of—creatures that boggle the imagination. Trees and stumps, forming strange and mysterious shapes. Reflections in water—stones and cratered rocks—it is all there. If we are to become successful in projecting images of other worlds, alien creatures, and the concept of time, we must study our own surroundings first.

I start with the presumption that you want to create convincing depictions of *real* worlds, even though they may be alien or futuristic in concept. The dominant element in the work of many illustrators is the human figure. Be it in costume or semi-nude, their illustrations revolve around the action of the figures. It is central to the drama in their pictures. Other illustrators make space and starships their specialty, and produce dramatic pictures which revolve around that motif. Many depict scenes with dragons and landscapes, and a fantasy theme as their favorite subject.

I have chosen to look upon science fiction as an opportunity to display epic scenes with vast spaces, structures, and armies, along with celebration and conflict; these are the themes I feel at home with. Sometimes I will build my picture around a meaningful symbol found in the story.

Whatever your choice in subject matter, take the one that excites your individual imagination—try not to copy others. To be influenced by other artists is natural, but in the end, to be successful you must create in a personal way. Your work must be your own.

In offering help to aspiring science fiction and fantasy artists, I present three important keys:

KEY I

You must *live* to create visual images. It should be a great passion in your life. Creativity as an artist comes first—science fiction or fantasy illustration comes after that.

KEY II

You should read—history, mythology, newspapers, fiction, science fiction. Be curious about past, present and future. Draw-draw-draw, and paint-paint-paint from life. Use and enlist the real objects, people and subjects around you. You will never know how to properly interpret photographs and scrap-pictures in a realistic way for your illustrations unless you do this.

KEY III

Take Keys I and II and dream. Use your imagination, and grasp an image that the story presents—one that *excites you.* You will know when you see it and read it. If you do this, your personal style will evolve, unlike any other. You will build images that are wonderful and different—even alien—but they will carry force and reality, and be much more convincing to the viewer than the shallow and false feeling that the contrived image will present.

I have been a judge in the *Illustrators of the Future* Contest since its inception, and have had the opportunity to see hundreds of entries. Now, as coordinating judge, I get to view all submissions, and have some thoughts to express about what I see.

My personal experience is with the realistic (and surrealistic) three-dimensional picture with a light source, revealing form, shadow and atmosphere—not the cutout-looking or flat, decorative style, which is certainly legitimate for the illustration of some stories, but simply not my forte.

If I have one major criticism, it is this: I see too many fragmented pictures with poorly considered ideas. It is nearly impossible to present more than *one* idea in a single picture (unless you are creating an all-over pattern or a purely decorative piece). In a dramatic illustration, representing a focused scene, one dominant idea will do. Anything more will confuse the viewer. It will not work to portray David slaying the dragon in one corner, and having the fantastic spaceship off to one side, next to the necromancer peering into his crystal ball—all of approximately the same size and importance. What is the picture about? What does it mean? Remember, that no matter how well you paint and draw, the most important function of the illustration is to *communicate*—and do it clearly. One idea is difficult enough to get across.

Another problem that I have observed is a lack of understanding about the use of color. The entries received are executed in black and white, and some are outstanding. However, in the workshops, when we get to look through portfolios, it becomes evident that few of the artists handle color very well. This deficiency brings me back to Key II. The observations that painting from life bring are not manifest in these works.

The influence of direct and reflected light are what make color. Many entrants paint the objects and people in their work in purely local color. Trees are green, branches are brown, metal is gray, flesh is tan, shadows are black or blue or flat purple and cloth is white. Think of your picture as taking place in a shadow box, with the walls painted green, and the floor painted red, for instance—and set a white egg upon a white saucer within it. Shine a warm light down through the top, and observe it closely. You will find that the surrounding colors are reflected around, and influence the color of all objects in the box. A white egg on a white plate, which sits on a white cloth, is anything but pure white. It is a riot of subtle color, and if carefully observed, will make a painting that looks *real*—not chalky or gray. The reflected light of the blue sky from the window will invade the shadows, and the warm light of the sun will give strong form and color to the objects, and pull things together, making a cohesive painting. Think of light as being warm or cool, and of how it influences the local color of the elements in your paintings.

In order to have a successful career in science fiction illustration, you must be able to produce full-color work. It's fine to do quality black-and-white illustrations, but the livable money is in full, color art.

Another shortcoming for some is poor drawing. There seems to be excessive emphasis put upon *rendering* figures and objects—concern with technique. If you will observe closely the real world around you, as well as the rhythm and structure of nature, technique will take care of itself. Don't concentrate on technique and expect it to solve your problems—it will simply act as a cosmetic that tries to cover weak perception. The viewer won't be fooled—bad drawing is bad drawing, no matter how well the surface is rendered.

I am going to conclude with the admission that most of the aforementioned criticisms have applied to me, personally, in my career growth as an artist, and that now, even at the age of sixty-five, I sometimes forget a basic key here and there. Don't become discouraged. Don't give up. Remember, illustration is a noble profession, unlike any other. Be proud, love what you do, be yourself, and always be reminded that better work lies ahead.

Enjoy it.

REQUIEM FOR A DEATHWATCHER

Written by
Carrie Pollack

Illustrated by
Oleg Dergatchov

Carrie was born on Long Island and began writing stories and poems as soon as she could chew on a pencil. She says that she flirted with a PhD in literature at the University of Illinois, but while working on her dissertation she discovered SF—inexplicably late in life. After reading fifteen Philip K. Dick novels in succession, she bumped into Tanith Lee's Flat Earth series. The touch of the true masters seems to have curbed her admiration for the fakirs so highly touted by "academia."

Wisely, she went AWOL from college and moved to the Southwest, where she began submitting to the Writers of the Future. There, she began raising her family and honing her skills. She's now moved to Massachusetts where her husband teaches computer science at Brandeis University and Carrie divvies up her time between writing and mothering.

Carrie says that she loves running, art museums, Indian food, and is a gluttonous and omnivorous reader.

Carrie has published numerous poems in small main-stream poetry journals and she is marketing a children's fantasy novel. She's also working on a book-length collection of poetry and a high-fantasy novel. If the very fine tale you are about to read is any indication, it won't be long until you find her work on the book shelves at finer grocery stores and gas stations everywhere.

About the Illustrator

Oleg Dergatchov was born in 1961 in Rostow on the Done, in Russia. He graduated from the Ukraine Print Academy in 1984, where he majored in graphic arts.

Since then, he has participated in over a hundred international exhibitions, where he has won several awards. His work has been shown in the Arlenhousen State Gallery in Germany in the Museum of Art in Moscow and in the Museum of Book Art in St. Petersburg.

I became deathwatcher here in Diryevnye over fifty winters ago, before we had either a proper burying ground or a church. Not until last winter did I fail in my office.

In the early days, I stood three inches taller—Serge the Dwarf, they called me—and my beard was black and fine as a newborn's thatch.

On the occasion of my first watch, we laid out the departed in a drafty barn, and drank strong tea and potato spirits to warm us through the night. Toward dawn, the wind's moan broke the stillness, or it may have been a wolf. Finally, at first light, we rose, bleary-eyed but grim, to nail the coffin and bear it out. When both the burying and the next night passed without incident, I almost wept with relief, and had to remind myself, *it will not always be so easy.*

For several years after, when a wraith rose during the watch, I would bellow oaths and prayers at it. Frightened witless, I sought comfort in the thunder of my voice. I would draw myself up, moist-palmed, roaring "Get thee back!" or "In the name of the Holy One . . . ," and thrust out an arm to point where it must go. Ziv, my teacher, before succumbing at last to madness, had taught me to keep a safe distance, lest I be turned to ice by the breath of the grave. That was my fear, you see, that some gibbering ghost might reach out and brush me with its fingers.

Spared that dread fate—for long enough, at least, that I gave up dreading it—still my work began to tell on me, and I lost the knack of youthfulness. Before my third decade was out, my temples went white and I chose to live apart in a hut obscured by trees. Ziv had warned of this, too, alluding to his own stark history: "How the dead envy us," he would mutter. "How they punish us for living."

In time, though, I came to see that the shades of the newly-dead trouble us not from spite, but because they are confused. If they rise, it is because they themselves are haunted by their own sloughed lives. As in a puzzling dream, elusive images flood them—the faces of loved ones, familiar objects, and scenes. And, thus, some of them wake, drift in search of these things, until we deathwatchers remind them to forget, soothe them back to their slumber. They bear us no ill will, though to look in their eyes is to be pierced with despair.

Once I grasped that my function lay in easing the dead from this world into the next, I began to address them differently. Each shade was as a lost child to me, in need of comfort and guidance; what cause had I to bellow at it? Rather, I wooed its compliance in low, soothing tones. People wondered if I'd gone addled, like Ziv, but since the balkiest wraith always turned back to its bier, no one challenged me aloud. Instead they watched the white forms yielding to my voice, like smoke before a breeze, and later asked me to their table, or sent their children with gifts of firewood and eggs.

That was in the first generation.

Later, they began to take me for granted. If a wraith turned back so readily, they reasoned boldly, that proved my efforts little more than ritual.

They didn't dare neglect the ritual, of course—they

weren't bold enough for that—but my inevitable fall from grace was underway. I saw that they would treat me as a charlatan in the end, and, now that I am white-bearded and stooped with age, it has duly come to pass. They smirk and spat in the dirt at my approach. At reckoning time, they grumble over my modest fee.

"Your work is so very demanding," they jeer, "anyone with feet could fill your shoes." As might be expected, however, none are overhasty to step forth barefoot. They claim they are too busy for such charades, but the truth is otherwise; they are glad it is I who stands to halt a wandering shade while they huddle safely farther back. Whatever their boasts and taunts, they cannot help but tremble when the dead waft into their midst.

For they have heard of Stepan the Fool, whose ghost leered at the mourners an entire night, slack-jawed and grinning; and of Vlad Kirilow, the innkeeper, too grasping a sort in life to part with his shadow easily. And their own parents watched the Drozyev infant appear in its mother's arms, squalling, unwilling to be wrested from her. For those three, I had to devise subterfuges, which Diryevnye may have called mummery afterward, but beheld round-eyed at the time.

I had Elena Drozyev rock her babe the night through, clutching it like a ball of mist as she crooned "Lullay, lullay," till her voice was hoarse as wind. As the final cradle song faded with dawn, both mother and child slept, and when Elena woke, her arms were empty.

Stepan I dealt with by having the pallbearers go masked, so he was unsure who to follow home from the burying ground. After bawling in terror for a bit, he sought the safety of his coffin.

And Vlad I outwitted by setting him a gamble; only if he could win every coin in my pocket by sunrise would he earn the privilege of haunting us. He cheated me out of all but one kopek, whereupon I had someone pinch a sleeping cock to make it crow.

And so these last years have gone, miserably but uneventfully, with Diryevnye's sneer fixed on me. Long past are the civilities, the gifts of firewood and eggs. Yet I am called before the priest. But that is only practical, for how could Father Josef entrust souls to Heaven without my first persuading them to leave the earth?

But, you are thinking, *what of this momentous failure you have spoken of? Surely Diryevnye has learned what can befall without your help and grown more careful of its manners?*

Alas, no, for once the ghost left off haunting the townsfolk, all they remembered was my failure.

Does age alone curve your spine? I see you wondering. *Is it bitterness as well, or shame?*

I tell you now: I am beyond either. Let me relate the story, so you may understand.

It was late last November, after the third snowfall in two days. At dark they came on their sleds to get me from my supper. Galena Rajevsky had taken her own life, they said as they blew on their frozen hands. I frowned, for Galena had borne a stillborn six days earlier—a bastard, buried in the sinner's ground, without Father Josef to bless its passing. For mourners, there had been Galena, myself, and a pig-eyed brother who shoveled the dirt on.

The Rajevskys looked up angrily as I crossed their threshold, as if Galena's suicide were my doing. I saw at once that it wasn't her loss which grieved them, but this second scandal, likely to remain fresh even longer than the first. The Rajevskys were one of Diryevnye's richest families—Anton Rajevsky owned half the soil the town was built on—and they chafed at being kept from their usual ostentation by the closed coffin in their parlor.

A handful of relatives and neighbors trickled in as the night wore on, but still the Rajevskys remained sullen. Anxiously rubbing his hands, Anton would greet each new arrival, while his wife sat stony-faced with her two daughters-in-law. Meanwhile, her sons—Alexei, the eldest; Semyon, the pig-eyed one; and Mikhail, the blond—paced nervously behind their mother's green settee. Once or twice, a servant went round with spice cakes and *blinchiki,* or black tea from the samovar. No one fawned over Anton or tried to curry favor with his wife, though they were delighted with the Rajevskys' disgrace.

Just before eleven, Galena appeared. Her once-black hair was as bridal tulle, and her eyes blazed like stars.

I held up my hand at her approach, and she paused, looking so deeply into me I forgot for a moment who I was. I felt myself drowning in her sorrow, her rage. If I have said the dead return because they are lost, and only need to be pointed at the portals of the afterlife, it was not true in her case. She had come with unfinished business.

Before I could find my tongue, she glanced away from me to accost her family and neighbors.

"I humbled myself to beg," she said, in her voice that was both a sigh and a heel on broken glass. "Still you refused mercy for my babe."

No one replied; neither her mother, whose lips had frozen in a nervous half-smile; nor Alexei, who gave money to the church and so had Father Josef's ear. All around me were ghosts, drained bloodless by their terror.

"Now it is I who will not forgive," she finished, and her fellow ghosts uttered little cries of dismay.

"But what is this?" I admonished. "If you bind yourself

to vengeance, you will spend eternity alone, while your babe goes uncomforted."

"When they condemned Marah's soul, they saw to it she would never know comfort!"

"Diryevnye has judged her cruelly, in truth. But who is to say Heaven will do the same? Marah's soul is innocent, after all."

"She was never baptized, and now she lies in unconsecrated ground!" hissed Galena. "How can Heaven open its gates to her? Besides, I have heard her crying. . . ."

"What is it you want, then?" I asked gently.

She held my gaze again, though this time there was only infinite longing in her eyes. "Tell them to give Marah a proper burial. Then I will go."

"But you will never join her in Heaven; your suicide has condemned you," I pointed out.

"At least Marah may find the peace she deserves."

I turned to my employers. "She has made her proposal. It seems reasonable enough."

Alexei hastened to my side, tugging at his collar. "Such things are not so easily arranged," he whispered in my ear, glancing up to see if Galena overheard.

She threw back her head and laughed, her hair tumbling about her like the mist at Kolyma Falls. Then she swooped down at him so suddenly he screamed, only to chuck him beneath the chin almost tenderly. "You were always such a buffoon, Alexei, much better suited to cards and drink than the pretense of God-fearing ways. Now, if you can buy your way out of hellfire, then surely there is hope for my Marah."

Alexei's eyelids fluttered, and I was certain he would faint. But Galena turned her attention from him to the others in the room. Uncle Vassily, the Danilovs and Gronskys, Olga Spitsyn and her crippled father. Galena looked long at each of them, her vaporous smile falsely sweet, then pretended to search for Semyon and Mikhail, who had abandoned their post behind their mother to stand whispering at the samovar.

"There you are!" she trilled, turning on them so swiftly that Mikhail broke out in sobs. "But what's this, Mischa? A grown man like you crying? For shame; think of all those times, not so long ago, when you and Semyon came to my room and amused yourselves beneath the nightclothes. Why, I never made a sound, though I wept inwardly for my chastity."

Next she drifted over to Mikhail's wife, trembling against Mrs. Rajevsky on the green settee. "Don't fret, Irina, for your husband has always had luck at concealing his debaucheries. He will never make a scandal for you."

"Stop!" cried Mrs. Rajevsky then, pausing briefly to compose herself; still the corners of her mouth twitched from time to time. "You must stop trying to bully us, Galena. It is unseemly."

"As was my swollen belly, Mother? Is that why you locked me in my room for six months, to spare our neighbors' eyes the offense?"

"We were thinking what to do. . . ." put in Anton Rajevsky, haltingly.

"For six months?" Galena's voice cracked with fury, the explosion of embers in a hearth. "This time, Father, you must think more quickly!"

"Galena is right," I said. "If she refuses to go from us by daybreak, the portals of the afterlife will close to her forever."

"And I will torment you twice that long!" Galena shrieked at them.

They all shrank into themselves again, except for Alexei, who had disappeared into a back room. Now he swaggered out, a tumbler of vodka in his hand. Avoiding Galena's eyes, he drawled, "Even if we gave Marah a Christian burial, how would we mark the gravestone? Her father's name is a *secret*." And he put a comic finger to his lips.

"It was Arpad," said Galena, to a rising chorus of gasps. "Arpad! Why should I protect him any longer? He swore to be my husband, then ran off when I quickened. No doubt he is in Balshoygrad this very moment, drinking and whoring on the proceeds from the Rajevsky silver. Yes! It was he who stole it, Father, and I guessed it months ago!"

Alexei hiccoughed. "Well, that's easy, then! Have someone talk to Arpad—if he allows he promised to marry her, then Galena's only half the slut we thought, and Father Josef may reconsider."

Stout Uncle Vassily cleared his throat and stood. "Is it true you were betrothed, Galena? Can this be proved?" he asked, in his best magisterial tone.

Galena turned her cold eyes on him, as if to say *Are we in a court of law?* and he crumpled meekly into his chair. "Why not go to Balshoygrad and ask Arpad yourself, Uncle? He is a bold enough sinner to brag of his treachery outright."

"Why trouble ourselves," slurred Alexei. "We'll send the deathwatcher. Let him earn his keep for once."

Heads began nodding eagerly, until I pointed out that no one, let alone an old man like me, could travel thirty snowbound miles and back by dawn. Even if I could, how would I find Arpad, assuming he was there? Then, Father Josef needed to be summoned, and Marah's tiny coffin had to be dug up and reburied in the churchyard. They would have to take Galena at her word, however they questioned it, or else steel themselves to biding forever with her ghost.

Cowards that they are, still they chose the latter. And, despite their waxen faces, I think Galena took it worst; as the neighbors began to leave, having lost their taste for gloating, she turned on me the desperate eyes of a drowning child. For all her spitefulness and threats, who would suffer as much as she?

The rest of the night passed in silence, until one by one the lamps sputtered out. By this time, only Galena's father and brothers remained, together with Andrei Danilov, who had agreed to help with the coffin. Even her mother had gone off to sleep, so it was left to me to try and console her.

"At least you will lie beside your Marah," I pointed out, but I think she was no longer listening.

The morning of the burial was a bitter one, its sharp winds laced with snow. Another week or two and the ground would freeze to iron, refuse to yield way for a coffin. We tramped after the sled, watching the white flags of breath rise up from deep inside our hoods. Like us, Galena refrained from speech, her form shimmering in and out of the snow flurries. Though always we felt her in our midst, we rarely knew where to find her.

They buried her next to Marah, in the shadow of a skeletal birch. The sinner's burying ground lies well outside the churchyard, and yet I thought I spied bald Father Josef peering out at us through a chancel window. Had someone told him Diryevnye had a ghost? Perhaps.

As they finished patting down her shallow grave, Galena knelt by the clutch of white stones, mostly sunk in snow, which was all that remained visible of Marah's tiny plot. Then I heard it, the faint cry, so like any newborn's, if a thousand times more desolate. And I understood the depth of my failure.

"Each of you must take a different path home," I instructed Galena's family as they turned to go, "and walk in as roundabout a way as possible. Otherwise, it will be easy for Galena to follow you. If you confuse her enough, she may be forced to return here, and her ghost will not trouble you. Go, now, and quickly—it is your only chance!"

I spoke vigorously, as if a happy outcome were certain, just so they would take their frightened eyes from me. It was not that my scorn for them had led me to indifference at their fate; through the decades of sitting deathwatches, my heart has grown heavy with an almost blind compassion. But I felt a terrible sense of unease, and wanted no one there to witness it. I had given them the best advice I could, in any event, and proceeded alone to the empty stone church.

It was no longer empty when I entered it: she had gone in before me, and came wafting out from the altar like a cloud of incense. I noticed for the first time how you could tell, even now, that her hair had been jet-black, its pallor misleading, like that of obsidian bleached by moonlight.

She caught my eyes, and I felt myself swimming in darkness.

"Why have you come here?" I demanded.

"I have chosen you to free me," she said, and drifted so close the scent of death was in my nostrils. It was not decaying flesh which I smelled, of course, but something far less noisome, like the damp spice of the trodden leaves of autumn. It filled me with a sweet melancholy, yet I shuddered to inhale it.

"Why not free yourself?" I countered. "I cannot believe that hellfire awaits you, when you have suffered an agony already. We have laid your bed for you. Go to it and be at peace!"

She shook her head. "How can I think of peace when my poor Marah has none? She sleeps in unconsecrated ground; that must not be! You have heard her crying. If you prove my good name, they will give her a proper burial."

"It may be that I cannot."

"Then at least convince them not to punish an innocent babe for its mother's sins!" The wind of her voice swept through me, and she seemed to grow larger, a billowing cloud.

Then she was gone.

How could I refuse her, knowing that she had chosen sin not from vengefulness but from devotion to her child? Ah, but I did, much as I longed to ease her suffering. A chill gripped me that very night, left me mute and shivering, helpless to do more than the simplest tasks. I sat three weeks at my fire, staring, seeing in the flames a black-haired maiden, one who might have roused me long ago, when I cared for such things. Impassive, I watched her flickering and dancing, often on the verge of pronouncing her name. Then at last she paled to the color of mist and my ancient blood began to boil.

Even when the chill had passed from me, I remained feeble for some time; it is a wonder I kept myself from starvation—or worse—that winter.

So it was that the first thaw came before I had word of Galena again—indeed, before I so much as remembered her appeal to me in the empty church.

Only then did I learn that Diryevnye had passed a difficult winter itself. All through it, Galena had been fully as vengeful as she'd promised. She'd blown her parents' windows wide each midnight, startled Alexei at his gambling, and caressed Semyon and Mikhail obscenely as they slept. Soon all the Rajevskys were haggard and dark-eyed. The town fared little better, never able to sit through an entire Mass without Galena appearing at the altar, lewdly stroking Father Josef's bald crown while he stood there stammering.

Karl Basayev, Ziv's nephew, reported all this to me when I'd recovered enough to haul my cart to his shop in town; my last sack of potatoes had finally gone limp.

"Does she plague them still?" I asked, surprised to find Karl, a particularly superstitious fellow, so cheerful on the subject.

He shook his head. "They almost sent for you—whether for your help or to drive a stake through your heart, I couldn't tell. Luckily, no one's died since Galena—that would have forced matters, no? But then she stopped coming, just like that. Now all she haunts is her bastard's grave, according to Nikolai Soltsyn, who's been tending the churchyard."

I set my kopeks on his counter and returned home. That evening, just before dusk, I went to the sinner's burying ground. As the light deepened to indigo she appeared, kneeling by the clutch of stones over Marah's grave. I blinked, uncertain of what had just happened; perhaps it was a trick of my eye and she'd been kneeling there all along.

Soon enough, things took on the look of a nightly visit—a kind of sacrament, even. The moon rose; Galena clawed at herself and moaned into the wind. The first stars brightened; she began to writhe with the force of her sorrow, her cloud of hair tossing, pale fists beating the air. When I tried to speak with her, she ignored my approach. I saw the angry glint in her eye, though, and knew it was meant for me.

Then, with the dawn, she keened a last time to the

chalky stars, and vanished herself. I rode for Balshoygrad that morning.

What can have been your purpose? you scoff. *For whatever reason, she had already begun to fade.*

That was my purpose, then. Let the others celebrate her evaporating like fog; let them smile when they had to strain to hear her weeping. To me her form was as bright, her voice as heart-rending, as ever. She hadn't changed; it was Diryevnye which had wearied of her. Who would have thought a ghost could be neglected, forgotten, much as the living? Certainly not I, mad Serge, the deathwatcher. And I could not abide it.

After three days' trudge through mud and melting snow, I reached the spires and domes of Balshoygrad. I had visited once before, forty-one years before, to be precise. Then, too, it was the dead who had spurred my visit. I suppose I had been touched for the first time by their anguish, and sought to lose myself in the mobs of the living. I found the city so filthy and brawling a place on that occasion, however, that even my barren life in Diryevnye seemed preferable. Today it was no different, though I viewed my surroundings as if from afar, some vaguely unpleasant scene from a former life.

No matter if half the time I forgot it was him I searched for, I found Arpad almost upon arriving. After choosing lodgings and settling with the hosteler, I decided to brave the public room, for the chill and damp of the ride were yet with me, and I fancied nothing so much as a tumbler of hot *kumiss*.

They ladled the frothing stuff out for me, and I hunched into a corner, letting the pungent steam moisten my brow and beard. As I downed one gulp, then another, I called to mind everything I knew of this Arpad—for I had scarcely dealt with him, and that a good two years ago. He had been a swarthy giant, I remembered, with the habit of pulling his cap down over his ears as he chuckled richly and avoided one's eyes. It had been an odd sound, that laugh of his, both generous and sly, like the eruption of mirth ringing in my ears at present. I clapped down my empty tumbler with a start and looked round; behind me, seizing a small red-haired man by the shoulders, was Arpad. He gave the red-haired man a hearty shake, his chest rumbling with amusement, before releasing him and retuning to his *kvass*. The red-haired man looked uncertain for a moment, vaguely flattered by Arpad's attention, but also alarmed by his unconscious strength.

As I approached Arpad's table I understood of a sudden why Galena might have given her heart to him. He was like the princes in children's storybooks, with their black curling beards and sapphire eyes. In his fur-trimmed cap and embroidered vest, he looked both robust and worldly, a man who has never known doubt.

He blanched when he saw me.

I frowned in bewilderment, then remembered my gauntness and white beard, my dark, worn overcoat. Perhaps I looked to him like the figure of imminent Death; it amused me to believe so.

When I fixed Arpad's eyes again, he had eased back into his air of bravado. With a clap on the back, he sent the red-haired man off in search of more drink. "Get some for our friend, too," he called after, indicating me.

I made no response to his overture, so he added, "You are a long way from home, deathwatcher. Better take care you don't sicken here; there would be no one in Balshoygrad to mourn your passing. No one but me, that is."

By these words I knew Galena had spoken the truth. He had wronged her grievously, and, suspecting I had come on her behalf—he must have gotten word that his child had been stillborn—sought to warn me not to meddle with him. Still I said nothing, even when the red-haired man returned and attempted to press a metal tumbler of *kvass* into my hand.

I stood in place, unmoving.

Arpad's brow began to glisten with sweat. Chuckling, he pulled his cap down over his ears and avoided my gaze. For once, it was more than duplicity which drove him.

"All right, then!" he shouted finally. "What is it you want?"

I explained.

"*Ach*, I knew she would come to a bad end. Dolt of a woman, thinking I would play at house with her when the brat was born. Though she was a sweet enough morsel before all that," he added, reflectively.

The red-haired man was staring at us both, wide-eyed, shaking in his boots, like as not. Arpad noticed him and cuffed him about the ears.

"Bring me a quill and paper and then be off with you!" he growled, and the man obeyed him as though he were a mere serving boy.

Arpad scratched at the paper when it came, his hand trembling with agitation or drunkenness, his eyes bright when he looked up at me afterward. "It makes little difference if you know the truth," he boasted, as Galena had said he would, "since I'll be off by the time anyone comes to look for me. But here, give Galena's mother this, for a less old-fashioned set of silver." And, reaching into his money-pouch, he tossed me three rubles.

Three days later, I held up Arpad's confession for Diryevnye's elders to see. Tearing it from my hands, they bent their heads over it a while, making little grunting noises and raising their brows at one another. When they were done, they eyed me warily and smiled.

"But this changes nothing," shrugged Boris Karpavich.

"No," concurred Lev Ternyinko. "Arpad never wed Galena, hence the Rajevsky infant is still a bastard."

I appealed to Galena's Uncle Vassily, who had shown such interest in proof of her betrothal, not so long ago. "Surely Galena deserves justice, now that the truth is known."

Vassily went red, then cleared his throat. "Justice? Why, yes, Galena deserves that. If Arpad returns to Diryevnye, he will be dealt with most severely. As for the rest of it, however"—here he cleared his throat again—"I do not see that justice has been miscarried."

Toward evening, shovel in hand, I paid a visit to two graves in the shadow of a birch bristling with new buds. *Marah's casket is so tiny,* I told myself, *one pallbearer alone may tend to it.*

The light was the deep pure blue of a match flame; as it went out, I noticed Father Josef's face in a window and recalled that I had no authority to break ground in the churchyard. I might raise Marah from one resting-place, but I could not sink her in the other. Then Galena's form coalesced before me, and I threw caution to the wind.

First, though, I lay down my shovel and knelt beside her to explain how things had turned. "We need no blessing to proceed," I whispered, "if that blessing comes from the mouths of arrant hypocrites."

She made no visible response; instead, she began to bat her breast and moan, as if helpless to do otherwise. But I sensed her listening to my words, her passionate assent with them.

I had thrust the shovel blade into the muddy earth

Illustrated by Oleg Dergatchov

but once, when Nikolai Soltsyn, the caretaker, came to stop me. I allowed myself to be led off; what was the point in resisting? But I called back over a shoulder as I went, advising Galena to rest assured Heaven saw the truth Diryevnye refused to. I was half across the field by then, but I could have sworn she turned her head toward me and smiled.

She appeared once or twice more in the following month, waking Father Josef or Nikolai with the echo of her weeping. But by the time the birch over her grave had donned its coat of green, she lay in unbroken silence. At least her mourning was at an end; either that, or the weight of her grief pressed so it kept her from rising.

She has not done with haunting me, though, and my dreams are full of black hair and the fragrance of new-fallen snow. We twine our limbs together, hers cool as mist, mine gaunt with age. The comely ghost and the skeleton. Even in my waking hours I see our coupling in my mind, and know the deathwatcher at my funeral will struggle to coax me to sleep. . . .

THE UNHAPPY GOLEM
OF RABBI LEITCH

Written by
Russell William Asplund

Illustrated by
Heidi Taillefer

About the Author

Russell was born in Edmonton, Alberta, and despite moving to the U.S. at the age of three, did not become an American citizen until last year. He says that the science fiction fan in him always enjoyed being a government-certified resident "alien."

By the time he reached the second grade, he knew he wanted to be a science fiction writer.

In college, at Brigham Young University, he waffled between studying computer science and English. It was at BYU that he heard about the campus SF magazine, The Leading Edge. While working as executive editor on the magazine he met and fell in love with his wife, Stephanie Rummler Asplund. He credits his success in part to marrying a good copy editor.

Russell and his wife helped form a rock band that played locally in Utah for several years, receiving good reviews from music critics for its decidedly "science fiction" sound. Many *of the songs and lyrics were written by Russell. Currently Russell works as a multimedia programmer, is an active member of the writing group Pilgrimage (along with fellow contest winners Scott Everett Bronson and Grant Avery Morgan), and is the father of three children.*

He read the first WOTF anthology years ago and began entering the contest, climbing the ladder from quarter-finalist to semifinalist, to finalist. He says he will never forget the first time he got a handwritten critique from Algis Budrys—that alone was enough to keep him writing for another two years. With the story you are about to read, he hit paydirt—garnering a first-place award and the chance to compete for the grand prize.

About the Illustrator

Like many artists, Heidi Taillefer began to draw at age two and never gave up. In fact, her parents encouraged her to draw—having her take art classes two hours a week from the time she was ten till she reached eighteen. This is the extent of her formal training.

At age twenty-two, she left college to pursue a career in art. Her work has recently been published in Airbrush Action Magazine, *and in the Spring issue of* Watercolor '95. *Heidi's next major project is a museum exhibit at the McAllen International Museum of Art and Science in McAllen, Texas.*

Heidi says that her personal tastes are a bit eccentric. She's fond of what happens after dark—the different, the bizarre, and the subversive. Her apartment in Montreal, Canada, is a miniature museum of collected masks, machetes, whips, skulls, and musical instruments. She likes to travel to dirty places, and has spent a good amount of time hiking alone in the Yukon and South America.

Golem." The old man's voice was soft, and dry as the Pharaoh's fields in Joseph's dreams, but it carried through the quiet house. "Golem, I need water."

The golem rustled where it lay in the kitchen corner. It had not been asleep—it did not need sleep as a man would—but it had been resting, watching the forest through the big kitchen window and dreaming in its own slow way. It could number each budding leaf on the oak and ash outside, knew every bird and squirrel sheltered among their branches. Left on its own the golem would stare for days on end, but at the sound of its master's voice it rose woodenly. Once it had been part of the forest, before Rabbi Leitch had carved it from the trunk of a fallen oak, shaping it lovingly into the form of a man and giving it life through the power of his faith and the holy name carved on its forehead.

It heard the old man coughing in bed, and hurried to fill a cup with water. The Rabbi was ill, though he would not call for a physician. "I will live or die as the Lord wills," he said. The golem hurried up the stairs, trying not to spill.

It was not large, for a golem—not much larger than a tall man. It had to duck only slightly to enter the darkened room where the Rabbi lay. The air was warm and humid, and had the stale smell of a room that had been closed for far too long. These days the Rabbi always felt

cold, and he would not let the golem open the windows
to let in fresh air. The Rabbi lay in the center of the room,
his wasted body dwarfed by the large bed. He looked
brittle and frail, but his eyes were still bright and he
smiled weakly at the golem.

The golem gently put the cup into the old man's
hands. He lifted it shakily to his lips, spilling some
water on his long white beard. "Thank you, my friend.
You are a loyal servant. Now bring me my books."

The golem did as the Rabbi asked, taking the old
man his beloved texts. The room was full of books, some
large and ornate, gilded with precious metals, others
small and poorly bound, but the Rabbi loved them all,
and the knowledge they contained. He was devout, and
he had been blessed to keep his eyesight. He still read
the Holy Word morning and night, and studied the
works of the great Cabalists when his strength permitted.
It was in these books that he had learned the secret of
animating the golem those many years ago.

"I have never given you a name," the Rabbi said as
the golem set the books by his bed. "The golems in the
texts all have names—Joseph or Isaac. Why haven't I
given you a name? Or have I?" The old man glanced
worriedly about the room, as if he could find the forgotten
memory on a shelf or hidden under a pile of blankets.
"Have I given you a name and just forgotten?"

The golem shook its wooden head. It could not
speak, but the Rabbi often spoke to it, and he understood many of the golem's gestures. The Rabbi had
lived alone for many years, since his wife had died.
They never had children, and the Rabbi preferred the
company of books to the prattle of strangers.
Occasionally, someone from the village came to ask a
question on a point of Law, or some other advice, but
they never stayed long, and the Rabbi liked it that way.

"I should have given you a name," the Rabbi said, choosing a small, leather-bound book from the pile. He tried to read, but his body was racked with coughs and he could not hold the book still. He looked back at the golem. "There is much I should have done for you. I should have given you a voice, but I valued my silence too much; this was selfish. I was a clumsy builder.

"Know that I will soon die, and return to God. When I die, you must go to Rabbi Meltzer, in the city. He will know how to make you whole. He is very wise. He will finish what I could not; he will make you a man."

The golem sat quietly at his side; it had heard the Rabbi speak like this many times. In truth it did not miss having a voice, although it may have once. When it was young it might have wished to be a man. But if so, that memory was gone with the termites and the dry rot. It had watched the Rabbi grow frail and gray, his limbs bent and gnarled like an old apple tree, had seen him confined to his bed, his strength gone.

What the golem wanted, secretly, in its dreams, was to be a tree, as it had been before Rabbi Leitch carved it and prayed it into being. Before the holy name on its forehead had given it life. Trees were strong and silent and long of life. Or if not a tree, a table or a chair—sturdy and reliable, passed down from generation to generation. But the Rabbi never asked, and the golem would not have known how to answer if he did.

The Rabbi sank into his pillow, breathing heavily. The golem moved to take the book from the Rabbi's hands, but he held tight. "Leave me my books, please."

The golem released the book and the old man lay back, clutching the book to his chest. His skin was ashen, and the golem heard him muttering a prayer under his breath. After a while he seemed to rest comfortably, and the golem thought he slept. It moved to return to the kitchen.

"Wait." The old man sat up in bed. The golem had never known him when he was young, but he remembered the Rabbi as a strong man of middle age, strong enough to carry in the trunk of a tree and carve it single-handedly into the shape of a man. For the first time in many years, the Rabbi resembled that man.

"The powers of Heaven are not granted lightly. I did not think, when I ran across the old texts—I was merely lonely, so I created you. But a golem, such a thing must have a purpose. More purpose than merely a companion to an aging hermit. Come to me." The golem moved closer to the bed. "Lean down, lean down."

The golem did as instructed. The old man took its head in his bony hands and stared closely at the golem's face. "Yes," he said at last. "It is as I thought. You must promise me, golem, to go to Rabbi Meltzer in the city. You must take my body there and give it to his care, for I will not last the night. He will give you a voice, and you must tell him the holy name carved upon your forehead. Will you promise me this?"

The golem did not answer right away. It had heard much of Rabbi Meltzer, from both its master and those who visited occasionally. Rabbi Meltzer was a powerful and holy man who could do what Rabbi Leitch said, but the golem did not want to be a man. The golem had not really thought of what it would do when its master died—perhaps just sit in the corner as if its master were away. But Rabbi Leitch still stared up at it imploring, his eyes bright and full of life, and the golem had been created to follow his orders.

"Promise me," the old man said. "Promise you will take my body to Rabbi Meltzer."

The golem nodded; this much it could promise. Perhaps Rabbi Meltzer would not think to give it a voice or finish what its master had started. The golem did not want any more purpose to its existence. It was enough for a chair to merely be a chair; no one asked a cutting block why it had been created.

But the golem would take its master's body to the city.

The Rabbi then explained the true pronunciation of the holy name that had given the golem life. He repeated it only once, but it was enough. Even the golem knew such a word was not given lightly, and it would not forget. The old man lay down then, a smile on his face. He did not wake again. By morning he was dead.

The golem cradled the Rabbi's body gently in its arms and carried him down to the kitchen. The sky through the window was bright and clear, the clouds still touched with pink from the rising sun. It was the month of Adar, and the trees were just beginning to bud. They had more leaves today than yesterday, and the golem knew there would be more tomorrow. A robin sang and a jay called from somewhere high in the trees. It had never occurred to the golem that it had feelings, but suddenly it felt very lonely. It held the old man tight to its wooden chest and hung its head. It stayed this way as morning passed.

It had promised to go to the city, and so it would. When the sun reached its peak, the golem set the old man down gently on the kitchen floor. Rabbi Leitch had loved his house, and the golem prepared it as if for a long journey. It latched the windows and put out any food that would spoil for the birds and wild animals. It changed the linens and made the bed, all as Rabbi Leitch had taught it.

When all was in order the golem lifted the Rabbi's body gently from the floor and walked to the door. It took one last look around the kitchen, feeling troubled. It knew the small home and the surrounding woods as well as it knew itself. They were part of the golem, its roots and branches. Everything seemed to be in place and the golem needed little for its journey, but it felt it had forgotten something. The golem had never traveled before, although it had helped its master pack on the few occasions he journeyed to the city. Even now the golem did not wish to leave, but the Rabbi's body lay heavy in its arms, and it knew that it must keep its promise.

Its master's books—that was what it had forgotten. The Rabbi never traveled without at least a bound copy of the Torah and his well-worn Talmud; he often carried several books of commentary as well. Certainly the Rabbi would not need them this trip, but it seemed wrong to leave them. The golem set the body down once again and fetched the books and a bag to carry them in. Perhaps Rabbi Meltzer would find them useful.

The golem slung the heavy bag across its shoulders and lifted its master's body once again. It locked the door behind it and made its way through the small garden. The soil here was loose and rich; the golem could feel it through its feet. Normally it would be helping Rabbi Leitch plant the garden now, with vegetables and herbs and a few scattered flowers. The bulbs they had planted last fall bloomed near the small fence. It took the golem a moment to gather its courage enough to walk through the gate and out to the road that led to the city.

It was a small road, poorly traveled, little more than two ruts that ran between the city and some more distant

land. The golem paused, remembering which way it had
seen its master travel.

The city was not far, but it seemed a long way to the
golem. Each step took it farther from what it knew. It felt
the small changes—the air was slightly warmer, the soil
sandier. The trees still grew tall and thick, and it paused
often to look up at them, knowing instinctively what
was oak and what was ash. It walked all day, slowly but
tirelessly, as the trees of the forest gave way first to
plowed fields, then small houses, and finally, as evening
fell, to the city itself.

It did not know the way to Rabbi Meltzer's home,
nor could it ask. So it made its way toward the city
square in hopes that word of its arrival might reach the
holy man, and he would come.

The ground felt wrong beneath the golem's feet,
packed so hard that only the heartiest of weeds sprung
up. The few trees grew stunted and yellow, and the air
smelled of smoke and humanity. Although it was late,
many people still walked the streets, and they stopped
to stare at the golem. Many Christians who saw it fled,
but the Jews seemed simply curious at first.

"Who is he carrying?" one asked.

"It looks like old Rabbi Leitch. He does not look
well," someone answered.

"Not well at all," said another. They began to follow
the golem, calling out to Rabbi Leitch.

The golem walked on, ignoring the growing crowd.
The buildings grew taller the deeper it went into the city,
until many were as tall as trees in the forest. Everything
was gray and stone; nothing grew here. The golem kept
to the largest streets, passing through the ghettoes and
into the commercial district where signs identified various shops. Rabbi Leitch had taught it to read some

Hebrew, but the signs were in a language it did not understand.

It had not imagined there would be so many people. There were Orthodox Jews, with long beards and fringed shawls; young professionals in high-collared suits; merchants; shopkeepers; Christians of every make and size. The golem walked on, stiff with fear, as the people stared.

"He's dead," a young woman said, pointing to the Rabbi still cradled in the golem's arms. "The monster has killed him!"

Several people screamed and the golem tried to walk faster.

How could they think it had killed Rabbi Leitch? For the first time it almost began to wish the Rabbi had given it the gift of speech. Why had he sent the golem to the city, if this was how it was to be greeted? And how would it find Rabbi Meltzer?

The avenue opened into a wide square where several streets met around a small, grassy park. Even the grass looked ill-nourished but at least it was alive. The golem hurried to it. A large clock tower looked over the city from one corner of the square. It struck the hour as the golem entered, the low chime ringing as mechanical saints circled the tower. The golem paused, looking left and right, wondering which way to go, and found itself surrounded. The crowd did not dare come too close; they circled at a distance. The golem searched desperately for someone who might be the Rabbi.

Two young toughs came forward. "Come, monster, give us the body."

The golem shook its head. It would be so easy to give the body to the crowd. Surely they would see that Rabbi Leitch was given a proper burial, but the golem had made a promise. It would deliver its master's body to Rabbi Meltzer, then it would leave the city and never come back.

Someone in the crowd began to cry and a few still called futilely to Rabbi Leitch. One of the toughs, a large Jew of dark complexion, handed his jacket to a neighbor and came forward. He barely reached the golem's shoulders, but he put his hands up like a wrestler.

"Give me the body. It is enough that you have killed a good man; at least let us bury him!" The golem shook its head again and tried to back away, but had nowhere to go. The large man's friend lunged and grabbed the golem's arm, trying to pull it away from the body. The large man moved in and took a swing; his fist hit the golem in the chest with a sickening crack.

The man screamed in pain. His friend pulled, but the golem's arm did not even budge. The crowd muttered angrily and drew in closer. The golem looked about in confusion and shook its arm, sending the man flying into the crowd. Whistles blew from across the square as the city guard arrived, mounted on horses. Darkness was falling fast, and the guards carried torches.

The golem began to panic. Little could hurt it, but its fear of fire was instinctive and overwhelming. Even when Rabbi Leitch lit a small fire, the golem felt nervous. Who knew what the guards would do?

"There he is," one guardsman shouted, and the horses pushed their way through the crowd. The golem ran, barreling its way through the people. It was not fast, but the crowd made it hard for the horses to pass.

It had no idea where to go, so it simply ran, followed by shouts of "monster" and "murderer." Some in the crowd threw rocks that bounced harmlessly off the golem, but it hunched over to protect its master's body.

It ran down dark streets, and alleys that smelled of rotting garbage, wherever it could spot an opening. It ran past taverns full of light and laughter, past laundries shut for the night, past stalls for kosher meats and cheap trinkets of copper and silver. Finally, near the Jewish cemetery, the golem turned down the wrong alley.

The golem whirled when it saw the dead end. The crowd watched from outside the alley as the guardsmen dismounted and stepped in cautiously, holding torches in front of them. The flames cast flickering shadows on the dark stone, and the golem tried to press itself tighter against the wall. When they saw the golem back away, the guards began to poke flames at it. The crowd cheered and laughed as the golem tried to dodge the torches while protecting its master's body.

"What is going on here?" A small man stepped forward, his voice carrying across the crowd. He wore a dark robe, and his beard hung almost to his waist. His eyes caught the flame of the torches. The mob quieted instantly. The guards poked at the golem a few more times, but the small man stared at them until they turned around. "I asked, what is going on? Will no one tell me?"

"We have caught a monster." The captain of the guard stepped forward. He was as tall and blond as the other was short and dark, and he was dressed like a Cossack in high black boots and loose-fitting shirt. "It looks like he has killed one of your Jews. Might have got more, if we had not been so quick to respond."

"A monster?" The small man walked deeper into the alley and eyed the golem critically. Several in the crowd called out to support the claim. The small man turned and looked at them sharply. "A monster? Did none of you think to look closely? What kind of monster would have the holy name engraved on its forehead?"

He turned back. "This is no monster; this is a golem.
And that," he said pointing to the body, "if I am not mistaken, is Rabbi Leitch."

The golem nodded, holding out the body. The crowd
murmured quietly, not quite sure what to make of the
small man's pronouncement. The city guard looked to
their captain, anxious to be about their work, but the
captain just shrugged.

The small man walked closer. "Fine workmanship—
I would expect as much from Rabbi Leitch. Greetings,
golem. I am Rabbi Solomon Meltzer. What may we do
for you?"

That was what the golem had been waiting to hear. It
knelt near the Rabbi's feet and laid the body of Rabbi
Leitch down carefully. Then it rose and walked out of
the alley. The city guard moved to catch it, but the small
man said quietly, "Let him go," as he knelt by the body.

The crowd parted as the golem passed. It began running as fast as its wooden legs could manage through
the crowd, down the street and out of the city.

It ran all night, until it reached the peace and safety
of the trees, until the earth once again felt alive and com-
forting beneath its feet. It sat against the trunk of an old
oak and tried to think. The golem had never had to
worry about what to do next. It had done whatever its
master had told it—fetching water, preparing meals,
cooking and cleaning, while the old Rabbi studied the
Word of God. Now there was no one to tell it what to do.

The golem was tired. The ground felt soft with the
fallen leaves of last autumn, their smell warm and com-
forting. The golem rested its head against the tree, just
sitting, as the night faded into morning. The tree rose
green above the golem, a few blossoms still clinging

Illustrated by Heidi Taillefer

amid the new leaves. Almost the golem could imagine it was part of the tree, an outgrown root just sticking from the ground. It could feel life below it in the soil, and above it in the branches, and it dreamed of being rooted to this spot. Yet even in this fantasy the golem was not quite content.

The golem missed the sound of voices. Not the nightmare shouts of mobs in the city, but the quiet talk of Rabbi Leitch with one of his infrequent guests, arguing over some finer points of the Law, or asking some small favor, always acting pleasantly surprised when the golem complied.

A robin was feeding its young in a nest above; the golem could hear the angry squawk of the chicks, and it watched the mother as she flew away to find more food. Once a small squirrel ran across the golem's legs, chittering at it briefly. The golem wondered if it should go back to the house it had shared with Rabbi Leitch, but there was nothing there for it now.

"Come back here, you feathered demon!" The shout shattered the silence of the woods. A large white goose ran by, its wings flapping wildly, kicking up dirt and leaves behind it. It honked as it passed the golem, then it was gone. The golem heard footsteps.

"Come back here!" The man came into view, shaking his fist at the retreating goose. He was stout, big-boned and obviously well fed. He breathed heavily. "I should have eaten you, do you hear me? I should have roasted you years ago."

He stopped to catch his breath, resting his hands on his knees. He wore the coarse fabric of a peasant farmer, though his clothes were neat and well sewn. His long beard and shawl marked him as a Jew. "Why do I bother," he said softly to himself, then yelled to the goose. "Why do I bother? There are plenty of others out here who would eat you. You would rather be eaten by a wolf? A complete stranger?"

The golem pulled its legs in closer to its chest. The man turned toward the tree with a big, friendly smile. "Hello," he said. The smile froze in his face when he saw the golem. The golem did not move, fearing a repeat of what happened in the city. The peasant stared, and when the golem didn't move, he took a small step closer.

"Hello there, wooden man." He took another step closer. "Did you move?" The golem tried to shut him out. It could feel the rough texture of the bark against its back, and it imagined that it too was covered, protected, rooted deep in the ground. Maybe if it sat still enough the man would leave. The peasant walked around it in a circle. "Who would leave a wooden man just sitting in the woods?"

There was a loud honk. The golem opened its eyes to see the goose standing at the edge of the clearing, its head cocked to one side. The peasant turned to it. "Just a minute, I've found something. If you want to be chased, you will have to wait."

"Look," he said turning back to the golem. "He must be Jewish. See, that is Hebrew on his forehead." He looked closer at the golem, as if he noticed that something had changed but could not decide what. He knelt by the golem. "Look, he is carrying a pack."

"May I open your pack, wooden man?" he asked. The goose waddled closer and honked again. When the golem did not answer, the peasant shrugged and opened the pack. He cried out with joy when he found the books. "Look! Look what he was carrying. He is a messenger from God, I tell you. Such beautiful copies of God's words, better than they have at the synagogue!"

The golem reached for the books and the peasant leaped away, dropping the pack. "You did move—I thought I saw you." The golem picked up the fallen books and placed them carefully in the pack. The peasant knelt down to help. "Please don't be angry. Those are lovely books; you must be a great scholar, Reb Wooden Man. Would you do me the honor of sharing my house?"

The golem looked up, surprised. In the city they had thought it a monster, and now this peasant thought it a scholar. But at least the peasant seemed friendly. The golem looked at the books. It could read a little Hebrew, but not much. Rabbi Leitch had loved these books, loved the knowledge they contained. He would not have wanted it lost.

The peasant watched the golem expectantly. It nodded its head slowly and stood. The peasant rose as well; he was not a small man, but the golem towered over him by a head. "Good, good. I have a farm not far from here. We will go there and you can tell me of the great things you have seen."

The golem shook its head. "You will not?" The peasant seemed to wilt. The golem shook its head; it had never been this difficult to talk to Rabbi Leitch. It pointed at its mouth and shook its head again. The peasant smiled. "Ah, you cannot talk. That's fine, I can talk enough for us both. Come this way."

He started to walk out of the clearing but was stopped by a loud honk. "My goose! I must catch my goose!" He turned around sharply and dove for the goose, but the goose dodged, and he fell to the ground. It waddled just out of reach and honked again.

The golem slowly and quietly circled around as the peasant rose, yelling at the goose to stay put. The goose was watching its master and did not notice the golem until it reached down with one large hand and picked up the goose. It fluttered and honked angrily as the golem handed it to the peasant.

"Thank you. See, I knew you were a messenger. Only a holy man could catch a demon like this so easily." The peasant held the goose comfortably in his arms. "Usually, it takes me all day to catch her."

As promised, it was not far to the peasant's farm. All the way there he chatted amiably to the golem, and sometimes to the goose as well. The farm was small—a few outbuildings, whitewashed and simple, but in good repair; a patch of garden, already planted with early peas; and pens for geese and goats. A small round woman waited at the door of the cottage and smiled when she saw them.

"Esther! Children! Come look what I have found," the peasant called. He walked to the pen and set the goose inside as several children poured from the house. The geese honked and the goats bleated and the children screamed and giggled. The riot of noise was as different from the peace of Rabbi Leitch's home as the city had been. But the golem did not find it threatening. The peasant threw his arms around his wife, then turned to the golem. The children circled around it, wide-eyed. "Children, this is Rabbi Wood. He helped me catch Pinochel."

"Did she get far this time, Papa?" a little girl asked.

He shook his head. "Not far, thanks to my new friend." He looked at the golem. "This is not the first time she has tried to run away. Some animals, they just don't like being penned up. But Pinochel is one of the children's favorites, so we go after her."

The goose stuck its head out between the slats of the

fence and honked. "This is Esther, my wife, and these are my children. Rachel and Rebecca, Joshua, Israel, and Daniel."

"What is he?" Joshua asked. His mother looked at him sharply.

"What is he? What does he look like?" his father asked. "He's . . . well, a wooden man, of course."

"A golem," Esther said, looking closely. "I think that he is a golem, like in the stories."

"I think he's a monster," Joshua said.

"No monster would be carrying what he has in his pack. Show them, Rabbi Wood. Show them your books."

The golem took off its pack and pulled out the copy of the Torah. It was a heavy book, with vellum pages and a thick cover of dark wood varnished to a high shine. Esther gasped a little when she saw it.

"No wonder you are Simon's friend. He cannot get enough of books, not that we can afford them. Sometimes I think that he would rather read than sleep. My husband, the Rabbi farmer. But where are our manners? Come inside!"

The cottage was smaller than Rabbi Leitch's house, but somehow they all fit in. The golem sat by a window in the kitchen as Esther prepared the evening meal. The children kept quiet at first, but as they got used to the golem they soon began to talk almost as much as their father. The golem sat and listened to the talk and the clanking of pots and pans, watching the children or staring out the window at the trees beyond. When the food was ready, Simon asked if he could see the Torah, and read a passage out loud before the meal began.

The golem helped clean after they ate. At first Esther wouldn't have it, but the golem was used to being a servant, not an honored guest. It ignored her complaints and simply started to carry away plates. She bowed to the inevitable and worked beside it.

They offered the golem a bed for the night. It tried to explain that it did not need a bed and would rather just stay in the kitchen. But it could not make itself understood, so they doubled up the girls and pushed a bed into a small room, just for Rabbi Wood. Somehow the name stuck, and they all came in to wish the golem a good night.

It lay down on the bed when they had gone. The headboards were rough pine, and the golem stared up, tracing the grain of the wood with its eyes. The bed was heavy and solid; the golem admired the workmanship, but it was not used to lying down. It got up and moved to the corner of the room, still looking at the bed. The golem imagined it was the bed, sitting in the children's bedroom, holding and cushioning the children through the night. It imagined them crawling in gratefully after a long day, or snuggling in on a cold night. It imagined what it would be like to be needed here, wanted here, and it found it did not want to leave the cottage.

The golem's thoughts were interrupted by a loud knocking at the cottage door. "Simon," someone yelled. "Simon, wake up." The golem rose and had almost reached the door when it remembered that this was not its master's house. Perhaps Simon's neighbors would not be as kind to the golem as Simon had been. The golem stepped back into its room as Simon walked to the door, dressed in a nightshirt.

"I'm coming, I'm coming," Simon said as he opened the door. "There are children in here, you know. Do you want to wake everyone?"

The golem stood perfectly still and watched through the door of its room. The peasant at the door looked visibly upset. The whiskers of his thin beard seemed to shake. "Come, Simon, you are needed in the city! We are all needed. There is a riot; some fear it will turn into a pogrom!"

"A riot? Is it bad?" Simon stepped back and pulled the old man in.

"A riot is never good; this you know."

"Sit down." Simon pulled a chair from the kitchen table and motioned the other to sit. "What is it this time? Another bad debt from the mayor?"

The man sat heavily. "Worse—there was a monster. Rabbi Meltzer made the city guard let it go, and it carried off some Christian children. They have the Rabbi in jail."

"How could Rabbi Meltzer make the city guard do anything? I have geese who weigh more than him." He waved down the man's reply. "I know, I know. It doesn't matter, as long as they believe it. Let me get dressed and we'll go see if there is anything to be done. Did anyone really see this monster?"

"Everyone saw it; even the Jews admit it. It was a wooden giant, ten feet tall. They say the Rabbi stared it down and chased it out of the city."

The golem saw Simon freeze and look over at the small room where it stood. Their eyes met briefly. The golem tried to understand, but it was not a quick thinker. How could they believe it had carried anyone away? They had watched it run out of town. It wondered what would happen when Simon said the monster was here. Would the riot stop when they took it in?

"Ten feet tall?" Simon said, hurrying into his bedroom. "You know how these things grow with the telling." He came back out, pulling on a pair of britches and tucking in his nightshirt. "I bet it was closer to eight. Come on, let's go."

The golem watched with confusion as the two men left the cottage. Surely Simon had realized that the golem was the cause of the riots. Why hadn't he told his friend?

"See, Mama? I told you he was a monster." The golem turned. Joshua stood at the door of his room, staring at the golem. Esther stood in her doorway, gazing at the door where the two men had left.

"Go to bed, Joshua." The boy started to argue, but his mother turned her gaze on him and he thought better of it. He went back into his room, closing the door behind.

Esther walked over and stared up at the golem. She stayed that way for a long time, just looking silently. "I hope my husband is right about you," she said at last and shook her head in resignation. "Where did you come from, Rabbi Wood? What do you want from us?"

The golem stood silently. It could not answer, even if it had a voice. How could any human understand what the golem wanted? Esther turned to her room, but stopped at the door to look back. "I will be watching you, Rabbi Wood. I hope you are our friend. But nothing will harm my family. Do you understand?"

The golem nodded slowly. "Stay in your room for now. We can't take a chance of anyone seeing you." She went into her bedroom and the golem stepped back into the small room the family had prepared for it. Why would they think it would harm the family? The desire to harm seemed to be a uniquely human trait. It sat in the corner waiting for morning, envying the bed.

Esther was already up and cooking breakfast when Simon returned, his face black from smoke and looking tired.

"Well?" Esther asked, setting a kettle of water to boil on the stove. The golem watched from its room.

"It could be worse," Simon said, falling into one of the chairs. "But not much. They are just holding the Rabbi for questioning. People are angry, though—ours *and* theirs. There were a few fires last night, a lot of shouting. But mostly it is still just talk—no one was hurt."

"What of the children?"

Simon snorted. "That would be hard to say, since no one seems to know who they are. No one has come forward to say that their children were stolen, or that this child is missing. But everyone seems to know that children were taken. It must be; there was a monster. There is even talk of the Blood Libel."

"Oh, no." His wife set down the pot she held and came to sit by him. It was one of the worst charges that could be brought against the Jews, and one of the most ridiculous. The golem had read about it many times, the belief that Jews used the blood of Christians, especially Christian children, in the Passover feast. It was so blatantly false it was hard to defend against. The accusation popped up whenever someone wanted to stir up trouble for the Jews.

"Where is Rabbi Wood?" Simon asked. His wife nodded toward the bedroom, and the golem stood and walked into the kitchen. "Ah, hello, my friend. You should see the trouble you have caused."

The golem hung its head sadly. "So, you think he is the monster, too," Esther said.

"Of course he is, unless he has a ten-foot-tall twin running around somewhere. But you did not steal away any children, did you Rabbi Wood?" The golem shook its head, but what did it matter? Like the Blood Libel, it was only what people thought that mattered. Rabbi Meltzer was in jail because of the golem. Innocent people were being hurt. But the golem had only been trying to keep its promise to its creator.

"What would happen if we turned him in?" Esther asked.

"Turned him in? How can you even say that?" Simon said. "Do you know who made him? They say he came in carrying the body of Rabbi Leitch. Do you think the Rabbi would have created a thing of evil?"

"I know he is not evil." Esther stood by the golem. "At least, he has not done what they say. But those in the city, they are our people. Do you think it would help?"

"I will not hear you talk like that. Do you see the mark on his forehead? To me, that means he is a Jew— he is our people. The Rabbi must have had a reason to create him, and who are we to stand in the way? Perhaps the Lord has sent him here for a reason."

Esther turned on her husband. "Perhaps he came to stop the riot. Perhaps that is the reason. Have you thought of that?"

"But he started the riot. Why create a golem to start a riot and then end it? It makes no sense. I will not turn him away."

Esther fell quiet for a moment, then hung her head. "You are my husband and I will do what you say. I will not turn the golem in."

She looked up. "But I will tell you this; if the golem came only to start a riot, then I say that he is a thing of evil, no matter who his creator. Even the Lord created evil along with the good. In a pogrom, *people* will die. He is only a piece of wood."

She picked up a basket and walked out the door, letting it slam behind her. Simon started to follow, then thought better. He turned to the golem. "Forgive her, she has lost family in the pogroms. Such things are a way of life here. She will come back in when she has fed the geese, and realize that it is not your fault."

The golem turned back to its room. "Only a piece of wood," she had said. The golem wished again that it were so. Maybe the riot was its fault. Perhaps its only purpose had been to deliver the body of Rabbi Leitch for a proper burial and after that it should simply have let them take it and do what they would.

The golem could hear Simon moving around, putting plates on the table. It smelled the warm bread cooking in the oven. Simon woke the children and they all poured into the kitchen, noisy and laughing. Here the riots seemed far away. The golem slumped by the bed. A large mirror sat across the room, and the golem looked at its reflection. Rabbi Leitch had created it well—its proportions were good, and the joints in its arms and legs cleverly fashioned to mimic a man's.

But it was all a fraud. The golem remained a piece of wood.

Only that wasn't true either. That was the curse that Rabbi Leitch had placed it under. It could no longer be just a tree, because it knew what it was like to be a man, but it could not be man, for it could not forget what it had been to be a tree.

Maybe there had been no purpose to its creation; maybe it had been a sin, an act of pride on the part of its maker for which the golem was doomed to suffer. Did its life matter?

The golem could not answer that question. It lived, whether it wanted to or not. Somehow giving up did not seem like the right answer, and it found it could not think of Rabbi Leitch as an evil man. It had been given life through the power of God; would such a thing be granted simply for the sake of pride? It looked in the mirror again and saw the mark on its forehead and raised one hand to touch it. The word came to its mind unbidden, the last word the Rabbi had spoken.

Perhaps it had not finished its purpose after all. The golem hadn't actually promised to do anything but deliver its master's body. How could it have done anything else? The crowd would not have simply stood by while Rabbi Meltzer gave it a voice. It tried to tell itself that it had done all it could, but its visage stared back from the mirror accusingly.

The golem heard the kitchen door open and the children greet their mother. It looked into the kitchen as Simon put his arms around his wife. "I should sleep," he said. "It was quiet when I left, but who knows what the night will bring?"

Esther leaned against him and nodded sadly. Could the golem stop the riots? If someone would tell it how, it would gladly try. Its master had been certain that it should talk to Rabbi Meltzer, but had he foreseen the riots? The golem looked again into the mirror. There was no one now to tell it what to do; it would have to decide. The mirror was framed with oak, and the golem came close and ran its hand along the frame. It looked again at the bed, and the wooden table in the kitchen. Their tasks were simple; they had a place and a purpose. They were part of the home.

The golem knew what its decision must be. It envied the chairs and tables and even the beams of the house, but the logs in the fire also served their purpose. They gave heat and warmth before they died. It would deliver its final message to Rabbi Meltzer.

The golem went into the kitchen. The children fell silent as it entered the room. Simon still stood with his wife, and they all watched as the golem walked past them to the books it had brought. It picked up all the books but one and handed them to Simon. The peasant took them, a confused look on his face. "Are you giving me these?"

The golem did not bother to answer; no one ever understood it when it tried. It picked up the book it had left—a copy of the works of Rabbi Adam, where Rabbi Leitch had first learned the secrets of making a golem. Perhaps Rabbi Meltzer would need it to give the golem a voice.

The golem walked out the cottage door. Simon followed. "Rabbi Wood, where are you going? Do you know what they will do if they catch you?"

The golem ignored him and kept walking. The geese in the pen honked noisily as it passed. The goats bleated. It was a fine spring morning, bright and clear, and the golem tried to take it all in, knowing it might be its last morning. The ground beneath its feet was rich and fertile, bursting with life—so different from the hard brick and stone of the city. But it had made up its mind. It would go to the city.

Simon ran along beside him pleading, till his wife stepped out of the cottage. "Let him go, Simon. Look at him—the golem knows what it is doing."

"But he gave me the books," Simon said. "Such beautiful books. I cannot just let him get himself killed by the city guard."

"He will live or die as the Lord wills. You said yourself he was a messenger; the Lord will take care of his own."

As the Lord wills. It was what Rabbi Leitch had said on his death bed, and it gave the golem some comfort. Simon stopped chasing. "Good luck, my friend," he said quietly, "and may the Lord be with you."

The golem was almost to the woods when Simon called to it again. "Rabbi Wood, if you are looking for Rabbi Meltzer, they are holding him in the courthouse, near the old town hall. Just look for the clock tower." The golem glanced back. Simon still stood by the geese, his wife watching from the cottage door. One of the geese, maybe Pinochel, was trying to work its way between the bottom slats of the fence. The golem turned and walked toward the city, hearing Simon's voice in the distance, "But he'll never find it on his own . . ."

The city looked different during the day, smaller and even more run-down, stunted like the trees that grew near its edges. The streets of the Jewish quarter were deserted, and here and there smoke still rose where fires had burned during the night. The smell was everywhere, and the streets were littered with ashes and broken glass. The golem followed the path it had before, ducking into doorways or alleys to hide from the few guardsmen who patrolled the streets.

Twenty to thirty people gathered at the Jewish cemetery around the raw, dark earth of a newly dug grave. The golem stood in the alley where it had met Rabbi Meltzer and watched as men lowered the rough pine casket into the hole. Streets that had been busy were silent now, and the golem could hear women crying. One man bowed his head and began to pray.

Hoofbeats echoed along the street as a mounted guardsman rode past the cemetery. He stopped when he saw the funeral. "You know the rules—no public gatherings," he shouted over the prayer. "Move along now, or I'll have to arrest you all."

The prayer stopped. A few mourners began to leave but many others muttered angrily. The man who had been praying stepped forward. "Please, sir, it is only a funeral. Let us have a few moments to say goodbye."

"I said move along." The guard put his foot on the man's chest and shoved him. The elderly Jew fell backward into the crowd. Some young men rushed forward, and the guardsman drew his sword.

The golem rushed out of the alley and most of the way across the street before it realized what it was doing. Several Jews screamed when they saw the golem, and the guard twisted around in his saddle just in time to see it bearing down. He swung his sword wildly, hitting the golem across the shoulder with the flat of his blade. The golem grabbed the guard's sword arm and lifted him up off the saddle.

The golem ripped the sword from the guard's hand and threw it clattering into the street, then dropped the guard, who scuttled back on his hands and knees into the crowd of Jews. To the golem's surprise they helped him up, trying to keep the guardsman between them and the golem. The guardsman took a whistle from around his neck and blew.

Several answering whistles echoed through the quiet streets. The golem looked down at the Jews, who drew back in fear. It hung its head. Couldn't they tell it had been trying to help? It turned away sadly and ran off down the street, listening to the hoofbeats of approaching guards.

The golem ran, but without enthusiasm. It heard the Jews cheer as the guardsmen arrived. The sound cut the golem in a way the guardsman's sword could not. It eluded the city guard for a while, ducking down alleys and hiding in looted shops. But the golem was not very fast. They captured it before it had even caught sight of the clock tower. It offered no resistance.

To the golem's surprise they did not simply kill it. It really did not know what it had expected—possibly that they would just burn it, or cut it into kindling. Instead the guards tied its wrists and led it through the city.

Word of its capture spread quickly. People peered from windows and stared openly from the streets. The golem hung its head so it would not have to watch. It knew that everyone it passed, Jew and Christian alike, was glad for the capture of the monster responsible for the riots. A few people cheered, but most watched silently as the golem lumbered behind the mounted guardsmen.

When it looked up, the golem recognized the city square with its large clock tower and realized it might get to see Rabbi Meltzer after all. Here in the center of the city, signs of the riot were less obvious—no broken windows or fires. People still went about their daily business, though they stopped to watch the golem pass. But the smell of smoke tinged the air, and Jews and Christians stood apart, glancing at each other nervously. The guardsmen led the golem across the square to a large stone staircase in front of the courthouse.

There they dismounted, and led the golem up the stairs on foot. Guards stopped them briefly at the door, and again before they could enter the courtroom itself. Each time the guards exchanged hushed words with those at the door. They waited outside the court until given the signal by those inside.

The courtroom was the largest room the golem had ever seen. The ceiling rose far overhead, painted ornately and leafed with gold, an artificial sky of clouds and Christian icons stained dark from the smoke of the torches that gave light to the room. At the far end, three judges sat on high black chairs, like austere thrones, the one in the middle a little higher than the others. The judges wore long black robes and peaked black caps to indicate their office, and the high judge wore a gold medallion around his neck as well. A crowd stood behind a railing at the edge of the room, watching. None were Jews.

In front of the judges a cluster of city officials, lawyers, and witnesses sat on hard straight chairs before a small table. The guards marched the golem toward the judges, their footsteps echoing in the massive room, as one of the lower judges spoke. He was huge and fat, with long dark hair and no beard to hide the rolls on his face, but his voice came deep and compelling. "You have said repeatedly that there was no monster to have taken away our children. And yet here it is for all to see."

All eyes turned to the golem. A voice spoke up from a corner of the room. "What I have said is true; there is no monster. It is simply a golem, a mechanical man—nothing that need be feared. If anything, you should count yourselves lucky to have seen such a wonder."

Rabbi Meltzer stood in a corner surrounded by several men-at-arms. He had been stripped of his robes and wore only rough prison clothing, but he still held himself proudly and his voice carried the same authority it had the night he silenced the mob.

"It doesn't matter what the monster is called, just look at it. It is not human, and it is not Christian. How are we to know that we are safe, while things like this roam our streets and the people who would build such a thing go unpunished? Where did it go last night; can you tell us that?"

"That I cannot say," Rabbi Meltzer said sadly.

"Cannot, or will not?" the judge asked, turning to the high judge. "I ask you to reconsider questioning the witness more stringently. We have now all seen the monster. Perhaps with a little persuasion, we can learn the truth."

The high judge was an older man, whose beard and hair were almost white. His deep-set eyes seemed to pass judgment on everyone in the room, and all were found wanting. He shook his head and spoke. "I do not believe we need to resort to drastic measures while there are still other avenues to pursue. Continue your questioning."

The lower judge sighed and shook his head, and there was some grumbling from the crowd. Obviously this was not the first time the issue had been raised. "What else is there to ask? We have seen the monster, and we have witnesses who say this man let it walk away."

"Perhaps," the high judge said. He turned to Rabbi Meltzer. "You say that this is a mechanical man. Did you create him?"

"No." Rabbi Meltzer shook his head. "I believe he was made by Rabbi Leitch."

"Maybe, then, we are holding the wrong man responsible. Where is this Rabbi Leitch?"

"He is dead. The golem carried his body into the city. I believe he died of natural causes; he was very old. I think the golem delivered his body for burial."

The judge thought for a while. "Do you see any reason that we should not simply destroy the monster? We cannot punish a dead man, and perhaps your only crime was in being too trusting of another's intentions."

There was a commotion at the back of the room. The door opened briefly, then slammed shut, the sound echoing through the room. Muffled voices could be heard arguing in the hall, then the door opened again. "Excuse me, Your Honor." Simon burst into the room, two soldiers struggling to hold him back. "I can prove the golem is innocent. Please, let me speak." The soldiers managed to grab his arms and began to pull him from the room.

"Wait." The high judge motioned to the guards. "Let him come forward."

The guards let go, and Simon crossed the wide distance to the judges, waving briefly to the crowd. "Thank you, Your Honor. My wife would kill me if she knew I was here—she thinks I'm out chasing a goose—but I couldn't let Rabbi Wood go alone. He cannot talk, you see, and I told him I could talk enough for both of us. Besides . . ."

"Silence," the lower judge ordered.

"Sorry." Simon looked abashed. He glanced over at the golem and smiled.

The high judge spoke. "What do you know about the monster?"

"I found him yesterday morning, out in the woods. He couldn't have been in the city when they say. I took him to my house and he slept under my roof. My son thought he was a monster, but my wife said he was a golem and . . ." Simon trailed off when he saw the look on the lower judge's face. "He was with me, all day and all night."

"Can you prove this?" the high judge asked.

Simon thought for a minute. "The pack he is carrying—in it you will find a book. It was one of the many he had when I found him. He gave me the others before he left."

The golem's guards took the pack from its shoulders, removed the book, and carried it to the judges. The high judge examined it carefully, rifling through the pages and running his fingers along the unfamiliar letters. The lower judge spoke. "A Hebrew book? What does that prove?"

"I am nothing but a simple farmer," Simon answered. "Where would I get books such as this? Send someone to my farm and they could bring the others here. That would show the golem was at my house."

"But it would not show when. He could have given them to you weeks ago, or perhaps even you yourself helped to create this monstrosity."

"That's impossible . . ." Simon began, but the high judge cut him off.

"I agree, but my colleague is right—the book proves nothing. If you have nothing but your word, I'm afraid I will have to order the golem destroyed."

Shouts filled the courtroom, turning it to chaos. Simon pleaded with the judge not to destroy the golem and the lower judge yelled that somebody must be punished, while several in the crowd voiced their displeasure at the judge's decision as well. The guardsmen's shouts for order only added to the confusion.

The golem stood passively in the middle of it all. It felt bad that Simon would feel sorrow at its passing, but maybe this was how it needed to be. Its only regret was that it had not been able to carry out the second part of its master's final request, but it did not think that it would live long enough to gain a voice.

"Excuse me, gentlemen. Excuse me." Rabbi Meltzer's voice cut across the clamor. Something in it commanded the attention of even the unruly crowd. "If it would please Your Honor, might I take a look at the book? I may be able to shed some light on this matter."

The high judge shrugged and handed the book to one of the guards.

"Surely you can't be serious?" the lower judge asked. "For all we know it is some book of arcane spells. Would you endanger us all?"

The high judge turned on him. "It seems to me that if the Jews had either the power or the intentions you fear, they would not be content to use their arcane powers merely to live in our ghettoes, sneaking out at night to do us harm. Why not raise up a whole army to conquer the city? Then they would be sitting up here, listening to overblown accusations about you and me."

The high judge turned to Rabbi Meltzer. "Take the book. Right now I would welcome light from any source. Keep in mind, however, that you are surrounded by armed men. Do you understand?"

The Rabbi nodded, and the judge motioned for the guard to give him the book. The small Jew took it and scanned rapidly through its pages. As he did, a brief smile crept to his face.

He closed the book. "Your Honor, if the golem were able to speak on his own behalf, would his testimony be acceptable in this court?"

The judge looked over at the golem. "Can he speak then? If so, then let him say his piece before we pass judgment."

"He cannot," the Rabbi said. "At least, he cannot yet. This book contains instructions on how he was made. I believe, if given some time, that I could give the golem a voice. Then maybe we can learn the truth."

The lower judge's face turned red, but the high judge ordered him to be silent before he could even object. He asked the Rabbi how long it would take, then ordered tools to be brought for the work. At the lower judge's request, he also sent for another unit of guards to watch the golem.

Rabbi Meltzer walked over to the golem. "Kneel down," he ordered gently. The golem did as asked. "I must put you to sleep for a while, but it will be all right." He reached up to the mark on the golem's forehead, the mark that gave it life. The golem felt a light touch, and then—for the first time since it had been created—it felt nothing.

"Wake up, my friend. Please." The golem heard the voice as if from a long distance. It remembered its master's voice, calling to it over the same distance on the day it had first awakened. Then it had not understood the words, but they had called it upward, as Rabbi Meltzer did now. "Wake up; I know I did not build that badly."

The golem opened its eyes. It lay on the floor, looking up at the clouds and cherubim that lined the ceiling, and longed for the real sky overhead. It felt different, more human—it was not sure that it liked the feeling. It rose stiffly.

The judge looked down. "Can you speak?"

The golem thought about it, then nodded. "Yes." The sound of its own voice surprised the golem. It was deep and percussive and the words felt strange in its throat.

"You have heard the proceedings against you?"

"I have heard what you have said."

"Do you have anything to say before I pass sentence?"

The golem thought for a moment, looking around at the judges and the hungry faces of the crowd that still pressed the edges of the room. "I do not understand what crime I have committed. I came because my master asked a favor before he died. If I have done someone wrong, then I will work to make it right. Tell me, who here have I harmed?"

For a long time the court remained silent, save for the shuffling of feet, then the high judge spoke. "Last night, there were many who knew of the destruction you had wrought. But today no one can be found who actually saw it. Rabbi Meltzer was only charged with obstructing the guards in the performance of their duties."

"You would destroy me, then, for the sake of rumors?"

The lower judge spoke. "Can you prove where you were last night?"

"You have heard the testimony of a good man." The golem motioned toward Simon. "Would you believe the testimony of a monster? Ask the Rabbi and those who were with him, ask the city guard. I gave my master's body to Rabbi Meltzer, as he had asked and I had promised, then I left the city, gladly. I walked until Simon found me. I would not have returned, had you not forced my hand.

"I did not ask to be made what I am, but who here asked to be born? Life was thrust upon me, as it was on all of you." The golem turned to face the crowd. "I have lived it as best I can. Judge me how you will."

It turned back to the high judge. "Your motives may be pure," the judge said, "but there can be no doubt that your presence here is disruptive. I am charged with keeping the city peaceful, as well as passing judgment. What would you have me do with you?"

Rabbi Meltzer spoke as the golem tried to think of a suitable answer. "Please, Your Honor, send him with me. I promise you that he will never again cause problems in the city. If so, as you have seen here, I can make him sleep as if he were dead."

The judge thought, then nodded. "You were originally charged with obstructing justice by freeing the monster. If you are willing to guarantee his removal from the city, then I can see no crime that was committed.

"However, I will ask you to turn over the book, so that no more of these creatures may be created. So this court finds. How say you?"

The lower judge could barely speak and his chins shook with indignant rage. "I cannot believe that you are going to let them go."

"I will take that as a no. How say you?"

The junior judge looked between his two colleagues. The lower judge glared at the young man, but the junior judge straightened his back and said, "Yea."

Some cheered, some booed, but the golem's bonds were handed over to Rabbi Meltzer, who led it from the building. Simon came along, congratulating the golem and patting Rabbi Meltzer heartily on the back.

"Do not thank me," Rabbi Meltzer said. "Thank the Lord for sending a wise judge among the Christians."

Simon ran to tell his wife that all was well. As they walked along the street, Rabbi Meltzer turned to the golem. "You have done us a great favor. Those who brought the charges against me have been seeking to stir up anger against the Jews for a long time. To lose such a public case will be a great setback to them. I would like to thank you.

"They may have destroyed your master's book, but they did not destroy the knowledge it contained. I saw enough that I can complete your creation. No one will be able to tell you from a man, and you can come or go in the city as you please."

"Could you create your own golem, if the need arose?" the golem asked.

The Rabbi thought for a moment. "Perhaps. There are still some pieces that I am missing. One in particular."

The golem knew what the piece was. It stopped and told Rabbi Meltzer the pronunciation of the name carved on its forehead, the name that gave the golem its life, fulfilling the promise it had made its master. The Rabbi listened closely, and smiled. "Yes, I could do it now. I'm sure of it."

"Write it down," the golem said. "Rabbi Leitch loved knowledge; he would not have wanted this secret to pass away with him. Write it down so that when the need is there, the knowledge will be too."

"I will, I will. Now, shall we make you a man?" the Rabbi asked.

The golem thought for a moment. For the first time since its master's death, it felt at peace. It knew what it wanted. "Rabbi Leitch wished this for me as well, but I am not a man and do not wish to be. I am grateful to Rabbi Leitch for what he gave me, and I am grateful for your offer. But there is another favor I would ask of you instead. . . ."

The rocking chair sat in the corner of Simon's living room, across from the large window, near the shelf on which he kept his books. It was beautifully carved of oak and finely stained. The scrollwork along its arm and backrest led to a single carved Hebrew letter. It was a wonderful chair; everyone who saw it said so.

Rabbi Meltzer had brought it a month after the riots, to thank Simon for his help. If it seemed a strange gift to Simon, he never mentioned it. They had placed it carefully in the living room, and Rabbi Meltzer had helped Simon plant a tree just outside the window. When the children had asked, Simon had shrugged, "It will be good to watch things grow."

The children loved to sit and rock, and Esther nursed their sixth child there and rocked her to sleep late in the night when nothing else would quiet her. Rabbi Meltzer often came to visit, and sat and talked with Simon, discussing the fine points of the Law while rocking contentedly.

When the children were grown, their children fought for a turn to sit on the old rocking chair, as their parents had done.

But everyone knew that it was Simon's chair. Every night before he went to bed he would sit in the chair, reading passages of the Torah out loud to no one in particular. And sometimes, before he went to bed, he would open the curtains and the children would hear him say, "Good night, Rabbi Wood."

And sometimes, the children said, the chair would rock by itself, on calm nights when no one was around. But they did not fear that the chair was haunted. They simply said that it was happy. And they were right.

A REPORT FROM THE TERRAN PROJECT

Written by
Scott Everett Bronson

Illustrated by
Patrick Stacy

About the Author

Scott began writing in the seventh grade by blatantly plagiarizing Walter Farley's young adult novel Island Stallion. *In the ninth grade, his drama class performed the play, then came onstage to "honor" the playwright by smacking him with brooms that had recently served as racing steeds.*

Not having learned his lesson, Scott continued to dabble in drama. He's acted in plays at Brigham Young University and in the local Actor's Repertory Theatre Ensemble—such roles as Kent in King Lear; *Henry in* The Lion in Winter; *and Tarleton in Shaw's* Misalliance. *He's also appeared on television in such movies as* Double Jeopardy *with Bruce Boxleitner and Sela Ward;* The Man with Three Wives *with Beau Bridges and Joanna Kerns;* Stephen King's The Stand *with Gary Sinise and Rob Lowe; along with episodes of the popular series* Touched by an Angel—*to name a few of his credits.*

He's written several award-winning plays and seen them produced; he wrote the lyrics for a musical tape, "City of Peace," composed by Arlen Card, who might be better known in SF circles as Orson Scott Card's brother but who is gaining fame as a composer.

Currently, Bronson is adapting Orson Scott Card's story "Quietus" for the stage, to be produced this next summer by the ARTE. Scott recently finished a mainstream novel and has it making the rounds; and has begun working on two more novels.

Bronson—who earned his Bachelor of Arts from Regents College in New York and once served as a missionary in Jakarta, Indonesia—lives in Orem, Utah, with his wife and four children, where he works as a medical supply manager for a nursing home.

About the Illustrator

Patrick Stacy was born in Mannheim, Germany, and lived there until he reached the age of eleven. He then moved to the U.S., where he recently received his Bachelor of Arts degree from the University of Massachusetts—Lowell.

Just before his marriage, Patrick won the Illustrators of the Future Contest, which will allow him to compete for the $4,000 grand prize with other illustrators around the world.

Patrick says that with the support of his new wife, he has been able to work diligently on his art, doing portraits and T-shirt designs.

ichael took another bite of his bread and, as he chewed, set the bread on edge and started pushing it across the table like a train, tooting "choo-choo" around the sticky mass in his cheeks.

I said, "Michael, stop playing with your food, please."

He ignored me of course, so I reached over and broke his finger. The pinkie of his right hand.

Michael dropped his bread and pulled his hand away, turning an annoyed glance at me. Then he looked at his dangling digit and said, in his irritating little child voice, "Hey!"

The twins, James and Tracy, both said, "*Eeuuoo!*" Abigail, smearing spaghetti sauce all over her highchair tray, looked up and laughed.

Michael held his hand up for the others to see and wiggled it, flopping the finger around. He laughed too, though I could plainly see by his expression that it also hurt a little.

"Practicing love techniques tonight?" my wife asked.

I looked at her and said, "I'm trying, Margaret. I'm honestly trying."

She grunted, as if to say, yeah, right.

"It's only a finger, Margaret," I said hotly. "It's not like it won't heal." It had only taken me three seconds to get red-faced, panting and heart-poundingly pissed.

Margaret dismissed my jealousy with a snort and said, "Besides, you'll have to do more damage than that if you expect to make an impression."

Michael put the bread on the table again and choo-chooed it slowly in my direction, giving the other children a sidelong smirk as if to say, watch me piss off Dad.

I grabbed his wrist and broke the other four digits of his right hand.

Michael screamed, "Don'! Don'! Don'! Don', Dathy!"

Each finger snapped loudly like a dry twig in a fire.

This time Michael cried.

I took his face in my hand and made him look at me. "I have told you a dozen times tonight that your food is not to play with. You are to eat your food and play with toys. Now, eat the rest of your spaghetti and green beans. If you act up anymore, I'll break your other hand and you'll go without dinner and dessert."

The other children had stopped laughing. When I cast my eyes about the table they all made themselves busy with eating. My gaze settled on Margaret. She had set her fork down and bowed her head as if offering oblations, though I knew she was not.

"What's wrong?" I said.

She threw her hair back in an endearing gesture that I normally found arousing, but this time, simply angered me.

Margaret didn't say anything; she just looked from me to sulking Michael then to me again.

"What?" I said. "You don't think a little discipline demonstrates my love?"

"In the first place," she said, "I was kidding. In the second place, he regenerates so much faster than the rest of us that it doesn't matter if you break a few bones. They'll heal before he's really had time to think about it."

Illustrated by Patrick Stacy

I glanced at Michael's hand. The pinkie finger had nearly healed.

"See what I mean?" Margaret said.

"So what are we supposed to do? Reason with him? The kid is nearly four and he still can't talk."

"He talks, Clark—"

"I know, I know, just not very clearly yet. And most of it is still that weird singing crap. It's not even Miranian, as far as I can tell."

"Clark, I'm not saying you're a bad father just because you break a few bones or tear a little flesh now and then. I mean, I've felt like doing it myself sometimes." She looked away and took a deep breath. "Actually," she said, still unable to look at me, "I have broken some bones. But it wasn't—" Suddenly her eyes teared up. One of those erratic female behaviors. "Last night I— While you were gone, Michael would not settle down and go to bed." Tears spilled from her eyes. "I broke both his arms and his legs and put him in bed. Five minutes later he was climbing the walls again." Margaret took another faltering deep breath. "I'm just saying that with Michael, it doesn't work."

Margaret picked up her fork and fiddled with the food on her plate. I was about to say something when she said, "Besides, it's a terrible thing to watch. I mean, like I said, I did worse last night, but sitting here watching you break his little fingers, hearing them snap—" She shook her head. "It made me sick to my stomach."

"I just—"

"I know. I said I'm not condemning you. We're both wrong though. *I* think."

I thought about it for a minute and, against natural inclination, said, "I don't know. I just don't know." I pointed at the twins. "It worked on these guys."

"They were never as wild as Michael has been. They didn't get half the damage done to them that we're giving Michael."

"Well, maybe you're right," I said, gritting my teeth.

Michael choo-chooed his bread again and I ached to smash his face in.

Any other time, any other place, and I would have done it.

I held my breath and counted.

The next day I had been home from my job and working on the garden under that hot yellow sun for nearly an hour when Margaret came barreling around the side of the house with murder in her eyes.

"What's wrong?" I asked.

"Michael."

The previous day I was chastised for being a bad guy, now it was clear to me that it was expected—no, demanded—of me to play the same role again, but on Margaret's behalf.

I sighed and wiped sweat from my brow with my sleeve. "What's he done now?"

Margaret extended an arm, pointing over the fence toward the front yard. She tried to say something, but the words did not quite form. Finally, in a quick burst, "He shat on the sidewalk!"

"What?"

"You heard me. He pulled his pants down, squatted, and took a crap right in front of the Miller's house."

"Shit," I swore. I sighed again and leaned against my shovel, twisting my back—realigning my overtaxed vertebrae.

Margaret only nodded as if to say, he's your job now.

"Where is he?" I asked.

"He ran away when I tried to catch him."

"All right," I said, dropping my shovel. "I'll get him."

I pulled my gloves off and dropped them on the back porch as I rounded the house. When I emerged from beneath the cover of the carport and looked down the sidewalk toward the Miller's, my eyes met a most excruciating sight. Michael, naked, danced like a demon around his little pile of shit.

Jodie Miller gazed on in horror while her three-year-old, Andy, laughed and shouted, "Michael doed poop! That Michael's peenie!"

Indeed, Michael's little penis, still larger than the average human penis of his age, was erect and wagging lasciviously as he danced and sang his gibberish.

"Michael!"

He didn't even stop to look at me. At the sound of my voice, Michael lit out like Tom O'Bedlam himself, and I lit after him.

His running away from me somehow opened the gate that freed the ancient impulses still attached to my genes. Shitting on the sidewalk was a pretty bad thing, but I'd been prepared to give him the benefit of the doubt: Maybe it had been an emergency or something. I was almost willing to let it be some kind of cute kid thing.

Now here I must stop and tell the truth. Margaret *unlocked* the gate that had been opened by placing me in this paradoxical situation—love the child, don't hurt him; now stop the child from being what he is.

The next thing to piss me off, to bring those impulses closer to the light, was when he ran into the street right in front of a man on a bicycle.

I followed Michael, and the poor faceless creature on the bike ran right into me.

Down we went and from the pavement I shouted, "Michael, go home! Now!"

"No!"

That brought my coldly reasoning anger to the forefront.

I shoved the cyclist into the middle of the street and took off after Michael again.

I got my fist into his hair just in front of our house and dragged him up the steps and through the door.

I kicked the door shut and tossed Michael into the hall. "Son of a bitch!"

Michael landed on his hands and feet, teetering against the wall. He stood up and glared at me. A rapid stream of gibberish assailed me from Michael's hot little mouth. Then he grinned a most superior grin that expressed, without words, more eloquently the sentiment he had just expressed in his meaningless musical language.

This final act brought my true, original self raging into the open.

I kicked him.

As hard as I could, right in the gut.

He hit the wall again. Harder this time.

Before his body had completed its bounce from the floor, I kicked him with my other foot on the side of the head. Tiny droplets of blood and spittle sprayed the wall. Piss soaked the carpet.

With frigid, calculated determination I kicked his groin. There, I thought. That should make a lasting impression.

Margaret laid a towel over Michael's pillow, then gently laid Michael on his bed with his face on the towel. The towel soaked up the blood that oozed in a steady trickle from Michael's mouth and the gash on the side of his head.

"Call the doctor," Margaret said.

"Where is she these days?"

"I don't know," Margaret said, testily. "Just get her."

I stared at Michael's limp little body for a moment, twinges of human guilt beginning to stab at my insides. Margaret turned to glare at me. I left the room.

In my office, I removed the Window from the safe and, though I didn't feel the same urgency that Margaret felt, I phased a brief but appropriately desperate message to the Project doctor. Not knowing where she was, I first phased the Window to search, then sent the message. If the Doc was on the other side of the planet, I'd probably be waking her up. I hoped so. I didn't like the Doc much. Though considered very attractive by Terran standards, I thought her eyes were too big, and everything else too small. Except for her ego, that too was unnaturally overgrown.

The Doc's holo-image appeared in the Window.

"What is it?" she said. The curtness and heaviness in her voice belied the cheery expression of her holo-image.

"I need you to look at my son," I said.

The holo-Doc's eyes closed for a moment, then she said, "All right." Her image vanished then the doctor herself stepped through the Window. Her hair was disheveled, her eyes full of sleep. All she wore was a sarong. She was naked above the waist. Her exposed skin shone with a thin layer of perspiration. It appeared obvious that she had been in the tropics still, I glanced down at the Window's setting to confirm my suspicion.

I smiled at her and said, "Thank you for coming."

The Doc ignored me as she pulled on her exam gloves. When she had them locked into place, she turned her blank expression to me and said, "Well?"

Bitch.

"This way." I led her to Michael's room.

She took one glance at Michael's mangled body and whispered, *"Yah shollah"*—dear gods—in Miranian. She removed one of the gloves, wet her fingers with saliva, and anointed her eyes.

My little knives of guilt sliced deeper and twisted.

The Doc replaced her glove, then rested her hands on Michael's head for a moment. She checked a wrist panel, touched a few bands along her arm, then placed her hands on his chest. She touched his neck with the tip of a finger; blood appeared for a moment. The Doc entered data and read panels on her gloves while Michael's neck healed. Then she put her hands on Michael's pubis.

"Will he die?" I asked.

"Of course not."

Margaret looked at me and her expression changed from disgust to fear. My rage must have been showing.

"You males are pathetic." The Doc spoke Miranian again as the gloves injected solutions into Michael's body. "You could learn a few things from the Terrans. They're not half as aggressive as Miranians."

The Doc stood and faced me, taking off her gloves. "Let me tell you something, let me try to remind you— you are no longer in competition with your offspring. Not on this planet. Genetic assimilation can stem that impulse to a point. Beyond that you must *learn* to control yourself. If you don't, Terran placidity will destroy us here, believe it or not."

"How?" I blurted, without thinking.

"Don't be stupid." The Doc jabbed a finger in my chest. "There's not a single culture on this planet that allows parents, let alone strangers, to murder their young."

"I know that. I thought you were implying something—"

"This level of abuse," she said, pointing at Michael, "would land you in prison if any Terrans were to discover it." The Doc looked at Margaret, then back to me. "This project will fail if you males keep killing your young."

"But you said—"

She stopped me with a wave of her hand. Then pointed at me. "We need to be very well established in every system that we possibly can before Miran dies or . . ." And she let it hang.

The Doc looked at Michael. "This child is a quick healer. He won't die from his injuries. And this may sound despicable, but, if we were to have lost this one, it wouldn't have hurt the project. In fact, it might have even helped."

Margaret's jaw fell open. She had learned to love very quickly. Her attachment to our offspring was nigh unto Terran.

The Doc ignored Margaret. "This child," she said, "is more Miranian than he is Terran in some ways. Throwbacks are not good for the project. Not yet, anyway."

"But—" Water filled Margaret's eyes.

"Don't worry," the Doc said. "You can keep him. He'll be good to learn on. But he won't be allowed to reproduce. I've already ensured his sterility."

Margaret gasped.

The Doc took a good look at both of us standing together and shook her head. "Pathetic."

We followed the Doc into my office. As she walked ahead of us she said, "I'll wager that your child is demonstrating some rather odd behaviors."

"Um, well, yes, he is," said Margaret.

"Gene analysis showed that his Miranian race-memory is nearly pure."

"What does that mean?" I asked.

"A lot of things." The Doc turned to us and stood in the middle of my office. "He's probably doing things that even you and I don't remember. His memory is ancient, and probably not as confused as ours. He may know lots of things we don't."

"Such as?" Margaret asked.

The Doc shrugged. "What the light of a red sun looks like, maybe."

That was something I expected to see every day, even though I had lived on Terra for more than eight years already, and Sol was the only sunlight I knew.

"Does he still speak Miranian?" the Doc asked.

"No," I shook my head. "He never has. Most of his language is some kind of sing-songy gibberish."

The Doc raised her eyebrows. "Interesting. During training, when we were still on the ship, they told me to be prepared for this sort of thing. Something like this happened to someone in the Pleiades Project, and the child began some strange sort of fecal worship. I don't know about that, though. I mean, do you think we used to worship our own shit?"

The Doc snorted and shook her head. She stepped through the Window and disappeared.

By morning the bleeding had long since stopped. All the bone fractures and skin lacerations were mended. Michael should have been in perfect health.

But he didn't move.

His eyes were open, watching anybody who came near, but there was no expression in them.

By evening my Miranian aggression came to a boil and I did my best to control it. It was plain that the little beast was trying to torture me with guilt. I wanted to kill him.

Margaret suckled Abigail and put her to bed, then spent an hour with Michael while I paced and molded my fury into a smaller, more manageable creature. Almost.

I heard Margaret come out of Michael's room and down the hall. "My feeling is that he loves you," she said in a soft, tentative voice.

I turned to her. I must have appeared completely baffled.

"I said—"

"I know what you said. I'm just trying to understand how that could possibly be."

"I think he's learning to love—*has* learned to love—and I think he loves you very deeply, and now—"

"You heard what the Doc said. He's more Miranian than Terran. Love is not a natural condition of Miranians. Especially males. The word doesn't even exist in our language."

"Yes, but maybe his Miranian dominance is only genetic. Maybe, in this ineffable concept the humans call the heart, he is more human than any of us."

The notion struck me like a comet.

I sat down and stared at the wall.

Margaret sat beside me and rested her hand on my thigh. "He loves you so much. And now you don't love him—he thinks. So . . . why should he live?" Why indeed?

"How do you know this?" I asked. "Did he talk to you?"

"No. I saw it in his eyes. I sat on the side of his bed and stared at them for an hour. I saw it all in there."

I waited at Michael's bedside all night, trying to read something in his eyes.

But I saw nothing.

For several hours I wrestled with myself while every particle of vestigial Miranian instinct told me to pinch his head off and throw it into a fire.

Michael watched my every move, every frustrated and angry gesture I made as I paced or pillared myself into a corner of the room, or against the wall, aching to kill the child.

Finally, near dawn, I knelt beside the bed and gazed again into Michael's eyes. Still, they would not open their secrets to me. Still, I tried. And soon, I saw that they were mirrors, and through them I could see into myself. My heart rate began to slow. My breathing deepened. I searched my Miranian memories, further back than I had ever gone before. What little I could make sense of began to give me an understanding of our history, our evolution. And I found that at some point in our past, we had loved just as well, or nearly as well, as humans.

And something else.

We weren't necessarily slaves to our DNA. The little tugs and nudges that nature used to alter, or shape, our behaviors were not the only things that caused us to evolve. Sometimes a great individual could decide that a change was needed, and if he or she were a great enough individual, the change might last.

I sat on the edge of Michael's bed and took his hand

in both of mine. Tears—actual tears, of guilt, fatigue and sorrow—fell from my eyes.

After several minutes I finally spoke the words that had become meaningless in our dying culture.

"Ku chinta klamu." I value/protect you.

After a moment, Michael smiled and sang, *"Eldo baszh."*

It sounded like—felt like—he said, I love you, in Ancient Miranian.

I could only hope.

DEVIL'S ADVOCATE

Written by
Syne Mitchell

Illustrated by
Kent Martin

About the Author

I first heard of Syne Mitchell from fellow writer Tom King who said, "Dave, I just had a visit from a young lady named Syne Mitchell, who will someday win the Writers of the Future—if she doesn't sell too many stories to qualify first. She's one of the most brilliant young writers I've ever met."

Now I see that his prediction came true.

Syne Mitchell began college at age thirteen and graduated summa cum laude *at age fifteen. At age sixteen she returned to college and earned her master's degree in experimental physics from Florida State University.*

At age twenty-one, she submitted her first story to Marion Zimmer Bradley's Sword and Sorceress #9, expecting to begin accumulating rejections, but instead got a contract. Since then she's sold several more stories to Sword and Sorceress and to Marion Zimmer Bradley's Fantasy Magazine. She contributes short fiction reviews to Tangent Magazine (an interesting publication that reviews nearly all of the short fiction in the SF field), and Syne recently attended

Clarion West, compliments of the Susan C. Petrey scholarship fund.

Syne currently lives in Washington with her companion Greg Nylund—an author of considerable talent who has recently sold several novels to Avon Books, a publisher who is noteworthy for quietly signing up many of the finest new writers of SF.

It won't be long until Syne joins him on the bookshelves. In the meantime, I hope you enjoy this rather delightful little tale as much as I do.

Sir, the devil's on line one. Again." Lisa-Marie's voice crackled over the age-stained plastic intercom.

"Just a minute," Murray murmured into the phone and tucked the receiver under his chin. He poked the plastic button with one pudgy finger. "I'm already on the phone with Bailey. Tell him I'll call him back."

Silence. "He says he already called twice this morning. . . ."

Murray sighed. "Fine. Put him on hold then. I'll get to him when I can."

"I'm putting him on line three."

"Who's on line two?"

"Antonio Genesco."

Murray winced. Genesco wanted Murray to represent him on racketeering charges. The problem was, Murray had evidence Genesco was guilty. It was unprofessional, and probably unethical, but Murray had been ducking him ever since.

The conversation with Bailey ran long. He insisted that Murray go over the items in the deposition a fifth time. By the time Murray got back to the phone, the devil had hung up.

It was just as well. Murray knew why he called.

Nine years before and two years out of law school,

Murray had a new wife, a new daughter, a new mortgage, and a failing law practice.

Murray thought the gaunt man who walked into his one-room practice that day was a customer. He was tall. His hair swept back into a televangelist's white pompadour. The stranger flipped back the bottom of his jacket and settled into the armless wooden chair as if it were a throne. Without speaking, he reached into his inner coat pocket and withdrew a red book of matches and a thick Valesquez cigar. The man bit off the end of the cigar and spit it on the floor. Then he flicked the book of matches open with his left hand. The smell of sulfur singed Murray's nostrils. The stranger's face behind the flare of the match was transformed. His white bushy eyebrows jumped in the flame's light and the hollows of his cheeks became bottomless.

"I'd like to make you an offer," he said.

Murray had thought the man a rival lawyer, come to buy him out. When he learned the true nature of his visitor, he became incredulous, then appalled. But, like others of his profession, he signed.

Now the debt was due.

Murray locked the door to his office and told Lisa-Marie to hold his calls. Then he removed the key taped under the pull-out extension in his desk and opened the strongbox in the bottom left drawer. Under a stack of bonds and his will he found the document. It was a stiff tube of parchment, tied with a red satin ribbon. Murray pulled the ribbon, and the parchment sprang open on the desk. He smoothed it with soft, damp hands and read the crimson script. It was the standard boilerplate. Murray's eyes skimmed to the bottom. The last line read: "In witness whereof, the parties have executed this Contract." Below, in shaky script, was Murray's signature, and Lucifer's.

Illustrated by Kent Martin

Murray called his wife and told her he would be working late. He removed his tie and made a fresh pot of coffee. Lisa-Marie went home at seven. Murray stayed and pored over the document until his eyes grew leaden and he sank onto the pile of unread contracts on his desk and slept.

Rapping at the door startled Murray into consciousness. He stumbled across the room, through the receptionist's office, kicked a pile of depositions on the Bronston case into white swirling chaos, and crashed against the front door. He opened it without thinking. The light outside was gray with the approaching dawn. Somewhere in the tract of undeveloped land to the south of the building, a whippoorwill called.

The devil stepped forward into the doorway and blotted out the sky. He pushed Murray into the room in front of him.

"It is time."

Murray sat down with a whump on Lisa-Marie's desk. The collar of his shirt was askew and damp. "Now about that contract. I have some problems with the way it stands."

The devil arched a thick white eyebrow.

Murray led the Lord of Darkness back into his office and pulled the vinyl-covered wing chair that he kept in the corner, reserved, for his special clients. The devil removed a cigar from his breast pocket and began to smoke. The heavy, sweet smell of tobacco mixed with that of burnt coffee and Murray's own stale sweat.

Murray sat forward and braced his elbows against his desk. "Before I render my soul, I want to discuss what I see as a serious breach of contract on your part."

The devil leaned back into the chair and removed the cigar from his mouth. He yawned. "How so?"

Murray poked his finger into a passage halfway down the document. "Line 46 clearly states that in payment for the surrender of the contractee's soul, the contractee will attain success in all worldly endeavors for a span not to exceed nine years." Murray gestured to the particle-board bookshelves and the polypropylene carpet with the melted cigarette patch near the door. "This hardly counts as worldly success!"

The devil crossed his right leg over and put his foot on his left knee. He blew two smoke rings in quick succession. "I've given you success. For the last nine years you've won every case that went to court. It's up to you to hustle and get the big clients."

"What about the McLarity dispute? The judge settled against us."

"Ah," the devil said, raising one immaculately manicured finger, "but your private investigator found that the main witness for the prosecution had been indicted for drug dealing seven years before. You never brought that up in court."

"The main witness was a juvenile when that charge was settled. The records were sealed. Those facts were irrelevant, illegal, and would have been immoral to use."

The devil smiled, "But you would have won."

"But—"

The devil uncrossed his legs and leaned forward. "Look," he said, gesturing with the smoking cigar, "you're getting paid. Most men in your line of work give me what I want for free."

The light came on in the outer office behind the devil. Murray heard a familiar whump as Lisa-Marie dropped her bag behind the desk in the next room. Then he heard water run as she readied the coffeepot for the new day.

"You're a good lawyer and a good man, Murray. I could tell you were going to give me trouble—so I made you an offer. I've kept my bargain. It's time to pay." Lucifer smiled, the wrinkles from his wide grin creased his chin into a sharp point. "You'll thank me, afterward."

The Lord of Lies had a point. Murray, defeated, gave the devil his due.

The devil's fingers were hot and dry and smelled of charcoal briquettes. A tiny tug on Murray's earlobe, and the wisp that was his soul slipped free. Murray watched as the devil opened his eelskin briefcase. He folded Murray's soul and placed it on top of a pile of others.

Instead of the sense of dread and loss Murray expected, he felt a new clarity. It was the same feeling as when he had the prescription on his glasses updated and suddenly he noticed the world was larger than he was used to.

The devil closed and locked his briefcase with a click. He shook the ashes off his cigar.

"Nice doing business with you." He rose and strode briskly past Lisa-Marie's desk and out the door.

"Rough night?" she asked, once the main door swung shut.

"Just some old business," Murray said. He stretched his arms and breathed in deeply. "Get me Genesco on the phone."

The phone rang through to Murray's office. He waited for two rings before he picked up.

Genesco's voice was slurred and angry. "Who's this?"

Murray tilted back in his chair. With the fees from Genesco's defense, Murray would finally be able to buy that Porsche he'd given up on. He smiled. "Genesco. It's Murray Taylor, your lawyer."

NARCISSUS RISING

Written by
Roge Gregory

Illustrated by
Richard Moore

About the Author

Roge Gregory lives in Staffordshire, England, where she spends a great deal of time caring for her four children, including a learning-disabled son—when she's not writing.

At thirteen she began authoring a hand-written novel. In the years since then, she's studied physiology and microbiology at the university level. She has won several awards for her writing in the U.K., and has placed some of her poetry and articles in the national press. She's currently working on three SF novels, and the first is nearing completion.

Narcissus Rising is her first sale.

About the Illustrator

Richard Moore was born in French Camp, California in 1966, grew up in Stockton and currently lives in Sacramento.

He has a no-thrills job that pays the rent but his passions are movies, writing, and art. He has been drawing since he was four years old. Richard has won several contests in high school, but had never entered a national contest until now. He is self-taught, gaining much information and inspiration from art magazines and the works of artists such as Patrick Nagel, N. C. Wyeth, George Petty, and Michael Whelan. He is a night owl and does his best work between midnight and 4 a.m. At present he is working on several comic strips and screenplays.

Vee, the clone, danced on the surface of Pharmacy like a godling. A gentle breeze pressed the silk of her shift into the curves of her body and fingered the firm muscles of her thighs. Giant orchids of lavender and lemon nodded their heads and laughed with her, drifted golden pollen onto her hands. She dusted the sparkling stuff over her shoulders, along the bridge of her nose and spoke aloud: "See what you're missing!"

Vellie, the master, far above and unconscious of the recycled, reconditioned air that susurrated through the cabin grilles, couldn't feel the contour couch beneath her. Under the enhancer, her limbs twitched in sympathetic reaction as her clone threw wide her arms, and she smiled drowsily at the laughter. She saw the green and blue of the orchid fields through closed eyes and felt the liquid sheen of the pollen on her own skin.

"To the east, Vee," she murmured. "Two degrees right of Carreebas. Survey says there should be some Scallybroke coming into bloom. Can you smell it yet?"

As the clone turned her head and tested the wind, Vellie sneaked a look at the warnings on the Survey display. Update tremors passed through it every few minutes and a weather report was included as a fixture. She avoided checking the monitors too often during contact, as the conflict between the inner visions from her clone and the messages from her own eyes created a confusing dichotomy. The island display showed ripe saffron inshore from the eastern bay, and she grimaced. Judging by the intensity of the transmitted color, Vee should have detected it long since. A reduction in perception levels was always the prelude to full sensory breakdown. She bit her lip.

"Yes," said Vee doubtfully, and swung to face the sun.

"Take a bike!" cried Vellie and sighed with relief when the clone mounted the cycle-drum that followed her. Vee was also becoming more difficult to control, more devious and recalcitrant. It was inevitable, Vellie thought, and checked as Vee triggered the gyropscopes and stabilizers and tucked herself in between the storage drums and the leading shields.

Carreebas shed a soft light—scarcely intense enough to cast even the most fuzzy and muted of shadows when at its height, and the clear air carried no clouds. Weather drones around the planet recorded the barometric changes that could precipitate one of the periodic windstorms. Vee might notice the first slight increase in the breeze, but with her senses dying it seemed unlikely, and with her judgment at next risk she might choose not to act anyway.

The wind, when it came, would lift the sweet sea over the islands, flatten the fragile flowers, shred the leaves to rotting tatters, and leave behind a brown and fertile medium for the spores and seeds and fruits that the water carried. Vellie had only seen holos, and they frightened her. It frightened her even more to imagine Vee exposed to the elemental fury. It was up to the masters to get their clones back into shelter in time. Sometimes one didn't make it. Natural attrition.

"What do I do with it?" asked Vee suddenly as the cycle-drum settled in the field of Scallybroke blossom.

"You should know. You've done it three times before," snapped Vellie. She felt Vee stiffen with offense and mumbled, "Sorry." If Vellie couldn't control herself, then she wouldn't be able to control her clone. Vellie's fingers touched velvet and silk as Vee stroked the massive blooms. Pale apple green at the rim of the trumpets deepened to forest at the neck of the flower, and faint smudged radials of russet turned to black in the throat.

"Beautiful," said Vee, happily, and stooped to inhale. A wall of sweet sickly perfume hit both of them, overpowering. Vellie gasped and tried to withdraw farther into the couch. Vee staggered and fell to her knees where she crouched, smiling idiotically. The odor of broken earth and of clean crushed mosses cut through the floral hypnotic. Alarm bells chimed.

"Vee," said Vellie quietly but urgently, "there's a storm coming. Take the harvest and get back to shelter." She had the urge to shake her own head violently, to transfer the motion to her clone to clear her mind, but the enhancer limited her movements and all she achieved was a gentle sway. The clone sneezed once, twice, and her thoughts began to clarify.

"Did you get me that dress I liked?" she asked too casually, craftily. "The one that drapes in tiers from the shoulder with a textual train and intellect programming. I wanted the Morovi silk. And in depth-cyclical aqua."

"On its way—it should arrive up here next shift, and I'll get it down to you straight away. Now . . ."

"And I could fancy some prawns when I get back. Those enormous ones from Demmony with the feathered heads. Proper ones, not recon, mind." There was a note of petulant spite in Vee's mental voice, an unpalatable development that grew stronger with each passing shift.

"It's done." Vellie would have promised anything to get her clone back to the safety of the dome, to the pro-grammed embrace of the automatics.

"Well, c'mon. Tell me what to do. I can't stand about here all day. The trouble with you people up there is you don't get to take any of the risks and you get all the benefits."

Vellie suppressed a sudden hot spurt of indignation. Vee knew—had known—how much she cared. This was just another symptom. And of course these flaws were in her own character, too. Vee got them from Vellie. The masters were never the most pleasant of people. Vellie sometimes wondered if she had the necessary strength of character, the self-will, the sheer conviction of her own superiority, that success required; then she looked in a mirror or listened to some puerile exchange between other masters or staff, and felt her essential flawlessness reconfirmed.

In the meantime her eyes stung with self-pity and her jaw clamped with the effort not to protest. "Take the scalpel—no the little one, you're only tapping the xylem flow, not packing the whole thing—and be careful! It's pointing toward you!" The deadly little instrument buzzed with menace as Vee fumbled at it. Vellie flexed her own fingers, twitched and shifted until suddenly her clone had it straightened out. "There. Now, a small slit diagonally down at the base of the style, as close to the placenta as you can get. Now. Stick a tentube on it to suck, and pump." She paused, watching through Vee's eyes.

"Another!"

Mother's milk, thought Vellie, as seven tubes filled with a viscous white glue: a specific against the neonatal morphotic plagues of the Hebrides and Anthea Systems

Minor. This stuff could ease a planetful of victims. And the younger flowers, the ones just breaking open to spill their perfume and dust into the rising wind . . .

Vee packed the tubes away with relative care and turned into the wind. Before she could say anything, Vellie spoke again. "A sucker. Quickly. There's still time." She could feel frown lines creasing Vee's brow, and the beginnings of objection. "You're the best one down there," she said softly, "the others never bring back as much as you do." She never used the word 'clone' aloud.

Vee suddenly remembered her skills and worked automatically, inserting the sucker nozzle into the fresh bud slits and activating the tiny power unit. One bud, too far gone, showered her with dark dust, which clung like a lover to her skin, in spite of the wind.

"Do try not to get it on your skin," breathed Vellie, but Vee wasn't listening.

"They say it's boring while the storms last," Vee mused. "I think I'll get Heller over."

Vellie wondered if Vee was trying to annoy her on purpose. "Oh, for God's sake," she muttered. "You could have anyone. Why him?"

"He's nearest!" snapped Vee. "It doesn't take so long sub-sea between the islands. And I like the way he looks at me!"

Vellie knew what she meant, but she didn't like the way Maxwell Hellman, Heller's master, looked at her, Adora Vellie. Again, she thought of deteriorating senses and sensibilities and wondered how much longer she would have with Vee. When a clone was decanted, the master-slave link developed as rapidly as consciousness arose in the clone. Only distance necessitated the aid of the enhancer, and once, months ago, Vellie had scorned its use. Now, more and more, she was coming to rely upon it.

As if on cue, her contact dimmed and flickered out into darkness. With a tiny inhalation she tried to rise, but the mechanical restraints held her back. Her eyes flicked open to check the progress of the storm. For a dizzying moment she had the swaying exuberant growth of Pharmacy superimposed on the hiss and click and liquid flow of the weather displays.

By the time Vellie's mind cleared, Vee was back on the bike under the shelter of the shell and riding for home.

The masters recognized Parfal Erriktor only as their own personal steward. A factotum and doormat. A general dogsbody. They seldom admitted that he—or indeed anyone else—might be able to manipulate their fractious moods, defuse their tantrums, optimize their relationships with their clones, and just keep them working. After all, the masters were—all of them—fault-less and exquisite. What need, then, for a Master Psychologist?

Vellie's towering rage was fed by the fact it took her a full leisure break to find the man. She was white and almost spitting with temper when she finally ran him down in the refectory, sharing luncheon with Maxwell Hellman.

"You have to do something," she stormed and leaned on the table with her knuckled fists, dwarfing him. The masters all dwarfed him. "I will not share my gym book-ing with Farrimond—he stinks even before he starts to sweat. And that's the second time he's infringed my booking!" To her annoyance, she gave an angry, dry sob.

"Sit down, Adora," said Erriktor. His face was

smooth, trained into blandness, free of all sign of emotion. Vellie wanted to smash it.

"Clone playing up?" remarked Hellman. He gazed at her with mocking interest. "Always the same with the first-timers. You've probably had her too long."

"Just because I can keep a clone longer than anyone else . . ."

"You should have freeloaded last night. I did. Didn't see you though." His shoulders shook. "Or is the link going? Did she cut you off? In that case, maybe we should try it for real," and his eyes flicked over her with such prurience that her skin crawled. "Though I doubt it would be as good."

With a shriek of outrage, she snatched the bowl of pasta that sat before him and upended it on his head, grinding the glutinous mass into his hair.

He sprang to his feet, glaring, red and oily juices running down the side of his nose, trickling off his chin. Lumps of real meat fell to the table, the carpeted floor. "You'll pay," he snarled, "believe me, you'll pay. . . ."

"Enough!" Although Erriktor spoke quietly, his voice carried the cadences of command, and both protagonists blinked and turned to him, startled. "Fined fifty credits, both of you"— even to a master, it was a large sum— "for lack of control." It stung, and he let them assimilate the charge until the opportunity for denial had passed. "Max, go and get cleaned up."

"She should have some respect for an elder," Hellman protested. He wiped globs of meat and oil from his cheek with long fingers, and flicked them contemptuously at the floor.

"Respect must be earned," responded Erriktor dryly. "And perhaps the veterans could learn something from Adora. Her clone holds the all-time record for survival."

Hellman glared at them from beneath dripping brows and made a noise like tearing calico. But he left without further argument.

"Now, Adora," said Erriktor gently, "sit down while I order for you. No, don't argue. You're not getting a choice."

Cleaner-bots fretted away at their feet until they moved to a clear table where prawns in cream appeared. Fleetingly, Vellie wondered if Erriktor had eavesdropped the contact tapes, but before she thought to refuse the prawns in pique, she had eaten them. Her hunger surprised her.

She listened absently to mildly scandalous and probably apocryphal gossip about retired staffers until her anger cooled. When she finished eating, Erriktor ordered an AmberFrog liqueur for them both and said, "I'll speak to Farrimond about his use of the facilities. He knows that repeated infractions can mean termination of contract. But," he touched the back of her hand, "that's not the real problem, is it?"

The finger resting on Vellie's hand was squared and stubby, with short—almost bitten— nails. Erriktor wasn't ugly, but the scattering of freckles on his pale skin, and the sprouting of ginger hair in odd places, compared poorly with the masters' elegance. They weren't all born that way, but they all bought a perfection to match their inner self-images as soon as they could. Vellie never stopped to wonder why Erriktor was the only man in the Section that she could stomach: she just knew he listened. The others either wouldn't or couldn't.

"The first time is always difficult," he said. "You know what to expect but it's still hard to accept. And the others don't help. It's a pity that you're the only freshman on board at the moment. And the only woman."

Vellie shook her head. Only another master could comprehend. Gender made no difference.

"At the moment, *you* are the only important one." Erriktor's eyes were a pallid hazel, Vellie noticed. His hands lay placid on the table before him, and only his chest moved slightly with his minimal breathing. "You need to be stronger for the sake of your clone. Clones. Without you, they are nothing. They don't even exist."

There was a fallacy in there somewhere, thought Vellie, but she couldn't quite pin it down. "Why do you never use her name?" she demanded.

Erriktor shrugged. "Because I can't help her," he said softly. "Tell me, how close is the end?"

Tears stung Vellie's eyelids and she suddenly wished she hadn't eaten so much. The corners of her mouth drooped but she managed to keep her voice steady. "I don't know," she admitted miserably. "There was a blackout during yesterday's shift and later we had a quarrel. I couldn't get her—*you* couldn't get her—something she wanted." Anger surged briefly and died. "Then she wouldn't let me back in. She doesn't seem to think like me anymore."

Erriktor looked concerned. "You mustn't let her bully you. Remember, there are always both physical and mental imperfections in the cloning. You *must* always be the stronger one, always know best."

"When she was first, you know, shuttled down, I could pick her up from the surface without any help. Now it's getting more and more difficult, even with the enhancer. Gods, how I miss that."

Erriktor nodded sympathetically. "Your empathy is powerful, but now is the time to learn the next step. It will come—the ability to let go, to draw a line under the one and simply be glad you could give life and make it happy for a while, take pleasure in your knowledge of worth. I sometimes think," he watched her closely, "that it would have been better if we had never found Pharmacy, if the drones had failed to identify the balms. It's not the only place where the human organism is the sole functioning computer, but it's certainly the most controversial."

Vellie rose. A little of Erriktor in philosophical mood went too far, but he put out a detaining hand. "Never forget that the clones are essentially incomplete—without the learned behavioral modifiers that you've gained from interaction, they're only partial people." He sighed and looked as though he would like to say more, but only added, "Feel better?"

"Um." She dredged up a wobbly grin to save his feelings. "I'll live. And thanks."

Contact came slowly at first, and with a dreamlike quality that was ominously new. Vellie wasn't sure what could be blamed on the disintegrating link and what was due to her clone's obvious hangover. She prodded Vee out of a rumpled and odorous bed and under a shower.

"Oh, Vee," she said in dismay as her clone scrubbed down. "You didn't get that pollen off, and now look at it." A fine and delicate network of mycelium, that glittered gold and amber through the droplets of water and gave off the scent of honey, covered the clone's hands and arms.

Vee hunched an irritable shoulder. "It doesn't matter. And Heller," she added maliciously, "likes it." However, Vellie insisted that Vee smear it with a biotic and felt a small thrill of achievement as her clone finally obeyed, although grumbling all the time. "And I'm not going out there again till the wind drops," Vee added.

"The blow's over," Vellie assured her. "So's the rot, and the green's already coming through. You know I wouldn't take you out into a mess, and this'll be like Spring on Home." She had to listen very closely for what sounded like a snort of derision in response.

Carreebas was still low on the horizon and the freshness of the early morning air seemed to invigorate Vee. Before Vellie could protest, Vee had grabbed the bike and was heading east. "Thought you said it was greening," she muttered, but Vellie could feel her lips pull back in a grin against her teeth. Shoots green as apples pushed through a light and fragrant leaf-mould.

"Stop a minute, Vee," said Vellie mildly.

The air was still and cool, crystalline. Shoots writhed spasmodically in the sun's substance, and new growth broke through the surface with an audible "pop." Moss was beginning to carpet the brown. Everything grew fresh and young all the way down to their toes.

"*Mmmyaahh!*" sighed Vee and stretched like a cat, the muscles of her arms and back rippling and flowing. "Whaddaya wan' today?" Her tongue felt thick and furred and couldn't seem to get round the words. "Stop shakin' your head," she added irritably as Vellie tried to focus more clearly.

"In the soil," Vellie whispered, "just under the surface, before it greens too much. Find the root mat, and at the edges, take the tips where the hairs are thickest and a smidgen of the soil. That's where the auxins concentrate."

"And wossit do to me?" demanded Vee acidly. "I maybe grow extra fingers? I've heard of this stuff." She sat back on her heels to sniff curiously at the friable medium. Fragments as fine as shaven fur clung to her skin and aromatic acids caught at the back of her nose.

"Don't crush it," murmured Vellie. It was a request born of instinct, not an order. She no longer had the confidence to issue orders, and in truth knew of no specific danger with the stuff, but felt driven by a native caution. "It's a constituent, a part ingredient, of the new-wave antigens."

Before Vellie could stop her, Vee licked her fingers. "Mmm. Tastes good. So now I live forever, yeah?"

"You're being very tiresome, Vee. You know perfectly well it's not as easy as that." Vellie sighed for a moment, hating herself, her clone and everyone she had ever known. "Oh, well, I don't suppose it'll do any harm. Let's fill up the rest of the cartridges."

"Yechn. I want to go to the sea," announced Vee when all the cartridges were filed in the bandolier and tucked into the stasis bank on the bike. Grit itched under her fingernails and streaks of dirt ran muddy with sweat down her exposed skin. She pushed her hair back with one grubby forearm. A rich redbrown scar slashed through the new verdure where she had been working. The surrounding orchid field had already grown waist-high. Vellie could only sympathize with Vee's desire, but although Heller's island would be less than a distant blur on the edge of the world when they got there, she would have preferred any direction other than east. Unconsciously her lips curled in distaste.

The beach was fine and firm, graded where the storm had drifted flour sand against the windbreak dunes into white, shades of yellow and pink. Vee stripped eagerly, anticipating the cool, and whimpered to herself as she managed to find a sharp edge in the coarser grades where the tide tugged at the land. The sea received her with a whisper of benediction, cool and cleansing.

Vellie sighed with relief as the mental and physical irritation eased.

Mindlessly, Vee swam out from the shingle, through wavelets that lapped at her and caressed her.

"Vee," said Vellie compellingly, "turn back." Beyond the double headland that guarded the bay, the sea was savage. Beneath the deceptive ripples that showed on the surface, feral currents raced between the islands. Eddies and undertows generated by the winds scraped the channels clean. Vee wouldn't stand a chance.

"Vee," hissed Vellie. "Vee!" Under the enhancer her scalp itched abominably, but her arms were too heavy and sluggish to lift to her head. Contact came and went in flashes and bursts of light, and then stabilized.

"Oh, all right," said her clone crossly, and turning on her back began to drift slowly back toward the shore. "Though I reckon I could swim it," she said, needling.

Vellie locked on again to Vee with grim determination: bright water streamed from sinews and muscles, sand crunched and groaned beneath her/her feet; a hand and shapely arm tendered for her/her shift, left lying in rainbow folds on the beach.

Vee screamed, a full-blooded, throat-tearing trumpet of sound echoing off the sky. Vellie produced a thin, high keen and screwed her eyes shut against pulsing dissonant images—her arm, wrinkled and old, the skin sagging over wasted muscles, decked with liver spots; her hand, gnarled and knotted with age.

"It's not that, Vee," she called urgently, as strongly as she could. "It's not that." For the reality that lay under the sensory collapse showed a golden network of pollen tubes breaking though the skin where biotic had been applied too haphazardly; breaking through in ridges and channels and rearing up into the mahogany splodge of fruiting bodies, the response to the new medium.

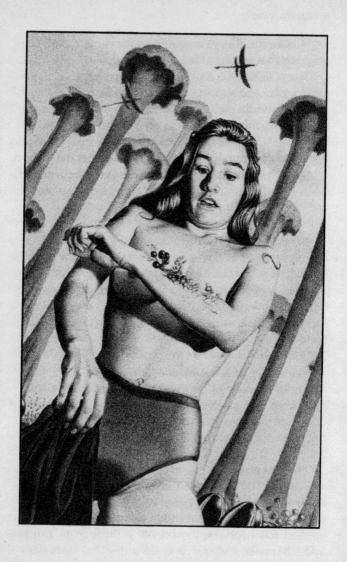

Illustrated by Richard Moore

"There's a cure," she cried, but her clone was running, running across the bluff into the sea-borne breeze, beyond Vellie's control, almost beyond her touch. "*He'll help me*," Vee shrieked into the wind of her flight and she thrust the image of Heller at Vellie, large, and moistly repulsive.

Vellie gagged. Wave after wave of revulsion swamped her and she threw out her hands in rejection. In that moment of negation, Vee, screaming fear, defiance and hatred, ran off the cliff and fell to the rocks and the current beneath.

The darkness inside her mind had the advantage of being comfortable. No criticisms, none of the constant challenges and irritations caused by the existence of others, living—existing—moment to moment, and sufficient to herself and each moment. Outside was light and movement, laughter and air; bitterness and envy, isolation. Once there had been a daughter, almost a friend; but all that friend had taught her was an extended misery of loss, and an ultimate descent into loneliness. Vellie wanted to stay with the warmth and the darkness. She didn't want to open her eyes. But someone kept calling.

The moon of Erriktor's face hovered over her like a captive balloon, oozing concern. Her arm throbbed with the recent memory of psycho-spray, and on the floor the enhancer coiled sluggishly, trying to sort itself out and tidy its component parts back into the fascia. The pneumopile of the couch was rough and scratchy against her back, as if stale crumbs abraded her skin, and her brain heaved at the inside of her skull. Vellie sat abruptly and her head collided with Erriktor's. Her mouth opened on an indrawn gasp of breath, and she glanced rapidly round the cubby like a trapped animal.

Erriktor gripped her shoulders. "Are you all right?" And without giving her time to speak, "You *are* all right." Hazel eyes held blue. "You're needed right now" (oh, slow kindling rebirth of hope; she warmed to Erriktor), "in Generation. Your clone is ready to wake."

Somehow, he got her up and walking, and through the integrity locks to Generation. He shared the needle showers and the radiant baths with her as far as he was able, talking all the time, a constant flow of words that washed over and through her forebrain, to be stacked by repetition against any time of need.

Vellie sat quietly in the recovery suite awaiting the pleasure of her clone. On the door the legend gave her indent and reference with the added information: "Clone AV#2: Full maturity." Drug-induced tranquility had allowed Vellie to enter the room with only the slightest tremor of guilt and sadness, and once inside she responded to the ambient peace. After all, she had helped the designers with that end in mind: to guide her clones through the trauma of birth; to bring them peacefully and trustingly to maturity.

Blue and lilac soothers rested her, encouraged her to slip further into a dreamlike state. The scent of camellias, very faint, triggered implanted subliminal memories of sunshine and shadow, mutual laughter, and a sense of belonging. Something disturbed her. Barely audible, the muzak marched out of tune with her mood. Irritated, she shook her head and tried to slow the pace to something of a more suitably funereal nature. The tempo failed to respond and remained annoyingly upbeat.

Half amused, half chagrined, Vellie realized that the manipulators were overriding her demands and using her own choices of sensory stimulation to lift her depression. Her mouth twisted wryly, and with a contraction of the throat that was something between a sob and a laugh, she turned her attention to the new clone.

The culture medium had drained away before her arrival, and the techs had been in an initiated breathing. Soapy vernix was drying rapidly in the warmth. White flakes drifted onto the satiny lining of the shell. The clone's breasts, perfect as her own, rose and fell gently with each movement of the diaphragm. The hair, less responsive than the rest of the body to the growth accelerators, clung moistly in short bronze curls to the scalp.

Vellie caught her breath. It was almost like looking into a mirror. Better, for this image would come alive, would empath with her. Erriktor's words began to come back to her. "Look to your strengths," he had said. "Build on them. The bond is the most powerful I have ever seen, and because of that, the clone's lifes pan will possess both quality and length. The love that you give is a part of this bond, and nurturing strengthens it, but it is also your weakness." Erriktor had looked at her anxiously, she remembered, as if he really cared, before the drifting clouds of antiseptic steam swallowed him. His voice had come to her disembodied. "When you give so readily, you open yourself to control. It's always a problem towards the end. Emotional blackmail. Just one more gem. Or holo. Or extended vacation." He sounded sad. "Try for a little discipline for both your sakes. They are, after all," and he laughed, "nothing but overgrown children, with the devious, incorrigible, obdurate cunning that all our young possess."

Some unrecognizable emotion spread through Vellie as she watched over the sleeper in the shell. It was, she realized, a good analogy: children—but without the messy smelly bits, and minus the years of waiting, hoping, for intelligent response. A full-grown child dependent upon her. She promised herself that she would do better by this one.

The last thing she remembered Erriktor saying as she entered the final cycles into Generation was, "They're all different. Don't expect a carbon of the last—you'll be surprised how much genetic identicals can vary," and he had squeezed her shoulder with a tenderness that had brought the sting back to her eyes.

Erriktor couldn't understand, though. How could he when he had never—could never—experience the full meeting of equals that she had? Vellie believed that even the other masters failed in full identification. The crude jokes about the clones showed the masters as insensitive, selfish oafs. Understandable, even excusable feelings toward the common herd became loathsome when directed at the clones. It would be like despising a piece of oneself. Unthinkable. And she leant forward, and with the back of one slim finger gently stroked the sleeping clone's cheek. She longed to whisper, "Wake up! Come and join me," but this time, everything must be perfect. Instead, she considered names, and what would be most effective to assert identity for this new creation.

The clone took a deep shuddering breath. Long, curved lashes fluttered on alabaster cheeks, opened upon eyes of a deep sky blue. Eyes you could drown in, thought Vellie admiringly, forgetting that they also belonged to her. Vellie held out her hands as the clone struggled to sit up, and for a long timeless moment they gazed at each other. Twin lips moved in the slightest of matching smiles.

Consciousness came swiftly with only a little pain. Vellie saw the clone's eyes widen in protest as the secondhand memories, hopes and certainties, fears and insecurities entered the receptive mind. Like writing on blank paper, dipping a hand into still water. It was a one-way process and she could only half watch through the curtain of herself. She wondered what it would be like to be the receptor.

The clone's fingers moved under hers, turned and grasped her hands more firmly. Vellie gasped with the brilliance of the smile that bathed her. Surely she had never produced any expression so beautiful?

"I love you," murmured the clone with total conviction. "Thank you for my life."

Vellie drowned in that smile, overwhelmed in the flood of emotion that poured from the clone. "Everything I have," she whispered with absolute sincerity, "is yours. All the ways of survival, all the elements of exchange." It would take time, she thought, even with the hypno-cells, for the clone to assimilate a full enlightenment, but they could take the run together while Vellie renewed her foundations. Her commitment was complete.

As Erriktor had said, the bond was exceedingly powerful.

"I was beginning to think," said Erriktor with a pleasant professional smile, "that we'd lost you to Generation." He hid his surprise at seeing the master, Vellie, in such proximity to Hellman. The masters were, after all, nothing if not fickle, and it seemed that the long separation had changed her tastes. "You have another success it seems. This current clone is even better than the last."

She sat beside Hellman, almost touching shoulders with him, and eating voraciously, savoring each mouthful as if it were a virgin experience. Erriktor found her air of avidity strangely repellent.

She stretched, and all the old familiar ripples moved through her muscles. Fingers spread, she rubbed at her scalp through the short bronze curls that the original Vellie had insisted they style the same, smiled at him sweetly, and with a few words put him at a distance. "I shall take care of her, believe me." Her voice was lower than she would have liked, carrying harmonics of both threat and promise, a combination that Hellman at least seemed to find attractive.

Erriktor blinked, and as she watched him flinch, she wondered for a nanosecond if something had gone wrong. But that was impossible. She had, after all, the right to the rank of master.

Where the bridging between master and slave became blurred, then the strongest emerged triumphant. Innocence had given her strength, and she had no intention of falling into the pit of longing and emotion that had trapped her progenitor. Future clones would find themselves handicapped before they could operate. She knew the ways from her acquired memories. She eyed Hellman speculatively as something crossed her mind.

Erriktor was looking worried, the fool, but she had no doubt of her ability to tie him up in philosophical knots until he became completely reassured about her.

"Have you named her yet?" His voice broke in on her thoughts.

She stared at him blankly for a moment before understanding came. "Oh, ah." After a moment's thought she pushed her lips outward in a calculated little *moue*. "Vex. Yes. Vex." She turned to Hellman with a giggle that she couldn't quite control. "Vex and Hex, how about that! You think they'll enjoy it down there?"

QUIXCHOTOL

Written by
E. Robertson Rose

Illustrated by
Gary McCluskey

About the Author

E. Robertson Rose began writing at high school and college, but decided while in school to enter a more stable, sensible profession: psychiatry. He hoped to disentangle the painful narratives of other peoples' lives rather than create his own.

However, in 1991, in defiance of conventional wisdom, he dumped his day job—closing his full-time psychiatric practice and moving to the San Francisco Bay Area, where he hoped the abundant bike paths and overall laissez-faire attitudes would help spur his creativity. In 1992, he made his first sale to Pulphouse, began doing some psychiatry on the side to pay the bills, got married, had a daughter, and gradually has found that his terse rejection slips have lately begun being replaced by kindly notes of encouragement. The rest will be history.

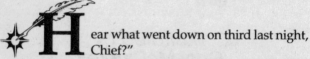

Hear what went down on third last night, Chief?"

Shepard's lean frame was jackknifed in his chair, his white boots kicked high on the auxiliary console. They squeaked against the old keyboard as he rocked back and forth, balancing precariously on the chair's rear legs.

"Yeah, I did." I nodded behind my paper. Scanning the classifieds in the *Park Service News* had become something of a habit these past several years, like coffee in the morning.

"What happened?" Timian asked, his voice straining to hold back a note of excitement.

"What happened?" Shepard's boots crashed to the floor with a bang. "I'll tell you what happened. A bunch of Zs got stuck in the outflow duct at plant seven. Almost caused a goddamned meltdown, that's what happened. Gonna cost Council two million to repair the damage. Check the board when you come in. If you're gonna be a ranger, you gotta know these things."

Timian's forehead puckered. "I thought the power plants were restricted. How could they gain access? Why would they want to?"

"Hell, they're Zs, kid! Who knows why they'd want to? I wouldn't be caught within a mile of that core. They must've waddled in through the outflow duct, best anyone can figure it. Can you imagine that, Chief, eight dumb Zs shuffling along in a neat little row, all getting fixed together in one ugly clump?"

"Yeah, 'fraid I can," I said.

"Amazing none of 'em died."

Out the side of one eye I spied Timian regarding me with those frail blue eyes of his. His stocky legs were tucked trimly beneath his chair, the image of a good cadet. I knew he wondered whether Shepard was bull-shitting him. I ignored his look. Ha! In the ads there was a position for a ranger open in Red Yosemite. A real park! At entry level wages. Damn.

A call buzzed in on the rescue line. Timian started, then sprang to the main console. His fingers flew smoothly across the faceted surface of the console, manipulating the grid. The kid was eager to redeem himself, show off his skills.

"A solo," he announced grinning. "From the Hill sector."

Shepard leapt to his feet. "The Hill? Not possible. There's never been a fix out that way."

Timian shrugged. "Called in from the Pink Paradis."

Shepard nodded. "Pink Paradis. Right. That's that new place, opened three, four months ago. Word on the Strips is they can't last a year. Can't compete, out there on their own like that." He turned to me. "So what in hell's a Z doing by the Pink Paradis?"

I tossed down my paper and snorted. It was a dumb question and Shepard had been around long enough to know better than to ask it. Why the hell did a Z do any-thing? Wasn't that exactly the point he'd been trying to make to Timian?

I swung around to grab an equipment pack. "Let's get moving, boys."

"Hell, Chief. Shift's up in half an hour, and I got me a pair of ladies waiting at The Lotus Pad, hungry for a real ranger. Come all the way from Planet Handelman. They'll be mighty disappointed if I don't show." He shot me a sly wink. "Can't it keep for the guys on third?"

Timian handed me the printout from the console. Not much traffic out there in the Hill. Not like the Strips. The Z could've been fixed all day before someone spotted it.

"Nope, 'fraid it can't wait. Your lady friends shouldn't have much trouble finding a replacement for you."

"Aw, come on, Chief," he said.

"Look. Last week you were late two shifts. Week before that I cut you a break and spring you early, then next day you call in sick. What's the problem, kid? Can't keep it zipped? You're a ranger. Remember?"

Shepard's eyes widened and his jaw went slack. He recovered quickly, however, his lips tightening into a broad grin that showed teeth. "No need to get sore, Chief. Just 'cause you never hunt the Strips. Know what they say, though: Every man needs a little companionship now and then."

I eyed him hard. "Shepard, how I handle my love life is none of your business; how you do your job *is* mine. Now we've got a fix to attend to, so let's move it!"

Shepard was a decent enough ranger when he felt like it. He was just young, and like so many here on Tesla, his sexual appetites tended to crowd out his work. Not that I'd never been tempted by the lure of the Strips myself. Packs of eager tourists streaming through the port on prepaid sex junkets, trying to cram all they could into their week away before crawling back to whatever drab world they were doomed to string out their lives on. All those excited, willing glances, all that smooth,

supple flesh. It could get awfully enticing, I knew. Hard
not to give in.

When I'd first transferred over from Vlad I'd spent
most of my off-duty hours reeling from one joint to the
next. But then I'd had an excuse: eight years of meditation training on a Monastic World with nothing but the
flat green line of the horizon for diversion. No sex, no
parties, no flesh to stare at but your own blurred nose.
In any case, I'd tired of the Strips after a few months.
Too much spectacle. Too much raw hunger unbalanced
by any real sense of beauty or intimacy. If not for the
arrival of the first Zs, I'd have put in for a transfer and
been off this world a decade ago.

The three of us hustled out of the station and piled
into the silver and black airvan with the Park Service
insignia holoed on the door. We cleared the perimeter
warning field and cut left then right around two busy
intersections, headed for the speedway. Not five blocks
from the station, opposite the flashing gold and lavender gateway to Strip Twenty-Two, we swept past a
small group of Zesh. They squatted by the side of the
road, their flat gray heads balanced on the thin coiled
stalks of their necks like some juggler's trick. I could tell
they were facing us because the respirators on their pos-
terior gill slits were out of sight, hidden behind chaotic
nests of tubules that glowed crazily in the lights from
Twenty-Two. The whole group seemed to stare rapt at
the roadbed. I say "seemed" because the Zesh have no
eyes, only tiny nostril-like apertures peppered across
the featureless planes of their foreheads.

Timian slowed the van and eyed me for a sign.
"Fixed?" he asked quietly. One of the Zs must've picked
up his thought because a slim tubule flicked out from
the tangle at its midsection. The movement was quick

and subtle enough that Timian missed it entirely. He slowed the van further and reached for the com-line to call in another unit.

"No problem, kid, they're mobile," I snapped. "Let's move it. This character in the Hill is solo, so he's gonna be fixed deep."

Timian cast a skeptical look back at the roadside Zesh, as though they'd gotten away with something, but he'd be sure to nail them next time around. With a hiss of acceleration the airvan leapt ahead and glided onto the broad speedway.

I really couldn't blame Timian for his mistake. He'd been with the Park Service on Tesla less than a month. It'd taken me a lot longer than that to get used to the Zesh's responses. How many of them had I pulled in on false alarms, their tubules flailing like a Medusa's head, even after the okay sign had been worked out? But then I was one of the first rangers to forgo the Strips for a chance at the Zesh. And that was before we realized they were telepathic.

The first time they brought one of the things into the station a bunch of us newer rangers had crowded round the autopsy table to observe. The peculiar chemical degradation they undergo at death was well underway. No odor whatsoever, but the Z radiated heat like a portable thermal unit. Its tubules had already gone rigid. They splintered off at the slightest touch. Before the med examiner even began to slice through the crinkly gray integument, the body lay in a slough of crystalline amber powder the depth of a finger, like pulverized glass, just from contact with the metal table.

I don't remember how many dead ones we hauled off the Strips in those first months before Council decided to make it a Priority Two matter. The Strip bosses were panicked. Didn't do much for their clientele's libido to have a new breed of alien turning up fixed or dead in their parking lots, pools, private beaches, secluded arbors, or whatever other improbable location you could think of. Nor could Council risk an "interstellar incident" with a species known to us under a year, a species we still hadn't been able to communicate with. Especially when the Croeb assured us they were peaceful and good-natured seekers of beauty and truth. It didn't hurt that they also happened to be under Croeb military protection.

So I got assigned to the Zesh detail, one of ninety rangers. It didn't take us long to determine that they were dying of neglect. Self-neglect. They would asphyxiate when their gill respirators lost their charge. We couldn't figure the damned things out—plain, seamless black boxes—and the Zs either didn't care to teach us or, more likely, couldn't. As the boxes lost their charge, however, the black color faded. With experience it became easy enough to tell about how much life was left in them. Armed with this crude skill, it became our task to rescue the Zesh when they got fixated, or "fixed." To save them from themselves.

If only we could've figured out what drove them, lemminglike, to their fixes in the first place. Or why, of all the planets in the galaxy, they chose Tesla, a Pleasure Park World, for their fatal pilgrimages. They didn't give a damn for our endless powdery white beaches; our perfect tropical climate; our three romantic sunsets per twenty-hour day, each in a different hue. And they certainly weren't here for the sex, legal and abundant though it was. The Zesh were a single-gender species—at least all the ones we'd cut open were.

So why had they appeared on Tesla alone of all the human worlds? Why had this Z we now pursued decided to fix itself in the unpopulated Hill sector? Meaningless, unanswerable questions.

Timian exited the speedway and threaded the airvan along a series of rough red dirt tracks. All around us the flat terrain heaved up into bouncing hills, dense with shrubs flowering in yellows, pinks, and whites. Outcrops of harsh brown rock jutted to either side of the van, looming dark against the flower-sprayed greenery. An occasional low tree crouched under the weight of its own limbs.

Beyond the hills, in the far distance, I could make out bank upon bank of coiled black spires taking aim at the soft yellow underbelly of the sky. The generating station was one of a network that enveloped Tesla in a protective high-density magnetic field, holding at bay the deadly flares of radiation that guttered constantly from the interplay of our three suns.

The airvan banked onto a steep incline. It slowed to a jogger's pace. Timian whispered a curse and jabbed the accelerator switch all the way forward with his palm. The van hummed defiantly, crawling forward no faster. It was designed for the flat concourses of the Strips, not these hills.

We crested the rise and off to our right the Pink Paradis bobbed into view—a maze of gaudy pink minarets and domed rooftops that seemed to have seeped across the entire hillside like a creeping fungal growth. Shepard, who'd been silent the whole trip, suddenly cried out, "Look!" He pointed toward the Paradis's huge holographic billboard, far larger than anything they would have permitted back on the Strips. It portrayed a handsome, dark, turbaned male fondling a svelte, slightly less dark female. His erection tented the rich crimson fabric of his djellaba. Her face was hidden by a full veil, but her ample breasts and thighs were bared without the slightest hint of shame.

Could Shepard really be so excited by this ridiculous display? I peered more closely. At the very bottom of the billboard, partially wedged beneath it, lay a small dark figure looking very much like a crushed insect. It was the Zesh.

Timian turned and said, "Chief, if it turns out this fix is related to the proximity of the magnetic field generators, we could have ourselves a real find, huh."

I snorted and shook my head. We'd rejected that hypothesis years ago.

But hell, Timian was new to the game. Hadn't I been the same way when I'd started? Bursting with theories about the Zesh and their fixations? Give Timian a few years—if he managed to stick it out—and that enthusiasm would wane.

So I let him chatter on about the magnetic field generators while he maneuvered the van as close to the billboard as possible. When he cut the engines I grabbed an equipment pack and bolted. Shepard sprinted out the other door to check the Z's respirator. He stooped beside the spindly body and shoveled through an armful of limp tubules to expose the black box. Grinning, he flashed me a thumbs-up. It might be this Z's lucky day after all.

I dumped the equipment bag out on the rich grass. We had a host of readings to take in order to satisfy the directives of the Council. They still hoped that, given enough data to play with, they could somehow make all the pieces fit together and solve the puzzle of the Zesh fixations. I followed their orders like a good soldier, but frankly, it was wasted effort.

We scanned for the presence of anomalous

electromagnetic radiation of any frequency, seismic perturbations, DNA, and amino acid fingerprints in the soil. Nothing. We assayed the geologic composition down to a depth of one hundred meters. We searched for unusual crystalline formations. We checked for the presence of ground water. We did everything but the sub-atomics scan; we couldn't get the bulky equipment in the van close enough.

I had just finished marking the precise location of the fix on the planetary grid when Shepard called out from beside the body of the Zesh. "Something strange here, Chief. Come have a look." As I approached he added, "Ever seen one of these before?"

Emblazoned upon the blackness of the Z's respirator box was a tiny golden emblem, like a starburst caught in a sine wave.

"No, I haven't," I replied. "But if I recall correctly, we were warned by Immigration to expect them, oh . . . 'bout three months ago, I'd say. That little insignia there is the mark of a priest—though the brains at Immigration had no idea what the concept 'priest' might actually mean to the Zesh. Just passing on what they'd learned from the Croeb. Nothing like our priests, though, that's for sure."

"A priest?" Timian asked with a frown.

I nodded. The first priest. Was there really something special that set this Z apart from the others? If so . . .

A pulse of excitement raced through my gut. My legs went weak and tingly. I stared up at the sky, rich yellow shading into dusky blue far off in the east. A faint, buttery fragrance lingered on the ghost of a breeze. I forced myself to breathe, slow and deep and even. The cool air filled my lungs. I felt steadier.

"Christ!" I muttered, shaking my head.

I, of all people, should know better. There was nothing here worth getting excited about. Just some Z with an insignia on its box, whatever the hell that might mean. Otherwise, it was a fix like any other.

Shepard said, "Looks like we've got ourselves a real V.I.Z., huh, Chief?"

"Yeah, a real V.I.Z." We all broke into laughter.

"Well, you'd better jack into this V.I.Z. fast, Chief. Its respirator might be operational, but it's as deep as any Z I've ever seen. Look at all the attention we've dumped on it—and not even a twitch in return."

Shepard was right. The curiosity and concern that spilled over from our thoughts should have been more than enough to jar the thing into flashing the okay, like the Zesh outside Strip Twenty-Two. Instead it lay unmoving, its jumbled tubules slack and heavy like seaweed stranded on a beach. That at least was a good sign.

I plunked myself down on the cool grass about half a meter away from it and eased my legs into a full-lotus. As I quieted my mind, I was struck by the chill in the air. The shadow of the giant billboard fell directly on top of us. Shadows were rare on Tesla. I stared up at the figures on the billboard. The woman's breasts and the man's erection loomed gargantuan. I stared down at the Zesh priest crumpled tight against the billboard's base. And I shook my head. How strange, that all my years of training on the Monastic Worlds should come to this—meditating in the shade of a billboard on a Pleasure Park World, hoping to prod an unresponsive alien back to consciousness with my thoughts.

I closed my eyes and sank into contemplation of my breath. I gathered my attention to a fine, focused point. And I thrust that point at the mind of the Zesh, pairing it with the image of that other Zesh on the dissection table, baking in a slough of shattered crystalline tubules. Then I opened my eyes and sat back waiting for it to rouse and flick me the okay.

A shudder rippled through its tubules. Several convulsed, darting out like startled minnows. They waved drunkenly for a few seconds, then slumped back to drowse with their companions.

"What!" Our mouths all fell open at the same time.

"What the hell is this?" Shepard whispered.

I knew I'd gotten through to the thing, no question about that. But this Z wasn't playing by the rules. Until I got an okay sign, the fix was still on. I closed my eyes and again thrust the image of death at it. Like a dagger. Deeper, deeper. Again. And still again. Son of a bitch!

I heard a soft rustling. I opened my eyes. The Z was nudging itself free. It took a full minute to scrabble out from its nook below the billboard. A lone tubule flicked out my way, then lashed back against its side.

We were done. At last. Mission accomplished.

I pried my legs out of the full-lotus, but before I could stand I experienced an inner sensation like that of fingers pressing at my mind—as if a blind person were attempting to penetrate and read my thoughts as braille. The sensation itself was not at all frightening, almost pleasant in fact. But on its heels came a flood of emotion that I'd encountered a handful of times before and that I did not find the least bit pleasant.

A vast sorrow burrowed into my chest, a pressured grief that threatened to explode in sobbing. I gasped, but the breath stuck in my throat. I forced it through, struggling to breathe as evenly as possible. In . . . out . . . in . . . out.

I shut my eyes and dropped back into meditation. Nothing here but grief, I reminded myself. A simple

emotion. Nothing more. Give it space and breathe
through it. Breathe, sucker! Inhale. Exhale. Breathe. . . .
Better.

An image from years earlier came unbidden to my
mind. I sat hunched beside a newly revived Z—my
fingers clawing at the smooth, impervious surface of the
roadbed we shared. I had just experienced its telepathic
groping for the first time and I felt devastated, utterly
devastated, by my failure to connect with it. Or so I
believed at the time.

Later I came to question the source of my emotion.
Had the sorrow I'd felt truly been mine? Or had I felt *its*
sorrow? Or some other Zesh emotion foreign to me, but
interpreted by my brain as sorrow? I didn't know, but
confusion turned to elation when I realized that here
at last lay a means of reaching the Zesh: through the
royal road of the emotions.

And so began half a year's worth of experiments in
which I was the star subject. Half a year's worth of
experiments that in the end yielded nothing. The Zesh
cooperated, of course. They let themselves be corralled
into the tidy white lab rooms and they squatted patiently
opposite me on the cool floor, their tubules flitting about
or matted soddenly together. But they never got fixed.
We were never able to reproduce their telepathic surges
of grief.

The memory vanished, but the sorrow of the Zesh
priest did not. Hang on and breathe, I urged myself. It
should let up any second now. Any second. It always
had.

But as breath followed halting breath, the sorrow
stuck fast. This Z refused to release me. I could still feel
it inside my brain, meandering through the neural
pathways, a lost child in a confusing metropolis of

thought, probing, searching—for what, damn it, for what?

For something to connect with. Yes, that was the answer. I knew it with a pained certainty.

I should open myself further then, to help it in its search, try somehow to forge a connection and receive it. It was a priest. Maybe . . .

What in hell was the matter with me! I seized the priest's sorrow and slammed it back. I envisioned a brick crushing the curious fingers probing at my brain. I could not receive them; no one could. They were the telepaths. We could only send. So why bother trying? Why risk the hope of true contact only to have it shattered again and still again, like so many tubules against the cold dissection table of reality.

The Z slid from my mind.

"That's right, priest. Back the hell off! I'm just trying to save your ass and do my job." Timian and Shepard stared at me. I hadn't realized I'd said it out loud. They'd probably both put in for transfers if I kept it up.

We brought the Z back with us in the airvan. No one spoke the entire time. It fumbled its way out at the station and waddled off toward the Strips, looking . . . well, looking very much like an unfixed Zesh should look.

I filed my report, making a special note of the priestly insignia for Immigration, then signed off to Petrie, our newest recruit from the Monastic Worlds. He beamed me a wide, beatific smile. I wondered how many months he'd last here on Tesla.

I fled the station and headed for Strip Twelve, the one closest to my living quarters. My mind was seething. I needed to get that priest out of my thoughts. Get some dinner inside me, preferably meat, some strong wine too . . . and, my God, yes, maybe even a woman for the night.

My belly full and my brain flush with a fine Headlands Cabernet, I was ready for the Strips. The cascading lights of Twelve outshone the sky above, muting its gentle pastels into a slurry of flickering bloodied grays. A dazzle of holo billboards beckoned to the tourists, promising delight upon sensuous delight.

I ducked into the Fontain Rouge with its famous trellised gardens. At either end of the lobby twin cupids spouted water from pursed lips. The water shimmered from within with a garish red glare, its source well concealed. Two easy arcs loped down above the heads of the tourists, gurgling contentedly into a large green pool at the center of which, on a tiny isle, Venus herself lay posed. Or more accurately, exposed. No statue this, but a live model replaced every two hours. Water sloshed at her ankles, stirred by the action of a submerged tidal agitator.

Even here in the lobby the tourists—mostly single, but also in clusters of two and three—pressed close on the broad cushioned divans. They eyed each other selectively. No music played. Instead, the splash of the waters mingled with a barely audible, breathless sighing, in alternate male and female voices, as if the walls themselves were coupled in delight.

I threaded my way through the glances of the curious and eager toward the party rooms in the back. Behind me the echo of the waters faded. I turned a corner and was greeted by a thick musky aroma that intensified whenever I passed one of the many ventilation grates in the floor. I sucked in the scent. My pulse quickened. A delightful, urgent heaviness settled in my groin.

Just ahead a door flew open and a woman, naked save for tight black gloves that hugged her arms to the elbow, scampered into the hallway. She was chased by a priapic man denuded of all body hair. Both wore party masks: his the Greek face of comedy, hers of tragedy. She spun and collided with me, then collapsed giggling into my arms. Her breasts compressed against my chest.

To keep from staring I dropped my gaze to the floor. The pheromones must not have hit me fully yet. I peeled her away, politely, and steadied her at arm's length until she regained her balance.

She peered at me through the mask, an exaggerated frown with a single, large teardrop dolloped below each eyehole. Her eyes glistened darkly within, but I could not make out their color. She placed a gloved hand against my cheek. The leather was almost hot, soft and inviting. I imagined her to smile beneath the mask as she gave my cheek a tender stroke.

Then her pursuer whirled her away and they were gone down the hallway. A slick of hot sweat streaked my arms where she had lain. I wiped them dry against my coarse uniform.

For a moment I hesitated. The woman's breasts, their jiggle, her giggle, the flesh-warmed leather, the musky tease of the pheromones, her touch—yes, her touch most of all—drew me forward. I eyed the door she and her companion had emerged from and I took a step.

But what was the use? She was gone, a brief faceless caress, nothing more. The mask she wore with its frown and tears—those were real enough; those lingered. And from behind them she had reached for me, touched me, tried to make contact.

An old sorrow burst upon me, familiar now, an ache in my chest too deep to find solace, even here.

It seemed I could not escape the Zesh. I turned and made my way slowly back toward the lobby.

The next afternoon we got another call from the Pink Paradis. A threesome doing the *Déjeuner sur l'Herbe* scene out in the hills, or "the Naked Lunch" as Shepard put it, had spied a Z.

We raced out, retracing our previous day's route. Timian and Shepard were silent the whole way. They probably wondered, as I did, why the repeat? Why the hill again?

At my command the airvan sighed to a halt on a verdant ridge top. We piled out and scanned the rolling hills for the dark blot of the Z. Timian spotted it first, out on the lip of a rocky precipice that hung below us about half a kilometer's distance. The precipice tumbled into a long steep drop. No road wound anywhere near it.

"They do pick the damnedest places," Shepard muttered.

"Well, boys," I said, "looks like this Z is going to bless us with a little hike." They groaned. "Hey, we can all use the exercise."

We distributed the weight of the equipment equally among us and set off, scrambling down the steep escarpment. In ten minutes we stood huffing at the lip of the precipice that held the Zesh.

I've never been crazy about heights, so I sent Shepard and Timian out to take the readings while I tried to determine where in hell we were on the planetary grid. From the corner of my eye I spied Shepard hovering over the Zesh, checking the respirator. His face went sour, his lips pinched. He scuffed at the dirt, sending a shower of loose gravel over the edge of the precipice as he trudged back my way.

"It's another priest, Chief. Maybe even the same one. Hell of a coincidence."

I started to curse, but simply shook my head. "You call it coincidence; I'll call it bad luck."

Shepard nodded. "Real bad luck. Its respirator's grayed out. Oh-point-one capacity, tops. The Z's been here thirty, thirty-five hours. Maybe longer."

"So it can't be the same one. Unless . . . Are you telling me it turned right around after we released it yesterday and came back here? Without recharging?"

Shepard shrugged.

We stood in silence. Timian shuffled up. He'd finished collecting his data. I ordered him back to the van to stow as much of the equipment as he could haul. That would save us precious time later if we were going to get this Z back alive.

I edged out along the precipice, hugging the hard rock with my back. It was plenty wide enough. I just didn't want to peer down over the ledge at that drop, not even accidentally.

When I reached the priest I carefully lowered myself to the ground. I brushed the loose gravel out from under me, dusted off my palms, then sank into meditation. I hurled the image of the dissection table at the priest and added my impressions from the day before, when it had finally flashed me the okay from under the shadow of the billboard. Its single tubule flying out. My relief. Its safety. I hammered them home.

And without my intending it, the rush of sorrow I'd felt the day before rose again in my chest. That endless, aching sorrow, lonelier than death. Like a mother torn from her child.

Before I could clear it, a word rang out in my mind. *Quixchotol.* I call it a word, but it was more a collection of syllables: brisk, sharp cadences rising and plummeting like the piping of birdsong. *Quixchotol.*

No such word existed in *my* psyche.

Oh, God. I must be receiving the Zesh priest.

I fought through the pounding of my pulse to remain focused. The word sounded again. *Quixchotol.*

"*Quixchotol,*" I shot back and heard the syllables repeated several more times. Here was the opportunity I'd waited a decade for. I took myself deeper, throwing my mind fully open to the priest.

Quixchotol! Riding the syllables came a flood of color. Intense velvety blues, vibrant pinks, salmons laced with airy sea-greens, sharp turquoises—they smacked into my mind with the force of a cresting wave, swirling, churning, blending into each other. They danced about me like living fountains, waters bright with teeming iridescent fish. And the fountains themselves danced and spun and twined in incredible arcs and spirals. Colors pulsed in what seemed thousands of unearthly hues, shifting every second, shimmering all about me. *Quixchotol.*

I penetrated deeper and saw that the vibrant splashes of color were merely the outermost surface of the *quixchotol.* For each shifting hue carried within it complex layerings of sound as well. Lilting fairy chimes effervesced with pleasure, bubbled over into throaty panpipe moans, which surged recklessly against the tense beating of a hundred hearts. And beneath the sounds, emotions. Such emotions! Taut strings of joy, yearning, passion, despair. They burst forth in riotous harmony, a chorus of emotions, each sounding its own unique tone, its own impossibly rich hue.

I wrestled to hold onto the experience of *quixchotol* without drowning in it. My body shivered. Such beauty. The rush and sweep of it. Such paralyzing beauty!

"I am a ranger." I forced myself to repeat the words

slowly in my mind. "A ranger. On planet Tesla. A ranger in telepathic contact with a Zesh."

But the onslaught of *quixchotol* was too much. I could not hope to contain it. My mind would crack open and dissolve any second now, flush with feelings, tones and colors, leaving me permanently insane.

With that thought the *quixchotol* subsided. I was left exhausted, like a swimmer washed ashore from a powerful riptide, clambering out from the surf on hands and knees. I felt Shepard tugging at my shoulder, his voice urgent, plaintive, yet so very distant. I could not open my eyes. I dared not. Not yet. I could not relinquish the beauty of *quixchotol*. Tesla's three suns would burn pale and dull to my eyes forever after, a mere facsimile of what light could be.

Shepard's voice finally cut through. "Christ, Chief, the Z's almost gone." I'd never heard his voice quaver so. "What the hell's the matter with you? Wake up!"

I blinked my eyes open. Shepard kneeled beside me. His face was drawn, his cheeks darkly hollowed. "You've been out ten minutes. What in hell's going on?" I could not answer.

"You okay?"

I nodded and smiled at him.

"You sure you're okay?"

I nodded, my smile widening.

"We're losing this one, Chief. And it's a priest, remember? V.I.Z.?"

I sighed. "Okay," I said weakly, "I'll give it one more try."

I shifted and pulled my spine erect, then struggled to focus on the litany of images I had broadcast to so many Zesh over so many years. But each time I imagined the dead Z on the dissection table a more powerful force wrestled it from my mind. In its place I heard *"quixchotol"* repeated over and over like a fevered chant: the priest inviting me to plunge into its world of splashing, sparkling color-tones and moods, drawing me into its embrace.

I couldn't break away. Nor did I want to. I sat rapt, my focus totally inward as color and sound ripped through me again. I didn't care about the Zesh, didn't care about the Park Service, or Shepard, or even myself. Only *quixchotol. Quixchotol.* There was nothing else.

And at last it dawned, a sliver of a thought . . .

This then was how they got fixed.

Shepard's voice intruded, verging on panic. "It's not responding, Chief. I think its respirator's shot."

I yanked my mind free of the Zesh and blasted it a jolt of alarm that redoubled what must have already been screaming into it from Shepard. *"Quixchotol!"* I shouted mentally, pairing the lilting sound of the syllables with the rough crunch of dried tubules. *"Quixchotol* means mind-loss. Death." Image of a dissection table. "You will die! Must stop *quixchotol!* Please!" I reached for the priest in my mind and imagined lifting it from the ground, shaking it violently over and over until its tangled tubules jerked back to life.

A sudden silence filled my mind—the peaceful, open silence of acquiescence. I'd gotten through to it at last. I rubbed my eyes open and waited for the okay sign. But the priest's tubules lay unmoving. If anything they appeared to shine with an inner tension, a tautness which, if it increased any further, threatened to snap them from within.

The Zesh was dying. This creature was dying and there was nothing I could do. Worse still, I understood.

It was a miracle we had ever managed to pry any of them free.

A savage grief swept over me. I clamped my eyes shut and thrust myself back into meditation. I prayed that the priest would pull me under once again and let me join with it, even in its dying. I groped for it like a child, refusing to let go of our contact.

I wanted, no, I needed it to know that I understood, that I had received it clearly. That Tesla was no shabby pleasure park, not to the Zesh. *They* didn't come here as we did, to drown themselves in mindless lust. For them it must have been a Mecca—the experience of *quixchotol*, a mystical union worth even the price of death itself. For ten years I'd regarded them as a lower life form, insensate and death-seeking. Now I knew the truth.

"Oh, my God." Shepard's voice broke through in a coarse whisper.

My eyes blinked open automatically to find every tubule in the Zesh's midsection, all seven hundred twenty of them, quivering at once. An agitated ripple of motion surged through them and they lifted and fell in unison, smoothly, fluidly, gracefully—like the arms of an anemone sloshed by a powerful ocean current.

I felt the Zesh grasp again for my mind . . . and the surrounding hillsides fractured into color, sound, emotion—even with my eyes open! A delicate, towering fountain of *quixchotol* geysered up from the precipice directly in front of me, only meters from where the priest lay. Another twenty or more dotted the surrounding hillsides, undulating like sensuous whirlwinds. They seemed to explode from the very ground of Tesla.

Shepard rushed to my side and grabbed my arm, concern taut on his face. He shouted at me, but I lost his words among the kaleidoscopic chiming of the *quixchotol*.

Illustrated by Gary McCluskey

It spumed out behind him, limning his features in a corona of flashing color-tones. I managed a weak smile and a nod—to let him know I was okay, yes, better than okay—but he didn't understand, perhaps could never understand. He tightened his grip, but the *quixchotol* was stronger. The pressure of his fingers dwindled and was soon lost.

My vision deepened, then, and I glimpsed underground rivulets swollen thick with the stuff. I saw how it settled in certain spots, gathering in intensity until the ground could contain it no longer and it burst forth toward the sky, sculpted by some property of Tesla into the slender twining fountains that only the Zesh could behold. The rivulets crisscrossed the hillsides in a bright, dizzying latticework of color. Yet all seemed to emanate from one location. They all flowed outward from the direction of the Pink Paradis.

The Pink Paradis? A gasp burst from me involuntarily, before I realized, before my face opened in a grin wide and childlike and brimming over with delight.

This then was the Zesh priest's parting gift to me. To understand that the *quixchotol* had its source *there*. That it was, after all, human in origin. That our mindless human pleasure, crude and simple as it was, could give rise to such beauty, such ultimate, universal beauty.

The fountains of *quixchotol* faded, absorbed back into the rocky green hillsides. I rubbed at my eyes and lurched to my feet. On the rock below me the Zesh lay fixed. I reached out to touch it, to make physical contact with this being whose mind I had shared so intimately. I laid my hand gently upon its tubules. A wave of warmth met my fingers. My hand trembled. Ever so gently I stroked at its tubules. They gave slightly, a stiff amber mass. One cracked, splintered off and rolled across the precipice. I watched it fall, to shatter with a tiny chime against the rocks far below.

"Oh, Christ, it's dead."

"Yeah, the son of a bitch didn't respond to anything you sent it. Not your fault, Chief. Don't worry, I'll back you up. It must've had a friggin' death wish."

I shook my head violently. "No!" Tears streamed from my eyes, leaving my cheeks wet and warm. I did not bother to wipe them. "No, it's not that. . . ."

Shepard stared at me. I gazed off at the hills to avoid his look. "It sent to me, Shep. This Z actually sent to me. And I received it. I know why they're here, why they get fixed."

I swallowed down a sob. "My God, my God, did I ever receive. . . ."

Shepard said nothing.

"Christ, Shep. I feel like I knew her. The priest."

Shepard nodded slowly several times in silence.

Together we hefted the body of the Zesh priest back to the airvan. It was not heavy, but the warmth radiating from it grew rapidly into a dry heat that stung at our bare palms. Timian met us halfway. He'd seen us coming and brought gloves.

THE HEART OF THE MATTER

Written by
Doug Beason

About the Author

Doug Beason was a Writers of the Future *semi-finalist in 1986. He has since published numerous short stories in such places as* Analog, Amazing Stories, Full Spectrum *and* SF Age—*among others. He has authored ten novels, many with collaborator Kevin J. Anderson, including the Nebula-nominated* Assemblers of Infinity; *their latest,* Ignition, *is soon to be a major motion picture. Doug holds a PhD in physics and served on the White House staff under both the Bush and Clinton administrations working for the President's Science Advisor. He's also served as Director of Faculty Research at the U.S. Air Force Academy in Colorado Springs, worked with* Apollo/Soyoz *astronaut Tom Stafford planning a mission to Mars for NASA, and has directed a plasma physics laboratory. Doug has been married seventeen years and is the father of two young daughters.*

've been unusually lucky—to have published so much as early as I have. I received no formal training in the craft of writing. I didn't take any creative writing courses, or enroll in writing classes while in college. In fact, I was twenty-nine when I first got the urge to write—I was ancient, by some standards in the SF field.

I learned the trade of creative writing by brute force: sending off for magazine submission requirements, then writing like crazy for several years before I got my professional sale.

But the upshot is that I've now sold everything I've written to professional markets. So something worked.

I learned to write by following a "hit or miss" approach, learning the craft by reading and by instinct. Every so often I'd pick up a book on writing and gain some hints that would steer me in the right direction. I attended one writing workshop after I sold my first novel, and that focused my efforts so I could write without constantly going back to the basics—because they became a part of me.

So certain parts of the trade can be taught—technique, hook, suspense, plot, point of view, character, theme, simile—the list goes on. That's called the *craft* of writing. It's the stuff that you can learn in a workshop, or by reading a book. You use it every day.

Remember that. It's never too late to start writing—if that's what you want to do with your life. And the craft of writing can be taught. So forget the fancy academic background, the English degree, or the masters in Fine Arts.

So what if you didn't take writing in college, or have any formal training?

But you'd better be a voracious reader and be ready to apply what you learn, because plenty in books is simply indispensable. Which leads us to the most important concern. Not the craft, but the *art* of writing.

Now, the art of writing is the stuff that breathes life into a story. It makes readers forget they're looking at words on a page, and instead start caring about what's going to happen to the character. It's what makes people laugh, or better yet, cry, when they become so attached to a character that what happens in the reader's head becomes as real as life itself.

The art of writing can't be taught. It has to come from the heart. No formula can show you how to do it.

Stan Schmidt, editor of *Analog*, once said he had read a technically perfect piece from a beginning writer—the work was grammatically correct, it had just the right number of adjectives and adverbs, it had an intricate plot and was populated with real characters. But the story didn't work. It was cold, sterile—devoid of emotion (and not purposely so). Why? Most likely because the writer was a young man who had not yet experienced life. He hadn't loved, or felt threatened in any way; he hadn't traveled, or interacted with people any more complex than the characters that you'd find on a TV show. In short, he was formalistic.

Once again: the art of writing has to come from the heart. If you aren't moved by your piece, then how is the reader going to be moved?

However, all is not lost. One way to write from the heart is to practice. And you can only practice by sitting down and writing. Not by talking about it, or by going around and telling people that you're a writer; or even getting together with other writers and doing "writer stuff." The world is full of people who like to hang out with writers and talk shop. But they never publish. Because they never sit down and write.

Writing. It's the only way you learn the art.

And it's hard. As are most things in life. You've all seen (or at least heard of) the old TV show *Beverly Hillbillies*. One character, Jethro, keeps saying he wants to become a brain surgeon. But he never applies to medical school, much less takes any premed classes. For many people, it's the same with writing. They say they want to be a writer, but they never write.

So the first bit of advice I can give new writers is just a variation of Heinlein's rules: first you *write;* then you *finish* what you write; then you *send it out* until someone buys it; and you *don't rewrite* unless an editor says they'll take another look at it. There comes a point where you have to stop tinkering with the manuscript and just get it out of your house and "on the street." By all means revise, but realize that there comes a time when it doesn't make sense to keep polishing your masterpiece.

When people ask "What's it like to feel you've got it made as a writer?" I can only stare at them and think, *huh?* What do you mean "got it made"?

You should know that writers *never* have it made.

You see, you don't get into this profession to get rich and retire. The money's not there. For every King or Clancy who hits it big, there are hundreds or thousands of people who have submitted works and have gotten no more than a form rejection slip. For many—those who want to be a writer for the money—it would be better to pursue something that really pays, like being a doctor or an engineer. Everyone's heard that the average yearly salary for a writer is on the order of $5,000. That includes the people who have hit it big, balanced by thousands more who practically have to give their work away.

The second reason writers never have it made is that writers never stop writing. Not because they have to keep writing for the money (reread the above paragraph!), but more importantly, because writers *can't* stop writing.

If you look at all the masters in the field, no one just quits writing, retires and takes up fishing. Why? Because the love of the art keeps them going. It's the reason why writers start writing in the first place, the reason why students take to scribbling vignettes in their notebooks at the risk of failing a course; why the mother of two small children, instead of flopping down in exhaustion while the kids are taking a fifteen-minute nap, picks up a laptop computer and types out the only 250 words that she'll create that day; or the office worker spends lunch typing out the next page and a half of his novel. . . .

You get the point. Writers don't write for their mothers. They don't write because it will make them rich. Writers write because they have to write. Something in their heads—a fantastic world of images, heroics, love and death—has to be communicated to other people.

They say you're only as good as your last book. In many ways that's true. Writers need to keep proving to themselves that they still have the fire in the belly to produce the written symphony that pulls myriad ideas, plot lines, threads of meaning, symbolism and emotion into a finite piece of work we call a story.

And it doesn't get any easier.

Remember, the art of writing is not formalistic. You can learn all the rules—and you should, especially if you're going to break them. But to get the emotion, you need to write from the heart. Don't talk about it, write.

Good luck, and hope I'll be reading you soon. But don't forget, if you're successful, you'll never stop. Because you can't.

IN THE ELEPHANT'S GRAVEYARD, WHERE SPACE DANCES WITH TIME

Written by
Sue Storm

Illustrated by
Patrick Stacy

About the Author

Sue Storm has known that she wanted to be a writer since she was twelve years old, when she wrote and directed a play about pirates. Sue got a degree in journalism back during the seventies, has worked as an artist in Eugene, Oregon, and currently lives on a farm in southeastern Oregon.

Five years ago she bought a word processor and began writing science fiction, fantasy, and horror, where she's had excellent success in the semiprofessional markets, with sales to anthologies such as Air Fish, The Magic Within *and* Palace Corbie, *and to such magazines as* Space and Time, Sirius Visions, The Silver Web, Dark Regions, Aberrations—*and literally dozens of others. Sue has stories* sold to such magazines as Pulphouse, Pirate Writings *and* Horror Story a Day. *She's twice been an honorable mention in both the 1993 and 1994* The Year's Best Science Fiction *by Gardner Dozois, was an honorable mention in the 1993* Year's Best Fantasy, *and has had preliminary nominations for both the Bram Stoker and Theodore Sturgeon Awards. Indeed, with nearly seventy sales to the semiprofessional markets, I believe that Sue holds the title as the most widely published new writer to appear in this contest. She even has a chapbook of her stories recently published,* Star Bones Weep the Blood of Angels, *available from CyberPsycho's AOD, P.O. Box 581, Denver, CO.*

Believe it or not, even with such credits, Sue is still eligible to win the contest, for the fine story you are about to read is her first professionally published tale.

Zatombi went to live in the elephant's graveyard when her eyes turned purple. Her mother locked her in the barn and sent a carrier pigeon to the village so the oxcart would come and take her away.

Six men tied her to the uprights of the cart. She could not move her head; she had to stare into the purple eyes of the girl tied across from her. The men stuffed rags in their mouths, but the other girl made sounds the whole way: "Ggggaaggaaggaa . . ." The sun fried Zatombi's head, wrung all of the moisture from her body. Dust swirled up and clogged her nose. She saw the spirits of the dead turning somersaults in the dusty air between her and the other girl. They wore bright red scarves and jigged about in complicated patterns, sometimes rushing by on the backs of iridescent impalas. The other girl saw them, too, but never for a second did she change the noise she made, and soon it became a drumbeat within their bones: "Gggaaagagga . . ."

Zatombi liked the elephant's graveyard spread across the side of a serpentine mountain. Icegreen moss covered the ancient bones, making them a broken, crooked forest. Orchids clung to the moss and sent their sweet, hungry odor out to devour the scent of rotting flesh. Not elephant flesh, of course. Elephants disappeared long ago. Only their giant skeletons remained to lumber the jungle at night. But famine, war, and finally, plague, placed the dead bodies of humans everywhere, as if someone's mad, giggling god felt compelled to decorate the earth with bits and pieces of humanity—in still life. Zatombi watched another girl carry around the tiny mummified carcass of a baby she'd found. She wrapped it carefully in banana leaves and, for weeks, sang to it every night, the same words over and over:

"Gwababa, gwababa, goduka . . ."

"Jackdaw, jackdaw, go home . . ."

The villagers called Zatombi and the others "mamba babies," because they believed such children—whose eyes turned purple at puberty—as dangerous and unpredictable as the mamba snakes dropping silently from trees like deadly black rain. Tradition forbade the killing of snakes; evil spirits flew free and ravening from a snake's dead body. So they appeased the spirits (and each other) by taking the mamba babies to the elephant's graveyard to live.

The new ones came with fresh and boiling confusion in their violet eyes. They screamed and ran in circles, often scratching dark, bloody furrows in their skin. Infection set in, killing many. Zatombi knew they wished for it, most of them. Death. They wished for death. Once, Zatombi wanted to die. But it was long ago, in another dream, long before she came to live in the elephant's graveyard.

She was four, and her mother Nomasa woke her before the sun and took her outside. Zatombi remembered staring up at the slowly bluing sky, her teeth chattering so hard she almost bit her tongue, as Nomasa sluiced her down with cold water from the pump. Then her mother tightly braided Zatombi's frizzy hair with bits of colored cloth. She dressed her up in the orange and blue dress made from cast-me-downs, and then she walked Zatombi over to the Big House.

Though Nomasa worked there every day, Zatombi had never been to the Big House, and she skipped with excitement through the pale warmth of early morning.

"Tula!" her mother said as they reached the huge front door. "Hush!"

But Zatombi's bare feet went slap-slap on the vast, shiny floor, and her voice squeaked in awe as she tried to look in all directions at once, craning her head at the tapestries, statues, and rich, shiny leather furniture. The Big House smelled of horses and pineapples and sugar cane.

When they reached a wooden door carved with the stick-thin figures of naked white women, Nomasa stooped and knelt down beside her daughter, plucking at her dress with nervous fingers and avoiding her eyes.

"You be good girl, Zatombi, hear?" Nomasa said. "You be real good. You do whatever they tell you."

Zatombi smelled her mother's sweat, sharp and musky. She looked up at Nomasa's deep black face and saw the lines and puckers there. Zatombi thought of how her mother smoothed her cheeks when she bumped her knee, how she smuggled home treats from the Big House, the way she made a warm, mushy lump for curling up next to in bed at night.

Solemnly, Zatombi nodded her head.

"You got to be good, baby, you just got to," Nomasa whispered, and then she stood up and opened the door, pushing Zatombi inside.

As the sun went down, making a fiery ball out on the edge of the dusty plains, Zatombi's mother waited for her by the kitchen door. One of the other women brought the little girl down the back stairs. The kitchen was full of the scents of roasting springbok and baking yams, and the yeasty smell of corn-beer fermenting in cool clay pots, but Zatombi did not notice. Her hair was all undone, wild around her face, and she had on different clothes.

Nomasa didn't look at her, didn't even take her hand. The blazing sunset made everything look red to Zatombi, or maybe it was the pain inside her and the way she felt for the first time how she was made up of more than skin and blood and bones, how there were things inside her that could hurt, and never even show.

Zatombi followed her mother home, stood still while Nomasa washed her under the pump again. Sat and ate, putting the food into her mouth in a slow, steady way, like the old-time robots in picture books.

When it came time to go to sleep, Zatombi pulled a blanket off the top of the bed and crawled underneath, way back in the corner. She lay and watched Nomasa's swollen black ankles walk back and forth, back and forth. She heard the bed creak over her head, felt the weight of her mother pressing down, pushing her closer and closer to Zatombi, but still too far away to touch.

Then Zatombi wanted to die.

She wasn't the favorite at the Big House, so some days she just sat and waited. As she got older, she made friends with a few other children. There weren't just black ones like her; there were three cream-colored blonde girls and one boy from trashtown. Their parents sold them, they said, seeming proud of the fact. They liked to play with Zatombi, dressing her in the exotic, lacy clothes the children wore in the Big House.

When the plague came, the blonde children were first to die. Most of the white people died, and a lot of the black ones. Zatombi and Nomasa didn't die. Nomasa had already had the plague when she was pregnant with Zatombi, and she survived. Now both were immune.

But Zatombi's eyes turned purple.

The mamba babies didn't make friends in the elephant's graveyard. They existed in too many worlds, and none of them coincided with each other. Alone, they scrounged for food, eating winged ants, locusts and caterpillars, kaffir plums, blackberries and wild figs. Sometimes, they found fresh bones and cracked them open to get at the marrow. The flesh they left alone. But bones formed the framework of their wild, demented lives. At night, when Zatombi lay inside her elephant skeleton staring out at the rib-crossed stars, she'd hear the soft, breathy notes of a flute made from the chin bone of a reedbuck, or the deep rumble of a hollow log pounded rhythmically with knobby human femurs.

Sometimes the elephants got up and danced, then, and Zatombi hung on to the pale bones, swaying in the moonlight. Clouds of blue moths descended out of the sky, covering her skin with their fuzzy tickle, like a faraway song she almost remembered.

Strange scenes wound among the stars. She saw an impossible world, round as a ball, chewing on itself like some demented hyena eating its own bloody leg.

When the sun came up, the elephant bones carefully rearranged themselves within their cozy coverings of moss, and Zatombi slept and dreamed of three-legged hyenas and Uthlakanyana, the magic dwarf who sat and laughed when the stupid animals grew hungry and chewed off yet another leg.

Green monkeys swung above her head, their loud "kek-kek-keks" waking her. Burrowing under a massive shoulder bone, she uncovered her cache of Cajun peas. While she ate, her mouth savoring the nutty taste, she thought of pictures she'd seen in books at the Big House.

A thing called "sit-tee," with tall buildings glittering in the sunlight and colorful metal carts that moved about with nothing at all to pull them. Streets and lives laid out in straight, narrow lines, turning corners with a sharpness that made her wince. She watched a sunbird land on an arching elephant rib. It preened its green, shiny feathers with a curved beak, its movements compact and fluid. A mongoose streaked across the ground with a graceful, humping gait. No sharp corners here, in the elephant's graveyard. Zatombi wondered if the sit-tees now rumbled with the restless quiet of old bones, if all the sharp lines had smoothed and crumbled into yet another graveyard. Or maybe the buildings still stood, and if you looked at them from far away, saw the sun glinting off of windows like a thousand eyes, perhaps you thought people still lived and played there.

How many travelers wept at the dust they found? Zatombi listened to the whining howls of the jackals wrestling over flesh left untouched by the mamba children. How many indeed?

Black clouds rolled suddenly over the elephant's graveyard, and rain burst out. Children hooted and screeched, running about in the warm water and banging bones against their heads, the slick skin of their thighs. Zatombi opened her mouth to the sky, felt the water slide down her throat, thick and hot like the mealies Nomasa used to make. She wondered: Would it feel the same when she peed it out? Would it climb the liana vines back into the clouds again? Again, and again, the same pieces of water passing through her body, kissing her tongue, and greeting her insides like an old friend. She stared at her purple eyes caught in the inky pools left among the bones. What if only a few important pieces—sky and earth, water and stardust—

passed through, over and over? Making a big circle, round and complete, just like that impossible world.

Zatombi went often to the edge of the elephant's graveyard and gazed at the dusty plains stretched like a hot, tight skin over the horizon. At the foot of the mountain, a lake stood, and a few animals gathered there to drink and wade. But beyond the lake, all was arid, parched ground. She climbed a liana vine, crouching in the trees with the monkeys, and wondered about the emptiness of the world. It bothered her, this emptiness. Somehow it pushed its way inside her and found the hollow cupped there, matching it edge for edge. Zatombi chewed on wild coffee beans and thought about doing something to fill up that space, both the one inside and the one outside. Her purple eyes saw tall waves of grass and the gently rocking necks of giraffes drifting along the green sea.

She climbed down again, and closing her eyes, sent her hands roaming over the rough surfaces of elephant bones. In her mind, they grew layers of scarlet muscles, tough gray hides, long eyelashes that framed amused and intelligent eyes. Clenching her fingers in sudden desire, she crushed an elephant's delicate foot bone. For a long time, she looked down at the calcium bits in her hand.

There must be a way, she thought. *A way to fix it.*

The adults brought a white boy one day, dumped him in a huddling heap at the edge of the elephant's graveyard. He ran screaming into the lush forest of bones, tearing at his neck where—though he wore nothing—he believed his white clothes still bound him. Zatombi followed and watched.

He screamed for a week. At night bush babies crept

up beside her, their huge red eyes watching along with her purple ones. They twittered like old women gossiping. During the day, tree dassies called out their displeasure, their groans spiraling up into shrieks that rivaled the white boy's.

Finally, he stopped.

Zatombi waited two more days, staring at the white boy huddled inside the skull cavity of an elephant. Something about him pulled at her. She dreamed once she hated white men. But that was long ago. It didn't happen here, among the chattering bones and ghostly butterflies and purple-eyed children. Not here, not in the elephant's graveyard, where space danced with time.

When Zatombi crept closer, she saw how the white boy shook all over. With unusual courage, she slipped through the leg bones of the elephant and squatted in front of him. The white boy wasn't big, not big at all. If he'd been like other white men, he never would've fit so easily into an elephant's skull. Long brown hair hung over his face in strands stuck together with dirt and oil. His hot purple eyes looked right through her.

"Sakubona," Zatombi greeted the white boy formally and waited. He didn't move, didn't even blink. She poked him in the chest. "Hey."

The white boy shuddered one final time and then grew still. His violet eyes slowly focused on Zatombi's. Some shadow of old pain floated out of her. She watched its gray outlines disappear into his chest.

"Uh!" she grunted.

The boy pointed down. "Wipe your feet," he said.

Zatombi looked where he pointed. A scattering of crushed mimosa flowers surrounded the elephant skull.

"You've come a long way," he said. "Evil may be on your feet."

Illustrated by Patrick Stacy

She ground her feet into the mimosa blossoms. A smell like burning bananas drifted up and away.

The white boy stared at her.

"Zatombi," she said, pointing to her chin. "Not so bad." She flung her arms out to the bones gleaming white and moldy green in the hot sun. Steam rose from disappearing rain. Overhead, a cuckoo whispered, echoing her words in tiny, whiplike syllables. "They leave us alone."

"Alone," he repeated, pushing his hair away from his face.

Zatombi nodded. She wanted to touch him, wanted to feel his skin. Her black fingers reached out. He was hot, burning-up hot, even in the shade of the elephant skull.

He winced, and Zatombi felt more pulled out of her, as if something slurped the grease from the inside of her bones. She stood and stumbled back. The white boy looked up at her, his purple eyes dizzy with pain.

"You're different," she said flatly.

His head fell forward on his chest, and he moaned softly.

"Different," he whispered. "I wanted to be different. Now the sky screams at me, and I live in an elephant's skull. You," he said without looking up. "They took you young, didn't they? People like my father and mother took you and brought you into their house, their big, fancy house, gave you sweets and pretty clothes to wear, and then they sat you on their laps and—"

"Tula!" she yelled. "You don't know that, you can't!"

She covered her face in sudden, inexplicable shame; her skin turned hot and cold. *Only dreams*, she told herself, *only silly dreams*.

He doesn't know.

"Oh, yes," he said. "Oh, yes." His face turned up to the steaming branches overhead, their green alive with the flash and twinkle of bright birds. "I thank the monkey god, and the leopard god, and the great elephant god himself that I don't have to grow up—and be the master of the Big House."

His voice grated on her unwilling ears like the sound of bone splinters crunching underfoot. Bravely, Zatombi reached out to touch him again. This time she felt a sudden dizzying lightness, as if they were both golden feathers rocking in the wind. Zatombi hung onto his arm and gritted her teeth against the pull of his magic, wanting it and not wanting it. *No one touched her, and she touched no one; it was always so. She had lived here all her life, and nothing came before, no sweet brown breasts for comfort as the wind howled around a stick and mud hut.*

"Zatombi." The white boy pulled her close.

She curled against him. The bumps and angles of her pain melted away, making her soft enough to fit exactly in his arms. Her heart leaped like a sudden wind; she closed her mouth to keep it inside.

Zatombi, she told herself, *you did not even know the heavy water jugs you carried.*

Spilled now, spilled and smashed. She groaned, not knowing what it meant.

"Zatombi," he whispered again. His voice was the wind rushing through wings—a thousand pink flamingos rising like a living sunrise from the reeds of the lake below. Her cheeks burned with tears like silverblue fire.

The moon looked down on them, its face the gaunt ivory of old bones.

"You screamed for a week," Zatombi said. Her voice was hoarse, as if she also had screamed for a week.

His hot body twitched. "My father, he saw my eyes and whipped me. He kept on hitting me. It felt like the blooming of hibiscus flowers all over my skin. I looked once, and he was a skeleton, a black jigging skeleton, with a grin as wide as the Big House." Zatombi watched his face, the sharp line where his jaw met his skull.

"Everyone . . ." His voice was a ghost whisper. "Everyone who came near, their secrets poured into me, like the spitting of snakes." He trembled against her.

Zatombi's hands stroked his jawline, touched his high forehead, traced the furrows there. This boy was different; magic lived in his skin. Hope wiggled and flopped like a lonely worm inside her emptiness.

Surely he comes for a reason. He will cut the cords binding the world. He is come. To us, to us . . .

A hoopoe landed on his shoulder, dug its beak into his tangled hair. Its tall, feathery crest made Zatombi remember. The master reading to her out of a gilded book. Colored pictures there; soft, fuzzy tints, round-featured faces.

"You can be our me-sigh-er." She pronounced the master's word, gripping his shoulders and shaking him. "You can save us, you will!" The graveyard slipped away, and she saw green creeping across the death-dust of the world, life tumbling like baskets of fruit from the sky.

The white boy stared at her, his purple eyes swimming with new and bizarre creatures under the pond-like reflection of the moon.

"I . . . I . . . I," he stuttered.

She pushed herself away. A hot ball of passion throbbed inside her where once lived only the emptiness of bones sucked dry. Zatombi curled her black fingers into fists.

"There's got to be a me-sigh-er!" she screamed.

Echoes of her obsession woke long-dead lions. They split the night with their roars, stampeding the elephants. Zatombi grabbed the elephant skull even as the head lifted and whipped through the air, raising tusks and trunk to trumpet at the moon. She straddled the convoluted spine, staring down into the elephant's brain cavity, into the white boy's blank eyes.

"There's got to be a me-sigh-er, don't you see?" Zatombi shrieked over the screeching of jungle ghosts.

He stretched his long white neck, straining to reach her ear with his lips. "Ouroboros," he muttered. "The worm that eats its tail."

Zatombi nodded fiercely, slinging her arms around his shoulders to keep from falling as the elephant rampaged down tiny paths meant only for dik-diks and the spotted civets who stalked them. The bitter scent of smashed sassy wood filled her nose.

"But it ends!" she yelled. "You. You will do this!"

Finally the elephants slowed, their bones floating to the ground to lie again among the busy worms.

"How do you know?" the white boy whispered.

Zatombi scrambled up a shifting pile of bones. "There." She pointed to the stars. "And there. And there. They tell me, at night. The whole, round world. Clean and ripe, like a white woman's breast. Waiting."

He crawled out of the elephant skull and stood next to her. He didn't look at the stars. For a brief second his eyes cleared, and when Zatombi turned, she saw a terrible truth there.

"Maybe it's you they're waiting for," he said softly. "Maybe it's you, Zatombi."

She shuddered. A swarm of bugs like tiny flames danced around the two children, burning holes in the night.

"Me-sigh-er." The white boy turned away, whispering to himself. "Fathers don't like me-sigh-ers. Fathers build fences, fathers keep things out. Talk, talk, talk all night long. Like jackals yipping, waiting for the next body to fall. I know, I know."

"I know, too, boma-man," she reminded him. "That's why. Why you're here."

Zatombi pulled his shoulder, forcing him back to her. Taking his pale face in her hands, she touched her lips to his. It was the first time she'd ever kissed anyone because she wanted to. The white boy's mouth was fire and ice. She pulled him down among the bone splinters.

"Me-sigh-er," he breathed, touching the skin of her belly.

They slept in the hollow of the elephant skeleton. Before Zatombi closed her purple eyes, she saw the black bar of a giant rib crossing the moon's face like a mouth. The mouth opened and poured out a haunting tune; it wove between the hollow beats, bone against bone, as the other mamba children drummed through the night.

The smell of death mingling with the scent of tulip trees brought Zatombi awake. She breathed in deeply, her body forming around the essence of where she lived. The warmth of the white boy's head numbed her arm. She touched his cheek. So white, as if the tulips grew inside his body and flowered on his skin. He opened his purple eyes and gazed at her. Zatombi knew the rising sun was behind her head, and he could not possibly see her face clearly. But his eyes pushed into hers anyway, diving down, down, until they reached her heart. Grasping, they pulled it out and held it up to the sky like some sweet and bloody sacrifice.

Zatombi's stomach growled. She shook her head, breaking the connection.

"Let's go," she said, gently untangling her arm. "Find something to eat."

He only smiled. His right hand dug through the pieces of bone, and he brought it out, unfurling his palm. On his white skin perched a small tangerine. Zatombi gasped.

"Go ahead," he urged. "Eat it."

Gently, she picked it up. She'd only seen tangerines once before, long ago in the Big House. A visitor came, a white man with a rare, kind face. He played with the children, chased them shrieking around the furniture. Afterwards, he opened a sack of orange fruit. Of course, the children snatched them up and hid them under their clothes, eying the man fearfully. But he only laughed, and they could not help but laugh with him.

Zatombi looked at the white boy, surprised. He smiled and nodded as if to say, "See, not all your memories are bad ones."

Turning away from him, she pretended to eat the tangerine. Instead, she slipped it into her neck pouch where she kept her other sacred things: a tiny piece of ivory she'd tried to carve into a round ball, several small crystals, and the dried twist of a dead baby's umbilical cord.

When she turned back, he grinned at her, the crooked set of his mouth pulling down one purple eye and pushing up the other, making his face a weird, fearsome mask.

"Will you wash my feet?" he asked playfully.

Zatombi stared at him. *Anything*, she said. Only not out loud. *Anything at all.*

A cool wind rippled down the mountainside bringing the scent of cedar and pink lilies, the faint aroma of child sweat. It swayed the vines overhead, sending out Zatombi's call to the mamba babies. "Come out," she whispered, and the breeze repeated it: *Come out, come down, down, down . . .*

The smell caught in Zatombi's throat, reminding her how she had doomed the white boy and herself. She bit the inside of her cheek, letting blood wash away the taste of tears. Fiercely, she made herself remember the round world, the empty sit-tees, the new life to be brought by the me-sigh-er.

Children slid down the liana vines, crept out from the elephant skeletons. They came from everywhere, crowding around the white boy. Zatombi squatted, touching his ankle with a timid finger; she felt the pulse of a thousand hearts. How had there come to be so many? Panic caught in her chest. She stood. In all directions, purple eyes stared out of ragged, haunted faces. Roughly, Zatombi pushed the white boy behind her, shielding him.

"It is too many." Her voice broke as she grappled with unfamiliar jealousy.

"Ayy-aayyah-aaayayya!" Voices rose in a slow murmur, joining for the first time in complicated harmonies. Bones picked up the new rhythm, steadily beating it out.

The white boy shrugged, pulled Zatombi to one side. *It will always be too many.* She thought she heard the words in her head as one by one, the lilac-eyed children stepped forward and touched the white skin.

Zatombi watched, helpless, as the children's accumulated pain drove the white boy to his knees. Soon he lay on the ground panting, his limbs twisting and his eyes staring blindly into the great orange ball of sun.

Still they came and touched him. Their thousand hurts crept out and writhed on the ground, red and smoking, as they pulled their hands away.

Zatombi held the white boy's head and dribbled water into his mouth. The sun moved across the sky and fell down the mountain into the great lake at its bottom, leaving purple and gold smeared overhead. The mamba babies chanted and banged their bones long into the night, until, finally, all had passed by.

Eerily, the song faded, leaving only the faint whir of bat wings in the air. The children waited, quiescent.

Zatombi kissed the cheek of the white boy and tasted his salt.

"Gone . . ." he whispered. "I folded them away. . . ."

"Will you eat now?" she asked him, blinking back purple tears. What had she done? He was so frail, she was afraid to let go, afraid the night wind and the fruit bats might pick him up and carry him away.

His eyes flickered, and then closed. Zatombi spent the night holding the white boy's head in her lap as he slept the sleep of the dead and the holy.

Around her, the mamba children moved quietly through the moon-laced dark, using their bones to grind up colored rocks and mix them with marrow, making a bright paste. They painted their bodies in stripes of red, black, and white. Zatombi saw a vision of young warriors with seven-foot spears and gleaming skin, their hearts hot with lust and glory. Somehow, she kept herself from shivering.

In the morning, the eyes of the white boy opened, and Zatombi did not know if he saw her, or even saw the thousand mamba babies standing among the elephant bones, silent as crows with their tongues eaten out.

He stood and slowly picked his way down the mountainside. The others followed, making sounds like rushing water as bones crushed and scattered under their feet. They walked through the hours of the day and the night, again and again, crossing empty plains. Dust got into Zatombi's mouth. It gritted against her eyeballs every time she blinked. She ripped off a piece from the shreds of cloth she still wore and tied it around the white boy's face.

The others rustled behind them, like the shuffling of elephants browsing at night.

After scattered pieces of time, broken only by the lifting and dropping of two thousand feet, dawn broke, and Zatombi saw the glittering edge of a village.

The sudden heat of day rolled in waves in front of her, and the sun sparkled off bright things held by the adults who stood, guarding their town. The white boy pulled the rag from his face.

Zatombi grew afraid. "Maybe," she whispered, "this is not—"

The me-sigh-er shook off her arm and leaped into the air.

"Ai-IEEE!" he cried, and came down running. Zatombi sprinted after him, and the thousand pounded into movement, shaking the ground as if an ancient, gracefully insane herd of gazelles bore down upon the village.

When they came close enough to see the white and black faces of adults, like stones chipped out of the air, the white boy raised his arm, stopping the mamba children all in a swirling cloud of dust. He stepped forward alone. Zatombi saw how the white boy's bones stuck out and the red and white welts of the whip crisscrossed his back.

"Father," he called. Across a chunk of bitter ground, brown and rancid in the morning sun, a man also stepped forward. A big man, he held a big gun, cradling it in his arms.

"I told you!" The man's voice echoed like cracking granite. "I never wanted to see you. Never!" His face twisted. "Never were you to call me by that name again!"

Before any hand twitched, the big man raised the gun and fired.

The white boy fell without a sound.

Both sides froze as time itself paused. Only the red blood moved, flowing from the white boy's chest. Scarlet and obscene, blood poured into the dead ground. Zatombi didn't know who broke the grip of time. She thought she screamed. But she wasn't sure, not really.

Even now, she is not sure.

And as for what came next—Zatombi saw the white boy's body fall into pieces, and the pieces turn into long, purple snakes. Moving like a wash of wind across the parched ground, the snakes slipped into the crowd of villagers, striking with bone-white fangs. People ran, screaming and firing their guns. Bodies fell bleeding, trampled under their neighbors.

One thousand mamba children watched, unafraid.

But Zatombi, with eyes dry as stones, gazed only at the blood-soaked ground where the white boy gave himself away. Her heart ground against itself and filled her chest with dust. She turned her back on the bright, sticky dirt. The elephants trumpeted their skeletal song, calling her home. Slowly, like the milling of ghost zebras at a water hole, the mamba children turned and followed. Through the timeless hours of their walk, the smell of blood lingered in Zatombi's nose, and the dust tasted like copper.

Sometimes at night, she hears him whisper, "It's you, Zatombi, maybe it's you they're waiting for."

The new plague, the plague of the purple snakes, wiped out village after village. Still, mamba babies come, making their own way now. They come with calm eyes the color of cool amethyst. Zatombi puts them to work, building houses out of bones, and lacing them over with banana leaves.

The old children grow older, and have babies of their own, sturdy, serene babies with bright plum eyes. They crawl to Zatombi at night, gathering around her in the pit of an empty elephant, its ribs stretching across the sky, and she tells them stories.

"There was a Me-sigh-er," Zatombi tells them, fingering the wizened tangerine in her neck pouch, "and He came to the world, and the world saw His light and liked it not, so the children of the bones took Him in and—"

But all the time, she wonders, Is it my fault?

Perhaps, once upon a time, one crazy, hurt child pushed another like herself, a boy scarred and insane from the whip of his father, pushed him to do the impossible . . .

Is it my fault?

For the rest of her life, she will atone.

". . . And the Me-sigh-er laid His hands upon the children with the violet eyes, and magic flowed from His fingers and bright peace rained down in the Elephant's Graveyard, and bread flowered from the ground, and sweet water ran from the bones, and all who watched gazed in awe at the miracles which He wrought. . . ."

GRAIL'S END

Written by
Callan Primer

Illustrated by
Anatoly Pristypa

About the Author

Callan Primer began reading and writing science fiction as a child after becoming interested in the gaudy illustrations in her father's books.

She began writing in grade school, but only recently began working at it seriously. As a part-time copy editor, she said she learned that editing can help any piece of writing and perhaps that has helped her work without worrying too much about how it looks on the first draft. So during her spare time—when she's not either tending her child or working on her freelance editing—she still likes to write and work on her reading.

Callan says that, like many writers, she went to school for an "unbelievable number of years," where she became a jack-of-all-academic-trades, but a master of none.

About the Illustrator

Anatoly Pristypa was born in a small town not far from Murmansk, in the north of Russia, but has lived most of his life in Nikolaev, in Ukraine.

In 1974 he graduated from school and began studying engineering, but for the past seven years has been studying art in the studio of R. J. Vineshtock.

Anatoly likes jazz, classical music, and enjoys collecting seashells. For the past few years he has been painting, doing graphic arts, and interior design.

Dr. Helen Burch stared at the niwa she intended to ride. The huge, flightless bird stared back, a hint of red in its implacable eyes. Helen's eyes were red too, thanks to an allergy she was developing to the omnipresent pink dust of the Aeolian lowlands, driven by the wind into every crevice she possessed and a few she'd forgotten. Her temper was beginning to rival the niwa's own, thanks to sleeping—or trying to sleep—too close to an Aeolian caravanserie. One day, she promised herself, she would find out if the Aeolians ever slept.

"And then," she said aloud, "I'll play back one of their mother-rotted songspiels at full blast." She smiled sourly at her empty threat; after her last report, she'd be—lucky to end up cataloging the family trees of Norway rats. The orders transferring her to the sewers of New York were probably already at the base station.

The niwa—its name a faint approximation of the two-toned screech the Aeolians used—stared steadily at her, making its own promises, none of them benign. Helen felt tempted to use a club to subdue it but reminded herself that when the Lady commanded respect for all living creatures, she had meant rabid Aeolian ostriches, too.

Helen took a firmer grip on the riding crook concealed behind her back and leaned left. The bird's head—more beak than braincase, and set on a heavily muscled neck—followed her.

"I am going to ride you today," Helen said in a soft, sing-song voice, swaying right. The niwa's head followed her to the limits of its tether. "I am going to the station and I need your strong legs." She continued swaying, the bird swaying with her. "I don't want to go." She slowly raised her free hand and untied the bird's tether. The niwa, unnoticing, swayed with her. "But sometimes we all have to do . . ." the crook came stealthily forward, kept low and out of sight. ". . . unpleasant . . ." she caught the dangling reins with the long-handled crook and twisted them ". . . things."

The small tug broke the niwa's trance. Without rearing back or raising its crest, it immediately slashed down. Helen sucked in her stomach and looped the reins over a hook in the niwa's saddle as the large, serrated beak went skimming by.

"Got you," she said triumphantly. The niwa squealed as its ugly, lethal head was snaffled. It thrashed but couldn't find enough play to attack. When it ungraciously accepted defeat, Helen began tying her pack to the saddle.

"You know, you're getting good at this." She swung into the saddle and gave the sensitive spot behind one of its vestigial wings a good scratch. "What a pity you're not going to get another chance at me."

The niwa looked back at her and raised its crest challengingly. Helen laughed.

"You say I still have to get off? Ingrate. How would you like to be clubbed every time I had to get on or off? That's what the knife-hands do when they want a ride." She gave the other wing a scratch, checked her saddle in preparation for casting off the hobble, then peered through the giant fronds that screened her campsite, taking a last look at the caravanserie.

The Aeolians, a dozen of the oversized kangaroo rats, were still at it. Yipping and howling with undiminished vigor, they hopped in random directions without straying far from the theoretical center of the group. They were still doing the story Helen had dubbed "The Silly Rocks Story," although in her records it was known as "Lowland Narrative Number Twenty-Three." Helen wondered how many versions they'd gone through since she stopped recording from sheer exhaustion the night before.

Tears—of exhaustion, she told herself—leaked from her reddened eyes. She wiped them away impatiently.

Think of your nice quiet carrel. Think of the mountains of data you haven't gone through. Think of the papers yet to be written, of the conferences where everybody speaks your language. Think of fresh, hot coffee and dawn breezes off the lake at home. But she continued to watch with the intensity of someone trying to memorize what she saw.

She blinked. Two Aeolians—whom she would have sworn weren't watching her—broke from the group and bounded toward her. Helen cursed and wheeled the niwa, but they managed to block her path. They bounced cheerily on muscular tails, bandoleers decorated with all their trade goods banging against their narrow breastbones. She eyed them sourly. She recognized these two. Her best bet was to cut and run right now, but she hesitated just enough for her professional instincts to take over. With a resigned sigh, she flicked on the recorder that hung on her belt.

She tied down the reins to free her hands. The human throat couldn't pronounce many Aeolian sounds, so she had picked up some hand talk that let traders be understood across dialects. It made an acceptable pidgin for most Aeolians.

<I see you,> she signed, using a polite gesture.

<I see you,> they echoed, jiggling. Their ears flicked back and forth in a pleased pattern.

<You go Earth home?> asked one.

"Too true," muttered Helen, but understood that they meant the base station and signed assent.

<Treasures give/take,> said the other. <Mix Earth luck/wish/story we?>

"Not again," said Helen bitterly. "Don't you two ever learn? We're snoops, not traders." She scowled, then signed <No treasure take/give.>

The Aeolians bounced as cheerily as before. <Big treasure,> offered one. <New treasure,> said the other.

<No treasure.> She slashed her hands for emphasis, effectively yelling at them. <Go hills, knife-hands eat.>

<Earth luck/wish/story big.>

Helen clenched her hands. They were playing out the stock scene from the "Hollow Peaks" story (Lowland Narrative Number Forty-Five). Nothing would convince them that they couldn't follow her to great treasure, magically protected by her luck aura. There was no point arguing. She tried to anyway.

<Go hills, knife-hands eat,> she repeated. <Earth wish/luck/story small.>

Their rhythmic bouncing never faltered. Helen leaned back in her saddle and once again faced the conclusion that it didn't matter what she said or did. They would follow her, believing in human luck and dreaming of human treasure until their hearts were ripped out by bone knives.

Illustrated by Anatoly Pristypa

Their cheerful expectations infuriated her. She leaned forward and gave them a hard stare until their bouncing became arhythmic and their ears drooped in distress.

<No mix Earth luck/wish/story.> Hands slashed emphatically. <Go hills, knife-hands eat. I laugh.>

Then she let the niwa loose.

No Aeolian on foot could keep up with a niwa. But they tried. Helen was congratulating herself on losing them when she turned back to check her trail. From the vantage of the foothill she was climbing, she could see much of the pale pink plain. A small dust cloud appeared to travel on the same line she did.

"You—you cretinous rodents!" Helen yelled. "You have worm chow for brains." She had one more chance to discourage them, and she had to do it, before they got farther into the hills. Reaching into her pack, she drew out a bright bundle of feathers. She tossed this in a low arc in front of the niwa, the feathers fluttering like a small, injured bird. The niwa raised its crest and in a few long bounds was on the lure, stopping to savage it. Helen climbed off in an instant, throwing the hobble on and then ripping off her packs while the bird tossed its prey up and down in an attempt to kill it.

By the time the niwa realized its prey wasn't edible, Helen was safely out of reach. It glared at her, straining against its hobble. Helen, despite her preoccupation with the traders behind her, laughed.

"You always fall for that one. Lucky for me." She pulled the beacon out of her pack and turned it on. If she were picked up by the skimmer, her trail would end here and maybe those two idiot traders wouldn't go farther into the hills. Maybe. They might decide to risk their own luck, but at least *that* wouldn't be her fault. She found a sun-warmed rock out of the wind and watched the pink dust cloud grow steadily larger.

The skimmer reached her just as the two traders got to the base of her hill. She loosed the niwa by yanking the long lead to its hobble, then climbed hurriedly into the skimmer. The niwa glared, but not seeing her through the transparent canopy that closed over her, promptly forgot she ever existed and took off as though a swamp ghost had its claws in its rump.

The two traders bounded determinedly up the hill. "Worm chow," Helen muttered as she strapped herself in.

"And hello to you too," said the pilot.

"Hi, Natalie, that wasn't aimed at you, just those two idiot Aeolians."

"Oh," said Natalie, languidly giving the skimmer altitude. "Then you weren't worried about that bunch of armed Aeolians."

"What!" Helen yelped. She strained against her harness. As the skimmer rose, she could see a dozen or so knife-hands, their gaudy ribbons streaming behind as they rode up the other side of the hill. The two traders still bounded upward, even though they had to have seen the skimmer.

Helen's head whipped back and forth as she watched the inevitable collision of the two groups. "No, no, no," she whispered. "Turn back, hide, you still have a chance." Then there was no more chance. The knife-hands flowed around the two traders. The forward momentum of both groups stopped, they coalesced, there was a swirl of activity in the center.

"Helen, what the . . . put that away! Are you crazy? Under a sealed canopy?"

Helen looked down and found she'd partly drawn the Gibbs. She looked at it, vaguely puzzled. She hadn't touched the damned thing since the jungles of Eris and only wore it because regulations said she had to. Below, the group shuddered, light flickering off bone-white knives. Helen tasted bile, and her professional facade broke.

"Natalie, please, the skimmer's got sonics . . ."

Natalie gave her a disbelieving look. "And how many rules would that break? The commandant would dismantle me down to my DNA."

The group dwindled as the skimmer leisurely gained more altitude, but what Helen's eyes couldn't see, her imagination filled in. "Natalie," she begged again, but could find no more words.

"I don't see any of us down there," said Natalie, but not without sympathy, and aimed the skimmer at the mountains. Helen stared back through the canopy, swallowing convulsively, her skin pallid despite the tan earned under a dozen alien suns.

"Leave it," said Natalie. "You can't interfere."

Slowly, Helen leaned back in her seat, a look of nausea on her face. "Too late. Too damned late."

They remained silent the rest of the flight. Too soon, the ancient caldera that housed the human base station appeared before them. The sun was beginning to warm the greensward of the caldera.

Natalie exchanged minimal recognition with ops. "It's me. I got her."

Masefield at ops returned the acknowledgment. "Right. Now it's Shelby's turn. He's given himself a real bad case of athlete's foot." A moment of silence, and Masefield said brightly, "Jaxon says, don't bother landing. Just fly by the commandant's office and drop Helen off."

Natalie quirked an eyebrow at the suggestion.

"Don't you dare," said Helen irritably. "Masefield, let

her know that I'll be in as soon as I unpack and clean up. I've been eating dust for a month."

"Uh, Helen, how about I carry your stuff to your carrel for you. She wants you now, pink dirt and all."

Helen, who was as familiar with the commandant's fanatical cleanliness as anyone, stared at the transmitter. "All right, Masefield, I'll trot right along and hope she doesn't have a prissy fit when she sees me."

"Too late," offered Natalie. "Too damned late."

Helen stared at the pilot, but Natalie maintained a bland expression all the way through landing and unloading, then waved cheerfully and uncommunicatively as she took off again. Masefield, who waited for Helen, had a worried look but was equally uncommunicative.

They had been through some hellish postings together; Helen wasn't going to accept this. She grabbed his arm and stopped him. "What's going on, Mase? What's got her tail in a knot?" There was no need to specify which "her."

He pushed her hand off his arm and kept walking toward the main gate of the station. "You'd know better than I."

Helen caught up with him. "Have things been bad?"

"When she's angry, she's a pain, and she's been angry for the last month. Since you took off against orders, as a matter of fact." He paused to work the gate mechanism, then set off again, not bothering to shorten his long stride.

Helen gritted her teeth and caught up with him. She was beginning to regret riding a niwa everywhere. It did nothing for aerobic conditioning. "In other words," she huffed, "situation normal."

Masefield stopped in front of the biolab, where the station branched into offices and living quarters. He frowned at her, then shook his head. Helen planted herself in his way, forcing him to detour if he wanted to pass.

"Mase," she said, "there's more, isn't there? I've gone AWOL before, and the crap just landed on me, no one else. What gives with her?"

He tossed her sample case into the biolab's decon hutch, then walked around her, not touching her. Before heading down the residential corridor, he relented. "Helen—this is different. For some reason, she's on the edge this time. Please don't provoke her. I know you enjoy it, but not this time. For your own sake."

"Mase," she called after his retreating back. "I do *not* provoke her. Not on purpose, at least."

"Helen," he called over his shoulder, "just don't keep her waiting this time."

"Waiting?" she muttered. "Who keeps who waiting?" She turned down the office corridor. "And I don't provoke her. She's self-provoking. *I'll* behave, and she'd better." But only a row of closed doors heard her declaration, which dribbled off the closer she got to the door at the end of the corridor.

"Damned anal-retentive control freak of a technophiliac," she whispered, then as the door shushed open called cheerily, "Good morning, Commandant." The figure hunched over her node monitor didn't look up. Helen had seen that posture in other primates, so she shrugged and went to sit on the window ledge. The window was sealed, of course—couldn't have pink dust over everything—but still showed a splendid view. The sun was just clearing the rim of the caldera, and the crystals in the west wall caught the light and threw it back.

A cold, formal voice addressed her. "Dr. Burch, do you remember anything like an executive order? It would have been just before you went on trek."

Helen allowed herself to start, just a bit, before turning to face the room. It was just enough of a twitch to inform the commandant that Helen had been oblivious to time passing. Unfortunately, the commandant hadn't bothered to look up. Helen smoothed her irritated expression, then said, "Which one?"

"The only one that applied to you." Her voice was calm, but her shoulders still hunched inward, eyes focused on the light pen twisting in her fingers.

Helen considered, swinging her legs so that puffs of dust came off them. "You mean the one forbidding ground travel in base sector?"

The pen snapped. "That's the one. Would you mind telling me why you felt privileged to ignore it?"

Careful, Helen.

"I believed that order was"—paranoid—"precipitous. I explained at the time you issued it that the muster of knife-hands hadn't reached critical mass for an attack yet."

"I remember your explanation. I also remember that you couldn't guarantee this."

Helen rolled her eyes at the word "guarantee," but repressed her first retort. "Let's just call it a statistically valid guess, given the pattern of past attacks on this station."

"Patterns in alien cultures are pure hindsight, Dr. Burch. Not something I want to risk my personnel's lives on. But none of this is relevant." She finally looked up, and Helen knew a moment of chill at the sight of those wide-open pale eyes. Mase was right. The woman was on the edge of . . . something. The commandant shuttered her eyes slightly and continued in her soft, controlled voice, "I still want to know why you feel you can ignore execs." Snap. "Perhaps there's a codicil in your job contract?"

Helen shook her head and managed to keep a bland expression. See, Mase, I'm behaving. I'm not even mentioning that she's issued more execs than every commandant I've ever worked with before, combined, and I'm certainly not mentioning that she uses them to replace simple management skills.

"Just for my personal information, why did you risk your life going into hills containing—and this is your own estimate—nearly three thousand armed and aggressive Aeolians?"

"When you last called a general staff meeting"—and demanded that I attend so I could listen to everyone complain about their offices—"I was on the trail of a significant narrative"—and you couldn't wait for me to come in on my own like every other mother-rotted com mandant I ever worked under did—"and the storytellers would have passed out of my reach if I'd waited until you decided it was safe"—fat chance—"and besides, I had the fastest niwa in these hills. The knifehands have chased me before."

Snap. "I didn't know that you'd been threatened by Aeolians before this."

Helen stopped swinging her legs and smiled, she hoped charmingly. "Some things you just don't tell commandants. They tend to worry."

The commandant's body seemed to explode outward as she kicked back her chair and hurled something at the wall. Pieces of the light pen pattered down. Frozen, they both stared at the plastic shards scattered on the floor. Slowly, very slowly, the commandant relaxed back into her chair, her face calm. She laid her hands on her desk and laced her fingers.

"So tell me again why you had to ignore an exec."

Helen raised her hands in a helpless gesture. "My

work is out there. I can't fulfill my job responsibilities by sitting around this station."

"You could always write reports."

The soft voice was inflectionless, but Helen caught her breath and stared at the other woman. So that was it.

"My report," said Helen finally. "You read my report. How did you get a copy?"

"There are those in division who think I ought to know what my staff is saying."

"That report was encrypted under section 4-c-9. It was read only by the standards and review committee. I repeat, how did you get a copy?"

"The standards and review committee decided not to officially notice it. So I received a copy along with the suggestion that perhaps the author could reconsider some of her conclusions."

"What?" Helen's voice began rising. "They're suppressing my report? They can't do that."

"They did. And I was privately advised that one of my field researchers was doing her best to ruin this mission. My mission. *My* mission." There was nothing left to break, so her hands clenched and unclenched on the rim of her desk.

"Why, you egocentric . . ." Helen found her voice rising to a screech and forced it back down. "Didn't you read the report? Didn't they? What are they doing, saying that the news is nasty, let's shoot the messenger? Cretinous bureaucrats." Helen slid down from the ledge and stomped to the commandant's desk, trailing puffs of pink dust. She grabbed the commandant's monitor and turned it so she could read it. "You *have* been reading it. Well, which part don't you understand? I realize this isn't your field, so I'll be glad to translate the technical terms."

"I'd like to understand how some pisspot xenologist gets such delusions of grandeur."

"Delusions of grandeur . . ."

While Helen, outraged, groped for further words, the commandant continued, "I was especially struck by this sentence: `In every contact of human and Aeolian lies the seeds of imperial domination.'" The commandant shoved her chair back. "Imperial domination. Why stop there? Why not say we were using them for slave labor? That would get even more attention."

Helen had herself under control again. "Now there's a thought. And maybe next time I won't encrypt, and maybe division will have one of its embarrassing leaks, and maybe the newsies will get a copy."

"You use a phrase guaranteed to bring every Gaean hound in the Senate down on our collective heads. Why? Why? *Why?*" Each "Why?" was punctuated by a fist pounding the desk.

"Because we've got to leave," Helen said in the reasonable tones of someone stating the obvious.

"Why?" The commandant was half out of her chair. Helen almost saw a complete rim of white around her irises. "You said we're destroying Aeolian cultures. I run this mission according to every single niggling, pisspot rule the Gaeans demanded, and I can document that. I'm ass-deep in status reports every day, with Gaean watchdog committees nagging me for more. I can account for every contact we've made with the Aeolians since landfall—except for yours. I have no idea what you're up to most of the time, so if anything's gone wrong, you turd-brained xenologist, it's your doing!"

Helen, startled by this burst of profane eloquence, said, "I'm sorry, I had no idea I was causing trouble for you with division." She didn't really feel sorry, but if things escalated any further, they'd come to blows.

The commandant relaxed enough to sit, and once more laced her fingers together atop the desk. She looked the picture of serene competence, except for the white knuckles. "Back to my original question. Why?"

Helen wondered if she'd have any better luck explaining things to her than she'd had with the Aeolians. The commandant may have read the report, but her eyes seemed locked on only one thing: the threat to her command—the same way the Aeolians could only see magic and treasure when they looked at a lone, scruffy human researcher.

So speak to her like she's an alien. Use her own metaphors, make what's happening personal, but don't make it her fault.

"The Gaeans are wrong, you know." Good, the knuckles were relaxing. "They thought we had to be hedged about with rules because otherwise we'd be out there, molding passive aborigines into our own patterns. But that's not what's happening. The Aeolians are molding themselves, in ways we have no control over." The hostility in the commandant's eyes faded marginally.

"The Aeolians are a metaphor-driven people. Most of the time I can't tell where their stories end and their lives begin. When we dropped into their lives, the only way they could handle our strangeness was to fit us into their stories. Fortunately, most of the stories involving us are benign. It doesn't harm the merchants to treat us like magical guardians, or the singers to ask us for oracles because we're obviously messengers from god. But to the hunters, the knife-hands, we're a gigantic, slow-moving <>."

"A slow-moving what?" asked the commandant irritably.

"This," Helen demonstrated the Aeolian hand-talk

again. "I don't have a word for it, but it stands for that elephantlike creature that roams the hills. Fast, large, very tasty, or so I'm told. It takes a group of knife-hands working together to bring one down. It's the only time Aeolians work together."

Helen began pacing. Movement always helped her to think, and she had to be very careful about her word choice. "They hunted their megafauna to extinction a geologic age ago, but the old hunts are still part of the knife-hand's myths. They still tell—they still live—the stories of hunts where a thousand hands brought down some huge creature. Now we're here. A giant, armored herbivore, so gentle it won't even step on the grass. The knife-hands are combining for the hunt, and I have no idea when it will stop."

"And we will repel them, as we have in the past, without harming a hair on their hides. I still fail to see how this is anything but an internal Aeolian matter. You haven't proved that we're interfering; you haven't proved that piece of tripe you were trying to send the standards and review committee."

Helen kept herself under control. "I haven't finished." She folded her arms tightly around her chest to stop from flailing them about. Stay professional. Don't yell. "This station provides a constant stimulus to the knife-hands. It never lets up. There's never a resolution. What do you think happens to the knife-hands we turn away? They have to hunt something. So they've started hunting other Aeolians."

"So?"

"So?" Helen's voice rose to a screech. A hint of satisfaction lit the commandant's pale eyes. So Helen pressed her lips firmly together until she could find cooler words.

"So," she tried again. "They've never done this before. I'm really afraid they're permanently breaking out of old roles. Like the tiger that tastes human flesh, they've developed a taste for easy prey. The only way to repair this is to leave *now*. If we stop stimulating them, they may snap back into their old patterns. Perhaps the stories of 'long pig' won't survive against the old stories. Perhaps. But we've got to leave now."

The commandant leaned back in her chair. Sometime during Helen's argument, she had relaxed. Helen stared at her suspiciously. "So," the commandant repeated the word for ironic effect. "It's an interesting theory, but it needs more rigorous proof. You rewrite this thing in consultation with Dena and Shelby, and I'll pass it to division." She tried to look like Solomon offering up a judgment, but the pleasurable gleam in her eyes gave her away.

Solomonic, indeed. Of the two xenologists, Shelby was the commandant's man and Dena had the attention span of a gnat for things outside her own research. They could spin out the rewriting process forever, which was what the commandant really wanted. Helen felt no more desire to pace; her arms fell loosely to her sides.

"Unacceptable," she said flatly. "Dena and Shelby are not experts in this field; I am. You can pass the report to division as it is, or see it plastered all over the newsies."

The commandant was unfazed. She smiled slightly. "Draft reports are classified under section 3-a-14. They can't be released to the media. And," she touched her screen in several rapid passes, "I am imposing a blackout on your communications."

Helen jerked. "You can't do that!"

"Thanks to your stated—and thank you for doing that—intention to go to the newsies, I can. Section 3-c-7.

Now you'll want to appeal all this, I realize. I'll file it for you. It may take a while to go through channels, of course."

"What is this to you?" said Helen, almost whispering. She couldn't trust her voice any louder. "Just some obscene game? Doesn't it matter that sentient creatures out there are dying because of us?"

"What matters is that you're careless and undisciplined. I wouldn't trust you to report on the weather."

Helen leaned over the desk. "Within a day's ride I can find enough mutilated corpses to fill this prissy office to the ceiling. Shall I do that? Would that be proof?"

"You're hardly a model of scientific detachment, are you, Dr. Burch?"

"And you're hardly a model of a human."

The commandant slowly rose from her desk and cautiously edged to its far side. Helen watched her, unblinking, until she realized that she held something in her hand. Slowly, unbelievingly, she looked down, and for the second time that day found the Gibbs in her hand. She stared at it, stared at the commandant, stared at the Gibbs again.

I didn't do what I just did, did I?

The expression in the commandant's eyes shaded from wariness to triumph, and Helen knew in a sickening instant that she had defeated herself. She found herself shaking. Provoked, outmaneuvered, and allowed to hang herself. She slid the Gibbs back into its leg pocket and wiped her hands down its seams.

The commandant seated herself, cool, collected, every inch the model administrator except for the gleam in her eyes, the gleam of a sated carnivore.

"This has been a stressful posting for you, hasn't it?"

the commandant said soothingly. "I should have seen the pattern earlier. All your insubordination has simply been a cry for help. Oh, good. Everything was properly recorded." She made rapid entries on her monitor. "Of course I shall recommend that this not be treated as a criminal matter." She beamed at what she saw on the monitor. "Yes, that's the section I want. Administrative request for therapeutic evaluation." She paused, and said delicately, "I'm right? You'd prefer therapy to criminal charges?"

The combination of fake solicitude and threat was too much for Helen. She felt her gorge rise, and, not seeing her way out of the trap, turned with an inarticulate grunt and ran for the door.

"Enjoy your therapy," the commandant called out as the door closed behind Helen's retreat.

Helen managed to reach a sanitary cubicle before losing the battle with her stomach. It only gave her a temporary respite. Before she reached her private quarters she had to slump down the wall of the corridor and put her head between her knees.

Fool, fool, fool, she said bitterly to herself. How could you let her get to you? Nobody will listen to you now, nobody, and the Aeolians will keep dying. What use are you, anyway, great researcher from Earth, with mountains of data no one will use because you're crazy?

A nearby node chimed. There was no one else in the corridor, so it had to be for her. She stubbornly burrowed her head farther into her knees. The node chimed again, then a third time. Then Masefield's voice, reflecting equal amounts of anxiety and irritation, came through the node. "Answer, Helen. I know you're in the building. What did you do to her? She's invoked nearly every fascist section in the rule book. I told you to watch out . . . what's that? No, I don't think she needs to know about that."

This last statement wasn't directed at Helen. She raised her head cautiously and peered at the node.

"Why tell her? She's not even supposed to leave the station anymore." Silence, then: "All right, all right. Helen, Jaxon says there's a female Aeolian at the east door, alone and on foot."

Helen stood too fast and had to clutch the wall for support. Fingers fumbling, she opened her side of the node. Her first words came out too hoarse to be understood, so she tried again, "Any gold around her neck?"

There was silence from Masefield, then, "Jaxon says yes."

Helen leaned against the wall. "An oracle. A mother-rotted oracle."

Masefield's voice grew soothing. "That's good. Why don't you come to ops and see?"

"No. Gotta talk to it—her. This is weird. They never leave their crèches. It's the singers who travel."

"Helen, she's filed a cultural contamination report on you. You're grounded until it can be investigated. And I've got to collect your equipment. *All* your equipment."

"But," she said slowly, "you haven't found me yet, have you?"

More silence. "Ten minutes," Masefield said. "And don't do anything terrifically obvious, will you, like try to set the commandant on fire."

"Ten minutes of discretion," Helen promised, though what she really expected to do with the time, she didn't bother to explain to herself.

An oracle—although the English word caught only at a shadow of the Aeolian meaning. Taller and more slender than the males. Never traveled, cared for by the singers. Helen had had very few chances to actually talk to one, although she had been privileged to watch something she had dubbed the god dance. Curiosity sped Helen along her way and shoved other problems to the background.

The east door opened, startling the Aeolian behind it into a clumsy fall. Helen took one quick look to confirm that it was an oracle before turning politely away. When she heard the yip that meant "human," she turned back—and caught her breath. The proud figure of the god dance was battered, filthy—and missing an ear. Helen stared, incredulous, at the bloody stump while the Aeolian crouched and flattened her remaining ear, quivering slightly.

Helen signed <I see you,> and the Aeolian straightened. Her remaining long ear stayed flat against her skull. Taking a backward bound, the Aeolian raised herself on the forepart of her long feet and began to dance. The god dance.

"Not to me, you idiot Aeolian," Helen cried despairingly. "I'm not your god, I can't do anything for you. Don't tell *me* your damned story."

The oracle ignored her. Spin, dip, leap. Sun rises, sun sets. Beauty and old stories, peaceful, peaceful. Then stamp, shake, lash. Knife-hands, flowing like red dust from the hills. Hunger. Homes burned. Hearts torn out. Fear. Running. Day/circle broken. The dance changed again. Stop. Justice. New luck, new wish, new story. Justice. New story. Change, change, change.

Helen squeezed her eyes shut briefly. "No new story," she said, opening them. "Just the same stupid one, pride and prejudice and anger. My pride, my prejudice, my anger."

"Helen." It was Masefield's voice, over the external speakers. "You've got a group of armed Aeolians at two o'clock, three kilometers. Get yourself and your lady friend in the door and we'll start up the sonics."

"Belay that." The commandant's voice also emerged from the speakers. "Aboriginal peoples are not to come in this station. And why hasn't Dr. Burch been confined and disarmed?"

"Commandant," started Masefield, "it's just the entryway, and as for Helen, I wasn't quite sure where she was until now. . . ."

Ignoring the squabbling, electronic voices, Helen peered in the direction Mase had given her. A slight fuzziness in the distance gradually became a dust cloud.

"Not again."

The oracle danced on, presenting her story to god/entropy/whatever, waiting for it to become a dialogue, for the story to change, for Helen to dance and sing with her.

"Not again," said Helen. "I can't . . ." She stood, arms dangling like leaden weights, heart pounding. "I can't . . ."

The dust cloud grew, and the oracle, oblivious, restarted the story.

Beauty, old story, peaceful, peaceful.

The speaker nagged at her. Something about her eardrums, and getting inside, but she was watching the individual riders take shape. There were seven, yipping and howling as they posted in their saddles, tails held straight up.

Hunger, burning, hearts torn out.

The quality of the knife-hands' howls changed, became the howls of successful hunters, their prey run to earth. Helen could see bone knives, held aloft.

Earth luck/wish story big.

You can't interfere.

Justice. New story. Justice.

"Yes," said Helen, "this time justice." Pulling out the Gibbs, she aimed carefully and pressed the firing stud. One rider spasmed and fell. The others didn't break stride. She could now see the pieces of bone they wove into their hair. "You aren't listening." She fired again. Then again. The remaining four broke off their approach, wheeling their niwas to look around, obviously puzzled. "Idiots," said Helen, then walked forward. Once she stood at the center of their attention, she fired again. Three more down. Their niwas tried to trample them. Slowly, reluctantly, Helen lowered the Gibbs. "And one left to tell the story." The survivor wheeled his niwa about, sending it toward the pass into the caldera.

The speaker was yammering at her. Something about mutiny, perhaps something about murder. Helen didn't pay attention. She pocketed the Gibbs to leave her hands free.

<New story. Knife-hands kill, kill knife-hands. Soon knife-hands hunt easy meat, meat no kill knife-hands.>

The dance had stopped. The oracle swayed slightly. Her sole battered ear raised, swiveled.

<New story,> the oracle agreed. <Bad luck/wish.>

"Probably," said Helen. When she had time, she would work out everything she had done, everything she should have done. She would probably have all the time she needed to think, once the Gaeans heard about this. Once the Gaeans heard about it . . . Helen began to smile. It wasn't a pleasant smile. The Gaeans, to show their concern for the rights of nonhuman sentients, would insist on a murder trial. Properly mishandled, it could turn into a huge embarrassment for division and a windfall for the Gaeans. The stink should be enough to blow this station off-planet.

The oracle looked droopy, probably from exhaustion, but Helen, feeling suddenly guilty, tried to reassure her. <Bad new luck/wish/story. Soon we leave Earth far home. Old luck/wish/story comes back.>

<Old luck/wish/story gone,> said the Aeolian. <All things change.> And with a decisive flick of her tail, she turned and bounded off.

"All things change," echoed Helen, staring after the oracle. "But why here? And why me?" She sighed, and said ruefully, "And the answer came back, `Why not?'" She watched a few seconds more, then whispered, "I won't fail you."

She heard excited voices behind her—babbles, cries, accusations. A small, satisfied smile curved her mouth as she turned to face her accusers.

It was going to be a great trial.

ABOUT THE WRITERS
AND ILLUSTRATORS
OF THE FUTURE

Written by
Dave Wolverton

About the Author

Dave Wolverton has been the first reader for the Writers of the Future *Contest since 1991, has edited volumes 8–12, and is an instructor for the annual* Writers of the Future *workshop, which for the past two years has taken place in Houston, Texas.*

When he's not involved with the contest, he writes science fiction—his latest novel being Lords of the Seventh Swarm, *the third book in his well-received* Golden Queen *series.*

In addition, to being a writer, he is the father of four children and enjoys gardening, fishing, and football—in that order.

Good things come in dozens—doughnuts, eggs, fishing worms. Twelve is considered a holy number or a lucky number in many mythologies: There were twelve apostles, twelve signs to the zodiac, twelve fingers on the god Quetzalcoatl. So perhaps the authors and illustrators in this twelfth volume of the anthology will find themselves in a particularly lucky or blessed state.

It does seem that we have some unusually talented people in this volume, many of whom show every sign of becoming serious contenders in the field.

This year, our winning authors hail from the U.S. and the U.K., while our illustrators come to us from the U.S., Canada, the Ukraine, and Croatia.

Twelve years ago L. Ron Hubbard initiated the *Writers of the Future* Contest to help discover and promote new writers of science fiction, fantasy, and horror. Five years later, its sister contest, the *Illustrators of the Future*, was formed to serve the same purpose for illustrators.

Over the years, both contests have been run along the same lines. All entrants from around the world may enter the contests free of charge, and both contests are judged only by professional authors and illustrators. The contests are sponsored by Author Services, of Hollywood, California; while Bridge Publications helps promote the contests by publishing this anthology.

Over the years, the contests have become international in scope, with winners having come from literally dozens of countries around the world.

Writers of the Future: Offers three prizes for our writers: $1,000 for our first-place winner, $750 for our second-place winner, and $500 for our third-place winner. In addition, each year our judges evaluate the four first-place winners and bestow a grand prize of an additional $4,000.

Beyond that, Bridge Publications, the publisher of *L. Ron Hubbard Presents Writers of the Future* volumes, pays each winner well for the opportunity to publish the stories.

Each author published in the volume is given the opportunity to attend the awards ceremony where he or she gets to meet contest judges and participate in a week-long writing workshop designed to help launch writers in their chosen profession.

This year our writing judges were Kevin J. Anderson, Gregory Benford, Algis Budrys, Anne McCaffrey, Larry Niven, Andre Norton, Frederik Pohl, Jerry Pournelle, Robert Silverberg, Tim Powers, Jack Williamson, and Dave Wolverton. Alas, one of our judges, Roger Zelazny, passed away literally as our annual writing workshop was in progress. Roger, one of the field's most talented writers, had been with the contest from its earliest days and always went out of his way to help encourage our winners. His presence will be sorely missed.

Illustrators of the Future: All of our illustrators also receive prize money, payment for publication and workshops of their own.

Each illustrator submitted a portfolio. Based on those portfolios, three winners each quarter receive a $500 prize and the opportunity to compete on a higher level. The three winning illustrators were then each assigned one of the prize-winning stories from their quarter and were given a limited amount of time to complete an illustration. Bridge Publications paid the illustrators for the right to publish the illustration for the story in the upcoming anthology, and the assigned illustration was then entered into the final competition.

The illustrator judges evaluated the twelve finalist pieces at the end of the year, then selected the grand-prize winner.

Our illustrator judges for this year were Edd Cartier, Leo and Diane Dillon, Bob Eggleton, Will Eisner, Frank Frazetta, Frank Kelly-Freas, Shun Kijima, Paul Lehr, Ron and Val Lakey Lindahn, Moebius, Alex Schomburg, H. R. van Dongen and William R. Warren, Jr.

We would like to heartily thank all our contest judges for their time and support.

Below you will find a list of our authors and illustrators for the year. In the past, we have published only the names of those authors and illustrators whom we published in the anthology; however, I've decided that too many of our finalists are noteworthy names you may want to watch for. For example, fine authors like Lois McMaster-Bujold, Kevin J. Anderson, or the up-and-coming Pat York (and many others I could mention) were once finalists in our contest but managed to slip past us, picking up novel contracts or making multiple short story sales before they won. Besides, during some quarters the competition was so tight that other stories could easily have come out on top. For example, we would have liked to have published Amy Sterling

Casil's marvelous and powerful tale "The Ballad of Johnny Punkinhead," but by the time we put this anthology together it had been purchased by the good folks at *The Magazine of Fantasy and Science Fiction*. So, from now on, I've decided to begin the tradition of letting you know the names of all the authors and illustrators who've been finalists for the year. We wish them great good fortune in all their writing endeavors:

Writers of the Future prize winners in this volume:

First Quarter

First Place	M. W. Keiper, *Ploughshares*
Second Place	Darren Clark Cummings, *Tempering Day*
Third Place	E. Robertson Rose, *Quixchotol*

Second Quarter

First Place	Edwina Mayer, *Dead Faces*
Second Place	Callan Primer, *Grail's End*
Third Place	Scott Everett Bronson, *A Report from the Terran Project*

Third Quarter

First Place	Arlene C. Harris, *His Best Weapon*
Second Place	Carrie Pollack, *Requiem for a Deathwatcher*
Third Place	Syne Mitchell, *Devil's Advocate*

Fourth Quarter

First Place   Russell William Asplund, *The Unhappy
                   Golem of Rabbi Leitch*
Second Place   Fruma Klass, *After the Rainbow*
Third Place   Roge Gregory, *Narcissus Rising*

Finalists

(Asterisk indicates that we chose to publish these finalists.)

Michael Brotherton of Austin, Texas
E. Stephen Mack of Berkeley, California
Richard Flood*
Amy Sterling Casil of Redlands, California
R. G. Riel of Wulguru, Australia
S. M. Azmus*
Sue Storm*
Noreen Doyle of Gardiner, Maine
Robert C. Osborne of Scarborough, New York
Joel Best of Niskayuna, New York
Elliott Robertson of New York, New York
Mark S. McCormick of Charlotte, Mississippi
Scott R. Parkin of Pleasant Grove, Utah
Kathy Watts of Half Moon Bay, California
Jerry Craven*

Illustrators of the Future prize winners in this volume:

Gary McCluskey
Ivan Gregov

Lionel Baker II
Kenneth Scott
Patrick Stacy
Anatoly Pristypa
Oleg Dergatchov
Kent Martin
Konstantin Sheverdin
Heidi Taillefer
Richard Moore
Brett Hess

Illustrator Finalists

Viktoria Dunaeva of Kiev, Ukraine
Konstantin Sheverdin of Lugansk, Ukraine
Joe Weider of Holmes Beach, Florida
Peter Sheverdin of Lugansk, Ukraine
Gordon Scott Manley of Portsmouth, Virginia
Korczok Zoltan of Vorosmarty, Hungary
Nikitina Liudmila Yurievna of Kiev, Ukraine
Oleg A. Mandrika of Lugansk, Ukraine
Jay French of Austin, Texas
Joseph C. Booth of Spokane, Washington
Frank Tamayo of Miami, Florida

CONTEST RULES

1. No entry fee is required, and all rights in the story remain the property of the author. All types of science fiction and fantasy are welcome; every entry is judged on its own merits only.

2. All entries must be original works of science fiction or fantasy in English. Plagiarism will result in disqualification. Submitted works may not have been previously published in professional media.

3. Eligible entries must be works of prose, either short stories (under 10,000 words) or novelettes (under 17,000 words) in length. We regret we cannot consider poetry, or works intended for children.

4. The Contest is open only to those who have not had professionally published a novel or short novel, or more than one novelette or more than three short stories.

5. Entries must be typewritten and double-spaced with numbered pages (computer-printer output okay). Each entry must have a cover page with the title of the work, the author's name, address and telephone number, and an approximate word count. The manuscript itself should be titled and numbered on every page, but the author's name should be deleted to facilitate fair judging.

6. Manuscripts will be returned after judging. Entries must include a self-addressed return envelope. U.S. return envelopes must be stamped; others may enclose international postal reply coupons.

7. There shall be three cash prizes in each quarter: 1st Prize of $1,000, 2nd Prize of $750, and 3rd Prize of $500, in U.S. dollars or the recipient's locally equivalent amount. In addition, there shall be a further cash prize of $4,000 to the grand prize winner, who will be selected from among the 1st Prize winners for the period of October 1, 1995, through September 30, 1996. All winners will also receive trophies or certificates.

8. The Contest will continue through September 30, 1996, on the following quarterly basis:

October 1–December 31, 1996   January 1–March 31, 1997

April 1–June 30, 1997   July 1–September 30, 1997

Information regarding subsequent contests may be obtained by sending a self-addressed, stamped business-size envelope to the above address.

To be eligible for the quarterly judging, an entry must be postmarked no later than midnight on the last day of the quarter.

9. Each entrant may submit only one manuscript per quarter. Winners in a quarterly judging are ineligible to make further entries in this or any future Contests.

10. All entrants, including winners, retain all rights to their stories.

11. Entries will be judged by a panel of professional authors. Each quarterly judging and the grand prize judging may have a different panel. The decisions of the judges are entirely their own, and are final.

12. Entrants in each quarter will be individually notified of the results by mail, together with the names of those sitting on the panel of judges.

This Contest is void where prohibited by law.

L. Ron Hubbard's

ILLUSTRATORS
OF THE
FUTURE
CONTEST

OPEN TO NEW SCIENCE FICTION
AND FANTASY ARTISTS
WORLDWIDE

All Judging by Professional Artists Only

$1,500 in Prizes Each Quarter
No Entry Fee   Entrants Retain All Rights

**Quarterly Winners compete for
$4,000 additional ANNUAL PRIZE**

L. Ron Hubbard's
Illustrators of the Future Contest
P.O. Box 3190
Los Angeles, CA 90078

1. The Contest is open to entrants from all nations. (However, entrants should provide themselves with some means for written communication in English.) All themes of science fiction and fantasy illustration are welcome: every entry is judged on its own merits only. No entry fee is required, and all rights in the entries remain the property of their artists.

2. By submitting work to the Contest, the entrant agrees to abide by all Contest rules.

3. This Contest is open to those who have not previously published more than three black-and-white story illustrations, or more than one process-color painting, in media distributed nationally to the general public, such as magazines or books sold at newsstands, or books sold in stores merchandising to the general public. The submitted entry shall have not been previously published in professional media as exampled above.

If you are not sure of your eligibility, write to the Contest address with details, enclosing a business-size self-addressed envelope with return postage. The Contest Administration will reply with a determination.

Winners in previous quarters are not eligible to make further entries.

4. Only one entry per quarter is permitted. The entry must be original to the entrant. Plagiarism, infringement of the rights of others, or other violations of the Contest rules will result in disqualification.

5. An entry shall consist of three illustrations done by the entrant in a black-and-white medium. Each must represent a theme different from the other two.

6. ENTRIES SHOULD NOT BE THE ORIGINAL DRAWINGS, but should be large black-and-white photocopies of a quality satisfactory to the entrant. Entries must be submitted unfolded and flat, in an envelope no larger than 9 inches by 12 inches.

All entries must be accompanied by a self-addressed return envelope of the appropriate size, with correct U.S. postage affixed. (Non-U.S. entrants should enclose international postal reply coupons.)

If the entrant does not want the photocopies returned, the entry should be clearly marked DISPOSABLE COPIES: DO NOT RETURN. A business-size self-addressed envelope with correct postage should be included so that judging results can be returned to the entrant.

7. To facilitate anonymous judging, each of the three photocopies must be accompanied by a removable cover sheet bearing the artist's name, address, and telephone number, and an identifying title for that work. The photocopy of the work should carry the same identifying title, and the artist's signature should be deleted from the photocopy.

The Contest Administration will remove and file the cover sheets, and forward only the anonymous entry to the judges.

8. To be eligible for a quarterly judging, an entry must be postmarked no later than the last day of the quarter.

Late entries will be included in the following quarter, and the Contest Administration will so notify the entrant.

9. There will be three co-winners in each quarter. Each winner will receive an outright cash grant of U.S. $500, and a certificate of merit. Such winners also receive eligibility to compete for the annual grand prize of an additional outright cash grant of $4,000 together with the annual grand prize trophy.

10. Competition for the grand prize is designed to acquaint the entrant with customary practices in the field of professional illustrating. It will be conducted in the following manner:

Each winner in each quarter will be furnished a Specification Sheet giving details on the size and kind of black-and-white illustration work required by grand prize competition. Requirements will be of the sort customarily stated by professional publishing companies.

These specifications will be furnished to the entrant by the Contest Administration, using Return Receipt Requested mail or its equivalent.

Also furnished will be a copy of a science fiction or fantasy story, to be illustrated by the entrant. This story will have been selected for that purpose by the Coordinating Judge of the Contest. Thereafter, the entrant will work toward completing the assigned illustration.

In order to retain eligibility for the grand prize, each entrant shall, within thirty (30) days of receipt of the said story assignment, send to the Contest address the entrant's black-and-white page illustration of the assigned story in accordance with the Specification Sheet.

The entrant's finished illustration shall be in the form of camera-ready art prepared in accordance with the Specification Sheet and securely packed, shipped at the entrant's own risk. The Contest will exercise due care in handling all submissions as received.

The said illustration will then be judged in competition for the grand prize on the following basis only:

Each Grand Prize judge's personal opinion on the extent to which it makes the judge want to read the story it illustrates.

The entrant shall retain copyright in the said illustration.

11. The Contest year will continue through September 30, 1997, with the following quarterly periods (see Rule 8):

April 1–June 30, 1996   July 1–September 30, 1996

The next Contest will continue through September 30, 1997, on the following quarterly basis:

October 1–December 31, 1996   January 1–March 31, 1997

April 1–June 30, 1997   July 1–September 30, 1997

Entrants in each quarter will be individually notified of the quarter's judging results by mail. Winning entrants' participation in the Contest shall continue until the results of the grand prize judging have been announced.

Information regarding subsequent contests may be obtained by sending a self-addressed business-size envelope, with postage, to the Contest address.

12. The grand prize winner will be announced at the L. Ron Hubbard Awards events to be held in the calendar years of 1996 and 1997, respectively.

13. Entries will be judged by professional artists only. Each quarterly judging and the grand prize judging may have a different panel of judges. The decisions of the judges are entirely their own, and are final.

14. This Contest is void where prohibited by law.

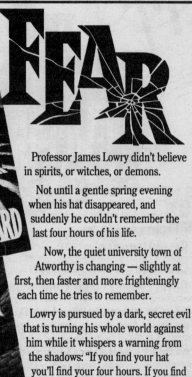

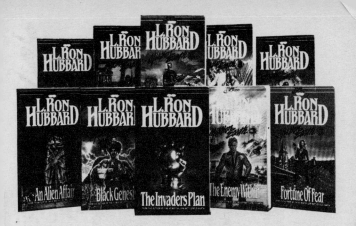

With a convicted murderess who trains giant cat-like animals, a doctor who creates human biological freaks, a madman who controls Voltar's secret police and a clandestine Earth base in Turkey, the stage is set for an alien killer assigned to sabotage the mission to Earth — the planet that doesn't exist.

"You will lose sleep. You will miss appointments. If you don't force yourself to set it down and talk to your family from time to time, you may be looking for a new place to live. Reading **The Invaders Plan** *is simply the most fun you can have by yourself... Remember how you felt the first time you saw* Star Wars? *This book will do it to you again."*
— **Orson Scott Card**

Paperbacks (Volumes 1-10): each $5.99,
Also available in audio (2 cassettes, 3 hours per volume): $15.95 each. Multi-cast dramatization.
